The Failed Queen

Audra Killian

Published by Audra Killian, 2024.

This is a work of fiction. Similarities to real people, places, or events are entirely coincidental.

THE FAILED QUEEN

First edition. November 12, 2024.

Copyright © 2024 Audra Killian.

ISBN: 979-8230535690

Written by Audra Killian.

Chapter 1

A^{*sh.*}
  Ash.

Aela's thoughts often wandered during her meetings with the elders. Their incessant arguing turned to buzzing in the background, yet that one word drew her attention with an inescapable lure.

Ash.

It resonated in her mind.

Ash.

Her gut churned with uneasiness.

"Where was the ash reported?"

The discussion around her died and silence pervaded the grand space of the throne room. The elders turned one by one to stare at her with obvious disapproval.

She restrained the urge to display her own annoyance. Though the words had not been spoken, the implication was clear enough: she was there merely as a placeholder for her brother the king. The elders had no desire to hear her thoughts.

After many moments of tense, awkward silence, Elder Berto cleared his throat and answered.

"Several villages near the KeyGil Mountains sent reports two days ago."

"Dirty snow, undoubtedly," another elder muttered.

"I think we can assume that the people who have lived near the border their entire lives know the difference between dirty snow and ash."

Again, tense silence greeted Aela's words. They preferred she sit quietly and not involve herself in state affairs. However, Aela had long succeeded at disappointing the elders.

She took advantage of their speechlessness and asked, "Why would there be ash falling from the KeyGil Mountains? Are the forests on fire?"

"At this time of year!" A voice scuffed at the question.

"Assuming it's not dirty snow," the man who had originally suggested the idea retorted. "It could be a fire."

"Those Frin'gerens are fire wielders," an elder named Hans stated. More an accusation than an observation, the statement had the intended effect.

A heated discussion erupted regarding the devious and untrustworthy nature of Dovkey's neighboring country. Aela sighed, realizing that nothing productive would come from this conversation. She half listened as the men spewed hateful and prejudiced commentary.

Finally, Elder Berto called the room to order. It took several minutes, but he quieted the remaining elders.

"I would remind you that our king is in Frin'gere currently on a mission of goodwill. It is imperative that we not jump to any conclusions at this time."

"Furthermore, we have strayed from the agenda," Elder Malcolm eyed her, making it clear to all that she was the cause. "The priestesses have received word that Immortal Council member Phoenix Son Aluz plans to arrive in Dovkey in time for the King's coronation ceremony."

Again, all the eyes in the room turned to her. Undoubtedly, they knew of the appeal that Aela submitted months ago for the dissolution of her engagement to the Immortal. Most did not approve.

"Has anything been decided regarding my appeal?"

"The king has not approved or dismissed it yet."

"Has it come to the king's attention yet?"

A hush fell over the room. They all refused to meet her stare.

"Has it?" Aela persisted.

"Your majesty, you are not implying that we would fail to present all pertinent information to the king, are you?" Elder Malcolm said with deceiving calm.

These political games of carefully chosen words and calculating tone of voice were among the predominant reasons that she spent so little time at the White Palace. Aela did not have the patience nor the disposition to play such games.

"Of course, I do not mean to imply any such thing. However, I cannot help but wonder why there is still no answer regarding my appeal. It was submitted over six months ago."

"The king has been very busy."

"It is a delicate matter."

"He's been preoccupied with preparing for his visit to Frin'gere."

The excuses came too readily to their lips. Aela recognized the truth in some of their claims. Her brother had inherited a tangled mess with the passing of their father less than a year ago. Furthermore, breaking a contract with an Immortal was no simple feat. Even she knew that.

As for preparing for his visit to Frin'gere, Aela saw it for the flimsy excuse that it was. Kesh visited Frin'gere frequently before becoming king. In truth, Aela wondered if his 'mission of goodwill' was merely an excuse to escape the elders and the demands of the crown.

"Of course," Aela submitted. Waiting to speak to her brother directly was more productive than arguing about it with the elders. "Is there something I may do to help prepare for Phoenix Son's arrival?"

"No, of course not. Your presence will be expected as you are a member of the royal family. However, all other arrangements having to do with the Immortal's arrival have been left up to the priestesses and a select few among the elders."

"In fact, Your Majesty, the rest of the meeting is trivial affairs that do not require the crown's attention."

Clearly dismissed from the meeting, she rose from the throne. With a dignified nod, she walked past the groups assembled on either side of the mosaic floor.

In as gracious a voice as she could master, she wished them a good day and exited the room. As the palace guards closed the heavy wooden doors behind her, she heard the voices of the elders rising in volume. The topic of their discussion obviously was of greater importance than they wanted her to know.

Across the hall, her personal guard waited. Four in all, the guards stood out from everything else in Dovkey. Rough, cream-colored turbans covered their heads and faces. Only the bridges of their noses and the hollows of their eyes showed. Simple woven fabrics of dull colors clothed every inch of their bodies, leaving no flesh exposed.

Without a word, Mar, Ter, Sey, and Anut fell into step beside and behind her. Aela allowed her thoughts to wander once again as she walked down the palace halls. Servants and palace guards scurried to get out of the way, bowing their heads to her in respect but eying her guards with suspicion and fear despite them being with her several for years now.

Ash. The word lingered, becoming more important than the outcome of her engagement.

She turned to Anut, the guard on her right. "Where is Menony?"

"She is in your quarters, still recovering from the trip here. Shall I retrieve her?"

"No, let her rest." Her maid and close friend did not well tolerate travel by boat. The voyage downriver from their hometown of Masia had been hard on Menony.

"Something troubles you," his deep voice rumbled gently.

She paused to stare at the vast ocean beneath the White Palace. The waves below spoke to those who were favored by Dovkey's deity, the Great Wave.

The waves had never spoken to her.

But the rivers had.

"I need to get to the river. Beneath the palace, through the old passages."

Her guard nodded and took the lead.

Aela paused for another moment to look at the sea. Even as she stared at the blue-green water, images of ash hovered on the edge of her consciousness. She prayed the river provided her with answers.

FINDING HER QUEEN IN the maze of the White Palace was not as hard as one might assume. With her quartet of massive guards, she was often easy to spot. Yet, Menony knew better than anyone that when Queen Aela wanted to escape notice she was quite capable of doing so, even with her guardians.

She started her search at the throne room, knowing that Aela was expected to stand in for her brother at the elders' meeting. The palace guards outside the room informed her curtly that the queen had left only minutes ago. She thanked them for the information and followed in Aela's path. Stopping occasionally to question another guard or servant, Menony soon realized where her queen was going.

Few knew that beneath the splendid White Palace existed ruins of an ancient temple. The forgotten space, dug by the first Dovkeyen nomads to reach the White Sea, was an intricate labyrinth of secret passages and rooms carved into the chalky stone cliffs. They tunneled all the way down to the sea.

As she approached the only access to the old passages, Menony glanced over her shoulder. As expected, no one followed her.

She soon caught up to Aela's group as they walked along the top of a wall that overlooked the Joining River. The Lesser and Greater Rivers, which flowed parallel to each other from the KeyGil Mountains, branched in many different directions before joining. Together they formed the Joining River, which ran along the eastern half of the country before splitting again. The Lesser and Greater flowed under and around the palace before spilling off the cliffs.

Aela turned to her with surprise. "I thought you were still unwell." The queen's light gray eyes surveyed her with concern.

"I am fine. Truly. Being out will benefit me more than waiting in your chambers." As Aela continued to examine her, Menony smiled. "I am fine."

Convinced, Aela turned and continued on task. Menony followed just behind her. "How did the meeting with the elders go?"

"As expected."

Menony smiled at her friend's disgruntled tone. Aela had never gotten along with the elders. "Surely, something interesting was said," she probed. The queen's pause told her that indeed something interesting had been said. "What was it?"

Aela succinctly summarized the meeting. However, something did not make sense. "Why are we in the old palace right now?"

A thoughtful silence followed. Menony waited patiently, knowing that she could not push for the information.

"There are reports of ash falling from the KeyGil Mountains," the queen replied softly.

The maid's brow furrowed. "And why does that worry you so?"

"I'm not sure, but I cannot shake the feeling that the presence of this ash is significant."

Menony nodded as she stared at her queen and friend with concern. "You're going to the temple pools?" She asked cautiously.

"No, no. I thought there might be some news on the water."

"You don't listen to the waves."

Aela turned her head to stare at her friend, "No, I don't. But I do listen to the rivers."

The paths leading to the old temple rooms were difficult and dangerous. Steep stairs accessed the caverns created by the rivers forced underground. Narrow bridges arched over the rapidly flowing water.

Droplets hit Menony's legs as they crossed a bridge. The water beneath was clear and cool. Once over the river, the stairs twisted into the cliff. The space was cold, dark, and narrow. A long, narrow opening in the stone allowed a slip of sunlight through. Nevertheless, Aela knew the way.

As the passages twisted closer to the cliff face, the powerful churning sounds of the rivers faded. Doors with hinges rusted by time stood firm and blocked doorways. Rooms overlooking the sea flooded with the spray of waterfalls, making the smooth stone slippery.

They went down a narrow set of spiral stairs. Through more chambers, some lit and some dark, they made their way down towards the ocean. After the final stairwell, they came to a chamber well-lit by natural light. Water from the cascading river above covered the window. The afternoon light passed through the waterfall and arrived on the other side in the form of colorful rainbows. Menony watched the smile brighten Aela's face. This was the queen's favorite place in the entire palace.

Aela took her sandals off before entering. A small crack in the bottom left corner kept the room from flooding. Menony and the guards lingered just inside while Aela reached out to the falling water. She closed her eyes while her fingers disappeared in the spray.

They waited patiently, and Menony watched Aela's face closely. The queen smiled at first, but her expression hardened. Finally, she pulled her hand from the water and opened her eyes.

"What? What messages did the river give?"

Aela's expression turned to one of confusion. "I'm not sure. I felt the waters of Masia; it felt like home. Then it changed. It was...different. I'm not sure what...but it didn't feel like home anymore."

She turned to face them.

Menony recognized the confusion on the queen's face, along with fear, and her worry deepened. She dreaded the river's whispers.

"The temple pools might provide clearer sight," Anut said.

Aela's face resumed the regal blankness that she was so skilled at enacting. "They will not work for me."

"You have not tried," Mar, the head of her guards said softly.

"I cannot hear the waves. I do not think it likely that the ancient pools will speak anything to me either." Her expression turned thoughtful. "But there might be news from those who dwell in the sea."

She turned her gaze to the guards. "It has been very long since you have been to the ocean."

"Indeed," Mar agreed.

Menony knew that the guards would do whatever Aela asked of them. Including visiting the creatures of the sea to discover what they knew. Each guard nodded silently. Mar walked past Aela and took over leading the group. Aela fell in behind him, Menony behind her and the remaining guards followed.

Even before Mar opened the heavy stone door that led to the temple pool room, Menony could feel the energy and magic contained inside its walls. Ahead of her, Aela bowed her head to pass through the low doorway.

Roughly carved steps lead into the chamber. The walls, unlike the stone elsewhere in the palace, were varying shades of brown, gray, and black. Centuries worth of smoke had stained the white stone despite the well-hidden vents. Several small pools circled the room, varying from a foot across to several feet across. The center pool was the largest.

The guards skirted the pools with great caution. Menony wondered if they too could feel the magic swirling in the water. She did not have the gift of water magic, but like most who were ungifted, she respected the power of it, nonetheless. Every time they passed through this room on their way to the ocean, she and the guards tried to leave it as quickly as possible.

She noticed that Aela was no longer in front of her. The queen wandered slowly around the pools, staring at the water. The water throughout the room began to swirl and sway gently. The change in pools momentarily distracted her. The water had not done this any other time they had passed through the chamber.

Menony turned back just in time to watch Aela step into the center pool. She called out as the queen sank beneath the surface of the water and rushed to the center pool with the guards just behind her. They knelt at the pool's edge, peering into the clear water. The queen disappeared.

"Where did she go? What happened?" Menony cried out frantically.

"The Great Wave called to her," Mar responded simply, though a note of concern laced his voice.

"The Great Wave?" Menony asked disbelievingly. "Why?"

"There are things that she must see," Anut said as they stared at the water intently.

"What do you see, brother?" Sey asked softly.

"Nothing. Listen to the waters."

They remained still, listening intently to the sounds of the pools. The rhythm had slowed but not stopped.

"She is safe," Mar said to Menony. "We must wait."

Menony was not reassured but sat silently at the edge of the pool to wait as long as needed.

THE WATER'S CALL WAS inescapable. She stared down at the temple pools as they passed, slowing to look at the water. Energy unlike she had ever felt before pulsed from the pools. Drawn deeper into the circle of pools, she looked from one to the other as the water began to move more vigorously and rhythmically. Entranced by the water, she watched as blackness rose from the depths and consumed the entire pool. Steam rose from the surface of the dark water, and swirls of sweet-smelling vapors circled her body, wrapping it in warmth. She touched her foot to the surface and felt the power of the magic drawing her down.

Warm water surrounded her as she sank deeper and deeper into the pool. The desperate pull for air faded from her lungs as the first vision came.

Her brother's ring, the King's Sapphire, on a dark and calloused hand that was not Kesh's.

A different hand covered in flames.

And a third hand made of ash.

Ash.

The hand disintegrated, and ash swirled all around her. Her vision-self held out a hand to the falling flecks of gray and black. The ash stung as it touched her skin, but the sting turned to burning cold. Horror filled her as she watched her hand turn to ice. Frost spread up her body until it reached her chest. The icy burn turned into crushing pressure as her lungs froze. She felt the desperate need for air as she tried to escape the vision, but the dreamscape around her turned to ash.

No fire.

Just ash.

A powdery gray face emerged. It was not one she knew, but the countenance was grave as it uttered the final warning of her vision.

"Evil has come to Dovkey, and it seeks you, my queen."

Chapter 2

Menony stood with Aela's guards around the temple pool, awaiting the reemergence of Aela. For hours, Menony sat at the edge watching the clear dark water sway gently on the surface. She wondered how deep Aela had been pulled under the surface for her to disappear or if the magic of the pool concealed her.

This was her duty, to wait until she was needed, and then she would serve whatever needs must be met. However, she had never been good at waiting peacefully in a corner to be summoned.

Her pairing with the queen was an ideal one. Aela rarely sought to call on another to do things, but she also did not object to Menony simply doing those things without being asked.

Those in her employment often formed attachments or basic affection for the ones they served. With Aela, she had found the sister that she never had, the family that she had always yearned for. The two of them had been of like minds and hearts. For this reason, she stayed with her friend despite all the many changes that life had brought to both of them.

A heavy hand rested on her shoulder. She glanced up to see Mar standing next to her. Though trepidation still filled her, she appreciated the calming gesture.

Not long after, Aela's head burst forth from the water. Sey and Anut stood on either side of the pool and gently pulled her from the water, waiting for her to regain consciousness. The soft fabric of her gown was made sheer by the water and clung intimately to her body.

Her skin glowed with a soft pink glow and steam rose up from her exposed limbs. She breathed slow and deep as if sleeping.

"What is happening to her?" Menony knelt beside her, desperate to do something but unsure what.

"She recovers still," Anut explained as he touched her trembling hands with his steady ones.

They continued to wait, the fear almost tangible. Aela took a deep breath and slowly opened her eyes. Menony continued to stroke Aela's hair as she looked around the room, appearing confused by her surroundings. Mar came into her line of sight and touched her face gently.

"You are in the temple pool room, where you were before going into the center pool."

Aela continued to look around with confusion. "I went into the temple pool," she said softly. Menony answered yes and drew Aela's attention.

"I saw you." Aela stared intently at her friend. "But, I can't remember what I saw. You just flashed through my vision and then you were gone." She turned her head and stared silently at the center pool before sitting up. Menony helped her.

"There were three hands," she said in a trancelike voice. Menony's heart skipped as she watched Aela crawl slowly to the center pool as if compelled by it once again. The guards tensed with apprehension as well.

However, Aela simply sat on the edge, running her fingers through the clear water.

"What of the hands?" Sey asked softly.

Aela remained fixated on the water as she answered. "One wore the King's Sapphire. His hand was dark and calloused."

"Kesh does not have dark skin or calloused hands," Menony said softly.

"No, he does not."

"Who else would wear the King's Sapphire?"

"Whoever he gave it to," Aela responded absently.

Menony objected without thought. "He would not give away the King's Sapphire."

The sharpness of her tone drew Aela's attention briefly. The trancelike gaze cleared for a moment, and Menony wondered what truth she saw. She felt wrong arguing the probability. Even she knew that the King's Sapphire could not be taken from its bearer, but had to be given of the wearer's free will.

The dazed look returned to Aela's eyes as she looked back at her fingers swirling in the water. "There was a hand covered in flames."

"The Phoenix Son; he is on his way here. He might be closer than we know," Anut said.

Silence filled the space.

"What of the last hand?" Menony gently prompted.

"Ash."

They waited for Aela to continue. "Ash and ice."

"What of the ash and ice?" Anut asked softly.

Aela quickly looked at him, her eyes sharp, the trance broken.

"Ash and ice are coming."

Aela stood suddenly and walked from the room, taking the path that led to the ocean.

"What does that mean?" Menony reached out to Anut, seeking an answer.

"I do not know. I did not have her vision." He looked to where the queen had left and to where his brothers now followed her. "She may not know either."

THE CHILL WAS STILL with her despite the warmth of the air. Aela wondered if she would ever be rid of it. Desperately, she wanted the sun on her skin, maybe then she would feel warm again.

The path to the ocean was just as twisting and challenging as the one down to the Temple Pools. A shiver crawled up her spine. Though she did not know how ash and ice played into her future, the message of the vision was clear as day.

Danger. Everything and everyone she loved was in danger.

Aela was unsure how she was expected to fight it.

Mar closed the distance between them and walked just behind her. After years together, she knew the feel of each one of her guards' presences. The energy that each exuded was unique and readily identifiable. Mar's had always been a quiet confidence and sense of duty.

"You have not had such visions before, my queen."

"No, I have not," she answered even though his words had not been a question. Aela, too, was troubled by the sudden occurrence.

The priestesses taught that only those specially chosen by the Great Wave were gifted with such forbearance. Unsurprisingly, the priestesses were the only group of chosen known to have visions, and one only became a priestess by passing the trials.

Aela was not among the young women who could claim that achievement.

And yet, she believed wholeheartedly that the vision came from the deity that had guided Dovkey since its founding.

She sensed that Mar had more to say but chose to keep his silence. And so, they descended yet another stair before coming to the most ancient and difficult of all the passages. The sound of the river cascading down the stone was stronger here, perhaps because the combined efforts of river and sea had thinned the walls.

The crashing of the waves greeted them as the stairs widened into a small landing. The ocean washed up on the stone to greet them, dancing in and out. The sky was encased with the dark blue-gray clouds of Dovkey, and backlit by the sun above. A slight breeze blew, but the day was warm. Aela felt the cold grip of her visions loosen as she stood with her face lifted towards the sun.

Looking back, Aela saw that all her guards stood solemnly on the landing, massive hands crossed in front of them. "The sea knows everything. I need to know what it knows."

They nodded solemnly.

Menony came to stand beside her and together they turned their backs on the guards. Her guards did not like to reveal themselves to other people, even her. Aela gave them the privacy that they would never ask for but undoubtedly appreciated. When she looked back several minutes later, only Ter remained on the landing. The others had vanished.

"Do you not wish to go too?"

"We will take turns. One of us will stay to watch you."

With a sigh, Aela nodded to the giant guard, knowing that it was useless to argue with Ter when his mind was made. He was the most serious and determined of them all.

She and Menony sat on the outcropping. Their legs dangled over the edge and into the water, where gentle waves pushed and pulled.

"Aela." She heard the concern and fear in her friend's voice.

Aela knew from the pause that Menony was about to breach a topic that she would not like.

"The priestesses were wrong." A few simple words with a consequential meaning.

"They were not wrong. I failed the trials."

"But you hear the water, and now, the Great Wave is sending you visions."

She remained silent before responding to Menony's argument.

"It is more than that. To pass the trials, a woman has to show that there is a deeper connection to the water. Magic, the ability to connect to the water, is not something I have."

"You haven't tried."

She turned to the woman she loved like a sister. The stubbornness in her tone was characteristic of Menony, and just one of the things that she adored about her. In this instance, her friend was wrong though.

"I have tried. For many years, I tried."

"You have not tried since the trials."

It was true. Aela had not attempted to connect with the water in a way that would allow her to manipulate it or do magic as some called it.

"There was no reason to. I stood on the beach that day and any magic that I had just left me. No matter how hard I tried, I couldn't do it."

They were quiet as Aela tried to block out memories of that day.

"Maybe the priestesses should retest you," Menony said quietly.

Aela laughed. "You only get one trial. There are no second chances."

"Perhaps there should be."

She turned to Menony. "Why does this matter so much to you?"

The other woman was thoughtful as she stared out at the ocean. "The elders use your failure at the trials as a reason to deny you the throne. It is your birthright. I believe you are meant to rule Dovkey."

Aela gently grasped her friend's hand, and they both stared out at the waves. She smiled when she finally turned back to Menony.

"I cannot thank you enough for your loyalty and faith in me, but I accepted long ago that my path did not lie in that direction." Her smile deepened. "Besides, Kesh rules Dovkey, and he will provide the next generation of kings and queens."

Menony's expression darkened, and Aela laughed softly. "I know that you think Kesh is erratic and impulsive sometimes, but he will do his duty to this country and its people. You'll see. Kesh will be a great king."

The maid's expression softened. "Many do not agree with you."

Aela's smile turned thoughtful. "Many do not know Kesh."

"No, they don't," Menony whispered beside her.

"They are returning," Ter said from behind them.

Both women rose and left the outcropping. They returned to the tunnel within the cliffs and waited for the guards to redress.

"My queen," Mar's voice called out.

Aela emerged from the cliffs and faced the tense guards. "Any news from the sea?"

"There is black current heading this way, carrying something unpleasant with it," Sey said as he finished tying the head covering.

"Black current? What does it bring?" Aela asked as she walked to the stone's edge. Sey's hand gently closed over her arm, pulling her away from the water.

"We do not know," Mar said. "It is still too far out, but it comes to Dovkey from the north."

"From the north, huh?" There was nothing north of Dovkey except the endless ocean. "Perhaps it is the Phoenix Son?"

Beside her, Menony snorted. "You think the Phoenix Son travels on a black current?"

Aela shrugged and replied dispassionately. "Perhaps."

"No, he comes from the south, and he will not come by sea," Anut said behind her.

She turned to look at him. "Have you seen his coming?"

Anut had been known to see things in the future, though he was never able to control when the visions came.

"No," the deep voice said. "But he will want the ceremony of arriving by river. He is an Immortal." The rare disgruntlement in the statement caused Aela to laugh.

"Dovkey greets its friends by river and its enemies by sea," Ter quoted the old saying as he too stared out to the ocean.

Legends concerning the White Sea said it was the home of the Great Wave, and deep beneath its purple-blue-green surface was said to be a white beach where the souls of Dovkey's dead went to join with their god.

There were other stories too...those of the sea people, who had once been allies of Dovkey, but were now thought to be nothing more than fantasy. Aela knew all the stories, but never had she heard of a black current.

The chill returned. Images of ash swirled in her head, and she could not dismiss the dread in her heart. She felt unsettled, sure that more bad news was to come. It was said to travel in threes.

"We should return."

Aela led the way back to the newer part of the palace. The journey was silent, and she wondered if her group felt the same foreboding.

Chapter 3

The days passed, and the elders' apprehension heightened each day that Kesh failed to return from his trip to Frin'gere. Aela sat quietly through their meetings, careful not to betray her own fear. However, like the elders, she felt it growing with Kesh's continued absence.

To Aela's surprise, Menony seemed to also be affected. She eagerly waited with the queen's guards outside the morning meetings. Her face displayed a mixture of hope and worry. The hope in her eyes dimmed each day without news of the king's return.

At night, Aela lay in bed listening to the waves outside her bedroom window. They had never spoken to her, but the visions in the temple pool inspired hope that maybe now she would hear the voice of the Great Wave.

Even though she prayed to her deity to reveal the vision's meaning, the waves remained silent. Alone, she could not decipher the significance of the images she had seen, yet the words of the ash man haunted her every night. They echoed in her head as sleep descended and ash filled her dreams.

Evil has come to Dovkey, and it seeks you, my queen.

She returned to the temple pools every few days, desperate for clarification in the form of more visions. Though Aela could feel the faintest tinge of magic in the water, it did not reach out for her as it had before. Whatever wisdom the pools contained, the water withheld it.

A week after Kesh's expected return, she once more snuck down to the temple pools with her guards and Menony in tow. Unlike her previous visits, she walked past the pools without hesitation. She continued directly to the opening in the cliffs that overlooked the ocean.

The Head Priestess reported to the elders in the morning meeting that the waves were unsettled. No clear message yet, but those attuned to the waves felt a stirring. With this vague news, the priestesses maintained their stoic calm while the elders blustered and argued.

Aela hid her own feelings of trepidation behind a calm demeanor. Though she did not show it, she was relieved when the elders dismissed her. With a respectful nod to both groups, she left the room and signaled her guards to follow her quick retreat.

Now, as she stood before the blue-green water, she struggled to find the source of her angst. The sea was calm as they stepped out on the small ledge, and the fog of the past few days still lingered to the north of the cliffs. Greatly disappointed, she realized she could not hear the waves any better than she had as a young girl.

She leaned forward to place her barefoot in the water when Mar threw his massive arm across her chest.

"No," his deep voice rumbled.

She noted the tense gazes of her guards as they looked out over the sea, and her own trepidation deepened.

"What is it?" she asked.

"There is something foul on the current," Mar said as he turned to Anut. "Can you see it?"

"No, but it approaches from the north." Anut stared at the gathering fog. His attention shifted suddenly in the other direction. "Another ship approaches from the south."

Aela turned to look at him. "There are two black currents?"

"No, just one, but whatever comes from the south is heavily shrouded. I cannot see if it is magic or nature that veils it. We should be wary of whoever comes on that ship."

"Threats are coming from all directions." Menony took a step toward the edge. "Nothing good comes from a still sea."

Aela stared out over the water, wishing that Kesh would return soon. Whatever approached, she knew that it was not good and that the elders would undoubtedly handle it with their usual ineffectiveness. As the thoughts of her brother and the challenges ahead of him occupied her mind, her eyes focused on the horizon.

With each push and pull of the tide, the black current crept evermore closer.

"Do you see it?" she asked.

The guards to either side of her tensed. Sey pulled her behind him so that three guards stood between her and the sea.

"It comes quickly," Menony whispered beside her.

"There is no reason to stay here waiting for it," Aela said firmly as she turned her back to the ocean.

"Will you tell the elders or the priestesses?" Menony asked as they ascended the darkened stairs. Hand-carved centuries ago and made more uneven by the salty air, Aela concentrated on her steps. When they finally entered the temple pool room, she looked over her shoulder at Menony.

"They would not believe me. Or worse, they would be suspicious of how I know such things."

"Who are they to say that you can't come into your magic later in life? Do they personally know the will of the Great Wave?" She protested adamantly.

Aela stopped to face her. "Why do you always insist on telling them these things?"

"They should know that they are wrong."

"It does not matter."

"If they are ever going to acknowledge your right to rule-"

"Don't." Aela's low response held all the authority of her royal lineage. "I will never be called upon to rule Dovkey. They will never need to call upon me because Kesh will rule as king. His children will rule after him."

Her tone forbade any argument, and Menony acknowledged it with a respectful nod. A tense silence filled the space between them. Aela felt her simmering temper heightened by the fear she refused to voice. As she stared at her closest friend, remorse mixed with the other emotions. She started to apologize, but Menony stopped her.

"You do not need to. You are the queen, and I crossed a line."

She bowed her head once again, before stepping around Aela and walking to where Sey waited by the exit.

The remorse only deepened as she watched her friend, knowing that the intention of her words was genuine. Aela had long ago stopped defending herself to the elders and priestesses, but Menony's steadfast defense of her continued to surprise and humble her even after all these years. However, she did not agree with her friend's beliefs. Even with Kesh's absence, she could not consider any situation that would end in her ruling Dovkey.

She glanced down at the pools. The water was black. Gasping as she knelt to look more closely, she wondered if the black current had spread so quickly. Before any of her guards could stop her, she put her hand out to the dark, glassy surface.

Blackness surrounded her. The rough water tossed her body back and forth. Panic propelled her limbs to swim upward, but there was no light to indicate where the surface might be. An icy chill seeped into her skin and spread throughout her body like a stain on linen.

She saw him, his face achingly familiar. Fear and pain hardened the features that were so like her own. His eyes stared ahead as he stood at the bow of a ship. The overcast sky behind him crackled with lightning. Violent rain pelted his face and body.

Unexpectedly, he turned toward her, his blue eyes meeting hers. His face softened, and he smiled. Reaching a hand out to her, his lips moved but no sound penetrated the darkness surrounding her. She tried to call out, but her lungs filled with water.

Her arms frantically fought against the blackness around her. She desperately needed to get to him. She needed to hear the words that he kept speaking, hear the message that she needed to receive.

She was in a pool of water, and he was a vision on a ship caught in the destructive power of sea and sky. Some part of her psyche recognized that he was unreachable, but still, she tried, despite her frozen body suspended in place.

He took a step towards her, again extending his hand. She reached for him, and this time her fingers met his. He placed something on her outstretched palm before smiling sadly. His gaze was filled with love.

"Some things you can't change, Aela."

Darkness swallowed his image.

She called for him, but there was no sound.

The meaning of his words was unclear, but she suspected that this was more than just another warning.

Remembering the object in her hand, she realized she held a card, worn and yellowed by time. Simple black swirls decorated the edges. She turned it over. The surface was blank for a moment, but she watched as a black ship emerged. It was the ship she had seen Kesh on in her vision. The lines of the ship blurred as the image ran like spilled ink across the surface.

The water allowed Aela to stare at the glossy black card for only a moment before it propelled her upward.

Her lips parted and gasped as the air touched her face. Opening her eyes, she found that once again she was in the temple pool. She turned side to side, examining the water around her. It was no longer black.

"You had another vision," Menony said quietly from the other side of the room.

Sey stood protectively behind her, one hand resting on her shoulder. "What did you see?"

"I'm not sure," Aela lied as Mar and Ter helped her from the water.

Menony's eyes narrowed as Aela avoided her stare. She pushed away Sey's hand and stepped forward.

"What did you see?" Her voice shook with emotion.

Aela's eyes finally met Menony's. "An old playing card with a black ship. I don't know what it means."

"The black current," Anut said from the corner of the room.

"Perhaps," Aela said as she wrung the water from her dress. "Perhaps there is a black ship sailing on a black current, or maybe the ship is symbolic of the black current." She looked back to Menony. "I don't know what it means."

The other woman nodded, satisfied with the answer.

Aela turned away from the water and toward the door. She paused next to her friend for a moment. Her hand squeezed Menony's before she walked silently out of the temple pool room. The others followed closely behind her as she led the way back to the palace. At some point, Sey slipped ahead of her. She doubted that any threats waited for them on the stairs, yet she let him lead.

Lost in her thoughts, she failed to hear the arguing voices as they entered the palace. Sey stopped her with a gentle hand against her abdomen. Only then did she hear the man talking on the other side of the hall.

"Is this how you treat all your guests?"

"You have arrived with the king's guard but not with the king, who was expected days ago. I'm sure you can see how your presence here is concerning."

Aela recognized the voice as belonging to Elder Hans.

"I'm not here to see the king, and I have no knowledge of his whereabouts. I am here to see the queen."

"You will be detained until more information on the matter comes to light."

Too curious to remember the soaked state of her clothing, Aela stepped around the corner to face the man who had arrived with Kesh's entourage.

She stood behind Elder Hans. Across from him, flanked by two palace guards, stood an unknown man. His hair was black and cut close to his scalp. Skin, tanned by a desert living, covered the hard features of his face and the toned musculature of his bare arms. He was taller than the elder, though she guessed not much taller than herself. He wore a tight-fitting tunic of crimson, with a looser robe of gold overlapping, and pants of dark brown leather.

Four men stood behind him, three of similar coloring and build. The fourth man had lighter skin and lacked the imposing warrior presence of the others. He stood with his head down, holding something close to his chest.

"Am I to stand here all day debating with you?" he asked the elder. "I am here to see the queen."

"She will be notified of your arrival," Hans sneered before turning to the palace guards. "You may take him to one of the detention cells now."

The elder waved his hands at the guards as he started to turn away. He caught sight of Aela. She stood several feet behind him, her soggy dress hanging heavily off her body as beads of water dripped to the floor.

"Your Majesty!" He cried in shock.

The dark stranger smiled as he quietly stated, "I think we can consider the queen notified."

Chapter 4

She was beautiful. More so than her brother had let on, Tarr thought with a slight scowl. Not that it changed his purpose in being here, but her beauty was a welcome boon.

Upon first glance, she had an appearance of vulnerability. Her willowy frame, large gray eyes, and porcelain skin were delicate in nature, but Tarr suspected that she was far from fragile.

He struggled to look away. She was a vision with her near-transparent dress and heavy waves of strawberry blonde curling around her face. He thought of enchanted sea creatures as he studied every detail of her appearance. Undoubtedly, she was aware of the state of her clothing, the curves and details revealed, but she appeared unaffected.

Instead, she stood regally as she considered the scene with the disinterested look of a well-trained royal. He smiled as he remembered how often Kesh had given him that same look. The queen executed it better.

"Your Highness," he said smoothly as he and the rest of the group bowed to her. He lifted his head enough to see the queen's guard lean down. Her gaze drifted as the behemoth said something in her ear.

She nodded once. The guard bowed his head and turned down another hallway, leaving his queen and the group.

Her focus turned to the elder. "Elder Hans, you may proceed with the introductions."

The pompous old man who had been sent to "deal" with him stuttered in shock, his eyes desperately seeking any focal point that was not the queen. Tarr smiled as the man huffed and puffed, his face heating like a clay pot in the fire.

"Your Majesty...perhaps, this is not the time...the time for introductions."

"Did I hear you correctly when you said that he returned with Kesh's men but not with Kesh himself?"

"Well, yes, and that was-"

She held her hand up to silence his objections. "Instead of treating him as a potential enemy, perhaps we should approach him as a person of interest who may have valuable information regarding the wellbeing of our king."

Tarr snickered from his bowed position. He waited for the elder to introduce him. However, a glance at the man revealed the elder's clear refusal to meet his queen's command.

Interesting, Tarr thought as he stood.

"As your advisor refuses to do the honors, allow me. I am Lord Tarr of Avengere." She studied him with that queenly gaze, her expression revealing nothing.

"Welcome to Dovkey, Lord Tarr of Avengere," her tone softened just a touch. "Avengere is a small province not far from the Dovkeyen border, is it not?"

"You are a scholar of geography, Your Highness."

He kept his tone pleasant, as he very obviously assessed her from head to toe. Taking a step towards her, he offered his hand. She placed her hand in his even as her eyes narrowed. He allowed himself to slip into the persona that he was familiar with, the one that was expected of him.

"And might I add that you are without a doubt a most...welcoming sight for any man."

He smiled and bent his head to kiss her hand. With a wink, he resumed his full height. Despite the flirtatious display, the queen's demeanor remained unchanged.

Her gaze was intense, and he saw the quick, unsteady breath that she took before the facade of calm resumed. She was not as unaffected as she appeared.

Falling even more into the act, he smiled seductively at her while leaning in to ask, "Do you go about like this all the time...Your Highness?"

"Frin'geren, you-" Hans bellowed in a highly offended voice.

Aela spoke before the elder could finish his sentence. "Elder," she said in a warning tone. "We must remember that our guest is no more accustomed to our culture than we are to his. What we perceive as vulgarity should be taken as a compliment."

Tarr felt his brow lift in surprise. Her reaction was unexpected. The old windbag behind him gasped with shock before he once again sputtered in anger.

"He insults you, my queen" the elder blustered.

"No more than I am accustomed to," the queen replied coldly.

Tarr was pleased to see the elder take her pointed meaning as he instantly bowed his head and took a step back.

Turning her attention back to Tarr, Aela's icy demeanor melted just a bit. "Forgive Elder Hans, it has been many years since we have had a visitor from Frin'gere."

"No doubt it has been at least a century since the likes of my people have been admitted to the White Palace."

Oddly, she appeared more pleased than upset by the sneering comment that was directed towards the elder. Tarr suspected that she felt a great deal of contempt for the Reformation.

"Elder Hans, will you see to it that a comfortable room is arranged for our guest?" She smiled sweetly at the elder when he would have objected. "And please see to it that he is shown to the library and refreshments are arranged."

The elder, clearly unhappy with the request, bowed his head to her before turning on his heel. He gave terse instructions to a few of the guards who flanked Tarr.

"Lord Tarr, these men will show to the library. I will join you as soon as I have changed." She nodded to the guards. They stood at attention and waited for him to follow.

"Don't feel the need to change on my behalf. I have no objections to your appearance."

Aela eyed him critically for a moment. "You are too kind, my lord. However, I must insist. You and your party will wait in the library."

Tarr hesitated a moment before turning to the guards. "Lead on, men."

The palace guards looked slightly offended by the commanding tone but were too well trained not to follow orders. He glanced over his shoulder and saw that Aela stood silently watching as they departed.

She was a delightful sight and an unexpected challenge. Tarr shook his head and laughed softly to himself as he walked away. She was going to be more trouble than he'd been led to believe.

However, he did love a challenge.

AELA WAITED UNTIL THEY were out of sight before following with her group and turning right. She hurried to her room, ready to be rid of the sopping dress that weighed on her. Her hair had fallen from the style that Menony had created that morning and stuck to her face.

"He's going to be a handful," Menony said as they turned another corner.

"I don't think we've even begun to understand the amount of trouble that Lord Tarr's presence is going to create."

Menony smiled. "Yes, I have a feeling he is going to be a thorn in the elders' sides, but I really don't think you understand how much of a problem he's going to be for you."

"Nonsense," Aela said. "He is just another man."

She waved away the statement as they entered her chambers. Quickly divesting herself of the gown, she accepted the robe that her maid offered.

"He's a very handsome man," Menony mused as she brushed out the queen's hair.

"Not important."

The little smile on her friend's face annoyed her. "A very handsome man with an interest in you."

Aela doubted that Lord Tarr's interest was genuine. She had seen the calculating glint in his eye and the way he watched for the elder's reaction.

"I have no doubts that Lord Tarr is here for reasons that do not include me."

Menony pursed her lips but did not say another word as she finished arranging Aela's hair. When she left to retrieve a dry gown, Aela stared at her reflection in the mirror. Even after years of seeing them, the gray eyes were still unfamiliar. The pale countenance that stared back at her had changed little over the years though.

She was a woman with unusual features, none of them unpleasant, but not beautiful by traditional standards. He had stared at her like she was beautiful though. Thinking of his appreciative looks and flattering words, flutters filled her stomach. They were novel and unwelcome.

Admittedly, the Frin'geren was pleasing to look at, but she did not trust him or his act of interest. Thinking of it only strengthened her resolve to discover his true motive.

Chapter 5

The library was a spacious room with floor-to-ceiling bookshelves, filled with ancient and new texts. The large windows looked out over the ocean, and a breeze carried the salty breath of the sea into the room. Cushioned sofas in white and beige formed a square in the center of the space. White china settings, two steaming pots, and trays of delicious pastries occupied the center table.

After quickly changing into a velvety green gown and having Menony artfully arrange her damp locks, Aela joined her visitors in the library. The palace guards positioned themselves on both sides of the door. Aela reminded them that the men inside were not prisoners, but the guards' commitment did not waver.

Two Frin'geren men accompanying Tarr stood near the window, one looking at the ocean below and the other scanning the room. The third man had stayed behind to prepare his lord's room. The fourth man, who did not fit in with the others, sat on a sofa alone with a scroll across his lap and a teacup in one hand.

Tarr reclined on the adjoining sofa, looking like a satisfied cat.

"You have quite the guard, Your Highness. Are they always with you, or is the visit of a Frin'geren a special occasion?" Though he smiled like a man without worries, he failed to mask the antagonism of the question.

Aela ignored it. "My guard is always with me, just as you see them now," she paused then added with a smile, "Your visit was unexpected, my lord."

He held out his arm to indicate an empty patch of the sofa, raising his eyebrow in what Aela assumed was either a challenge or an invitation. She decided against both and sat on the couch opposite the other guest. Tarr made a show of disappointment, but she ignored it.

The foreign lord refused her offer of tea, so she poured only for herself. She blew gently on the steaming liquid before bringing it to her lips.

"As my future wife, what terms of endearment would you prefer?"

Aela barely avoided spewing tea across the room as Tarr's words hit her. Her fit of coughing went unnoticed by the Frin'geren.

"Honey...darling...sweetheart...cuddlebum, maybe?"

She recovered from the coughing fit and glared at the Frin'geren, who had continued to lounge on the sofa. He appeared completely at ease, but his sharp eyes watched her reaction.

"We have a pet name that is widely used in my country, one that I have always been fond of," he paused. "Puss."

Aela choked on her tea again. As she cleared her throat, she heard Sey's soft rumble of laughter behind her. She would scold him later.

"Lord Tarr," she began with another clearing of her throat.

"I don't think we need to keep up the formalities, do we, darling?"

"Lord Tarr," she said in her most regal voice. "Before we dispense the pet names, you are going to explain to me why it is that you think we are getting married. I find that I need more than brief introductions to consider matrimony."

Tarr sat up, amused by her response. "I find that I needed nothing more than the sight of you."

He waited for her reaction. She schooled her face into an expression of boredom, refusing to react to his provocations.

When she did not respond, he continued more seriously. "You are undoubtedly beautiful, my queen, but we both know why a man would strive to have your hand in marriage."

Again, she remained silent.

"Power, wealth, position..."

"I have a thorough understanding of why a man would want to marry me; however, Lord Tarr, I don't understand why you think you would be able to achieve such an honor." She paused. "Is that the reason for your visit- that you wish to propose to me?"

"I don't need to."

Aela lifted a brow and asked in a deceivingly sweet tone, "Oh? And why is that?"

"Perhaps," the man on the other sofa cleared his throat, "my lord, you should explain about the game."

Aela looked to Tarr. Irritation showed on his face.

"Game?" she prompted.

"Your brother, King Kesh, and I entered into a game of Seer's Fortune," Tarr began. Some of his bravado faded. "His wager was your hand in marriage, and he lost."

Aela sat in silence. Her face displayed the absolute disbelief she felt despite her attempts to hide it. She couldn't imagine her brother doing something so foolish. No one would play Seer's Fortune unless they knew that they had the abilities of a seer. Or they were a complete fool. Only a true seer could win, and Kesh was not a seer.

"This is not possible," she said in a quiet voice.

"I anticipated the news would not be well received," Tarr said. "That is why I brought Harold with me. He is the owner of the deck we used. With him," Tarr pointed to the scroll sitting on Harold's lap, "is the contract signed by all involved."

Without knowing why, Aela looked at Tarr's hands. She hadn't given them any attention before, but as the images of her vision in the temple pool resurfaced, she knew which hands were his even before she looked.

The King's Sapphire encircled the middle finger of his dark, roughened hand. She heard rather than felt the teacup shaking in her grasp. Putting it down with overt care, Aela leaned towards Tarr.

"Your hand," she commanded.

The Frin'geren took heed of the intensity in her face and readily obeyed. Her pale slender hands cradled his. She stroked her fingers over the ring as the room watched silently.

"The King's Sapphire cannot be taken from its owner; it can only be given. It will disappear from a thief's hand and return to where it belongs." Her voice sounded distant even to herself as she stared at the ring.

"Yes, I know," Tarr's soft tone drew her attention to him. Sympathy warmed his eyes.

"Why did he give it to you?"

"So you would know he was not forced into the game."

She stared at the jewel, stroking it slowly, a wide array of blue shades reflected in the faceted surface.

Pulling away reluctantly, Aela turned to Harold. "The scroll, please."

He quickly rose from his seat and laid the scroll on her upturned palm. She waited for him to reseat himself. Though she had pulled away from him, Tarr leaned forward with his elbows on his thighs.

Aela felt like she was in a dream. A part of her was living this while another part of her stood apart, outside watching everything unfold. Everything she saw seemed blurred around the edges and noises seemed far in the distance. Even as she unrolled the scroll, the crackling of the paper seemed too far away to be in her hands. With a steadying breath, she looked down at the three distinct handwritings that explained the events that transpired. Kesh had challenged Tarr to the game, Tarr had accepted, and Harold signed as the witness.

Beneath the challenge, Kesh had written out his wager...*by my divine right as the King of Dovkey, I offer a betrothal of marriage between my sister, Queen Aela of Dovkey, and Tarr of Avengere.*

However, no wager was written beneath Tarr's acceptance of the challenge.

"Your challenge was not written down. That makes this incomplete," Aela said to Tarr.

"No, Your Majesty," Harold objected. "Lord Tarr's challenge was written there; I saw it myself before the game started."

"It is not here now."

"The winner's challenge disappears once the game has been played out. It is of no importance, anyway," Tarr said.

"It is of no importance? And how many times have you played Seer's Fortune?" Aela exclaimed. It was a rare moment of uncontrolled temper. "This does not make sense." She stood and began to pace in front of the sofa.

"What is of importance," Tarr began.

"No," Aela interrupted, "there is nothing to indicate why my brother would do something so foolish. And am I correct in believing that you are not willing to share with me what your wager was?"

Tarr bristled at the harshness of her tone. "I am not required to disclose that to anyone other than my opponent. I assure you King Kesh was aware of what I was willing to offer."

"Your Majesty, we cannot force Lord Tarr to reveal that information. It could bring the wrath of the cards," Harold said shakily.

"Yes, I am well aware of the consequences involved with Seer's Fortune. It was indeed fortunate for you, Lord Tarr, that my brother would choose a game in which such consequences are death. When Kesh returns-"

Tarr's hardened expression silenced her. She looked to Harold, whose head hung low. "What are you not telling me?" she demanded.

He met her glare head-on. "I don't think you're as knowledgeable of the game as you think, Your Highness." He paused. "King Kesh did not just lose... he tried to cheat the cards."

"No." The breath left Aela's lungs.

"He picked the death card," Harold said softly.

The black card in her vision. The black ship. A ship of death. The meaning of the vision was devastatingly clear at this moment.

Aela fell back onto the sofa, a hand held to her mouth as if that could contain the scream rising in her throat.

"Guards," she said quietly, and both the palace guards and personal guards moved quickly to her side. "Show Lord Tarr and his party to their quarters."

Tarr reached for her. "We are not done talking."

"We are for now." Indifference filled her voice as she looked away from him. "Rest after your long journey." She turned to her left and gave a nod to Sey.

Over Tarr's objections, Sey herded the foreign lord from the room. Aela sat in silence as the space emptied.

Startling with the gentle squeeze on her shoulder, she looked with wide eyes at Mar. No words passed between them, yet she understood the comfort offered.

As the light of the fading sun dwindled in the room, Aela rose and walked to the window. She looked out on the calm ocean and evening sky. In the distance, the black current darkened the blue-green waters. Now, she knew what it would bring.

AELA RETURNED TO HER room with a look that Menony knew well. Something dire had transpired in her meeting with the

Frin'Geren, Menony was sure of it. She also knew from the firm set of Aela's lips that she was not ready to discuss it with anyone.

The queen scribbled a note to the elders demanding a meeting with them in the morning. After dispatching a guard with the note, she crawled into bed and succumbed to a deep sleep.

Menony stayed nearby. After tidying the room and straightening the queen's clothing and vanity multiple times, she settled into a chair near Aela's bed and watched while she slept through whatever horrible news the meeting had brought.

As the day passed into night, Menony lit candles around the room. Aela awoke to the soft glow.

"You're awake," she said in her gentle voice. "I heard there was unpleasant news in the meeting with the Frin'geren." Silence. "Are you okay?"

"I don't know," Aela's voice broke with emotion, and Menony moved to sit on the bed. She took Aela's hand in her own. She let the love she felt for her friend pour into where their hands met.

"Please tell me what happened."

"The black card I saw in my last vision..." her voice broke. Sniffling, she tried again, "Kesh challenged Lord Tarr to a game of Seer's Fortune."

Menony pulled back in shock. "No, no. He didn't."

Aela nodded. "He did. I saw the contract that they signed. The owner of the deck is with Tarr's group and ready to give testimony of what happened."

Menony stood up from the bed. Her grip on Aela loosened as she stepped away. One hand went to her abdomen and the other to her lips. "And the black ship, how does that relate to this?"

"Lord Tarr accused Kesh of cheating. In Seer's Fortune, the consequence of cheating is death." Aela's voice quivered. "Why would he do it? Why would he play *that* game of all games?"

Menony shook her head. "Are you sure? Maybe the contract is fake. Maybe the man is lying." She heard the desperate edge to her voice.

"Ony, Tarr has the King's Sapphire. He could only have gotten it if Kesh willingly gave it to him."

"What if...what if something happened to Kesh and this Frin'geren took it?"

"You know it doesn't work that way." They pondered the truth silently.

As Aela crawled out of bed, the pins from her hair fell to the floor. Menony rushed forward to pick them up. "Leave them; I'll get it," she instructed when Aela reached down to help her.

"I can help."

Menony pushed Aela's hands away and continued to gather the scattered pins. "You deal with it in your way, and I will deal with it in my way. You sleep, and I do." Her voice was quiet but firm.

Aela did not argue. "I'm sorry. I should have told you when I came back, but I just couldn't take anymore. I needed time to understand it, to absorb it." She ran a hand through her falling hair, and more pins fell to the floor.

Menony allowed her to kneel beside her this time and gather pins.

"I should have asked for more information before I sent the Frin'geren away. I need to talk to him again."

Menony took the pins from her and carried them to the vanity. She arranged them carefully as she considered everything Aela told her. Discretely, she wiped away the single tear that slid down her cheek. When she turned around, she saw Aela pacing the room.

"The contract...I saw it in Kesh's handwriting that he bet my hand in marriage to Tarr. And as the winner, Tarr..." the sentence dropped as her eyes sought Menony.

"You're betrothed to Lord Tarr? A Frin'geren?" Menony did not hide the shock.

"I don't care that he's a Frin'geren," Aela retorted with a display of her temper. "I care that Kesh played that stupid game to begin with! I care that he did something so, so idiotic and dangerous."

Menony's sentiments and emotions aligned with Aela's; however, she forced calm into her voice when she asked, "What will you do?"

"I have called a meeting with the elders and priestesses for tomorrow morning. I do not know enough about the game to determine a way out of it."

"They will not be happy. Despite your appeal, there is still talk that you will soon be wed to the Phoenix Son."

"I don't wish to be wed to anyone, not the Phoenix Son and not the Frin'geren. Can I not just be known as the barren queen who lived alone until old age took her?"

Menony gave a sad laugh. "You do not want to be alone your whole life. You will want someone to share the joys and pains with."

"Do you want someone to share your life with, Ony?" The edge of anger in Aela's voice only cut deeper.

Menony tried to keep the sadness from her expression as she smiled weakly. "At one time I did."

Aela stopped her pacing to stare at her. The question was in her eyes, but Menony spoke quickly before Aela could pursue it.

"When will you speak with the Frin'geren again? He has information you will need before you talk to the elders tomorrow. Maybe you should request to meet him in the morning also."

"No, I will go tonight."

Menony's eyes widened. "It is quite late. You slept for several hours. Dinner was served and cleared at least three hours ago."

"I'm sure he will be up. I will go to his room and take as little of his time as needed."

The corner of Menony's mouth quirked in a half smile. "Is it proper for you to go to his room at this time?" Teasingly, she asked, "What will the elders say?"

Aela shot her an annoyed look. "I do not care what they think. Besides, they cannot think any more poorly of me than they already do." A small smile formed, "There's no point trying to please them so why not enjoy frustrating them?"

Menony laughed. "Good for you." She stepped forward when Aela turned to the door. "But you cannot go like that."

"Why not?" Aela stood with her hair lopsided from sleeping on one side, her eyes still droopy, and her wrinkled dress hanging off one shoulder, oblivious to her state. "I do believe he has seen me worse than this," she said as she straightened her dress.

Menony studied her queen and friend. Somehow, Aela had grown into a stunning woman without any understanding of her beauty. She would never think to seduce a man with her appearance or with a pleasing smile. Part of that mentality came from being a queen who was raised to give orders and had the expectation that they would be followed. Part of it was simply Aela's personality, too direct and rational to consider a different approach. And the rest was a lack of experience in the matters of flirtation.

Despite the closeness of their ages, Menony felt almost maternal in this aspect. Her experience undoubtedly exceeded Aela's.

"I don't think he was particularly objectionable to your appearance earlier." Menony laughed at Aela's glare. "If you won't do it to impress him, then think about this: people will see you, either entering or leaving, and you look like a woman who just got out of bed. If you leave his room looking like that, it could be assumed that you got that way from being in *his* bed."

Aela considered it. "I see your point." With a sigh, she trudged to the vanity and sat down.

Menony smiled as she took out the few remaining pins. With gentle strokes, she brushed Aela's hair, allowing herself to focus on the task instead of what had happened with Kesh. The king had confided in her that his trip to Frin'gere was more than a diplomatic one. However, she never could have imagined that he would participate in something as consequential as Seer's Fortune.

Her heart broke for Aela...for everyone who would be without the king now. She felt the tears gathering in her eyes, but she refused to shed them. The way was set now, and though she did not know where it would lead, she would respect the sacrifice that Kesh had made to make it so.

She stared at Aela's reflection in the mirror. The sad, lost look was gone. A look of determination replaced it. A smile parted Menony's lips. She sincerely hoped that the Frin'geren knew what he was in for. His job would not be easy.

Chapter 6

A half-hour later, Aela stood outside Tarr's door with Sey. A pearl-beaded net contained her unruly curls, and she wore a simple deep blue dress that hugged her curves demurely. Menony had chosen the dress with care, explaining to Aela the importance of conveying the right intentions.

Aela agreed. She wanted to convey power without intimidating him and welcome his confidence without projecting a desire to know him intimately. Fortunately, Menony was a skilled maid and a knowledgeable woman who knew how to accomplish that.

As they approached his room, she noted that one Frin'geren and one palace guard flanked the door. Aela felt a prickle of irritation at the guards. She had not wanted to deal with anyone but Lord Tarr.

The Frin'geren guard smiled grandly and bowed deeply as she approached. "Your Highness," he said almost reverently. His skin was a few shades darker than the guard next to him, and his eyes were a pleasant brown.

The palace guard straightened and rigidly bowed with a murmur of acknowledgment.

So, he is one of those, Aela thought. She discovered soon after returning to the palace the guards' loyalty was divided along clear lines. Most of the palace guards, those who had been raised and trained almost from birth to be palace guards, felt their allegiance belonged first to the elders and then to the king or queen.

The soldiers, some of whom rotated through palace guard duty, came from all over Dovkey. They were boys from the country, sons of fishermen, and heirs to merchant fortunes. Unlike the palace guards, the soldiers had not been groomed from a young age by the elders' ideals. They were men with strong loyalties to the monarchy, taught by their parents the old system before the Reformation. It was another example of the disconnect between those who lived in the palace and the rest of the country.

Aela knew that news of her visit to the Frin'geren would surely reach the ears of the elders by way of the palace guard. Though she was pleased by the elders' inevitable disapproval, she recognized the potentially damaging uses of such information and began to counterplot how to use the situation to her benefit.

"Have you come to visit Lord Tarr, Your Highness?" The Frin'geren's question brought her attention back to his smiling face.

"Yes. I realize the hour is late..."

"He will not care, Your Highness. My lord will be very pleased by your visit. Allow me to inform him of your presence."

He bowed again before looking sharply and briefly at the palace guard. The latter huffed and glared with disapproval.

Seconds passed before the door was thrown open, and in the doorway stood a half-dressed Tarr. His shirt and boots had been removed. He wore only a long swatch of scarlet cloth around his waist. It hung to the floor, but Aela could see that he wore nothing on his feet. He braced his hands on either side of the door and leaned towards her with his characteristic leer.

"Why, Your Highness, to what do I owe the pleasure? Have you come to determine our affinity for each other?"

The palace guard visibly tensed. Tarr grinned wider.

"Matters were not settled earlier. Forgive my appearance so late in the evening, but I wish to finish our discussion." Her tone was polite but firm.

"I am always agreeable to engaging in deeper discussions with you...Your Highness," he infused the statement with innuendo.

She speculated that the undertone to Tarr's statement was more to irritate the guard than seduce her. His widening grin validated her theory.

A soft snort behind her indicated that Sey was also amused. She refrained from glaring at him.

Tarr stepped aside and welcomingly gestured for her to enter. "Shall we?"

Unable to keep his silence any longer, the guard blocked her entrance and said, "Your Majesty, I can arrange that the library or perhaps one of the studies be readied for a meeting with the Frin'geren. Perhaps one of the elders would like to join in the discussion."

"I very much doubt that," Tarr muttered behind the guard.

The guard turned on him, his face reddening, and a threatening look that alerted Tarr's own guard. The other Frin'geren emerged from within the room and stepped in front of his lord, ready for a challenge. They stared at each other, a breath away from violence.

"I do not wish to have an elder included in my conversation with Lord Tarr," Aela directed at the guard. He turned from his staring match and eyed her with a mixed look of confusion and disapproval.

"But it is not proper..."

The disapproval set off her temper. In a sharp voice, she snapped, "I do not need you to lecture me on what is proper. I do not answer to you."

Being tall for a Dovkeyen woman, she stared levelly at the guard. He seemed torn between standing his moral ground and showing the proper reverence. She waited silently for him to decide between the two, knowing that each passing second was more worrisome. Sey tensed behind her, ready to intervene. She held up a hand to stay him. The guard would need to make his decision without interference.

He nodded his head, "Of course, Your Majesty. It was not my place. Forgive me."

He bowed deeper than when she had first approached; however, she was not comforted. The palace guards were more loyal to the elders and their Reformist ideas than she realized. She would have to move around the palace more carefully in the future.

She remained silent, knowing that her temper still burned.

"Now, if you don't mind stepping aside," Tarr said from behind him.

The guard turned only briefly before resuming his former position, eyes blank and fixed straight ahead. Tarr's guard also resumed his position. Aela turned to Sey, who gave a reluctant nod. He assumed a position opposite the other guards, his big hands crossed in front, and his legs in a wide stance. His imposing figure put both guards on alert.

Aela smiled as she imagined the grin hidden beneath his face covering. She knew that Sey enjoyed the perceived threat the guards took from his presence. As she entered the room, she felt certain that her guard would keep the other two in line.

The room was pleasantly warm, lit by many candles and a few lanterns that Aela did not recognize.

She stared so intently at one that Tarr commented, "I brought those with me, from Frin'gere. They give off less heat and more light. They are created by some of the best fire magicians in Frin'gere. That one bottle of oil will burn for years."

She nodded in acknowledgment as her gaze drifted over the room. The small sitting area was sparsely furnished and lacked windows. To the side, a door stood open, and she saw more of the foreign lanterns glowing on either side of a bed.

Tarr followed her gaze. "Straight to the point. I like that in a woman."

She felt the heat of her anger dissipate as a small smile formed. She forced it away and resumed her royal composure.

"I must apologize, Lord Tarr. You have not been given adequate quarters, though I know those were the instructions I gave."

He leaned against one wall watching her, a lazy smile parting his full lips. "Oh, they are adequate...and nothing else."

"This is unacceptable. You should have been given one of the ocean-side rooms."

"I am content not having that swishing and swashing sound haunt me all night as I try to sleep." His frown conveyed how much the thought disturbed him.

"Then a river facing one," she persisted as she went further into the room. Sturdy but easily replaced pieces furnished the room. The exquisite mosaics, paintings, and pottery that typically decorated the room of any other visiting diplomat were absent. A plain rug covered the white stone floor. Drawn by her anger, she turned from the sitting room to the bedroom.

Again, the small size of the room failed to meet her expectations. The linens were clean but not gracious or inviting. Rather like the elders, she thought with rising anger.

"I will have you moved to a more appropriate room tomorrow. Accept my apologies for this mistake. As I said, it will be corrected."

Tarr leaned against the door frame, arms crossed over his chest, and watched her with interest.

"And why is it that you find it so unacceptable when the elders did not?" He asked with amusement and curiosity.

"Because I am not a prejudiced, uptight, disrespectful Reformist," the words were out before she could stop herself.

Tarr threw his head back and laughed. Then he slapped his hands together. "Thank the gods for that!"

Color rose up her neck to her cheeks. "I should not have said that."

Tarr pushed away from the doorway. "No need to apologize to me, nor to pretend. I'm not a prejudiced, uptight, disrespectful Reformist either; though, I'm not too sure about your guard out there."

"Sey?" she said with confusion before realizing he meant the palace guard. "Oh, that one. The palace guards are not my guards," she said with a bit of irritation.

"Yes, I noticed that you seem to have your very own entourage." He approached her with an intent gaze as if searching her eyes for secrets.

"Just as you have your own personal guard," she countered.

He stopped in front of her. She was surprised by how much their height difference pleased her. She disliked being a tall woman in a land where the men were rarely as tall.

"True, but I'm a foreigner in a hostile country. What is your reason?"

"You think Dovkey is hostile?"

He raised an eyebrow and let his eyes sweep over the room before looking back at her.

She laughed. "I'm almost as unwanted as you, maybe even more."

"So unwanted that you need protection?" The tone was mocking, and yet his eyes were serious.

"I don't think the elders are going to kill me, no. The priestesses might." She was pleased to see he smiled at her joke. "I don't fear assassination attempts."

He moved closer, crowding her with his body, and his voice turned soft in response to her somberness. "What do you fear?"

The intimacy of his nearness and the warmth of his voice triggered her internal alarms. Somehow her defenses fell in his presence, and she failed to notice his seductive advance. She took a step back and stared at him, wondering how he got past the defenses so easily. Straightening her shoulders, she resumed the look of indifference she had been taught as a child.

"Earlier, you were telling me about the game of Seer's Fortune," she prompted.

His eyes narrowed for a moment before he responded in an equally indifferent tone. "Yes, I was explaining to you how your brother cheated the game and revealed the death card."

She took a deep breath to calm the temper simmering near the surface. "Yes, I believe that is where we left off."

She looked around, realizing for the first time their proximity to the bed. Stepping around him, she headed towards the door. "We will continue the discussion in the sitting room."

Tarr stepped in front of her so smoothly and quickly, she almost ran into him. "But of these disappointing chambers, I assure you this one is much more adequate."

"That all depends on what you think is going to happen."

He smiled at her response, and she realized her retort was not what she had intended it to be. "We will be discussing the game that you and my brother-"

"I do love *discussing*," he said as he herded her away from the door.

She knew she was being maneuvered, yet she allowed it as she avoided his touch. Her retreat was interrupted when the back of her knees hit the chest at the base of the bed. A commanding and apathetic retort evaded her. The temptation to return his suggestive remarks warred with irritation.

He continued his advance in silence. Aela stilled as she watched him. He leaned down, circling his arms around her. She felt the breath leave her in a barely contained gasp. His body exuded startling warmth as it hovered just above hers.

The chest behind her opened, and she heard the clink of glasses. "I find that discussions are always a little better with this."

Stepping away, she saw that he held a dark green bottle partially wrapped in a rough, brown cloth.

"Wine?" Puzzled by his actions, she asked, "How does wine make your discussions better?"

He smiled. "You, my darling queen," he leaned towards her, his voice dropping in volume as if conveying a secret to her, "are Dovkeyen and oblivious to the finer things in life."

He stepped around her and walked into the other room. She stood in confusion for a moment before following.

Tarr stood at a small table with one of his lanterns on it and the chairs pulled out. He poured the red wine into two generous glasses. Looking up expectantly, he waited quietly as she took her time joining him. He watched as she took a seat before seating himself and sliding the wine across the table.

She picked it up and twisted the thin stem of the glass in her fingers, watching the liquid swirl.

"You do know that drinking is permitted only with dinner. It is thought to be overindulgent to drink after the meal when there is no food to be complimented by its presence."

"Will they hang me for it?" he asked with avid interest as he took a long taste.

"Under Reformation law, you would be heavily fined." She continued to swirl the liquid.

"It's a good thing I'm not a Reformist then. It's an even better thing that I'm Frin'geren, and nothing less than overindulgence is expected. You will have to tell me more about the Reformation, but not tonight." He took another drink, his eyes noting the untouched glass. "Shall I take yours since you do not have the good fortune of being Frin'geren?"

She looked up from the wine and found his expression softened. Lifting the glass to her lips, she took a small sip. The rich liquid hit her tongue, and she decided it was the best wine she had ever tasted.

"I find that I am curious to discover how wine improves discussions. Now," she set the glass down and turned her focus fully to him, "Lord Tarr, how did you and my brother become involved in a game of Seer's Fortune?"

He sighed. "I'm afraid that you're missing the benefits of the wine." He shook his head sadly and leaned back in his chair.

"What?"

"The point of the wine is to help you relax. Drink more and perhaps you will not charge into each new conversation topic."

"It is late. I wish to make this conversation as short as possible as I am sure that you are tired from your journey."

He leaned forward. "I find my stamina is always renewed by a beautiful woman. Besides, if we finish too early, they'll never believe that I had enough time to bed you."

She stared at him. Silence filled the room.

Suddenly, Aela laughed. She tried to contain it but failed. No man had ever talked to her the way Tarr did. As the future queen of Dovkey, she was treated with respect. Men did not approach her with flirtations or make suggestions of lust. Even without the strictures of Reformation law, such things were not done.

"You assume that I want people to believe that you seduced me?"

"Of course you do." He drank leisurely. "That is why you came here so late."

"I came so late because I need to be well prepared tomorrow when I face the elders with the news of your claim." She took another drink.

"Leading them to think that I seduced you could keep them off balance."

"Leading them to believe that you seduced me would only harm the integrity of your claim. A woman is weakened by lust and easily manipulated by a lover," Aela said mockingly.

Tarr paused in bringing his glass to his lips. "In what world is that true? Where I'm from, it is not a man who leads a woman around. In fact..."

Aela laughed and took another sip. "No," she held her hand up to stop his objection. "The only thing this meeting will accomplish outside of giving me information is to irritate the elders."

"You enjoy irritating them?"

"Disapproval is the only sentiment I can stir from the elders." They grew quiet for a moment as she stared thoughtfully into her cup. "Tell me what happened, please." Her voice softened but was no less commanding.

"Kesh and I had met on a few of his other travels to Frin'gere. We drank and gambled before. He was surprisingly fun for a Dovkeyen." He took a drink and stared over her shoulder, gathering his thoughts. "This last time he contacted me, and we met at Harold's tavern, not far from the border. We played a few inconsequential games before he suggested that we up the stakes. He suggested Seer's Fortune, and I agreed."

"Are you a seer?"

"Drink more, you're charging again." He smiled and waited until she took a drink before continuing. "No, I am not a seer, but I knew that Kesh was not either. Since he was the challenger, I had the advantage. Don't ask what I wagered; I won't tell you."

She stared at her wine. "Why would he challenge you to that game?" She looked at him. "How did he cheat?"

Tarr shrugged. "I have no idea." When she would have objected, he continued, "I only know that he cheated because the death card appeared. I am told it only appears when someone cheats. I am not sure what he did to get it. As to why...he was a man grieving. He was not ready to be king, too immature and unwilling to accept the challenges of being king. He wanted to pass it to someone else."

Aela disagreed with his opinion of Kesh, but she did not argue with him. Instead, she switched tactics.

"I'm afraid that you were misled on what you would really be getting out of this deal. According to Dovkeyen law, only a member of the royal family may rule. By marrying me, you would gain little political power." She took a drink. "You wouldn't even be called king."

"What?" Tarr seemed surprised for the first time since she had met him.

"You would only be a prince. Titles of king or queen are reserved for those of direct royal blood. Did Kesh not mention that?"

"No, he did not." Tarr took another drink.

"I know that the reward in a game of Seer's Fortune cannot be denied. But is there another way to nullify the agreement?"

Tarr raised an eyebrow but answered anyway. "If the winner refuses the winnings without the influence of duress, which I will not do."

"I see." She stood.

"Are we done?" Tarr asked with amusement.

"I believe I have the information that I need. Thank you for the wine." She bowed her head and walked towards the door.

Again, he moved so quickly that she didn't realize it until he spun her around to face him. He held her arms in his hands and stared down into her eyes. "Did you discover how wine improves discussions?"

His tone was so deep and seductive that she couldn't help smiling. "Yes, it relaxes the other party enough that the process of getting information is much easier. I'll remember it in the future." She tried to turn away, but he continued to hold her.

"Stay," he commanded softly and disappeared into the other room. He returned and held a dried leaf to her lips. "It will cover the smell of the wine. I would hate for the queen to be heavily fined."

She smiled and took the leaf from his fingers. Taking a conservative bite, she found the plant had a subtle mint flavor.

"Thank you. Good night, Lord Tarr. I wish you a restful sleep." Again, she tried to turn away, but he held her.

His hands drifted from her arms down to her hands and past her fingertips. His fingers tangled in her dress, crimping the material in his hands. She stood still, unsure of his intentions. He continued to gather the dress until the hem rested at the top of her thighs. Dropping the now wrinkled material, he ran hands up her waist, skimming the sides of her breasts. His fingers gathered at the base of her head threading into her contained curls. Without warning, he pulled the beaded netting free and tangled his fingers in her hair.

She unknowingly arched towards him as his hands continued to mess with her hair. With a soft groan, he whispered into her ear. "They may not believe you were bedded, but you do look seduced."

Aela pulled away to look at him. "I would be neglecting my duties as a womanizing Frin'geren if I let you leave looking any other way."

Despite herself, she smiled, and this time when she turned, he let her. He opened the door and smiled at the astonished guards as she walked regally by them with her rumpled dress and tangled hair.

Aela did not spare either of the guards a look as she headed towards her room. However, she heard the soft rumble of laughter from Sey behind her as they turned the corner.

Chapter 7

Tarr closed the door as she slipped from sight. His head rested against the wood as a sigh escaped his lips.

The enormity of his purpose in Dovkey weighed heavily on him. He knew it wouldn't be easy to do what he'd promised, but the realization of just how difficult it would be exhausted him. The role he played was not new to him, but he found that he resented it now.

The world expected the worst from a Frin'geren. Rumors of his homeland were varied and often scandalous. In a place as secluded and conventional as Dovkey, such rumors inspired fear and disgust. Undoubtedly, places in Frin'gere were as wild and unscrupulous as the tales. Yet, he doubted that there was any country in the world that didn't have its own cesspools, maybe some better hidden than others.

She was not completely fooled by his act though. He liked that she either did not trust his act or saw through it. It was another way that he had underestimated her.

Kesh had warned him.

As he stepped away from the door, images of that night returned to him. He poured himself another glass of wine, emptying the contents in one long swallow. Unfortunately, it would take a much greater quantity of wine to keep the memories at bay.

He could almost hear the raucous voices of the tavern patrons and smell the tangy mix of sweat and beer. They had sat in at a corner table that night, away from the crowd. The night was not any different than other nights. Two old friends, a steady supply of drinks, and a game of cards.

◈

"I THINK WE SHOULD RAISE the stakes," Kesh said. His sad blue eyes stared across the table.

Tarr's gaze shifted lazily to the cards in his hand, and he sorted them as the man across from him waited for a response. Two empty glasses and a melting candle stood between them. The remains of their game, a worn deck of cards and two piles of gold, occupied the remaining space on the table.

He raised his glass, signaling to the passing serving wench his silent request for another drink. His stare turned to Kesh.

Finally, he responded, "As a Frin'geren, I am always ready to raise the stakes. Is it not enough for the King of Dovkey to gamble away the country's wealth?"

Despite the cacophony of the tavern's drunken occupants, the men remained undisturbed at their table in the darkened corner of the room. They had passed the evening undisturbed with the fickle favor of fortune indulging them equally. The table between them was nothing more than a few weathered planks of wood nailed to rickety legs. The chairs upon which they sat were of the same materials and quality of build. A lantern with fogged glass hung nearby and cast a dim light on their space. Though the floors were clean, the air smelled of spilled ale and a faint tinge of brine.

Kesh, the King of Dovkey, eyed the similar stacks of gold on the table, arcing an eyebrow. The Frin'geren's laugh was deep and untroubled.

"Men like you come to Frin'gere to lose themselves in debauchery, but you have a deeper purpose. A darker reason for being here." He studied the man across from him. "So, if not your country's riches..."

The king leaned forward, his eyes scanning the room with a caution that bordered on paranoia. Blonde hair fell over his light blue eyes. The faint tan of his skin glowed in the light of the candle, which cast his features in shadow. A well-grown goatee formed under his nose and around his lips. Quietly, he said, "I am prepared to gamble more than that, Lord Tarr."

Tarr was silent for a moment. Finally, he drawled, "Dovkey is a very rich country. What else could you possibly give?"

Kesh took a steadying breath. "I have the authority, now that my father is dead, to marry my sister to anyone I feel is worthy."

"And you find me worthy?" Amusement filled the question.

"No. No one is worthy of Aela, but I have no greater treasure to offer."

Tarr laughed. "I've never known any woman to be so valuable."

"You've never known Aela," the king replied softly.

"So, you bet your sister's hand in marriage? How is that more than the riches of Dovkey?"

"She is Dovkey. She will inherit the crown."

"You bet the rule of Dovkey then?" As Tarr tilted his head to the side and the corner of his lips rose slightly, the light from the hanging lantern struck his amber eyes. "And what could I possibly wager against that?"

Kesh's expression remained serious; his tone strained. "You know what to bet."

Tarr's smile faded as he nodded his head gravely. "Very well." He looked down at the table and shuffled the cards in his hands. "Ace's Keeper is not the game for so large a wager. Did you have another game in mind?"

At that moment, the serving wench returned with drinks.

Kesh thanked her as she set them on the table. Tarr looked at her with a sly smile as he put his arm around her waist. "My dear, we will need something stronger than this."

Her mouth opened in outrage, "After I bring you these, you want different ones?"

Tarr picked up one of the gold coins and flipped it over his fingers. "No, we want these and something stronger," he handed the woman the coin. Her expression showed a hungry pleasure.

"I think I can handle that then," she said sweetly as she took the coin. She turned to retrieve the men more drinks, and Kesh watched as she walked away. He turned his intense focus back to Tarr.

"Seer's fortune," Kesh said in a grave voice. The air around them condensed, and the sounds of the drinking house faded from hearing. It was as if the burden of fate realized weighed on their shoulders. The two words spoken clicked into place events that had always been destined to happen.

Tarr's heavy brow sank further over his eyes. "That is the game for high stakes," Tarr sounded calm and indifferent, but his eyes darkened with an indecipherable emotion. "Seer's Fortune it is."

The king nodded.

They sat in silence until the sweet-eyed serving girl returned with their drinks. She carefully placed a shot of dark amber liquid in front of each man. Tarr smiled up at her as he handed her two more gold coins. "One is for you, the other is for the owner of this establishment. You will go tell him now that his presence is requested here."

She nodded and smiled shyly. Then she turned and rushed back to where the tavern owner wiped the wooden bar with a worn cloth.

He listened to the girl while she handed him a coin. With a mild look of curiosity, he looked from the coin in hand to the pair of men sitting in the secluded corner. He rounded the bar and approached Tarr and Kesh's table with a friendly smile.

"Good evening, sirs. What may I help you with? I hope everything has been to your liking."

"Yes, thank you," Kesh was quick to reassure.

"Do you have a Seer's Fortune deck?" Tarr asked briskly.

The man's entire stature seemed to sink. The contented look withdrew from his face as he clasped and unclasped his hands in front of him. "I do. Most barkeeps in Frin'gere have one."

"We have need of it," Tarr said in a smooth voice. "And your discretion."

The man nodded and mumbled that he would return shortly.

Kesh watched the man return to the bar. The tavern owner approached a plain woman of little height with a frown of irritation on her face. She was undoubtedly his wife. Fear replaced the annoyance as the tavern owner whispered in her ear. He slipped out from behind the counter ignoring the raucousness of the oblivious drinking crowd and passed through a door opposite the bar.

"What is she like?" Tarr's quiet question drew the Dovkeyen king's attention away from the bar. Kesh stared at him as if he did not understand the question.

"If I am potentially to marry your sister, I'd like to know what kind of woman I am binding myself to."

Kesh smiled. "She is...not what you would expect."

Tarr mockingly gasped, "Is the princess of Dovkey not an ideal specimen of acquiescence and grace?"

Kesh laughed, and his face relaxed. "Aela is far from acquiescent. And she's a queen, not a princess."

"I thought all Dovkeyen women were tame creatures,"

"She will not be easy to manage," Kesh said with a soft smile.

"A challenge it is then. I prefer it that way."

Kesh shifted his attention once more to the bar behind Tarr. The tavern owner's wife picked up the abandoned towel and wiped it over the counter. She watched the bar and tried not to draw attention to her husband as he once again crossed the room with a small, glossy, black box.

He carried the object with extreme care, anxiety evident in his eyes. He walked straight toward the table in the back, passing men and women too far into drink to concern themselves with what he carried. The man held the box in his shaking hands as he stood before Tarr and Kesh.

The owner threw his head back in a silent prayer, hoping that any or all gods would be with him. "I have the cards with me." He held them out to the two men. "Do you wish to inspect them before playing?"

Tarr shook his head. His expression was neutral. "There is no need. The cards check themselves."

The owner looked nervously at the box. "And you, sir, would you like to inspect the cards?"

Kesh also declined as he ran the back of his hand across his mouth. His eyes looked down at the table.

The man looked at the box again. "I will inspect them," he declared bravely. "I won't have death seeking me."

He gently put the box on the table. His wife timidly approached and set another candle between the two men.

"Should you do this, Harold?" she asked nervously.

"I have no choice. They are my cards and to refuse them could bring bad upon us," he responded gravely as he took the silken-wrapped object out of the box.

Pulling the wrap off one side at a time, Harold revealed the stack of worn and faded cards. The edges of the hand-length cards were torn and burnt. Stained by every use, the background on the cards was a dull yellow. Harold spread the stack flat across the table. He revealed the four symbols: leaf for earth, droplet for water, flame for fire, and swirling wind for air. Each card possessed one of the symbols, except one. The black card, as glossy and beautiful as the box, stood out from the others.

"The death card is here as well as the four elements. I see four queens, four kings, four ladies, four knights, four pages, four banners, and four beggars. I believe the whole deck is here."

THE FAILED QUEEN 61

"Very well, let no harm befall you," said Tarr. He looked at Kesh. "Are you sure this is the game you want to play?" The intensity in his eyes was disconcerting.

"Yes, I am quite sure."

Tarr exhaled slowly and sat up straighter. "Do you know how to play the game?"

"Of course, I know how to play the game," Kesh's voice rose with irritation.

"I will explain the rules to you anyway." Kesh tried to interrupt, but Tarr silenced him first. "I will not win by your lack of knowledge. If you lose, then no one, not even the cards, can hold me responsible." Tarr looked at the cards spread before him. "When was the last time you saw a game of Seer's Fortune?" he directed the question to Harold.

The owner stated that it was not more than a few years ago that the game was played at his drinking house. "Good, then you can correct me if I explain anything wrong."

The owner nodded.

Tarr returned his attention to Kesh. "Only five cards are played in this game. You will pick four of the five, and I will pick the last one. I will then shuffle those cards since you are the challenger. After that, I lay the cards on the table in front of you, and you pick my card."

"Is there anything else?" Kesh tapped his foot impatiently on the floor.

Tarr put his fingers on the cards. "Do you know that it is said that the cards can tell if you are a cheater even before you have cheated? They know all intentions simply through touch. To cheat is to sentence yourself to death, for it comes to all who try to deceive the cards."

"Are you ready?" Kesh leaned forward, staring calmly at Tarr.

The Frin'geren picked up his shot and threw it back in one swallow. He then leaned in and whispered, "You are truly going to risk your life for this? On nothing more than a show of luck?"

"Luck or skill," Kesh responded.

Tension hung in the air as the two men stared at each other.

"Well then," Harold said uncomfortably. "Please state who the challenger is."

"I, Kesh Ingrand Nico Gero, King of Dovkey offer a challenge of Seer's Fortune."

Even as Kesh said it, the barkeep's eyes widened in shock, and his wife gasped behind him.

"I, Tarr of Avengere, accept the challenge." He took a long drink of his ale.

"Well then," Harold stuttered. "What do you challenge, your...your highness?" he began.

"My sister's hand in marriage," Kesh said calmly. Stunned silence followed in the wake of his words.

"Do you have the paper and quill?" Tarr prompted impatiently.

Harold's wife put the desired items in front of him. "Are you sure you want to do this?" he asked Kesh slowly.

"This is the choice that I make," Kesh said with a sincere smile. He picked up the quill, drove it into his fingertip, allowed the blood to cover the edge, and then signed his challenge on the paper. Tarr did the same, and Harold signed as a witness. His wife rolled up the sheet and stepped behind her husband once more.

"And you, my lord?" Harold managed to ask despite his shock.

"My wager is written on the paper. Unlike the challenger, I do not have to disclose it," Tarr said sternly. Slowly, Tarr looked back at the king. "What would you play with?"

"I chose the four queens. It seems appropriate since I wager the queen of Dovkey." Kesh seemed less comfortable than he had been only minutes ago.

Tarr sorted the four queens out of the deck and picked a fifth card. He placed the remaining deck in a stack to the side. He shuffled the five cards and lay them face down in a row, and then leaned back on his chair, staring intently at the king.

"Show me the King of Water," he ordered.

The king of Dovkey held his right hand over the cards, hovering no more than a few seconds above each. Tarr rubbed his goatee, his brow pensive.

Kesh blinked his eyes as his hand paused over the card second from the left. Finally, he moved his hand to the middle card, his fingers resting gently on the surface. Tarr leaned forward over the card. He forced Kesh to meet his eyes. The tension that passed between them filled the space, and after a few pregnant moments, an understanding seemed to pass between the two men.

Kesh sat straight in his chair and flipped the card over. The queen of fire showed underneath his shaking fingertips. The card, stained as all the others, showed a brilliant picture of flames dancing around a beautiful woman. Despite the size of the painting, the detailed face with cupid bow lips, fiery red hair, yellow eyes, and high cheekbones showed clear as day. The woman of the card stood seductively between the flames. The red dress parted to reveal her legs, and her arms rose above the low neckline and over the crowning headdress of gold and rubies. Yet, as they stared at the card, the queen's lovely painted face melted away in front of them. The flames blazed, and the queen's body burned as it swayed with the dancing fire. Blackness filled the space around the card, and as the queen became undistinguishable, the blackness swallowed the flames.

A shadowed ship rose from within the black. Unseen waves beat it from side to side before finally crushing it back into the darkness. The death card lay on the table with its glossy surface reflecting the light.

Harold's wife gasped. Before her husband could stop her, she spread the stack of cards on the table and saw the card of death gleaming in the center of the deck. She quickly looked back at the row of cards and watched as smoke rose from the middle one, leaving the untarnished Queen of Fire behind. Smoke rose from the others and the face of each card appeared as the smoke dissipated. The Queen of Earth held the right end, while the Queen of Air held the left end. The Queen of Water rested next to the Queen of Fire on the right side, and the King of Water rested on the left side.

Tarr closed his eyes briefly for a moment almost looking remorseful; however, as he opened his eyes, he smiled coldly. "Has it ended the way you saw it?"

Kesh did not answer as he swallowed the shot of amber liquor.

"What does this mean? Why did the card turn black?" Harold's wife whispered to her husband.

He solemnly responded, "The king tried to cheat the game, and the cards have punished him with death."

"But he almost had it," she objected. "Didn't you see it? His hand stopped on the King of Water first. He might have won the game."

Harold silenced her with a severe look. He hesitantly gathered the cards, covering them once more in the silk before returning the bundle to the box. "Come," he said to his wife as he herded her back towards the bar.

Tarr stared into his ale before taking another drink.

Kesh took a ring from his finger, admiring the brilliant sapphire at its center. It reflected varying shades of cerulean, turquoise, and indigo. He handed the ring to Tarr, who did not immediately take it.

"That is a water sapphire, belonging only to the royalty of Dovkey."

"Which you will soon be," Kesh countered.

Tarr took the ring. "The ocean supposedly whispers to the bearer of such stones. Did the ocean whisper to you?"

Kesh snorted softly. "Show it to my sister. She should believe the contract and everything that you say when she sees it."

Tarr laughed mirthlessly. "I doubt even this rarity will be enough to convince your sister of what you did tonight."

"She must believe it. You must make sure she believes it. All of it."

Harold returned, clasping and unclasping his hands. "Your Highness, if you would like to stay here tonight, it would be an honor to me and my wife."

"Thank you. That is very hospitable." Harold nodded nervously, prompting Kesh to add, "Death will not come tonight. You have nothing to fear. I will find it on a ship."

Harold bowed his head to the king. "I am so sorry even if..." He could not bear to finish the sentence.

Kesh nodded in return, and Harold joined his wife in seeing to the other customers. The Dovkeyen king peered over Tarr's shoulder at the room full of drunkards, slightly amused that the fate of a country changed in a few short moments, unnoticed by those no more than a few feet away.

"What sort of things does the ocean whisper about?" Tarr asked as he studied the gem.

Kesh looked back at him and smiled. "Ask her. The waters will whisper to Aela."

The note of sorrow in Kesh's voice caught Tarr's attention. He looked up with compassion in his eyes. "I will take very good care of your sister."

"I'm sure you will," he retorted skeptically.

Looking away, he sighed. He seemed relieved, freed from a great burden even as he whispered to himself, "At sea. At least fate has chosen to be kind."

Chapter 8

Neither group of advisors received the news of Kesh's involvement in Seer's Fortune well. Aela purposely withheld the king's cheating and the appearance of the death card. The tavern keeper, whose presence she required at the meeting, agreed not to reveal that knowledge to the assemblage unless instructed to do so by her.

Both sides flung angry words at each other as Aela's patience dwindled. Several of the priestesses were knowledgeable of the game. One, named Sonea, had seen the game played. She explained that it was meant to be played by skilled seers, and she made her disapproval of it being played as a tavern game obvious.

In the game Sonea witnessed, the wife of the seer who lost refused to hand over the crystal that had been wagered. Her husband pleaded with her, but she would not relent. She immediately became sick, but still, she refused. Within days, she passed. In his grief, the seer forgot to hand over the winnings, and he too became sick. However, when he relinquished the crystal, the illness resolved.

Many of the elders refuted a card game as having such influence; however, the priestesses remained steadfast that the game's winner could not be denied his winnings.

Aela was not surprised when the subject of her engagement to the Phoenix Son surfaced. The elders quickly argued that the consequences of breaking a contract with an Immortal were dire. Aela pointed out several times that the easiest solution was to have the contract nullified by the Immortal Counsel. Both sets of advisors contended that the Frin'geren could forfeit his claim.

Before they started arguing again, Aela spoke. "He will not. I spoke with him last night, and he is not open to discussing alternatives."

The group hushed.

"Elders, priestesses, I feel that we cannot act yet. We will await the arrival of the king or the Phoenix Son and ask his counsel. This may be a matter that only the Immortal Council can settle. The Immortal may agree to annul the contract."

She turned her gaze to Harold.

"I thank you. You have made a long journey to ensure that your duty to the cards was done. I feel confident that you may consider that duty fulfilled and return to your home. Do any dispute this?" Silence answered her question, and she turned back to Harold. "Sir, you may leave tomorrow with the ships sailing east. I will see to it that additional transport is arranged when the river has carried you as far as it can."

She nodded and gestured to the door. He eagerly exited the room.

After another hour of discussion, the two groups settled on the same conclusion Aela originally suggested. She slipped from the room, knowing that her presence would not be missed, and wandered down the halls.

She heard footsteps trailing her but failed to recognize the different cadence of the gait. The presence fell into step behind her and felt familiar enough that she continued without verifying which guard it was.

"Could you hear the meeting from where you were?" She sighed with exasperation. "It was like dealing with children. No, worse than children. Children aren't that ignorant."

The laughter behind her did not belong to one of her guards, but it was familiar. She stopped so suddenly that he collided with her. Their bodies bumped against a wall though Tarr's arms came around her and cushioned most of the impact. He continued to laugh in her ear as she regained her balance.

"Lord Tarr, forgive me, I did not realize that it was you. I thought that one of my guards..." She turned in the cradle of his arms to face him.

"I see no need to apologize. I'm quite happy with how this worked out." He smiled, and his arms tightened around her. He continued to hold her, seemingly content to wait for a response. When she gave none, he said, "I wanted to thank you for the new quarters. They are more than adequate."

She smiled in that genuine way that few people saw, and her voice conveyed her satisfaction. "I am glad to hear that it was taken care of so quickly. Are you and your men comfortable?"

"I'm very comfortable." His amber eyes studied her for a moment before his arms fell away. "My men will only be staying one more night, but they too are comfortable."

Her eyes narrowed in confusion. "You are leaving, my lord?"

"No, my men are leaving with Harold in the morning."

Aela continued to stare at him with confusion. "Why are they leaving without you?"

"Are you suggesting that I will need armed protection while I am in your palace, Your Highness?"

"It is not my palace; it is the elder's," she admitted. "And, yes, you do. You are a Frin'geren in a foreign land. Is there not always someone around who would want to kill you?"

"I feel that I should be insulted," he laughed.

"No, not by me. I have no desire to kill you, but I would not trust the motives of others here."

"If it is so dangerous for me, then I suggest we get married as soon as possible so that I'll have the protection afforded to your husband." He leaned in with a suggestive smile. "I am quite eager to claim my husbandly rights."

"You would be safer not married to me…at least, you'd be in better standing," she mumbled as she stepped around him and continued down the halls.

Following her once more, he resumed the conversation. "How is that this is not your palace, they," he indicated the two guards who passed them warily, "are not your guards, and that you are so disliked that people would kill you?"

Aela slowed before stopping to turn to him; she had no desire to collide again. His touch affected her ways she didn't want to ponder just now.

"There have been tensions between the elders and the monarchy since the Reformation. The Reformists sought to do away the monarchy altogether, but it was not well received by the people. So, instead, a mess of laws was created to restrict the power of the monarch, which has slowly declined over the ensuing years. With my father's illness, the elders overtook many of his responsibilities in running the palace. Thus, those who live here and work here are of a Reformist mindset. In that mindset, I should be nothing but ornamental."

"Is that all?"

"That is enough for now." She took a few steps and turned back to him. "Do you really intend to send your guard away?"

He nodded. "I have no plans to leave Dovkey. As unadventurous as this place may be, I plan on settling in."

"Very well, I will assign one of my guards to you. Sey will join you shortly. Good day, my lord," she bowed her head to him as she always did and continued down the hall at a brisk pace.

AELA SAT AT HER DESK of white-washed wood when Ter entered the room. Closing the door behind him, he waited patiently for her to address him.

"Is something wrong?"

"There is a guard here to see you. Tevor is his name. He has concerns that he would like to address."

The queen sat in quiet surprise before telling Ter to allow the man in.

Aela watched as a palace guard entered. He kneeled before her desk with his head bowed, waiting for her to acknowledge him.

"You may rise."

He rose, staring at her with a touch of awe and an abundance of respect. She was momentarily taken aback by the display. "Your Majesty, it is an honor to serve you."

"You are one of the palace guards?"

She had not lived in the palace for many years and was not familiar with all the guards. However, the man before her exuded a reverence that she had not encountered among them.

"I am a captain in your army. Every soldier is required to fulfill a rotation with the palace guard."

Aww, Aela thought. That explained his unexpected attitude.

"Captain Tevor?" He nodded. "I thank you for your service. My guard said that you had concerns that you wished to discuss with me."

"Your Majesty, there have been multiple reports from the border that are of a concerning nature."

Ash.

"Are you referring to the reports of ash coming off the KeyGil Mountains?" He nodded. "Yes, I have heard of those reports. The elders do not think that it presents any immediate threat."

She watched his face tighten with disapproval at her mention of the elders. Her lips twitched before she could completely suppress the smile. The novelty of disapproval directed at the elders and not herself was amusing.

"I can see that you do not agree."

He pondered his words before responding. "The presence of so much ash is not a common phenomenon, especially in the absence of fire." Aela agreed that it was indeed not common.

"It may coincidental that at the appearance of the ash, a Frin'geren arrives at the palace with incredible claims, and the king has not returned as expected."

Aela's gaze sharpened as she studied the man in front of her. She had not realized that news of Tarr's claim and Kesh's absence were known throughout the palace. As she assessed Captain Tevor, she believed him to be a shrewd and intelligent soldier with strong loyalty to the crown, not the elders or the Reformation.

She sat back in her chair, her hands carefully folded in front of her. "Coincidental perhaps. You are very knowledgeable for a guard, Captain Tevor. More so than I would expect."

His gaze shifted away for a moment before he straightened and met her stare. "I am not a simple palace guard, Your Majesty."

Aela's lips twitched again. The captain did not like being compared to other guards.

"It is my sworn duty to protect you and the people of Dovkey from threats, both within and outside our borders. I have talked with a few of the men who have seen the ash. It is unnatural."

He paused for a moment.

"I know several of the men in King Kesh's private guard. The king ventured to Frin'gere more often than most are aware of, and he often took the same road. It is not well known, and it passes through the KeyGil Mountains. Reports of ash come from the same section of the mountains where the king often travels."

Aela was aware that Kesh had often snuck off to Frin'gere before their father's death. He enjoyed the pleasures and freedoms found in their neighboring country. She also knew that he did not travel the main roads on his excursions. She was surprised and troubled that his ventures were not as secret as he had thought.

"I can see the reason for your concern, Captain. What have you heard regarding the Frin'geren visiting the palace?"

"He won a wager with the king and is here to collect his winnings."

That was true enough. "And do you know what those winnings are?"

He shook his head. "I do not. But the fact that a Frin'geren is here, having recently won a wager with the king, yet the king is...unaccounted for..." He let his words trail off.

"Have you shared these thoughts with anyone else?" The wounded expression in the captain's eyes convinced her that he had not. "If you have come simply to express your concerns, consider your duty done. I have heard them and will consider their relevance." He appeared ready to object. "However, I have the impression that there is something more."

He bowed his head. "Yes, Your Majesty. I would like permission to leave my post with the palace guard and travel to the border, to the road that King Kesh would likely take on his return into Dovkey."

Aela considered the request. She agreed that the reports of ash near the border, Kesh's tardiness in returning, and Tarr's arrival were more than mere happenstance. The elders refused to take the news seriously and take action. Yet, she could not deny the twisted feeling of dread she felt.

"Lord Tarr's guards will be accompanying a man who traveled with them back to Frin'gere in the morning." She saw the question on the tip of his tongue and stayed it with a gesture. "It is not relevant who the man is. I will travel with him and the Frin'gerens. I will request that you accompany our group."

"Your Majesty, if there is a threat at the border, you would be safer here at the palace," Captain Tevor carefully objected.

"Possibly." She smiled at his mutinous expression. "I'll travel as far as Masia. The town has been my home for several years, and I find that I miss it. From Masia, you may travel on to the border with the Frin'geren envoy. My presence in Masia will allow you to easily communicate anything you find without putting me in danger."

Relief shone through his eyes as he bowed his head. "Yes, Your Majesty. I will await my orders from the general of the palace guard and then prepare for the journey."

Aela nodded. "And you will not speak of anything discussed in this meeting."

"No, of course not, Your Majesty."

"Until tomorrow then." He bowed again and left the room.

The door closed behind him and reopened as Ter entered.

"We are leaving in the morning to accompany the tavern keeper back to Frin'gere."

"All the way back to Frin'gere?" he questioned.

"No, we will stop in Masia. Captain Tevor will continue with the Frin'gerens."

Ter approached her desk. He stood silently in front of her.

"What? Tell me your thoughts" Aela broke the silence.

"The black current continues to approach the palace."

Aela rested her folded hands under her chin. "Yes, I know."

"But something dark also approaches from the mountains."

Her gaze shot to him. "Have you heard something? Has Anut seen something?"

"You saw something." She stared at him in confusion. "You saw ash, and there is ash in the mountains."

"We don't know that they are connected."

His silence conveyed that he did not believe that. Neither did she.

She instructed him to tell the others and make whatever preparations were needed. Menony hurried to pack Aela's things. The question was in her eyes, but she did not ask. Aela would explain it once they were on the river.

She debated calling all the elders together for the announcement that she planned to leave the palace in the morning. Instead, she found Elder Berto, who was more gracious than the others.

He was in one of the libraries, books spread out on the table in front of him.

"Elder Berto, if I may have a moment of your time."

He removed the small rectangular reading glasses from the tip of his nose. "Of course, Your Majesty. How may I be of service?"

"I feel that Kesh's involvement in the game of Seer's Fortune should remain undisclosed for the time being."

He nodded. "Yes, the elders would be in full agreement with you. Knowledge of this unforeseen complication is strictly confined to the elders and priestesses."

"The tavern keeper from Frin'gere has knowledge of the game."

Berto's brow furrowed with concern. "Yes, he is a variable that will be harder to contain. Do you believe he will spread the word of what happened in his tavern?"

She doubted it. Harold's solemn vow of secrecy was genuine; however, the elder did not need to know that.

"I cannot say with certainty, Elder Berto. We have no means to control what tales he spins once he is back in Frin'gere, but we could control what is done while he is in Dovkey."

The elder nodded enthusiastically. "We could send a chaperone of sorts to monitor and intercept if needed."

She nodded, grateful that Berto had taken the bait. "That is a splendid idea. Who will you send?"

He frowned. "It would have to be someone with knowledge already. One of the elders or priestesses...none of which can be spared at the moment."

She wondered when any of the elders had last been among the people they supposedly represented.

"Perhaps I may go instead," she suggested.

Berto started to object but paused to contemplate the ramifications.

"Lord Tarr will go with us. It will be an opportunity for him to see Dovkey, away from the grandeur of our White Palace. He will see that Dovkey is a place far too reformed for the sensibilities of a Frin'geren. I would take this opportunity to dissuade him."

"Do you really think you could convince him to renounce his claims?" He asked eagerly.

Aela thought the odds were not in their favor, but again, the elders did not need to know that.

"We must try, mustn't we?"

"Oh, Your Majesty! It would be quite the endeavor to take upon yourself. You would have to travel with the Frin'gerens for days."

She almost snorted at his concern but managed to contain herself. "Sacrifices must be made for the sake of Dovkey."

He beamed. "This is an opportunity we must seize. I will inform the rest of the elders of your intentions."

The prospect of changing the foreigner's mind won the elders' enthusiastic approval. Her advisors wanted nothing more than to have Tarr out of the way. When she requested the addition of Captain Tevor to her party, Elder Berto readily complied and assured her that everything would be ready to sail tomorrow.

She ignored the mild irritation at the elders' eagerness to send her, the last member of her family aside from Kesh, on a potentially dangerous venture. Their king was unaccounted for, and she was next in line. However, the possibility that she would ascend the throne never seemed to cross their minds. She pushed the irritation away, reminding herself that their disregard worked to her advantage.

Having managed the most pressing logistics, she sent Ter to arrange her meeting with Tarr. Of all the pieces to manage, she suspected the Frin'geren was going to be the most difficult.

Chapter 9

"There'll be talk if we keep meeting like this," Tarr teased as he sauntered into the room.

Aela faced away from him, staring out the ocean-facing window. A soft breeze tangled the loose strands around her solemn face.

Stepping further into the room, Tarr paused for a moment to note the guard assigned to him and another standing in front of the closed door. No one in or out without their approval, he thought to himself.

Kesh failed to mention that she had four massive bodyguards. They concealed their bodies and faces, a practice he had not encountered anywhere else. In all his travels, Tarr had never met men with such imposing height and build. Nor men possessing such stoic silence. The few hours spent with Sey were quiet; the guard was not forthcoming.

Despite the temperate climate of Dovkey, Tarr watched Aela shiver in front of the open window. She ran her hands absentmindedly over the exposed skin of her arms.

Spying a delicately woven throw hung over the back of the sofa, he grabbed it as he approached her. She seemed unaware of his presence until he draped it over her shoulders.

Startling for a moment, she turned to meet his gaze. Long, dark lashes framed her serious, pale, gray eyes. He stared into those eyes, feeling as if they possessed the ability to peer deep into his soul. The feeling was disconcerting, and he looked away first.

"Couldn't wait to get me alone again?" He questioned with a perked eyebrow.

He watched with satisfaction as her face softened, undoubtedly the only bit of emotion she let show. However, it satisfied him.

"I have decided to leave tomorrow with the tavern keeper. I will accompany him to the border."

He pondered her statement. "A lowly tavern keeper merits the queen's escort?" He attempted a teasing tone but realized a hint of suspicion seeped in as well.

She turned from him and the view of the ocean below. Pulling the ends of the throw closer, she perched on the edge of the nearest sofa. He followed, eager to hear her answer. Her steady gaze followed him as he took the seat opposite her.

Tarr noted the nervousness that her poised bearing failed to conceal and wondered if his presence unsettled her or if something else was the cause. He decided to test it and forwent the sofa. Her gaze sharpened as he sat on the low table right in front of her.

"This is better, is it not?" He smiled while settling his legs on either side of hers.

She silently watched him, disapproval clear in her pale eyes. His nearness agitated her, but not in a nervous way.

"The sofa would be more comfortable," was all she said.

Tarr smiled at her again. "I guess it's all a matter of personal opinion." She continued to stare at him, and he realized that she was not going to make this easy. "Why, love, are you accompanying Harold back to Frin'gere?"

"Your game with Kesh needs to remain undisclosed for now."

"Ah, but you could just send soldiers with him to ensure that he doesn't squeal," he mused.

"I could, but I'm not."

He huffed in feigned frustration. "If you can't share your most intimate," he leaned in close, trying to fluster her, "thoughts with your fiancé, who can you share them with?"

To his great surprise, she called his bluff and leaned into him, separating their faces by only inches.

"And what intimate thoughts do you expect me to share with you, Lord Tarr?"

He reached out to tuck an errant strand of hair behind her ear. "Nothing is more intimate than the truth. Why are you going on this trip?"

She contemplated her answer, and he prepared for another frustratingly obtuse response. However, she surprised him again.

"I'm concerned about something happening near the border. I need to see it with my own eyes."

"'Something happening'... Does that imply danger?" She did not respond. "I have a hard time believing that the elders would allow you to head into something dangerous..."

"We have differing views on the importance of this particular topic."

He leaned back. "I happen to be from the other side of the border. Perhaps I could shed some light on the topic."

She smiled. "Some would say that your place of origin makes you a less trustworthy source of information."

His eyebrows rose. "You think Frin'gere is challenging your borders?"

She watched his reaction carefully, not saying anything.

Tarr knew his irritation showed, but he failed to remain silent.

"I'm only the first wave of invasion, is that it? I've done away with your missing king, and now I have my army waiting at your borders, ready to invade." She still did not respond. "That is what your advisors think, isn't it?"

"I do not believe their imaginations have ventured so far."

"So, you alone know that there's a threat?" He failed to contain his anger.

"I am one of a few people who believe that there is a threat at the border. However, I did not say that I thought it was Frin'geren."

The silence hung heavy between them.

"You don't trust me, do you?" The question surprised even him.

She was equally taken aback. "I've only just met you. Why would I trust you?"

"Your brother trusted me."

"Did he?" A whispered question was full of emotion.

"Yes."

This time, she broke eye contact and pulled away from him.

"The elders do not trust any foreigners, especially Frin'gerens. Your way of life is the antithesis of their Reformational values. No excesses of any kind, no uncontrolled magic, no disorder."

"There's no such thing as no disorder."

She smiled at that and stood. The throw dropped down her shoulders to the sofa.

"The boat upriver will leave at dawn. Am I correct in assuming that you will be accompanying me?"

"As opposed to staying here with your disapproving elders?" He sneered. "Where else would a devoted fiancé be but at your side?"

She rolled her eyes at his flattery, and he failed to hold back the harsh laughter.

"Sleep well, Lord Tarr."

He reached for her hand as she started to walk away.

"Just Tarr," he said softly, his gaze drifting up to her face. She nodded.

"Sleep well...Tarr."

He released her and watched as she walked to the door. Just as her guards prepared to open it, he asked, "Aela, what's really at the border?"

She turned back to him. "I don't know."

He growled in frustration.

"Reports of ash coming off the mountains between Dovkey and Frin'gere."

"Fire magic does not produce ash," he stated solemnly.

"I know. I'll see you on the river tomorrow."

She left the room, one guard following and the other staying.

THEY TRAVELED UP THE Joining River on a beautifully engineered barge. Light filtered through the dark blue-gray clouds overhead. The brilliant green of the rolling country on either side of the river was a refreshing change to the stark white of the palace. The ivory sails filled with the wind and steadily propelled the vessel against the current. Barges of similar size sailed past them easily.

Too long away from the river, Aela thought as she reclined on the deck cushions. She loved to sail, but duty had placed other demands on her time. With a fleeting moment of resentment, she realized that in the last year, she had done very few of the things that she loved. First, the death of her father a little over a year ago, and then the observation of Dovkey's grieving traditions. With Kesh's coming coronation and trip to Frin'gere, the elders had insisted that she leave her home in Masia, declaring her presence in the palace was needed. However, in her time there, she had nothing more than attend meetings without the authority to speak her opinions on issues.

She shook her head to clear it and focused only on listening as the river lapped playfully against the sides of the barge. Her eyes closed, and the sun warmed her face while the smell of the water filled her nose. She breathed it in and tried to lose herself in the perfection of the Great Wave's creation.

What had once started as small villages on the river's edge had grown into thriving towns. Each town was a tiny shipping center, carrying the goods from outlying farms to the network of rivers that transported wares all over the country. The fruits and grains came from the lowlands to the south and were among some of the goods that Dovkey sold to its neighboring countries. However, it was the finely crafted wares of varying artisans and rare oils that brought the most wealth to the people of Dovkey.

Little had changed since the arrival of Dovkey's ancestors. The small ancient houses made of bleached wood and white stone still stood, though newer constructions of stone were intermingled with the old. Dirt roads coming from the surrounding country turned into stone-paved streets. A single structure rose from the center of each town and looked much like the window tower of the palace.

Despite the varying ages and heights of each tower, they all served as a guide to the rivermen. Built with similar layouts and materials, a simplistic elegance pervaded all the communities. The well-thought out designs created towns that were not only open and welcoming but organized and easily navigated. More subtle details distinguished each one from the next. In each area of the country, a strongly unique style of art existed.

The barge stopped at each small port. The white banners of grieving hung for Aela's father over a year ago still adorned the doorways of each house. Yet, such happiness filled the air that the loss of a king was far from thought. Rainbows of ribbons waved in the breeze at all the ports, and crowds of people stood on the riverbank waving excitedly to their queen.

"It would seem only the elders don't appreciate you." Tarr stood at Aela's shoulder, looking out at the port as they approached.

She turned to him, the smile on her face fading. "The Reformation was the elders' attempt to restructure the country. It was also an attempt on their part to abolish the monarchy.

Obviously, they failed in that goal. The people of Dovkey allowed them to make many changes, but that was not one of them."

"So, the elders simply dislike the monarchy? It felt as though there was something personal in their animosity towards you," he remarked casually. When his prying failed to elicit a comment, he sighed, "Fine, keep your secrets...for now."

He walked away leaving Aela to ponder his words. Looking at the people gathered on the docks, she felt joy. From a very early age, she knew that these people would be her purpose in life. Though she did not have names for the faces that beamed at her as she made her way from the dock to the center of town, she knew who they were. They were the men and women who worked day in and day out on their fields and crafts, returning home to nurture their growing families. The people who looked to her for guidance, and who shared in her losses and achievements. Their presence brought her a sense of peace that few other things did.

AELA'S GROUP PARTED ways at Bewyl. The easiest passage through the KeyGil mountains was south of the Greater River. Tarr's men reluctantly left with the innkeeper. Whatever orders or reassurances he gave them proved enough to send the men on their way. She wondered if Tarr felt vulnerable without his men to watch his back. Not that he showed any signs of concern.

The remainder of the passengers continued to Masia. They traveled with unexpected speed up the Joining River and then the Greater River. It was almost as if the winds from the sea propelled them with all due haste towards Masia.

The sailing had been smooth up the Joining River, but after only a day on the Greater, ominous clouds gathered in the east. The captain of her barge, who had sailed the rivers many times, assured her that it was a mountain storm sure to disperse before it hit

Dovkey. She remembered watching the storms gather on the peaks of the KeyGil Mountains when she lived in Masia and knew that they rarely came down the mountain.

Another day passed, and Aela watched with growing dread as the clouds drew closer.

"I don't think that it is a mountain storm," she told the captain as they stood together on the stern of the ship.

"It does appear to be moving in this direction, Your Majesty. But it will not keep up momentum for much longer. We might catch only the tail end of it."

Aela nodded, but she was not convinced. As the day passed, she continued to watch the black clouds grow. Her wind-propelled ship and the encroaching storm were destined to meet on the river as the sun began to set behind them.

She stood at the railing with her eyes fixed on the horizon. Tarr came to stand next to her.

"Is it wise to sail into that?" he asked.

Captain Tevor joined them, standing on Aela's other side. He bowed to the queen and nodded his head in respect to Tarr.

"I'm not sure," she admitted. "The captain assures me that the storm will run its course before we meet with it, but I don't believe it will. It seems to be growing the closer we get."

"I would agree. If we continue at this speed, we will reach the storm just after nightfall," Tarr observed.

"Yes, we will."

"What towns are between here and Masia?"

Aela turned to him and noted the tension in his face. She attempted to lighten his mood. "Not one for a little rain?"

Tarr frowned. "That," he pointed to the clouds, "will be more than 'a little rain'. What towns are there?"

"There are no more towns," Tevor answered.

"What?" Tarr leaned forward to stare at the soldier.

"Masia is the easternmost town in Dovkey. The closest towns are Bewyl, which we passed several hours ago, and Shuesh, which is inland to the north."

"We should go back to Bewyl for the night."

"The captain is very experienced. He has handled stormy waters before. We should not be worried," Aela interjected.

With his usual perception, he retorted, "But you are. Don't deny it. I've watched you all day while you've tracked those clouds. There's something unnatural about that storm. You feel it, do you not?"

Beside her, Captain Tevor shifted uneasily.

"I have thought the same things, Your Majesty. The crew is loyal to their captain, and they trust him. But there is worry on this ship. They know this storm is not common for the area."

"It looks like the kind of storm that blows in from the sea," Tarr added as he stared at the clouds.

Aela couldn't deny it. The sensation of something ominous had been with her since first seeing the clouds. A sense of restlessness agitated the current of the river, and the water carried a message of warning.

"Yes, I feel it. I fear that no matter which way we go, that storm will catch us," she turned to Tarr and then to Captain Tevor. "We cannot avoid it now."

Tarr nodded and remained at her side as the ship continued to sail into the heart of the storm.

Chapter 10

The last rays of the sun sank beneath the horizon as the first torrents of rain hit the ship. Malevolence fell from the sky in the form of a storm. Aela felt it on her skin like a thick coating of oil. Magic infused the droplets that fell, but it was a kind of magic unknown to her. She had never experienced something so evil.

"Is this water magic?" Tarr yelled as he struggled across the deck towards her.

"No, I...no...I don't think so, but there is something of water magic in it."

He stared intently at her.

Captain Tevor stood beside her, yelling to be heard over the crashing of the storm. "You should move into the cabin, my queen."

"Have you ever felt anything akin to this in your studies?" Tarr persisted as he gripped the rail.

Aela shook her head as her footing slipped on the deck. Tarr moved to catch her, but he was not close enough.

Mar's great arms wrapped around her from behind and lifted her. She gave him a quick smile of relief. While he stayed with her, Aela noted that her other guards stationed themselves at other ends of the ship, ready to prevent anyone from going overboard.

The waters below thrashed like the waves of a stormy sea and violently rocked the boat from beneath. A savage wind tore at the deck from above.

"This is strange magic," Mar said to Aela as he placed her back on the deck. She grabbed the railing as the boat again threatened to topple her.

Aela agreed as she studied the black clouds above. "I can almost feel traces of water magic, but this is not water magic."

"How do you know?" Tarr asked as he appeared next to her.

She pushed the hair out of her eyes as she turned to him.

"It's twisted. Water magic is neither good nor bad. But there is evil intent in this magic. Can you feel it?"

He shook the water from his clothes. "I wasn't sure what it was, but it feels like it's trying to seep into my skin."

A sickening heaviness settled deep in her gut. Suspicions took root. If her worst fears proved true, then the people of Dovkey were in great trouble. She clung to the hope that this was a storm like any other. She prayed that they would sail through it unchanged and unharmed but struggled to deny the feeling that the worst was yet to come.

Mar insisted on tethering her to the ship with a rope anchored to the mast. Tarr, the captain, and many of the crew were tied off as well. None of her guards had safety lines, but Aela did not fear for them. She knew that none of her guards needed safety lines. For them, the water below posed no more threat than the raindrops falling from above.

She feared for the crew and herself when the winds threatened to capsize the ship. Tarr insisted only once that she take refuge with Menony in the captain's quarters. A scathing glare was the answer he received. The deafening thunder from the clouds made speech inaudible. He accepted her refusal and stood with Mar and Captain Tevor bedside her. Together, they stayed above deck as the crew weathered the storm through the long night. All of them hoped that dawn brought with it a break in the storm.

THE RISING SUN PENETRATING the clouds was the first sign of the storm breaking. The winds faded, and the waters calmed. By the time the sun was nearly directly above, the black ominous bringers of battering rain had dispersed, leaving only the drenched crewmen and a damaged barge as proof of their existence.

Aela stood stubbornly on the deck, soaked to the bone and chilled to the core. Despite Tarr and Captain Trevor's attempts to persuade her to leave, she had steadfastly remained at the railing through the wind and rain.

Her hair was a tangled mess around her face. Her clothes, heavy with water, hung limply on her body. She pushed the damp strands away from her eyes as she leaned over the railing. Tarr stepped closer, unwilling to risk her falling over.

"What is it? Do we have a hole somewhere?" he half-jested while examining the ship.

"The barge took a beating, but nothing that will impair the rest of the journey. We are very close to Masia." She uttered the words with a tone of dread.

Tarr's heart nearly jumped out of his chest as she leaned even further over the railing. "What are you doing?"

"The river," Aela said sadly.

"Other than being much calmer than it was last night, what about it?"

"There is nothing but despair...and pain."

"Perhaps the water did not enjoy that supernatural storm any more than we did." Tarr turned his back to lean against the railing. He removed his shirt and wrung water from the garment.

"No, it's not that," Aela said with frustration. "It's telling me of something that has happened...something horrible."

"I'd say that storm was horrible," Tarr responded. "You should get out of those wet clothes. Go down to the captain's cabin and let Menony get you warmed up."

"No."

Tarr groaned. "Do you enjoy shivering? Are you planning to catch your death out here?"

Aela turned to glare at him. "Why don't you go downstairs and..." She noticed then that he was shirtless. "You can go below deck and warm yourself."

"Aela, you and I are the only ones still standing on this deck, freezing in our wet clothes." She looked around and saw the crew had changed into drier, heavier clothing. "Well, you, me, and your guards, but I have a feeling that they are less affected than we are."

She shook her head, turning away from him, and Tarr had the urge to shake her. Maybe he could rattle some common sense free if he did.

"There's something in the water."

He looked over the side and saw nothing but the gentle current. When he looked back at her questioningly, she sighed.

"A message of some sort."

"A matter of minutes... that is all it will take to change and warm you. Then you can return to your post."

He gently grabbed her arm and pulled her away from the edge. With his other hand, he undid the rope around her waist. Her eyes stayed focused on the water, but her body moved with ease as he guided her further away.

"Ash. All ash..." she mumbled. "Death and ash..."

He paused with her last words. "What did you say?"

Her gaze was completely unfocused. He shook her gently, but she remained in a trance. A heavy hand fell on his shoulder. He glanced over to see Mar standing behind him.

"Let her go to it," he said in a deep voice.

"Let her go where?" Tarr asked with irritation. He wondered if he was the only one who saw the danger in her staying in sopping clothes.

She slipped from his grip as he questioned the giant guard. Realizing that his fingers no longer held her, he turned frantically to see that she had slipped back towards the railing of the ship. He called her name, but she did not answer.

To his horror, she leaned out towards the water, repeating three words over and over.

Death and ash, death and ash, death and ash.

In a second, she disappeared over the side of the ship.

He screamed her name as he raced to where she had just stood. Had it not been for the large arm wrapped around his chest, he would have dived in after her.

"Where is she? Where is she?" He shouted.

"The river called to her, and she had to answer. She is safe. You must let her see this through." Mar commanded him.

Tarr rejected the explanation, but he could not break the vise-like grip around him. The other guards gathered around them; their attention focused on the water.

Distantly, he heard the shouts of the crew call for help. The queen was overboard. Tarr knew that they would have no better chance of getting to her, and though it went against his instincts, he settled himself to wait...trusting that the river would protect her under its icy surface.

AELA COULD FEEL THE death. She hadn't understood the growing heaviness in her heart, but now, she knew that only death could feel so weighty. The death of what she did not know, but she could feel it, and it was profound.

She needed to be closer to the water. If only she could skim her fingers over the surface, then she might know the full meaning of the words the river whispered to her.

Aela heard Tarr's voice distantly before she felt the coolness of the water envelop her, but it did not matter. She needed to be in the water to know the truth. As in the temple pool, a vision of stunning clarity came to her under the surface.

She saw the town she loved, in every magnificent detail that she could remember. She saw the clouds forming just to the northwest and moving with frightening speed. The rain poured down from the sky, but it was not normal rain. This was burning. Each drop seeped into every surface it struck, and everything became ash with the rain's touch. The images played out in her head as she watched raindrops falling on the unsuspecting people who then became ash.

Aela tried to warn them. Water filled her mouth as she screamed out, but no one in the vision heard her.

Except for one person.

A diver she knew well turned to face her. She peered into his terror-filled eyes, and he said only two words as their gazes met, "*Save us.*" His voice was scratchy and just above a whisper.

The image of the diver and the death all around him blurred as Aela felt her body being pulled to the surface. The world above the water seemed less real than the vision she was in. She felt the heaviness of her limbs, and her eyes saw the blurred world as she was hoisted onto the ship. Worried voices speaking incomprehensibly buzzed around her as she was laid out on the deck. Concerned faces filtered in and out of her vision.

She knew them. Menony, Mar, Ter, Sey, and Anut were there. The faces of the crew were hazy shadows in the background. However, the one closest to her was Tarr. He placed his ear on her chest. His angry words were unclear as he lifted his head and looked down at her. His dark eyes filled with something she had never seen before.

Fear, maybe, she thought.

A hard pounding on her chest, and then Tarr leaned over her again. This time his fingers pinched her nose, and he placed his mouth over hers. Air was forced into her lungs. She tried to push him away, but her body would not respond. It was still so heavy. Again, he forced air into her lungs and pounded on her chest. His lips moved with furious words, and his eyes darkened still.

Tarr pushed Mar aside. Menony knelt next to him, placing a calming hand on the clenched fist he had slammed into Aela's chest. He looked down at her, the despair so deep in his eyes that Aela wanted to assure him, to say something, anything that would drive it away. She tried once more to move her body.

However, as Tarr again tried to give her breath, her vision blackened, and she saw only the face of the diver.

"Death and ash. Evil magic brought death and ash. Beware, my queen, it seeks you too."

Chapter 11

Aela sat up with such force that she knocked Tarr off balance. He fell backward and stared at her in shock as she gasped for breath. Even as her breathing evened and turned to heaving sobs, he remained motionless in disbelief. When they pulled her from the water, her skin was blue, and her chest was unmoving. Her body had been on the verge of death, and he desperately had done everything he knew to return breath to her lungs. His efforts appeared ineffective, but her cry filled his ears even as his eyes watched the pink glow of life return to her skin.

"Aela," he whispered her name as he reached tentatively for her.

Anut stopped him. "It must pass first."

"What must pass?" Tarr asked angrily as he struggled to free his hands. However, he was no match for Aela's guard.

A look passed between Anut and the other guards. They acknowledged each other with a nod and pushed back the crew.

Tarr looked from the retreating crew to Anut. "What's happening?"

Menony spoke before Anut could answer, her pale face turned intently toward Aela. Her hands hovered just inches away, but she paid heed to Anut's warning and refrained from touching the queen.

"Do you really think she was having a vision, Anut?" she whispered. The guard nodded. "Another one in such a short time. I don't think that she's ever had one outside the Temple Pools before."

Tarr painfully looked away from Aela to Menony. "I didn't know she had visions."

"Why would you?" Their eyes bore into each other. Tarr looked away first with a curse rolling off his lips.

"Has it passed yet?" his impatience clear.

Anut leaned forward, gently reaching out to Aela's shaking, sobbing form. His fingers brushed the surface of her face, and she stopped. She lifted her tear-filled eyes to him and in an eerily calm voice said, "Masia is ash."

"What?" Menony exclaimed.

"Masia was burnt to the ground?" Tarr asked.

She shook her head, and her focus remained on Anut. "I saw it- the approach of the storm and the unnatural rain falling. The people turned to ash as it touched them."

"The rain turned people to ash? This is what you saw in the river?" Tarr asked with a hint of disbelief in his voice.

Aela turned her vacant gaze to him. Her face was pale, and her lips still held a tinge of blue. "Yes. The river wanted to warn me. It called me into its waters. That is the only way for me to have a vision; I must be submerged." Her eyes narrowed. "I can see that you don't believe me."

Tarr started to object, but she continued in a hard tone, "I saw you before you came. A man who was not the king wearing the King's Sapphire, and soon after, you arrived. Believe what you will, but when we sail into Masia, we will find nothing but ash."

There they stared at each other in silence.

"Come, my queen," Menony said as she wrapped her arms around Aela and helped her to stand. "You are soaked, and the winds have not yet died down. Let us get you dry and warm."

Aela went willingly, but Anut reached out gently to stop her. "Was there more?" His voice was low and soft.

The queen stared at him, her body beginning to shake. "No, that was all."

THE FAILED QUEEN

Still, Anut would not let her go. Tarr watched the exchange between them with wariness. They stared at each other intently, secrets and stubbornness in their eyes.

Finally, Anut spoke. "There was great warning in the water. I do not think it meant only to show you Masia's fate."

"That is all I saw."

Anut released her, and Menony helped her to the captain's quarters. Tarr watched them go. His heart still thudded heavily in his chest. Fear unlike any he had ever known had filled him when he saw Aela's lifeless body on the deck of the barge. Desperation to save her had governed his actions.

He tried to calm the stress response with controlled breaths and found himself at the railing once again. His eyes watched the water lap against the vessel. Bracing his weight on the rail of the ship, his head fell forward. He never doubted Kesh's words of warning, and he did not fear whatever dangers threatened Dovkey. However, the depth of his feelings towards Kesh's sister was a surprise and potential complication. A wholly unwelcome one...even though the King of Dovkey had warned him of this eventuality too. He turned to look at the door she had taken to the captain's quarters. She would be the death of him, in more ways than one.

Even though she thought that he did not believe her visions, the truth was that he did. As he turned back to stare at the river, he dreaded what they would find when they reached the town of Masia.

※

THE SUN HUNG JUST ABOVE the western horizon as they sailed on the outskirts of Masia. The storm pushed them farther back than anyone had realized, and they spent most of the day making up ground.

Aela stood alone at the bow wrapped in a heavy cloak. The blue hue had left her lips hours before, but the chill was still with her. She stood like a statue as the wind blew the first flakes of ash down the river. Men and women and children who she had known floated in the air past her, but she had no more tears left to cry. They had all been spent. She felt frozen inside and doubted any source of heat was hot enough to thaw her.

She heard the whisperings of the crew as ash filled the dusky sky. They had not heard her prophetic words, and though they did not know the source of the ash, they felt the evil in the air.

Aela dreaded what they would find around the next river bend. She had seen the destruction in her vision, and she was not eager to see the reality.

With a quick glance back, she saw the fear in the faces of the crew. Despite the captain's hardened expression, Aela knew that he too was worried. Menony watched the ash with tears in her eyes. The guards stood solemnly to either side of her, though they remained distant enough to honor her solace.

As Tarr approached, she turned back to the river.

"This is what you saw?" he asked softly.

"Death and ash," Aela said without looking at him.

They passed a few moments in silence. "Will there be anyone alive when we reach the town?"

"No."

"How could this happen?" He asked aloud, though it was unclear if he meant for Aela to answer.

"Look for yourself," Aela said with a gesture of her head.

They rounded the bend, and the fading light of day illuminated the gray city. The current slowed and bucked the ship the closer they came.

The buildings were gray, sculpted ash. The wind skimmed a thin layer away with every gust. Soon, everything would be blown away, and little would remain of what had once been a thriving port.

"Should we search for survivors?" one of the crewmen called out. The crew gathered at the railing, looking mournfully out at what remained of Masia.

"There are none," Aela said in a firm voice. The soft mumble spread through the crew.

The young crewman started to object, but Aela spoke first. "There are no survivors. What happened to this city was done by evil magic."

The wide-eyed men nodded in agreement.

"How do you wish to proceed, Your Majesty?" the ship's captain asked.

"You can dock at the first pier. My guards and I will go into the town and return within an hour." She turned to the crew. "And then we will sail back to the White Palace and let them know what has happened here."

Expressions of fear and shock met her words. She started to turn away from them when Tarr's hand gripped her arm. He leaned in close so only she could hear his words. "Are you sure that is safe? You don't know what happened here."

"Yes, I do." He stared at her, clearly unhappy with what she planned to do. "The storm brought the destruction, and it has passed. All that remains is the ash." She saw the worry in his eyes, and she hoped to bring him comfort with her words.

"I'm going with you." His statement did not surprise her.

"I request to join your guards, Your Majesty," Tevor said with a bow of his head.

Aela nodded. The elders would need to hear about the devastation from another. Her guards would not testify, and any statement made by Tarr would be viewed with suspicion.

A half-hour later, the barge docked. Aela departed with her guards, Tarr, and Captain Tevor. Mar and Ter walked ahead of Aela while Anut and Sey walked behind her. Tarr and Tevor brought up the rear.

The group was quiet as they approached the ashen town. Like thick gray mists, ash swirled in the air and obscured the fading light of the sun. Soon, there would not be enough light to see; however, Aela did not plan to linger in the town for long.

"What has the power to do this?" Captain voiced the question.

Aela was sure that everyone shared her fear, but to say it aloud was more frightening than thinking it.

"This is not fire magic," Tarr stated firmly as they entered the main street of the town.

"No, it isn't," she confirmed as she paused in front of an ash person.

Aela's heart broke as she looked at the anguish captured on the woman's face. This was someone she knew; she knew almost everyone in Masia. The features were softened too much to identify who exactly it was. She turned away, and the pain in her heart only deepened as she looked out at all the other anonymous figures gathered on the main street. So many robbed of life.

Captain Tevor made a gagging nose as he knelt in front of a figure so small it could only be a child. Despair filled his watery eyes as he looked at her. He stood, cleared his throat, and turned away from the child.

"I know you said there were no survivors, my queen, but may I have your permission to search the buildings? Just...to be sure."

She nodded her approval and watched as he walked away to search for life.

Tarr stood beside her. "The amount of magic this would take..." He shared the same horrified look as her captain.

"It could only be one thing."

"Don't say it."

"It's a wrangrent."

"Aela," he chastised.

"You can deny it if you want, but this is evil and twisted. I can feel the strains of elemental magic. It's been corrupted."

"That is a bold and terrifying statement, Aela," Tarr said quietly. "There hasn't been a wrangrent in over a hundred years."

She turned to him. "What is this?" She gestured to the ashen people and buildings all around them. "What is this?" Her voice grew in volume.

"You think I'm not terrified to say that word? I am. Thinking, now knowing, that there is a practitioner of magic so powerful and malicious that they can twist elemental magic into this..." she pointed to the woman. She covered her mouth as a cry of sorrow escaped. The tears fell silently down her face. "Tarr, I have never been so terrified of anything in my whole life. I don't know how to fight this."

He did not have a response for her, and she turned away, allowing the tears to fall silently down her face.

Aela wandered deeper into Masia, and Tarr wondered silently next to her. The others walked the streets and alleys that branched off the main road.

A breeze blew gently as night approached, and she sobbed harder as a man and woman locked in each other's embrace disintegrated. Bit by bit they were swept away and lost.

"This was my home. These people welcomed me, sheltered me. They were my people."

She stood in front of the couple, her hand stretched out to them. Her fingers closed around the ash floating in the air as if she could collect all the pieces and put them together again. Knowing that every one of them would disappear angered her. Families were wiped from existence, and she wondered who would mourn an entire town. Brushing the wetness from her cheeks, she swore to mourn them. To celebrate their lives and send prayers that their souls passed safely to the White Beach. She would not let them be forgotten.

"We will lose the light soon," Tarr said gently.

Aela nodded.

"I'll gather the others," he offered.

Her guards quickly rejoined her. Though she could not see their faces, she knew they felt the same sorrow she did. Masia had been their home too. The first they had truly known. Despite not understanding who or what the guards were, the people of this town had accepted them as easily as they had their failed queen.

Captain Tevor returned with Tarr beside him. Devastation darkened the soldier's face. "I could not find any...any who were spared," he said quietly as he stopped in front of her.

"I know," she responded quietly. "We will return to the White Palace and tell the elders of this. We will do everything in our power to ensure that this does not happen to any other Dovkeyens."

He bowed deeply to her before continuing to the ship. The crew quickly surrounded him when he boarded. They shouted out questions and demanded to know what he had seen. He answered each one.

By the time Aela and her guards were on board, the sailors' curiosity had been sated, and they returned to their tasks with heavier hearts. They bowed their heads in respect to their queen, but they did not engage her.

With silent haste, the crew prepared to embark, and soon they were sailing away from Masia. Aela watched it until the river's bend hid it from her sight. She stood with her eyes fixed in the direction of her home long after the night had fully settled.

Chapter 12

The exhilaration of twisting magic, forcing it to go against its nature, had always been the wrangrent's deepest passion. However, as they stared out over the ashen remains of Masia, they realized that destruction was so much more fulfilling. The immense power it had taken was exhausting. Even now, with their back bowed from the weight of conjuring the storm and blood trickling from their nose, they felt alive and powerful. Weeks would pass before another show of magic could take place, but for now, the wrangrent was satisfied with their accomplishments.

The queen's sorrow only sweetened the moment. Originally, she was meant to be among her people, in the place that she called home. They intended to have her ashen body stand with the rest, but the timing had been off.

However, seeing the devastation on her face was far better, and now, they knew that she would not perish until the end. Now, she would suffer with each step along the wrangrent's journey. She would be an integral part of it. The country would watch as they grew in power and the queen weakened.

Yes, the idea of breaking Dovkey's queen was perfectly delightful.

Destruction was akin to creation; they knew that now. Creating something new from what already existed. A city of ash where people once thrived. A moment frozen in time, delicate and fleeting. This was the kind of power that would drive the world to its knees. And the world would be theirs.

THE WINDS ROLLED OFF the KeyGil Mountains with avenging fury, propelling the vessel down the river with astonishing speed. The current eagerly assisted in driving the queen and her party to the White Palace with all haste.

Dutiful crewmen silently completed their work on deck with fear lurking in their eyes. Aela wanted desperately to give them comfort, but she had no words to offer. The evil magic that had destroyed Masia was undoubtedly that of a wrangrent, a sorcerer who used twisted elemental magic for the purpose of destruction. It had been almost a century since the last known wrangrent, and his reign of destruction had spread far and wide, lasting decades. elders all over the continent still told tales of the cruelty and devastation. For this reason, Dovkey and many other countries closely monitored the practice of magic.

A wrangrent was not easily defeated. He was first a master of one of the four elemental magics- water, earth, air, and fire. From this knowledge, he learned to twist the magic against its nature and used it to inflict his will to harm. Only with great power and skill could one twist the magic against its own neutrality. Aela could not comprehend the power it would take to turn a city to ash.

Her elementary knowledge of water magic was minuscule in comparison to that of a wrangrent. There was only one force that she knew of strong enough and knowledgeable enough to defeat one: the Immortal Council. She found that she was grateful that a member of the council was expected. Phoenix Son Aluz would be able to act as an intermediary between the Council and Dovkey.

"They will not be easily convinced."

Tarr stood beside her on the deck. Aela turned to him and nodded. "You are right, they will not be. They will simply have to hear the testimony of everyone on this ship. Dovkey cannot afford to have them do otherwise."

"Aela," Tarr paused to consider his words. He looked behind them; seeing no one, he continued in a low voice, "You do understand the magnitude of this?"

With a spark of temper, "Of course."

He ran his hand through his hair with a sigh of frustration. "You cannot take this on alone," he muttered to himself.

"I have no intention to," Aela said irately. "This is a matter for the Immortal Council." She pushed angrily off the railing, but Tarr grabbed her before she could take more than two steps.

Mindful of his voice, he said softly, "You had a vision in the river. How long have you had visions like that?"

"Do you mean visions of Masia or visions of things that I have not otherwise seen?"

"Both."

Aela was silent before deciding to respond. "I rarely get visions. In fact, I have only had them in the temple pools before."

"What are those?"

"They are ancient pools of magic located beneath the palace. They were once used by our ancestors to commune with the Great Wave. Elaborate ceremonies were performed there. Now, though, they have all been forgotten. Few know of the passages."

"But in the river-"

"That has never happened before. I can sometimes hear the voice of the river, but it's never called to me for a vision before." She tried to pull her arm free, but he persisted.

"You haven't told anyone of these visions?"

"No, Tarr. Only my guards and Menony know because they have been present when I've had the visions. Otherwise, I feel that we're all entitled to our secrets, don't you?"

His expression hardened. She pulled away and avoided him for the rest of the trip.

THE WATER BECAME CHOPPY and violent as they sailed onto the Greater River. Thunder boomed in the distance and dark clouds gathered on the horizon.

"Do you think it's another of those unnatural storms?" A sailor beside Aela asked.

She turned to him, seeing his need for reassurance. Looking down at the water, she listened for any message it might carry. With her eyes closed, she heard nothing but felt the strong anger.

"No," she looked back at the old sailor, "I don't believe that is the same kind of storm up ahead."

He nodded but did not question how she would know that. Relief replaced the fear on his weathered face as he returned to his duties.

"What do you think it is?" Menony had taken the sailor's place. Softly, she asked, "What does the river tell you?"

"There is anger. I'm not sure whose, but it fills the waters."

The source of the anger became more apparent to Aela as they neared the White Palace. The white edifice was gray in the dark light of the storm raging around it. Rain beat the stone, and the ocean sprayed around the palace, threatening to rip it from the cliff. What had sounded like thunder was the shaking of the earth as the sea crashed against it again and again.

"What is this?" Tarr asked as he tried to pull Aela from the railing, watching as they neared the palace.

"The Great Wave. This is his anger. His anger and his despair for his people in Masia," Aela said without turning to him.

"We have to go inside the cabin; the waters are too rough out here," he yelled over the howling wind. The ship had sailed into the rain's path, and it pounded furiously against the deck.

"No, you go inside. I am not afraid of the water."

"Why, because the river won't let you drown?" he asked angrily. When Aela just ignored him, he turned to the guards, "Help me get her somewhere safer."

However, the guards simply formed a half circle around her, barring Tarr from her side.

"It is not safe out here!" he objected.

"Go inside, Frin'geren. Our queen will be safe where she is," Mar said.

Tarr turned and escorted an objecting Menony off the deck.

THE BATTERED SHIP ARRIVED at the port of the White Palace in one piece. The docks were abandoned; however, with the help of Aela's guards, the crew anchored. Tarr watched as Aela instructed Ter to take care of her maid, Menony. The seasickness that Menony was well known for had left her weakened and faint, and she did not appear to have the strength or the desire to fight Ter when he picked her up and carried her into the palace.

Sey stood behind him, indicating that he would escort Tarr. He looked at the guard and then approached Aela. "I think I'll go with you."

"Not to see the elders," she said as she strode down the dock.

"I will testify to what I have seen." He kept pace beside her.

"You know that your word will mean little to them, Tarr."

"Damnit, Aela!" he said when his path was blocked by Sey. He watched as she and the other two guards continued. "It is not safe for her. Why can she not see it?"

"Is it your concern?" Sey asked quietly.

Tarr's angry eyes flashed up to the guard's hidden face. "I want to collect on my winnings."

Sey's stare bore down on him though he could not see the other's eyes. "Maybe there is more to your concern than winnings."

"Do not mistake me for anything more than a greedy Frin'geren."

An amused snort followed his words. "People are never what they seem." A silent moment before the guard added, "Kesh was not a fool. He would not keep someone he distrusted close to him."

Tarr's gaze narrowed at him. "We were just two men playing a dangerous game in a grimy tavern."

"You are still playing a dangerous game." The guard stepped closer, his body towering over the Frin'greren. Tarr did not doubt for a second that it was meant to be intimidating, and he hated to admit that a part of him was worried. Kesh had told him many details about his sister over the years, but he had never mentioned the quartet of giant guards. He was still bitter over that particular omission.

"We do not know Kesh's plan, but you are a part of it. My brothers and I respect that and trust that Aela's brother had his reasons for bringing you here. Do not mistake, though, our loyalty is and will always be to her. Should you at any time present a threat to her, you will be taken care of without a second thought."

He did not doubt Sey's threat for a moment. Tarr could not see the other man's eyes, but he directed his stare to where he assumed they were.

"I am not a threat to your queen. I cannot tell you everything that Kesh had planned...I cannot tell her either. However, I am here to see that his wishes are fulfilled. First among them, the safety, well-being, and happiness of his sister."

Another snort of amusement followed his statement. "I believe you will protect her, and I think you may even bring her happiness. If, she lets you."

Unsure how to respond to that last bit, Tarr silently nodded his head.

"Now," Sey's tone even more jovial, "Are you to be carried also?"

Another grunt of amusement as Tarr glared balefully at the guard. "Let us go then."

THE PALACE SHOOK ALL around her as Aela hurriedly walked the halls to the dining room where she was told the elders gathered.

"The great father feels much pain," Anut said beside her.

"Yes, he does."

"Our peoples will feel it too."

"Yes, they will." She shook her head. "How did it come to this? How did something so evil come to Dovkey?"

"Evil can go anywhere at any time," was the guard's solemn reply.

"Why Masia? Of all cities, why my home?" Rage filled her voice.

"The Great Wave is not the only one who feels much pain," Mar said from her other side. "Perhaps that was the purpose."

Aela stopped and turned to stare at them. "You think Masia was attacked because of me? That the wrangrent wants to wound me personally?"

"Evil seeks you, my queen," Anut said.

Aela gasped at hearing the words that had haunted her every time she closed her eyes since Masia. "You had a vision?"

"I had your vision," Anut responded.

"My vision," Aela repeated in shock.

"We are sworn to protect you, but that is not possible if you do not tell us of the dangers you see," Mar scolded gently.

She rubbed the bridge of her nose. "I will not have you lose your lives because of me."

"Lives given by you," Anut said.

"I know! And I won't have them lost!" She took a deep breath and lowered her voice. "Your deaths are not the repayment I seek. There is no debt to be paid as far as I am concerned, and nothing makes my life more valuable than yours."

"You are the queen," Mar began.

"And you are princes," Aela interrupted.

"We have left that life."

"It does not change who you are."

"Of land and sea, we chose land. Thus, you are our queen," Mar's arm crossed his chest, his fist pounded once over his heart. Anut followed suit.

"There are two paths before you. One will take you to safety. He will offer you this path." She suspected that the "he" Anut spoke of was Tarr. "The other path will take you into danger. There are some things that even we cannot protect you from."

Aela looked down the hall towards the dock they had just come from, but it was the opposite direction that drew her. "Then I'll pray for the Great Wave to protect me." She turned and resumed her chosen path with her loyal guards beside her.

"WHAT IS THE MEANING of this?" Elder Malcolm exclaimed when Aela and her guards entered the dining hall where the elders and priestesses were gathered for the evening meal.

The thunderous sound of the waves hitting the palace was accompanied by the rattling of crystal and china.

"I have news that cannot wait," Aela said with authority.

"Do you bring news from Masia?" Berto asked with concern.

"I bring news of Masia."

"Is this the reason for the Great Wave's discontent? Is your coming the reason that the White Palace is being assaulted?" George huffed. A murmur of assent went around the table.

"The pounding of the waves is of little consequence-" Aela started.

"The Great Wave's will of is little consequence! Do you hear such blasphemy?" the murmur of disapproval grew.

"Elders, I believe the queen has something of great importance to tell us." Bena quieted the group.

"Masia has been destroyed," Aela said before she could be interrupted again. Her voice rose with temper. "The 'assault' on the White Palace is the Great Wave's anger and anguish over what has happened to his children in Masia."

Voices of fear, anger, and confusion debated the news amongst themselves. They flung question after question at her. She explained as calmly as she could the events again and again. The elders struggled to hear her words. They clung tightly to disbelief.

"There is a wrangrent in Dovkey." The simple statement silenced all in the room. Faces of shock, skepticism, and horror looked back at her.

"Queen Aela," Bena said cautiously, "to make such a statement is…bold and unwise without the proper knowledge needed to understand the complexities of magic."

"I know what I saw, and what I know what I felt."

"Did you go into the city?" Elder Hans asked anxiously.

"Yes, I did. My guards, Lord Tarr, and Captain Tevor went with me."

"How do you know that the city was not burned? I believe that Masia is very close to the Frin'geren border, is it not?"

There was a general nodding of heads around the table.

Aela felt her face reddened with outrage. "Are you suggesting that Masia was attacked and burned by Frin'gerens?"

"I think that it is a possibility to consider."

The patronizing tone and calm expression of the elder made her want to scream, to berate them all for their foolish denial. She watched as the notion of a Frin'geren attack settled into the minds of the elders.

"It was not the Frin'gerens!"

Malcolm turned to her with a sneer. "How can you be sure, Your Majesty? You suggest that this is a magical transgression, but you are not qualified to evaluate magic on that level, or any level as it is."

She contemplated telling them of the vision, but it was likely they would not believe that either. The visions were a long-held secret, known only by her guards and Menony. And now, Tarr.

"We will send a small company of soldiers to Masia to determine the nature of the attack and search for survivors." The last of Hans' statements was pointedly said to Aela.

"Yes, we must determine what has happened!" Another elder exclaimed. "When the King returns..." his statement trailed off before it could be finished.

No one knew where the king was. Aela had her fears regarding Kesh's well-being, but that was also not something that she wanted to share with the elders.

Discussions erupted all around the table, and Aela realized that she was dismissed. She was not the ruling monarch, and the advisors felt no obligation to include in her in the discussions.

The elders quickly forgot her presence as they began discussing the possibility of a Frin'geren attack. She was tired, and her sudden arrival had somehow left the elders feeling threatened. She would take a few hours of the night to rest, to reorganize her thoughts, and in the morning, she would demand their attention. The threat of evil magic in Dovkey was real, and the people of Dovkey needed her to convince the elders of the truth.

With an exasperated huff, she left the room unnoticed. Her guards followed behind her.

"They would not listen," Anut said beside her with a note of disbelief in his voice.

"No, they would not."

"They are fools then," Mar's deep voice rumbled.

"Yes, they are, but I will not allow their foolishness to hurt my people," she said as they walked undisturbed to her quarters. "Tomorrow, you will gather the crewmen and Tarr to testify to what was seen...the storm and the city." There was a grunt of acknowledgment.

They walked the rest of the way in silence. At the door, Mar left her to confer with his brothers and to decide if they would seek information from another source. Anut stationed himself outside her door, despite her attempts to persuade him otherwise.

Aela wished them a good night and threw open the door to her room, the temper she usually kept tight control of, blazing like a wildfire.

"I would venture to guess that it did not go well." She turned to find Tarr seated at her desk. "What are you doing here? I told..."

"You what? Told your guard to put me to bed like a good little boy?" he mocked.

She turned from him, seeking the view out the open window.

"I told you that it would not be easy."

"I know what you told me!" She instantly regretted lashing out at him. He was not the cause of her anger. He was not the source of her pain. "I'm sorry."

"Pssh, that was mellow." He waved away her apology.

She crumpled onto the bed, holding her thought-burdened head in her hands. "Do you believe me?" Her voice was soft, but he heard her question, nonetheless.

"I was there, remember. I saw you fall into the river and come out talking about raining ash, and I then saw the city you spoke of."

He rose from where he sat, and she could hear his steady footsteps coming towards her. She felt him looming over her before she felt his hand gently lift her chin. "Anyone who was there can testify that something unnatural happened to that city."

"The elders suggested that it was merely burned in an attack." She pushed off the bed, the anger rising anew. "As if I couldn't tell the difference between fire damage and something more sinister."

"They are fools."

She smiled briefly at that. "Yes, they are." She turned to Tarr. "Someone suggested that it might be a Frin'geren attack."

Aela watched the slow, steadying breath that Tarr took even as his fists clenched and unclenched. "I don't believe that for a minute, Tarr. But the elders...they jumped on the idea like a pack of starving dogs. If they continue with this notion that one of the Frin'geren states attacked us-"

"Do not worry about Frin'gere. If the elders truly do want to pursue a fight with their neighbor, it will not be a fight they win. I assure you of that."

He reached out and gently stroked her cheek.

Her eyes darkened with unshed tears. "Someone destroyed my home, Tarr. Someone killed my people...my people." He brushed away the single tear that fell. "The elders cannot be depended upon to protect Dovkey."

"No, I don't believe that they can." He continued to stroke her face, his dark eyes studying her features. "What will you do?"

"There is an Immortal lord on his way to Dovkey as we speak. I will wait for his arrival and seek his aid with the Council. Until then, Mar and Anut will gather the crewmen to testify to what they saw; though, I don't know if it will make a difference. I would have you testify, but I'm not sure if that would be best at this time. I want Sey to stay with you until the elders can be convinced that there is not a threat from Frin'gere."

"You think that I can't protect myself?" his question more amusement than offense.

"Of course, you can. I will feel better though if you were not alone in the palace."

"Very well, I will accept your guard." He waited a moment before asking. "Why is a member of the Immortal Council on his way to Dovkey?"

The smile of relief faded from her face as she turned away from him. "Dovkey has a contract with the Phoenix Son Aluz."

His gaze sharpened. "You are purposefully being vague."

The gasp of surprise escaped before she could contain it. "You cannot expect me to tell you state secrets."

He studied her, and she silently cursed him for being so observant. "No, I think there is more to it than that. However, I will not push tonight. You need rest."

"Yes," she quickly agreed. "I will wish you good night now. We both are in great need of rest."

"I could stay here, Aela; lessen the burden of your guards. They would have only to watch over one room." His arms came around her, pulling her into his body. "I would watch over you all night, hold you close to me."

They were the words of the arrogant Frin'geren lord she had first met, but the honest emotion behind the words was the Tarr that she had come to know. She was not sure which to believe though she knew she was tempted to accept his offer.

"No, no." She shook her head as she pushed away. "I'm sorry, Tarr, but-"

She did not finish the statement because he pulled her closer. She felt herself melting into him just as he pulled away. His dark eyes stared into hers. "You have no reason to be sorry. Do not forget though, my queen, that you are in danger, and when I find the source of that danger, I will personally destroy it." He kissed the top of her head. "Sleep well, Aela."

Before she could respond, he was gone from the room. Leaving her to deal with the confusing emotions swarming inside her. Unable to sort through them, she pushed them out of her thoughts and went in search of Menony. She would check on her friend before succumbing to sleep.

※

HER EYES CLOSED HEAVILY as she rested her head on the pillow. Sleep came easily, but she did not find the rest she needed.

Aela saw his face in her dreams. A memory from when they were younger.

She stared out a window at the sea below. Just beyond the White Palace was a spot in the vastness of waves where the sea had parted, and her mother's body had been taken to the White Beach.

Her mother had been the great Healing Priestess of Dovkey, the most magical of all water wielders in Dovkey. She had worked tirelessly to save those infected by the Exchromy fever, but even with all her blessedness, she had succumbed to the fever too.

Guilt flooded her heart as she thought about her mother tending to Aela day and night despite the fever raging through her own body. Had she spent less time caring for her daughter, the Healing Priestess might have been able to fight the infection.

She would not have passed onto the White Beach.

"You are not the reason," her brother's voice carried over her shoulder. She did not turn to face him, and she did not agree with him.

"Had it not been you, it would have been another. She refused to avoid the sick. It was her duty and her calling to heal. How could she not do that in a time of such great need?"

"If it had not been me, she would have taken better care of herself. She would have rested more, given her body the strength to heal and fight."

"She was past the point of recovery when you became sick," he said sadly.

"You do not know that," Aela said.

"*I do.*" He said it with such authority that Aela did not bother trying to contradict him.

Hundreds had succumbed to the fever. Excromy fever did not have high survival rates. Aela, was to her knowledge, the only Dovkeyen to survive. The fact did not give her relief. It only deepened her guilt.

"It was meant to be," Kesh said as he folded her into a hug. "You cannot see it now, but it was meant to be."

She buried her head in his chest and cried. Great sobs of grief so deep she feared she would never not feel it.

"I am useless now," she whispered to him.

"You will never be useless, Aela," there was a hint of mirth in his tone.

"I have failed the trials, and I can no longer conceive the next generation. It was my duty to provide the heirs while you ruled. I cannot do that now." The rare survivors of the fever were always barren.

"Then you rule, and I will provide the heirs," he commented lightly.

She pulled away and hit him on the chest. "This is not a joke, Kesh."

"No, it is not. I think I would enjoy begetting heirs much more than ruling the country." His smile was infectious, and she could not help but return it with one of her own.

She shook her head. The priestesses had convinced her father, the reigning king, that she would benefit from recovering away from the palace. She wondered if, in his grief, he preferred not to have her close. She was now a reminder of too many painful things.

Her aunt resided in the faraway border town of Masia. It was decided that she would go there. Hurt filled her when she thought that no place in Dovkey could be further away than Masia.

The memory shifted. The setting remained, but the words spoken were not from the past. These were not part of her memory.

"It's time, Aela." The memory version of her brother looked at her with dire seriousness. "I have done my part as best I could."

What part she wanted to ask, but the dream version of her could not speak.

"One day, you will see the whole thing laid out, and you will understand. I am sorry that confusion and doubt will precede the understanding, but it could not be helped. I leave you with everything and everyone most important to me. I know you will protect them as I have tried to protect you."

What was he saying? Why was her mind twisting and changing a bittersweet memory?

"I have loved you, my sister, since the day I first looked upon you and saw the greatness you were destined for. It was my great honor to be a part of your journey." He leaned forward and placed a gentle kiss on her forehead.

"Death came by sea, and I am grateful."

She woke with a sob on her lips. The memory was one she did not like to revisit, but the twist at the end was even more devastating.

The waves below continued to pound against the palace, and she was amazed she had fallen to sleep at all. She threw the covers off and stood at the window.

It was more than a dream.

More than a memory.

It was a vision and a goodbye. Tears rushed down her face as she silently wept the passing of her mother in memory and the passing of her brother in a vision.

Chapter 13

The black ship appeared on the horizon two days later, heralded by the arrival of the black tide.

The elders argued about what to do while the priestesses finally warned of the ominous water. The two groups were forever feuding. Aela sat silently in their meetings as sorrow seeped into her being. She wanted to look at her brother's body to confirm the vision, but in her heart, she knew the truth.

As the ship neared the coast of Dovkey, wave upon wave beat the White Palace. Each hit was stronger than the last and each seemed to bring with it the threat of destruction. Heavy rain poured from the sky, but it was not the nurturing rain common to the season. Instead, it battered Dovkey with the same ferocity as the sea. The rivers swelled, and some worried the White Palace would flood as it never had before.

The elders consulted their histories, and the priestesses listened to the waves. Yet, they learned only that their god was angry. Aela knew that their god was grieving also. If the waves had been under her command, she too would have crashed them repeatedly against the palace. She would have flooded the rivers and let them carry the White Palace off the cliff and into the sea. She felt very little love for the place despite the role it had played in the history of her people.

When the rain and waves finally ceased one morning, the black ship lingered in the shadow of the cliffs. It was weathered and beaten, with a torn sail and a broken mast. The elders waited for a crew to disembark; however, when no one departed after several hours, a small boat was rowed out from the cliffs. Aela knew the men rowing towards the ship had orders to look for disease and burn the ship.

They found neither disease nor the bodies of crewmen. One body only occupied the ship. In the captain's quarters, they found King Kesh's body, gray and cold. With heavy hearts, the soldiers recovered the body of their king and left hungry flames to devour the ship as the sun sank into the ocean.

Aela stood on the steps of the tower as the men lifted his body from the boat, carrying it up the white steps as the priestesses followed behind with their chanting. She stood on the steps even as they passed, yet her eyes remained fixed on death's ship. Red and yellow flames reached up to the dark sky as they consumed the broken vessel. She stayed on those steps until the flames were drowned in the black waters and the ship sank into the White Sea. She watched, her face still as stone and her eyes as dry as the Frin'geren deserts.

Sorrow pervaded the palace as preparations were made for the king's funeral. As with most things, the elders allowed her little input in the proceedings. They assured her over and over that King Kesh would receive the greatest honors to send him on his way to the White Beach.

Dignitaries from all around Dovkey were invited to the palace. Much to her disgruntlement, her cousin, the Healer Priestess of Dovkey, was among those sent for. Her mood turned irritable as she waited to put her brother to rest.

Only Tarr seemed to understand her frustration.

"How long are they going to wait? There will be nothing left of him by the time your elders finally bury him," he griped upon entering her study. She looked up from her desk.

"His body has been preserved," she replied. "And we do not bury the dead. We send them to the White Beach."

"What is that?"

"The realm under the waves where our god, The Great Wave, is said to reside. All souls in Dovkey join him at the White Beach."

"Do you believe in the Great Wave?" He asked as he sat on the corner of her desk.

"Yes, I do."

"You believe he is an all-powerful force that governs our fates?"

She thought carefully before responding. "I believe that he sets all things in motion. He has a plan for each of his people, and to each, he gives the strengths and skills needed to fulfill his plan."

"Hmmm," he looked at her skeptically, and she smiled.

"Are there no deities in Frin'gere?"

"There are hundreds of deities in Frin'gere. The problem isn't choosing to believe in one, it's choosing which one to believe in."

"And which ones do you believe in?"

His expression was thoughtful. "I'm not sure I believe in any." Her brow rose in surprise. "From what I have seen of life, the gods care little for us. We are passing amusements for them, and here and there, they may choose to bestow a blessing on the faithful. I prefer to believe in my own abilities to change the world."

Aela smiled. "That does not surprise me."

They sat in comfortable silence for a moment. "Who is the Healer Priestess? I hear she is the one that the elders eagerly await."

She could not refrain the eye roll or groan of irritation. Tarr smiled amusedly at her response. "Not someone you are fond of?"

"Ishea, the Healer Priestess, is my cousin and the highest-ranking priestess in Dovkey. Her presence is expected at proceedings such as the funeral of a monarch. However, I do not rejoice at knowing she will be here."

He laughed. "Oh, I must know. What about her drives you so mad?"

"I don't wish to speak of her," Aela said as she pushed out of her seat. She circled the opposite corner of the desk, but Tarr moved quickly to intercept her.

"So, we will not speak of her." His hands rubbed her upper arms. "Would you rather we talk about your brother?"

Her body tensed. "What is there to talk about? He is dead. The result of foolishly playing a game that he could not win." She tried to pull away from him, but Tarr held her tightly.

"You cannot see his reasons now, but I promise in time, you will understand the why," he said softly.

His words reminded her of the similar ones Kesh had spoken in her vision. The realization that so many things she did not understand were in play, that there were so many secrets that she did not know, solidified more each day. She wondered more and more what Tarr's true purpose for being in Dovkey was.

"Why are you here, Tarr?" She asked softly.

"I've become bored and restless in my rooms."

She glared at his obvious misinterpretation of the question. "What are you doing in Dovkey?"

His expression hardened. "I'm here to marry the queen that I won in a card game."

"Not untrue, but not the full truth."

He shrugged. "Kesh wanted me here. Even I don't know all the reasons why, but...this is where he wanted me, so here I am."

She accepted that for now but knew there was more he was not telling her. She was sure of it.

THE HEALER PRIESTESS arrived within five days of the black ship's appearance.

Tarr watched as the elders fawned over her. The priestesses, to his surprise, greeted her with restrained courtesy. He expected a warmer welcome; however, Aela explained that an old rivalry existed between the palace priestesses and those outside the palace.

The Healer Priestess was a beautiful woman. Slightly taller than the queen, she dressed in flowing garments of white that accentuated her lithe body. Her white-blonde hair piled atop her head in a loose but elegant bun. And, unlike the icy reserve of the queen, she was warm and friendly.

He smiled as he watched Ishea greet Aela first as protocol dictated and then with enthusiastic fondness. Aela remained rigid as Ishea enveloped her in a hug. The priestess fussed over her as they reentered the palace.

Aela stoically endured the affection and fuss. Though, Tarr suspected she was miserable. He followed in amused silence as the two women joined the remaining elders and priestesses in the dining hall.

Aela took her seat at the head of the table while Ishea took the seat to her left. Tarr stealthily occupied the seat to Aela's right where he could continue to observe the interaction between the two.

Ishea reached across the table and cradled Aela's hands in her own. "My queen, my cousin, I cannot tell you how great my sorrow and the sorrow of all Dovkey is at the passing of our beloved king and your treasured brother."

"Thank you, cousin. The loss is felt by all of us."

"The loss is even greater for you. My heart aches, and I find that I wish I had the magic and skills to heal emotional hurt."

Aela nodded in that regal way of hers. Tarr was fascinated by how she often used it to avoid commenting or responding.

"When will we send him to meet the Great Wave?" The priestess asked.

"In the morning, your holiness," an older man further down the table responded. Tarr had not bothered to learn the elders' names beyond Berto. He was the only courteous one among them. Even now, he received sneers and looks of disapproval from the others.

"Yes, he should join the creator without haste."

Aela's eyes started to roll back into her head, but she managed to restrain herself before it was noticed by anyone else at the table. Tarr attempted to smother a laugh. The poor attempt earned him the Healer Priestesses attention.

"Oh, I do not believe we have met, sir." Her pale green eyes gazed warmly at him.

A moment of silence passed while she waited for introductions to be made. Ishea glanced between him and Aela. He sniggered again, wondering if he should be offended that Aela refused to introduce them.

Finally, Ishea prompted, "My queen?"

Aela sighed, "This is Lord Tarr of Avengere."

"A Frin'geren?" The priestess inquired. Aela nodded. "What brings you to Dovkey, my lord?"

"My fiancé actually." He smiled at Aela who remained silent as she cast him a glare.

The comment did however gain the attention of the elders, who immediately denied the validity of his claim.

"That has not been finalized!"

"There are procedures, Lord Tarr!"

"How very presumptive!"

Their objections filled the room.

"Enough." Aela's voice was low but full of authority. One word managed to silence the room. "We will not discuss this on the eve of my brother's funeral. As is custom, we will adjourn to our personal spaces for the night and prepare our prayers for the king."

Solemn silence eclipsed the room.

"Of course, Your Majesty," Ishea said. "I would like to join the palace priestesses in their temple this night and pray for King Kesh's arrival to the White Beach on the morrow."

The Head Priestess nodded as she stood. Ishea bowed to Aela before she joined the other priestess. However, she glanced over her shoulder and smiled at Tarr before leaving.

He wondered when he would see the Healer Priestess again. Soon, he wagered.

THE LOOMING INDIGO clouds of Dovkey parted enough to allow a few shafts of light. On this day, however, the Great Wave honored the dead king and showered the palace in the sunlight. The highest tower, where the watchmen kept the guiding fire, glowed a soft bluish-purple, and just above the ocean, the stone reflected blue and green. In the center of the cliffs, a string of lights starting at the highest tower glowed with bright intensity.

At the base of the cliffs, ancient builders had hollowed out a great cave. Stairs spanned the width of the cave and led into the ocean. The stairs disappeared under the water, and it was said they led to the White Beach where the Great Wave and the dead resided. Despite the constant wearing of the ocean's motions, the steps seemed untouched, each edge as sharp as the day it was carved. Rivers tumbled off the cliffs on either side and scored the face of the stone; however, the sound of the ocean drowned out the rushing water.

Aela felt the misty air that the wind blew against her cheek and looked out over the sea. Its movements were calm. Behind her stood the palace staff, the elders, and the priestesses. Above, next to the rivers, gathered the sorrowful subjects of Dovkey. The white veil on her head gently flapped against her lips. Dovkey traditions honored the dead by wearing white as it represented the deceased's final descent into the land of the Great Wave.

The guards, who also dressed in white, carried Kesh's burial boat down the stairs. They lowered it and gave it to the sea. The water swelled onto the stairs, wetting even those who stood on the higher steps. Aela stood tall as the water rose above her waist and lifted her brother to her height. She peered into the boat at the peaceful face. She reached for one of his hands resting across his chest. Noticing the king's sapphire ring was missing, Aela remembered that Tarr had it. She wished that she had requested its return.

A sensation on the back of her neck prompted her to turn. The Frin'geren stood at the top of the steps in front of her guards. His eyes focused on her and something in the way his face softened pulled at her heart. She felt the tears that she was determined not to cry gather at the corners of her eyes. As if reading her thoughts, he slipped the King's Sapphire from his finger and descended the stairs towards her.

She reached for it, and he laid it gently in her palm, his fingers lingering over her hand for a few extra seconds. Turning from him, she looked once again at her brother. With the utmost care, she lifted his left hand and placed the ring on his finger where it was always worn by a king of Dovkey.

A gasp behind her conveyed one of the elder's disapproval. She did not care. The ring would go with him into the afterlife for he was the last male descendant of her line and the last king of Dovkey.

The priestesses behind her cleared their throats, and she relinquished his hand. They surrounded the boat, flinging bundles of flowers and herbs onto the body. Then their voices harmoniously sang the ancient song of the Great Wave.

The five priestesses pressed the boat down, filling it with water. Aela watched as Kesh's image sank further and further. The women released their hold on the boat as it disappeared completely. Only the current carrying it away from the cliffs showed. The mourners stood in silence until the world began to shake. Far out into the White Sea, a coral peak of white rose out of the ocean, showing everyone that the king had arrived at the White Beach. A series of waves hid it once more.

Aela turned from the sea and ascended the stairs leading into the palace, where she waited for everyone to pass her. She lowered her head. Menony and her guards stood behind her, and she felt their strength seeping into her.

Her brother's soul had finally returned home, and there it would rest for eternity.

Chapter 14

The ancient rituals of grieving were among the few laws left untouched by the Reformation and remained beliefs that the people of Dovkey had never strayed from.

Long, unfurling banners of white hung from the walls and tower of the White Palace. Servants walked the halls solemnly with heads hung low. Even the elders dressed in the traditional white robes to honor the dead.

As Aela looked out over the Joining River, she imagined the docks of Masia. In her mind's eye, she saw the white streamers tied to the wooden piers waving in the wind. She imagined the warm, happy spirit of the river town subdued by the grievous news that had spread to all parts of the country. She longed to walk among them in her period of grieving, but Masia was no more.

According to the ancient laws, the grieving observed a week of silence. They were to not speak a word to another, and none were to speak to them. Aela had passed two other weeks of grieving in the palace. Both times she had had Kesh, first for her mother and then for her father. Now, she faced a week of silence without the man who had always been her constant. Never again would she feel his presence in times of sadness and fear. Never again share her joy in times of happiness. Never again would she take her strength and guidance from the person she had loved most in the world.

The clouds had cleared enough that light shone on the palace once more, but there was no light here. Every space she entered was filled with ghosts and figures of white that moved without sound through the halls. She knew that life continued in the hallways and rooms beyond her, but she had not been a part of palace life for years now.

That was why she needed Masia. She could walk through the streets and take comfort that life continued even if she was not allowed to participate. At home, people knew the language not spoken with words, the language of assuring glances, comforting embraces, and a warm presence. Her period of grieving was for Masia as much as it was for Kesh.

Here, the palace was full of people hastening to leave her presence. She had not seen the elders or priestesses since the burial. The dignitaries that had come to the palace for the funeral left to observe the week of silence in their own homes. Ishea returned to the village near the Domean border where she was treating an outbreak among the old and very young.

Aela's guards had been silent out of respect for her. She knew she had only to ask, and they would disregard the traditions and forgo the silence. Until that time, their presence, though distant at times, was reassuring.

Three days had passed, and she had seen Menony for only a few brief moments during the day. Her friend's avoidance hurt more than the entire palace full of silence. During their few encounters, she had seen the dried tears, the reddened eyes, and the shadows of sleeplessness. Menony had always been a tender soul, and she and Kesh had been good friends. His passing was a great loss to her as well.

"Have you been hiding these last few days?" It was strange to hear the voice of another after three days of silence, even if the voice was familiar.

Aela looked over her shoulder and saw Tarr leaning against the wall with his arms crossed over his chest. His eyes were dark with concern though he wore a smooth smile. She often thought that he wore a mask, but it failed to hide the truth of his eyes.

He looked away for a moment and the concern was gone, vanished like all the other times. She smiled sadly as she wondered why he hid.

"Have you been avoiding me?" he asked with faked offense.

Aela felt a smile tug at her lips then frowned as she remembered the circumstances that had brought her to stare out longingly at the Joining River. She turned from him, shaking her head. A few words and a look of concern had made her forget her loneliness for a moment. They had made her forget the reason for her silence. She turned from him and walked away.

His footsteps followed behind her until she saw his feet in front of her. She stopped suddenly, almost unable to avoid running into him.

"Now, I know that you are avoiding me."

Aela reluctantly smiled.

He was so close she could feel the heat of his body. It seemed so welcoming. All she would have to do was step forward, close the distance between them, and be enveloped in warmth she had not felt since Kesh had left all those months ago.

They stood inches apart. He seemed to know her longing for company and waited patiently as she soaked up everything she needed. The wind blew into the open corridor, tugging at the white veil she was required to wear in the presence of others but did without when she was alone. Yet, Tarr stood above, studying her face. Breaking every tradition with his very presence here.

He reached out to her, his fingers gentle and slow. They grazed the bare skin of her arm. His touch was warm on her goose-bump-covered flesh. With extraordinary care, he let his hands travel higher up her arm until his fingers kneaded the tension from her shoulders.

She wanted to stay there, taking in his warmth when she felt nothing but cold inside her heart. Aela wanted to fall apart while his body protected her from the wind, while his defiance protected her from all the expectations of the world.

Looking into his eyes, she saw the dark pools of feelings and didn't know the depths of those pools. She looked away, refusing to give release to the tears in her eyes. His hands tightened on her arms as she tried to turn away from him. With pleading eyes, she looked up to him, hoping to convey her thoughts in a look.

"I know the rules," he said softly. She released a pent-up breath. "I'm not Dovkeyen though." He smiled. "I'm not bound by any vows of silence."

Her eyes pleaded again, and he gestured for her to be silent though she made no sound. "You can't talk. But I can. As I see it, this is what every man dreams of; being alone with a beautiful woman who won't talk back or interrupt or argue or correct..." He smiled as he looked down at her face.

Tears gathered in her eyes, yet she smiled a small smile, shaking her head in amusement.

"I would be a fool not to take advantage of this. Technically, I'm breaking no laws as a Frin'geren and you break no laws, so long as you don't say a single word in the next four days."

She shook her head again.

"I know it will be hard to resist proclaiming your love for me, but you'll just have to control yourself." She held back a laugh at his ridiculousness. "Who knows, you might like what I have to say."

His hand gripped her chin and lifted her gaze to his. "And there are so many other things we can do with our mouths." He leaned in closer as she made a face of objection. However, his lips touched gently just below the outer corner of her eye, first one side, and then the other.

TARR HAD WATCHED HER wander around the palace alone for three days. Though her guards followed at a distance, she looked so abandoned. Her skin was pale, and he assumed she was not eating as she should be. Her gray eyes were rimmed in shadows from lack of sleep.

The grieving traditions of Dovkey were new to him, but he could not say that he agreed or even liked them. How isolation aided in the passing of grief, he could not figure. People needed warmth, compassion...contact when sorrow was so deep.

In those first few days, he had tried to honor her country's traditions. With each passing day though, he worried more and more that she would just fade away in her isolation.

He refused. Refused to let her be so lost and alone.

Thus, he refuted Dovkeyen tradition and broke the silence. The grief and the relief that filled her tears confirmed his decision to stay with her until the week was over. She would not feel the cold emptiness of solitude, and she would not have to carry the burden of her grief unaided. His commitment to see her through this was resolute.

He filled her days with tales of desert nights told in loving detail, of riotous bar fights that tempted her to laugh out loud, and of boyhood adventures that briefly brought tears to her eyes.

He touched her in ways meant to be comforting. His family had always expressed love in a tactile fashion. It was what he knew, what comforted him. His urge to caress her, hold her, soothe her with his hands only intensified as she surrendered to it. The enjoyment she took from it was obvious, and he found that touching her was unavoidable.

From that first afternoon overlooking the Joining River, they met in various places throughout the palace. Her guards aided in arranging the meetings. Despite his defiance of the country's traditions, he respected the ways of her people in their presence.

She wore her veil as they walked down the halls in silence, passing servants, elders, and priestesses. Each looked at the pair with confusion, unable to understand how two people would pass the time together in silence.

Three days passed. On the fourth, Aela took Tarr to the waterfall room. She casually took his hand and led him on the secret path to the ancient room. Enjoying the feel of her hand in his, he smiled as he followed her lead. Her guards followed distantly behind, obviously knowing the path that she took. When he looked back, he found that they had parted one by one, no doubt securing her privacy.

Before entering the chamber, she took off her sandals and motioned for Tarr to do the same. He eyed her questioningly before reluctantly complying. Unable to contain her excitement, she rushed down the last few steps and splashed into the water. It wrapped around her ankles, swaying in and out of the drains on the floor.

Though he relished her joy, he entered the chamber with uncertainty. Warily, he eyed the water that sloshed around his legs and wet his pants. A soft sound drew his attention. Aela held her hands over her mouth as she tried to contain a laugh. He could almost read her thoughts. *Desert boy.* She walked to the large window and closed her eyes as she leaned toward the water with contentment.

"This is a special place for you," Tarr said from beside her.

She looked at him with a smile and nodded. She was relaxed. The comfort and ease of being together the past week had gradually deepened. He wondered if she felt a lightening of her royal burden when it was just the two of them. He hoped that was true.

AELA COULDN'T FIGURE out why she felt relaxed with Tarr. The days in his company, unable to say anything had been more a relief than she had ever thought silence could be. She did not have to consider her words carefully or measure them in terms of how they would be received. She didn't have to calculate her tone to accomplish goals of diplomacy, reprimand, or faked interest. In the quiet moments with Tarr, she felt her truest self.

Tarr was different than she expected. She had no doubts that he was a clever, manipulative, and persistent man. However, she was not sure to what use he put those qualities.

Their time together had taught her that he was also highly observant, learning her expressions quickly. They had spent days now communicating with her expressions and his words. He was sensitive to her moods, knowing what stories to tell at what times, depending on if her need was for humor, wonder, or reflection. Most importantly, he knew when silence was the only balm for her aching heart.

They stood next to each other looking at the cascading water. Aela leaned out the window, letting the spray caress her face. She closed her eyes and smiled. Somewhere in the thunderous rush of the falling water, she could hear the faint voices of the river.

"What does it say?" Tarr's whisper brushed the skin of her ear.

She startled slightly, her eyes opening. He stood close, studying her face.

"You looked as if you were listening," he responded to her unvoiced question. "I have heard rumors that the priestesses listen for messages from the ocean. Do they do the same things with the rivers?"

The priestesses did hear the voice of the Great Wave through the sounds of the ocean. However, she had never heard of another person who could read messages in the river. She had not known of them during her priestess training. The first time she heard the river whispering to her was in Masia.

In response to his question, she slowly shook her head. "But you do." He looked away, his expression deep in thought.

Aela touched his face as he turned it away. At the feel of her fingers, he turned back to her. His slow smile was soft and full of surprise. Her fingers lingered on his cheek as she watched him lean closer.

She began to shake her head, but it was too late. One hand cradled the back of her head, the other wrapped around her waist, and he pulled her body into his. He paused just a breath away from her lips, allowing her the chance to pull away.

Aela didn't want to pull away. Curiosity replaced the doubt she felt only moments ago, and she wondered what it would feel like to have his lips on hers. The role of a queen was a lonely one and never had she been held like this. She tilted her head up silently permitting him to continue.

His lips were softer than she expected. He pressed them to hers, and she exhaled the pent-up breath. Her eyes closed as she felt his grip tighten, bringing her closer to his body.

The kiss was soft, almost lazy as if there were no other pressing matters in the world. Despite her inexperience, she knew he was experienced. Not only was he a handsome Frin'geren, but his touch was also confident and natural as if he had done this a thousand times. The thought irritated her, but as he shifted her body against the window ledge, she allowed it to slip from her mind.

He nipped at her bottom lip as he pulled away. She sluggishly opened her eyes and found him studying her face. No leering satisfaction, no censure, no concern...just a look of simple contentment revealed by his warm eyes and indolent smile. It mirrored what she felt inside.

Laughter filled with surprise and joy bubbled up, and she failed to fully contain it.

Tarr's face hardened just slightly though he continued to smile. "Is that a complaint? Because I've never had one of those before."

The sulkiness in his voice was so uncharacteristic that Aela held in another laugh. His face hardened more. Before he could respond, she gripped the back of his neck and went up on her toes as she pressed a quick kiss to his lips. She did not linger as he had but merely sought to offer reassurance.

Tarr eyed her curiously. "You'll have to explain that later." It was the first time in the week that he had not been able to read her thoughts.

Aela acknowledged him with a nod and turned to look out the window.

The silence between them was not uncomfortable.

"You're wet...again," he whispered in her ear. She smiled because it was true enough. The spray of the water had seeped through both their clothes. "It seems to happen to you quite frequently whenever I'm around."

She turned to him with amusement. Then she gestured toward the waterfall in front of them. "It could have something to do with that." He admitted with a smile. "Do you miss it?"

Aela nodded as she stretched her hands out to the water that carried a piece of home with it.

Tarr turned her back to face the water and lifted her to the edge of the window. "Go on, get a bit closer."

She leaned back with his strong arms supporting her. The moment of fear was swiftly replaced by elation as the spray soaked her clothes to the skin. She felt its coolness spread over her body, and she heard the voices of the river. The calming river voices were wordless waves of condolence and empathy, but they became voices that she vaguely knew- the brisk tone of the baker, the gravelly voice of a diver, the innkeeper's wife's high-pitched timbre. They were the pieces of home that she had needed so desperately. Found with the help of a stranger in a room of rainbows. The joy she felt brought tears to her eyes. She stayed in the spray until she felt the complaints of her lower back. When she reached for Tarr's shoulders, he pulled her in.

He lowered her slowly to her feet and placed a kiss on her forehead. No other words were said, but Aela felt a well of emotion filling the space between them. Realizing that she was not ready yet to examine those emotions, she stepped out of his embrace.

He acknowledged the distance with a slight frown but said nothing.

Sometimes, silence was the only thing needed, Aela reflected as she returned to the upper levels of the palace with Tarr. They walked slowly side by side, seemingly both lost in their own thoughts. Aela did not want to be in her head any more than she wanted to be in her heart. Sorrow and pain filled her heart, but confusion and doubt clouded her mind. However, she could not shift her thoughts when the source of her confusion brushed against her causally. It was impossible not to be aware of his presence.

She knew that some thought of her as cold, and in times of doubt, she thought they might be right. Aela was aware of how she handled difficult situations. She pulled away and turned from the problem. In that way, she supposed, she and Kesh had been alike. They both ran away when things were beyond them. He ran to Frin'gere, and she escaped into an inner sanctum that no one could find.

They passed the first of her guards, Ter, and he fell silently in step behind them. Anut and Sey did the same as Aela and Tarr passed them too. The group had entered the newer parts of the palace when they encountered Mar. Aela paused.

Tarr's fingers found hers, brushing them playfully before turning her palm down. Bringing the back of her hand to his lips, he placed a gentle kiss on her skin. "Until tomorrow."

He bowed before walking away with Sey as an escort.

Aela watched him leave. A tempest of emotions swirled inside her. Fear won out, and she turned away, refusing to allow herself to dwell on thoughts of Tarr.

Chapter 15

The first few days of mourning passed in a blur. Menony wondered at times if she would survive the sorrow that she felt, but she pushed through the pain of grief. She had not failed in her duties during those difficult days, but she also hadn't been as aware as usual. From Aela's guards, she learned that her queen had spent several days of her mourning period with Lord Tarr. They had also disclosed that the queen was happy and relaxed during her time with him.

However, Aela now spent most of her time in her quarters. She studied maps and old law. When her eyes grew strained from staring at scrolls and books, she stared listlessly out the window. Aela did not share her thoughts as she sat alone looking at the sea.

The guards' refusal to follow Dovkeyen tradition was an unexpected blessing. Mar revealed that when Aela did leave her chambers, she instructed the guards that she wished to avoid Tarr, which was quite a task for the Frin'geren was determined to see her.

Tarr requested a meeting with her several times, though she denied all of them. Sey was assigned the task of dismissing Tarr each time he called on her, and Menony was sure that the guard found amusement in the task. He was also the one tasked with following Tarr when Aela wanted to know his whereabouts. Part of her success at avoiding him was attributed to always knowing his location.

On the last night of their grieving period, Menony prayed for forgiveness from the Great Wave as she broke with tradition and asked the question that had been on her mind for days.

"What happened with Lord Tarr?"

Aela turned from looking out the window with a shocked expression.

"In five hours, the official week of grieving will be over. I hardly think the Great Wave will condemn us for ending it now. I hope not anyway," she said almost to herself as she folded a discarded shawl.

Aela laughed, and the sound was a welcome break from the silence. "I find that there is some wisdom to the silence when it comes to grief, but a week is too long a time. I have missed talking to you, Menony." Her smile fell. "Are you well? The first few days..."

Menony nodded, fully aware of how withdrawn she had been. "I am. Not healed, but that mostly comes with time, does it not?"

Aela nodded knowingly. Menony had been with Aela through the loss of her mother and father. Both had devastated the young queen, but she found joy in the years since their passing. However, she suspected the loss of Kesh would take many more years to fade. The two siblings had been very close.

"Again, I ask, what happened with Lord Tarr?"

Aela countered by questioning why Menony would think anything happened.

"Your guards are gossips."

Again, the sound of Aela's laughter was a warm and welcome sensation.

"They told me that you spent much time with him throughout the week and that you took him to your favorite place in the palace."

"They truly do have loose tongues, don't they?" Aela said with mock censure as she rose from her seat by the window.

Menony patiently waited her out. She could see the thoughts gathering in Aela's head as she started to absentmindedly pace the room.

"He was...distracting. Comforting," a small smile betrayed her thoughts.

"And yet, you have spent the past two days in this room, refusing to see him."

Aela bit her nail, a rare tell of discomfort. "It was too much."

"What was?"

"What I felt when I was with him. Too much. I, I can't allow myself to be distracted by all these feelings that I...I don't know what to do with them when there is so much going on."

Menony stood in front of her, taking her friend's face gently in her hands. She lifted Aela's face until their gazes met.

"Aela, they trained you so well to be a pillar of strength and authority to your people. First, your parents laid the burdens of a queen upon you and then the priestesses. They all scrutinized you while watching for the manifestation of a prophecy. More and more they piled upon you, and you slowly became less of a person.

"Fate dealt you one heart-breaking loss after another, and somehow in all of that, you were blamed for a failure that was never yours. You took it all in as your own. In doing so, you started to believe that you were the failed queen, and every day since you have tried to deny your need to prove differently. You've been torn between thinking the worst of yourself and being a paragon of restraint and duty. Neither of those things is who you are.

"You are the queen of Dovkey, and you are a woman with wants and needs. You can be both and accomplish everything that needs to be done. Kesh," her voice broke as she said his name, "He believed with everything he was that you were the future of Dovkey. And he would have wanted you to be happy."

Tears streamed down both their faces as Aela pulled away. Silence filled the space between them before Aela said quietly, "I think I should pass the rest of my grief in silence. Thank you, Menony. You are dismissed." She turned away and resumed her seat at the window.

Menony felt a moment's worth of irritation at being dismissed. However, concern quickly replaced it. She had been by Aela's side for many years and had watched the woman become more and more withdrawn, convinced that the events of her life had made her unworthy of the things that every person wanted and deserved.

Tarr brought out feelings that Aela had not allowed herself to feel in a very long time, and he made her want things that she had been told she could not have.

As she left for her own room, she wondered if Kesh had suspected Tarr's ability to break through Aela's walls. The deep ache of loss filled her chest again at the thought of Aela's brother. He had once told Menony similar words and had convinced her that she could fulfill her duties and have love. She trusted that he would have found a way to do the same for his beloved sister.

THE QUEEN RESUMED HER duties the first morning after the end of her grieving period. She attended meetings with the priestesses and elders every day. The discontent between the two deepened with each encounter. Their feuding carried past the closed doors of their meetings and drew the attention of the guards stationed outside and those who passed in the hall. The strain of their constant bickering wore on their queen, her exhaustion more evident after every meeting. Added to her frustration was the elders' refusal to accept what had happened in Masia. Several messengers returned early in the week with reports that confirmed the queen's story. Two of the palace priestesses had traveled to the destroyed town also. Since their return, the priestesses sat quietly as the elders argued with the queen regarding Masia.

To the disagreement of her guards, Aela continued to insist that the Frin'geren be kept at a distance despite the obvious pleasure that she had taken in his presence.

THE FAILED QUEEN

Anut remembered the first few days he and his brothers had spent with the queen. Her aunt, who lived in Masia with her, had just passed. Her grief was heavy and carried with it the smell of spring rain. Aela was barely a woman of eighteen, but when his powerful father had come to her, requesting that she shelter his illegitimate sons, she had accepted with the confidence and maturity of someone much older.

Living in Masia had not been easy for any of them. Far from the ocean, they longed to feel the salty sea on their skin. Instead, they covered their appearances, out of fear that their father's adversaries would find them and fear of rejection from the townspeople.

She pushed through her grief and taught them the ways of the land. With her encouragement, they walked the streets of Masia, bought the wares of merchants in the square, dove with the divers for pearls, and eventually became a part of the community.

Aela showed them the rivers, where they heard and felt again the voices and power of the water. She gave them life on land and showed them how to remain connected to the water.

Her grief had faded after a time, and joy filled many of her moments in Masia. However, they had never seen her truly happy.... truly free from the burdens of her perceived failures and unexpected losses. At least, they had not seen it until her time with the Frin'geren that King Kesh had sent to look over her.

Neither he nor his brothers understood the scheme set in motion by Kesh, but he believed that her brother wanted her happiness as much as they did. And for this reason, they ignored her command to redirect Lord Tarr.

Three days after the end of her grieving, Mar and Ter led the way as they exited her room and descended a set of spiral stairs, continuing down the hall. She continued walking down the hall unaware of Tarr beside her until he spoke.

"You have been avoiding me."

She jumped in surprise at his voice. Stopping abruptly, she stared at him and then at her guards. She glared at each in turn. The Frin'geren's touch on her arm drew her attention back to him.

"I cannot talk now."

"Actually, this is the first time in a week that you can talk," the man did not bother to hide his own irritation.

"I have to go-"

"Well, I will not delay you, I promise. In fact, I will walk with you as we talk." He took her elbow and began to walk forward.

Aela's temper flared as she pulled free of his grasp. "Where do you get the idea that it is acceptable to touch me like this?"

"Would you prefer I touch you in other ways?" He asked quietly as he leaned closer to her ear, obviously unaware that her guards had excellent hearing.

Sey chuckled, and Aela stopped suddenly to glare over the Frin'geren's shoulder. He pulled her close to his body, seeming to think that Sey would crash into her. "Which reminds me of another topic we will have to discuss at some point." Before she could respond, he propelled her forward again, the guards falling into step.

She pulled her arm away but continued walking. In a more reasonable tone, only slightly laced with disdain, "Lord Tarr, it is not the custom for people to physically intimidate others in this country. Furthermore, I am the Queen of Dovkey."

The Frin'geren eyed her with cynicism.

She took a deep breath, and continued in a calmer tone, "Tarr, we both have titles to throw at each other and ideas of our own importance, but I have never treated you as anything less than a respected diplomat. It is not beyond reason that I ask you to respect my standing as the queen in return."

"I have a great deal of respect for you."

She was silent at his unexpected response.

"I am confused about why you have been avoiding me though."

Aela looked to Mar, the oldest of the brothers. He silently took a step back, the rest following his lead. Her scowl expressed her displeasure.

Turning back to Lord Tarr, "You are distracting."

"The very best sort of distraction, I hope." He gripped her tightly around the waist until Sey cleared his throat. Obviously, not a fool, the Frin'geren realized he was given an opportunity and should waste it by pushing too far. "Is a distraction so bad?"

Uncharacteristically, she groaned and let her head fall backward. "Yes, it is. The elders refuse to accept what happened at Masia and are constantly at odds with the priestesses, who have become withdrawn and secretive. That concerns me greatly. There is a wrangrent in my kingdom, hundreds of lives have been lost, my brother," her voice broke, "is gone, and an Immortal is on his way here as we speak."

"An Immortal? Who called upon the Council? Surely, if the elders or priestesses went to such lengths, they accept that there is a threat in Dovkey."

She groaned again. "No, he is not coming because of the wrangrent."

The Frin'geren's eyes narrowed as he quietly asked, "And why is an Immortal coming to Dovkey then?"

The queen hesitated. "After I survived the Excromy fever, my father entered me into a betrothal with a Phoenix Son."

"You are engaged to an Immortal?" His voice took on a sharper edge. Aela nodded. "Did your brother know of this?"

"I would think so, especially since I submitted several appeals to him."

"Appeals?"

"Yes. I have no desire to enter into an arrangement with the Phoenix Son. As the king, Kesh had the power to absolve the contract."

"So, as the queen, you have the power to absolve it?"

"Once I have officially been crowned the next ruler of Dovkey, yes, I will."

"Good. That should be one of your first orders of business, especially considering that you're already engaged."

Her eyes widened. "No, I am not. I was wagered in a foolish game like a pile of gold."

Lord Tarr stepped closer to her. His hands tried to cup her face, but she pulled away. He tried again.

"Careful, Frin'geren," Mar warned.

The man nodded in acknowledgment. "Aela, I promise that none of this was done to hurt you." She stared at him with doubt in her eyes.

When he once again tried to cradle her face, she let him. "I was sixteen when they told me that I was betrothed to an Immortal. My father told me it was an honor. I told him I was honored, but I didn't want to leave my people." She paused. "He then told me that I had failed in my other duties to Dovkey and becoming an Immortal was the only thing left for me to do."

"Your father was a bastard."

The corners of her lips tilted upward for a moment. "Kesh knew how much I hated the betrothal, how…insignificant it made me feel. I doubt that he didn't know how his wager would affect me. So, I must disagree with you when you state that there was no intention to hurt me. He knew it would wound, and he did it anyway."

They stared at each other in tense silence. "Our 'engagement' is the least of my concerns right now. You will excuse me while I see to the more pressing ones."

She stepped around him and continued down the hall.

"We are not finished with this conversation, Aela," he called out to her.

Anut and his brothers fell into step around her. She waited until they had turned the corner before quietly speaking. "I do not know what your intentions were, but do not disobey an order like that again."

The meeting had not gone as intended, but the Frin'geren had gained a great deal of knowledge that he had not had before. Anut hoped that he was astute enough to use it wisely.

TWO DAYS LATER, THE tower watch reported that a small vessel bearing a flaming sail approached on the Greater River. The Phoenix Son had arrived.

Even if the priestesses had not demanded that she formally greet the Phoenix Son, Aela would have requested a boat take her out to meet the Immortal's. It was customary for the queen or king to escort the vessel of an important visitor into the port cave. Some things were too deeply ingrained to be forgotten.

Menony dressed her in a fitted, soft gray gown overlaid by a robe of sheer teal fabric. The neckline of the gown was square cut, and the hem dragged at her feet. The formal attire had been made at her last visit to the palace on Kesh's insistence, but she had not had time to have the gown altered. The thought of Kesh brought a sharp pain to her chest, but she ignored it.

As she stood in front of the mirror, she wished that she had had the gowns hemmed before the arrival of the Phoenix Son, but little could be done now. She had only a few minutes before she needed to be on the river.

Thankfully, Menony emerged from her closet with heeled sandals. She still remembered when Kesh had brought them back from Frin'gere where many women wore elevated footwear. She had taken one look at the shoes and laughed. They looked as impractical and uncomfortable as wearing bricks strapped to her feet. The heel was made of braided rope and satin ribbons of dark gray wrapped across the top of her foot, behind her ankle, and up her leg where

Menony tied them off with a bow. The height increase was only an inch or two, but it was enough to compensate for the length of the gown.

"I would never have admitted this to him, but they aren't as horrible as I once said," Aela said as she tested her balance in the shoes. They were easy enough to walk in and would last her the rest of the day. Menony would hem the other gowns for tomorrow.

Aela heard the soft snicker as her friend knew to whom she referred. Menony had a gentle smile and a far-off look on her face as she appeared to be reliving the memory in her head.

Aela's blondish red curls were arranged on top of her head, and a small pearl tiara was fitted into the mess of curls. She wore a single matching string of pearls around her neck that hung just above the neckline. After a final look in the mirror, she decided that she was presentable enough.

With her guards in tow, Aela walked to the port cave. The priestesses and elders gathered on the docks to welcome the approaching guest. Aela shook her head as she remembered the less-than-enthusiastic welcome she had received weeks ago.

Men, darkened by hours of work on the waters' edge, loaded and unloaded the dock full of boats. They looked up from their work as the queen and her group of guards walked along the wide stone dock. Excitement and awe buzzed in the air. The news of the Phoenix Son's arrival had spread throughout the palace, and people other than the dock workers gathered. Many had never seen an Immortal, and it was a great honor to just be in the presence of one.

She nodded her head to each and waited while a beautiful boat made of a light golden wood was readied. A crew of five was all that was needed to man the boat, but it could carry an additional ten. Aela and two of her guards boarded.

As the oars rowed rhythmically against the current and away from the port, she studied the scene on the docks. The priestesses were dressed in their ceremonial garb of blue robes and silver cords. They stood shoulder to shoulder on the dock with identical expressions of meditative calm. She knew from meeting with them earlier that despite the calmness of their faces, nervous excitement filled them.

Unlike the priestesses, the frantic emotions of the elders could not be hidden. They argued and awed with each other over the great honor of the Immortal's arrival. They too were dressed in the formal garb of their position. Robes fitted long ago for some, tight and straining around some abdomens, were a sea foam green and lined in gold on the lapels and cuffs.

Aela went to the ship's captain shortly after departing, instructing him to meet the approaching vessel of the Phoenix Son before it reached the docking cave. The captain, a veteran on the rivers of Dovkey, assured the queen that they would reach the Immortal's boat without any difficulty. With the reassurance, Aela took her seat at the base of the sail.

It was an old tradition to meet approaching vessels on the river, and Aela was sure that it was the start of that old saying; Dovekey greets her friends by river and her enemies by sea.

The captain was true to his word, and in only a short time of sailing, the flaming sail of Aela's guest neared. She stood and watched as the crew dropped the sail, causing the boat to slow in the gentle water. The Phoenix Son's boat did the same, and soon the two vessels rocked next to each other. Aela stood near the railing, waiting for the crew to put a plank across the boats.

As the wooden sides of the boats scraped against each other, a man of tall stature and lean build appeared on the railing also. Along with his crew, he aided in positioning the plank. With the help of Mar and Anut, she crossed.

Aela studied the strong structure of the Immortal's face and the soft amber eyes under a jutting brow. Despite the handsomeness of his distinct features, the warmth of his smile was most attractive.

He offered his hand as she stepped onto his boat. She noted that his skin was warm and smooth just as she would have expected it to be. He stood taller than Tarr, towering above her, yet not as tall as her guards.

Mar boarded as the Immortal gently led her away from the side of the boat. Looking over her shoulder, Aela watched as the hulking guard crossed the narrow board and was impressed as always by his grace despite his massive size.

"I had not expected such a splendid escort, Your Majesty. I marvel at the thoughtfulness you show after such a tragic time." His voice was smooth and warm like his skin. He spoke with a gentleness that was soothing and disconcertingly intimate at the same time.

Aela turned her full attention to him. He was a dazzling man and would have been even before being gifted with the phoenix breath. He studied her features as she studied his. She had no memory of him, but she knew that he would have one of her.

As if able to read her thoughts, he said gently, "You were very young and ill when I saw you last. You had just come through the fever, and it was a great triumph and surprise to your people."

"It was what the Great Wave wished," she gave the standard reply when people remarked on the miracle of her recovery. She was still uncomfortable talking about her illness and survival.

Seeming to sense her tension, the Phoenix Son changed the subject. "May I offer my sincerest condolences on your brother? He was so young and taken before he had the chance to make his mark on the world."

Aela dutifully thanked him though his words annoyed her. Kesh had made his mark on the world. All those who had truly known him were better for it.

Aluz studied her. "You have no memory of me, do you?"

"No, I do not. I was very ill, as you said, and much from that period of my life is hazy."

"Of course," he seemed disappointed by her admission but continued in a more formal tone. "Allow me the introduction; I am Aluz Calla Phoenix Son, member of the Immortal Council." He bowed deeply over her hand.

When he stood, Aela bowed over his hand, "We are honored to have you here, our Immortal Lord. The elders and priestesses have eagerly prepared for your visit."

"I must insist that you call me Aluz." A look of concern came over his face. "I wonder if you have been told the actual reason for my coming here."

Aela wanted to sigh out loud but managed a forced smile instead. "Yes, I was informed of our betrothal many years ago."

He studied her again. "I cannot help but feel that you are not happy with this arrangement."

"My Immortal Lord-"

"Aluz, please."

"Forgive me for seeming underenthused, but much has happened in the past months. I have only finished grieving my brother with a week of silence. Before that, one of our towns was destroyed, and many lives were lost."

"It would seem that Dovkey has suffered greatly." Much to her surprise, he did not ask further about the town and the lives lost. Instead, Aluz stepped closer to her, taking both of her hands in his. She stilled at the forward gesture, uncomfortable with his nearness. Tarr was the only other man who had dared to be so close.

"What can I do for you? What is it that you need? You have only to tell me, and I will see it done."

He stared down at her, his eyes showering her with compassion and concern. She found that she was not comforted by it. Giving his hands a reassuring squeeze before prying her own free, she took a step back.

"Your concern is..." she was suddenly at a loss for words, "comforting," though it was not. "Thank you. Other concerns are far more important right now."

"What could be more important than you?"

Aela was confused at the mild irritation she felt. She had no doubt that his concern was genuine, yet she was unsettled by it.

"Perhaps you need more time to grieve. You mentioned the week of grieving I know is a tradition of your people, but you need more time. There is no need to rush such things. I will speak with the elders. There will be no requests made of you."

The irritation grew. She disliked being told what was best for her and having decisions made for her.

"Aluz, that will not be necessary. I have a very firm understanding of what I need, and more silent grieving is not it. Especially when there is so much that needs to be addressed. I thank you," she stopped him before he could interrupt, "for your concern. I am honored by it, in fact. But there are still many other things that you do not know, and they must be dealt with."

The plank between vessels had been removed, and Aluz's boat sailed towards the palace once more. The other boat followed the Immortal's back in port.

"What things do you speak of?" His voice was pacifying.

Her temper flared, but she kept her tone respectful. "There is the issue of our betrothal. It is Immortal Law, if I am not mistaken, that an Immortal cannot occupy a position of ruling power among mortals."

"Yes, that is true. However, that was discussed when our betrothal was first arranged. Your father assured the Council that you were not the ruling monarch and that there would be no conflict."

"That was true before Kesh's death. However, with his passing, the crown will come to me."

The Phoenix Son stood in quiet contemplation. "Yes, I see how this is a problem. The Immortal Council will be very distraught to hear of this news."

"I plan to nullify the betrothal contract after I am crowned."

Aluz's expression darkened. "A contract with an Immortal can only be made void by the Immortal."

"Considering the present circumstances, you will void the contract. Will you not?"

Aluz turned to her. He was not a man of youth, nor did he seem to be a man of many years, but his eyes were those that had seen centuries pass. Aela wondered if perhaps it was the internal glow that radiated from all around him that gave the impression of youth or perhaps it was the long braids that hung tied back, a style that only younger men wore. Whatever his age, he held considerable power as an Immortal.

"I'm afraid that it is not that easy. I have the power to void the contract, yes, but that decision would have to be discussed with the Council."

The bit of hope that she had felt regarding the situation dimmed. "How long will it take for them to make a decision once they are notified of the situation?"

"I cannot say for sure. There were other matters that you were speaking of?"

"Yes, I'm afraid so. It so happens that I am illegally betrothed to two men."

Aluz stared at her in silence. "Forgive me, but did I hear you correctly? There is another who you are to wed?"

"Yes."

"A man of your own choosing?" he asked quietly.

"No. My brother played a game of Seer's Fortune, and he wagered my hand in marriage."

"And he did not win?"

"No."

"How did you come to know this? Did King Kesh tell you himself before he passed?"

"No, Lord Tarr, the Frin'geren he played with, arrived before we discovered my brother's fate. With him came the owner of the deck and signed witness of the game. He brought the contract signed by both men. Lord Tarr had the King's Sapphire which cannot be worn by anyone other than the king or someone he willingly gives the ring to. There was no way to dispute the claim."

"He is here already? This Lord Tarr of Frin'gere."

"Yes, he has been a guest of the White Palace for some time now." Aela turned to look out over the river. "I know that you fully understand the consequences of refusing the victor of Seer's Fortune his prize."

"Why would your brother do this? First, it is pure insanity to enter into a game of Seer's Fortune unless one is a true seer; but your brother was not, was he?"

"No, he was not. I have no other answers to give as to why he would do this."

"There is no shame on account of you. From what I have heard, your brother was not a conventional man, and his actions could not be restrained."

She bristled at the hint of disapproval in his tone.

"He can choose to forfeit his winnings in favor of something else."

"He will not. I have already pursued that option with him."

"Perhaps there is something that I may offer him. Is his interest wealth, power..."

"I honestly do not know what his motivations are," she said quietly.

"We shall find a solution to this," his voice was reassuring but his eyes were doubtful.

They approached the dock where the gathered crowd bowed deeply. "Think of this no more for tonight. There is a celebration in your honor, and you should enjoy all the hospitality that my country has to offer. You are our honored guest."

Aluz appeared on the verge of saying more, but to Aela's relief, he was immediately swept up by the elders and Priestesses. The two groups played a verbal tug of war with his attention from the moment that he stepped off the boat. Cheers from all the gathered observers echoed through the cave with increasing strength and volume. It was the sort of welcome that made her proud.

Chapter 16

The elders led the Phoenix Son away enthusiastically while the Priestesses trailed behind them. Aela did not see him again until dinner that night.

The most splendid of decorations dressed the formal dining hall. Candles in artful arrangements aligned the center of the long table, and sconces lining the walls created a warm glow that illuminated the ivory stone. Crystal china set the table and dinnerware of silver rested beside the sparkling plates. Flowers of pinks, reds, and oranges, colors picked in honor of the Phoenix Son's immortal flame, created centerpieces of dazzling heights. The finest table dressings of linen and silk covered the white wood table and the high-backed chairs. The room was enchanting and elegant.

The elders occupied the left side of the table, and the priestesses occupied the right. Aela sat at the head of one end, and Aluz sat in a position of honor at the other end. Servants stood against the wall, some holding silver pitchers of water and wine, watching for the opportunity to refill someone's glass. Others waited to serve the first course.

The Phoenix Son answered question after question, all the eyes in the room focused solely on him. He had changed into a tailored suit of red silk, and his cooper braids hung loosely around his face. His skin glowed more brightly than early in the day as if it soaked up the candlelight all around him. He gave his attention generously to those around him with a pleasant but neutral smile. Once his attention turned to her, and his smile was no longer pleasant. Appreciation reflected in his eyes as they took in the sight of her.

Aela tried not to fidget under the attention, returning his smile with a pleasant one of her own. She struggled to hold his intense gaze for more than a few seconds. Taking a drink to hide her discomfort, she thought of Tarr. He never hid his appreciation or attraction to her; however, she did not feel the same discomfort with his attention as she did with Aluz's.

Aela looked around the table and realized that Tarr was not present. Motioning for a servant, she asked about his whereabouts. "Did he refuse the invitation?"

The servant stared at her blankly, unsure of the answer to give. "Was he invited to this dinner?" Aela asked with mild irritation.

Again, the servant stared at her in bewildered silence. "Never mind. Send someone to find him and tell him that his presence is requested."

"My queen," the girl began to object.

"His presence is requested by the queen. This is my table," Aela said more forcefully than she intended.

The girl nodded and quickly left the room. Her departure went unnoticed.

The first course served shortly after was an assortment of small loaves made of dark grains and glazed in honey, thick slices of a white loaf with a hint of pepper, and crisp slices of sourdough bread sprinkled with spices and a delicate drizzling of oil.

The conversation remained focused on Aluz's end of the table, and Aela found that she heard very little of the discussions taking place. Most of the commentary centered on praises of the Immortal, which he accepted graciously.

Aela waited for Tarr. She worried that he would not come. With surprise, she realized that she dreaded this evening without his presence.

Servers cleared the first course as the door to the dining hall opened. Tarr sauntered in, dressed in formal attire that Aela had never seen him wear before. The cut was similar to that of the Phoenix Son but lacked the extravagance.

"Forgive my tardiness," he said in an unapologetic tone.

"What, what?" Malcolm began to huff.

"Lord Tarr," Aela said as she rose and motioned to one of the servants. "We were not sure if you would be able to join us. It will be just a moment as they prepare another setting."

The servant hesitated only a moment before gathering the needed dishes. He paused again looking to Aela for guidance.

"I think that we shall place Lord Tarr between Elder Berto and Elder George." In the middle of the elders was another place of honor for guests.

The arrangements quickly came together, and Tarr sat with a smile at the serving girl who poured him a glass of wine.

"I am honored, Your Majesty, elders, priestesses, and," he turned his head to Aluz, "you, our Immortal Lord. I have never had the great privilege of an Immortal's company."

Silence descended as anxious gazes flitted between the two foreigners. Aela noted that both men evaluated each other with a critical eye.

"It has been a long time since I have dined with a Frin'geren. It is entirely my honor to be at the table of so great a queen, her council, and her guest." The tension in the room dissipated with the Phoenix Son's words.

The slightly spiced soup of shellfish and fish was the second course, followed by a dish of roasted vegetables and lamb accompanied by a herby mint sauce. The conversation returned, though it was less jovially than before. Tarr's presence seemed to unsettle the elders, though the priestesses seemed less affected.

As the last course before dessert was cleared, Tarr turned once more to the Phoenix Son. "Have you been to Dovkey before, my lord?"

Aluz smiled and briefly cast a glance in Aela's direction. "I have had the pleasure of visiting Dovkey before. Sadly, the last time that I was here, the people of Dovkey were just recovering from a devastating plague. I came as part of the aide and found that I was charmed by so many things in this fair country." He gave Aela a warm smile that drew the attention of everyone. Curious eyes turned to her.

A single pair of narrowed eyes looked at her before looking once more at the Immortal.

"Yes, there are some very charming aspects." Tarr smiled, but it lacked warmth. "Though I've also found Dovkey to be-"

"You were going to tell us of your latest travels, Lord Phoenix Son," Malcolm rudely interrupted.

On the verge of giving the elder a public set down, Aela paused when Tarr gave her a slight shake of his head. Reluctantly, she let the issue rest.

"I am most happy to share those stories with you, Elder; however, I would take this opportunity to speak with your other guest." Aluz turned his attention back to Tarr. "What part of Frin'gere do you hail from, Lord Tarr?"

"Avengere."

"That is near the Dovkey border, is it not?"

"Yes, it is. Have you been there, my lord?"

"No, I cannot say that I have, though I have seen parts of Dinya."

The brief look of surprise on Tarr's face disappeared so quickly that Aela wondered if anyone else had seen it.

"I have seen many parts of Frin'gere, but Dinya is not one of them."

The Phoenix Son's lips rose in a pleasant smile. "I have always admired the hospitality of Dovkey. How long have you been a guest here, Lord Tarr?"

"Several weeks."

"And news of King Kesh's death came only a week ago, I was told."

"Yes."

Aela wondered about the reasoning for his interrogation.

"Were you and the king acquaintances for long or had you just met the night of the game?"

Tarr's expression hardened. "We had met on a few previous occasions, played a card game here or there. Though I admit I was surprised that he suggested a game of Seer's Fortune."

Aluz looked concerned. "He suggested it?"

"Yes, he did. The queen and the elders read the contract and can testify that it was stated as such...my lord." Hints of hostility grew between the men.

Aluz considered this as he folded his fingers in front of him. "Are you aware that the queen was bound in contract to me several years ago?"

"Bound in contract to you?" Tarr's brows raised in interest as he turned to glance at Aela.

"The betrothal," Aela clarified before any untoward suggestions were made.

"Ah, yes, I recently was made aware of that." He turned to Aela. "You are in demand, aren't you, my darling queen?"

"Yes, she is," Aluz's tone was cold now. "I'm sure that you know there are severe consequences for anyone who breaks a contract with an Immortal."

"Just as there are consequences to denying a winner of Seer's Fortune."

"I believe we can find something that will persuade you to retract your claim."

Tarr's smile was unkind. "Oh, I doubt that."

The tense exchange between the two paused as a dessert of sweet custard and berries was served. The servants had barely moved back from the table when Aluz rekindled the conversation.

"Have you heard of the Exchromy fever?"

Aela felt her body tense involuntarily at the mention of the devastating plague that had swept through her country. She knew that the topic would come up, that someone would use it as a way to dissuade Tarr, but she had not expected it at dinner.

"I have. There has not been an outbreak in Frin'gere for over a hundred years."

"That was the sickness that had befallen Dovkey when I came with aide."

Feone, the youngest of the priestesses and one closest to Aela, looked at the queen briefly with concern before daring to interrupt the Phoenix Son. "My Immortal Lord, perhaps now is not the time to discuss such things." Her voice was timid but succeeded in silencing the Phoenix Son.

Aluz's gaze shifted first to the priestess and then to Aela. Whatever he saw produced a softening of his tone. "Of course. Forgive me, Your Majesty, for speaking on matters that would be best explained by you."

It was hardly an apology, Aela thought. However, she bowed her head in acknowledgment. "Thank you. That is most gracious, my lord." The heat of embarrassment mingled with that of her temper.

"Oh, now I must know." Tarr looked from Aela to Aluz, his eyes hard though a smile parted his lips. "My queen, I must know." The firm undertone to his voice made it clear he awaited her explanation.

"The fever, which affects only females, was contracted by many in Dovkey, including my mother, who was the Healer Priestess at the time. I also contracted the fever, and she treated me, among many others. Sadly, she died of the fever."

"You survived," Tarr said slowly.

"Which means-"

"I know what it means." Tarr's dark eyes softened only momentarily as he looked at her. Turning away from her, his voice was lighter, "It matters not. I have no burning desire to sire young." He turned his attention to the Phoenix Son. "I find it interesting that an Immortal Lord would bind himself in marriage to a mortal."

"The binding is more than marriage. Queen Aela will join me in the phoenix fire and become a Phoenix Daughter, taking her place among the Immortal Council. It is a great honor."

"Indeed. I say it is fortunate that I have the power of Seer's Fortune behind my claim."

Aela found Tarr's provoking tone amusing.

"Fortunate...yes," Aluz looked thoughtful as he smiled at the Frin'geren. "Is it in Avergere that you met the late King Kesh?"

A hush fell over the table. The entire group avidly watched the two men, who continued to stare intensely at each other.

"Actually, it was in a small town further north. I would tell you the name but with our present company, I don't think that would be wise. I would hate for the poor deprived souls of Dovkey to find their one escape from oppression lost because I carelessly told their government of it."

Offended outbursts filled the room. Aela shook her head at the disorder that one statement could cause. Tarr knew exactly how his comment would be received, yet he chose to say it, nonetheless. She also knew that he was a calculating man. He was not the carefree, oblivious philanderer he played. No, she knew that he was careful and manipulative, and there was a reason for eliciting this reaction.

"You insult your hosts greatly."

"How dare you!" someone bellowed.

"We protect our people from the evil ways of your country."

"Elders, please, let us discuss this," Aluz tried to calm. "Let us hear the reasoning the Frin'geren offers for making such a statement." The Immortal's voice had lost all its warmth, and his stare hardened when he looked at Tarr.

The Phoenix Son's words failed to quiet the enraged elders. The priestesses sat quietly watching the scene, leaning closer to whisper amongst each other.

"Enough!" Aela's firm voice projected to the far end of the room and effectively silenced the group. She took advantage of their surprise. "We will not argue like children in the presence of our guests."

"But the Frin'geren has made blasphemous statements-" Malcolm protested.

"He has stated his opinion, which he is entitled to. Just as you are entitled to view him as amoral and corrupt. However, there will not be any further insulting at this table. Do not forget elders, that Lord Tarr is also a guest of Dovkey."

"Wisely said, Queen Aela," Aluz commented. "Your people are fortunate indeed to have you as their ruler."

"Of course, if she is expected to uphold her contract with you, Phoenix Son, she cannot also be expected to rule Dovkey. Perhaps the elders have planned for this outcome all along." Tarr said causally as he took a drink of wine. His eyes met Aela's for a brief second, and she understood his motive instantly.

"What do you speak of?" One of the elders exclaimed.

"It is Immortal Law that an Immortal cannot be connected to any political position outside the Council. Now, either he plans to void the contract with our lovely queen, or he intends for her to give up her throne."

Stunned silence greeted his words.

"It is not that simple," the Phoenix Son finally said. Irritation laced his voice.

The rest of the table sat in quiet contemplation. Aela noted that the elders looked from one to the other, anxiety and concern playing over their features. They tensed in their seats, and their eyes avoided her and the priestesses.

"It is a great honor for one of our own to be considered as a future member of the Immortal Council; however, the line of Gero has ruled over Dovkey for generations. Their line was blessed by the Great Wave. That cannot be easily forgotten or dismissed." The Head Priestesses' tone was somber and severe.

"Maybe," Elder Malcolm said quietly, "The House of Gero no longer has the blessing of the Great Wave."

"Only the Great Wave can appoint or dismiss a ruler. It is not in your power to make such a decision," Bena, the Head Priestess, said in a strained voice.

"No decisions have been made," Berto tried to reason.

"There have been discussions of this though?" the Phoenix Son asked.

"There have been discussions of this since the Reformation." Aela drew the attention of all. "And there will continue to be discussions of this; however, they will not take place tonight. I call for everyone to return to their chambers and let the matter rest for tonight. We can discuss the ramifications of the current situation tomorrow."

Her tone forbade any objections, and she was pleasantly surprised when the elders began to rise from the table, bowing their heads first to her and then offering wishes of pleasant sleep to the Immortal. Berto was the last of the elders to rise. His eyes were sorrowful as he looked at her. She felt a moment's worth of sympathy for the unfortunate position she knew he was in. She offered him a bow of her head in return.

The priestesses rose silently. "Would you accept the honor of showing the Phoenix Son to his rooms?" she asked the Head Priestess.

The woman bowed her head in acknowledgment and stood beside the Phoenix Son.

"I would talk with you," he commanded as he stood.

It irked Aela, but her tone remained only firm when she responded. "Yes, but not tonight. We will hold counsel in the morning."

"I insist that we speak tonight."

"Your journey has been long. You will rest tonight, and in the morning, I will address your concerns and questions. Sleep well, our Immortal Lord."

He wanted to demand more, but decided against it, seeing her stony expression. She would not relent on this. Gracefully, he bowed to her across the table.

"I wish you a restful night as well." He turned to leave, but not before his attention paused on Tarr, who remained comfortably seated. The Phoenix Son's face hardened, but he said nothing more as he allowed the priestesses to guide him from the room.

Chapter 17

Only Tarr and Aela remained at the table. The servants began clearing away the dishes as the two stared at each other.

"Leave it for now. I will have a moment alone with Lord Tarr," Aela said in a strained voice.

The servants quietly left the room, only their curious looks betraying any thoughts. Her expression remained aloof and regal, but Tarr knew that she was furious with him.

"You do not seem pleased, my queen."

She waited for the door to close behind the last person before she turned the full force of her anger on Tarr. Her gray-eyed stare pierced him like a dagger strike. "I'm wondering where you learned diplomacy," she said in an icy tone.

He laughed. "It had to be addressed. Why dance around the issue?"

"How do you even know the issue wasn't already resolved?"

He leaned forward. "For one, he was staring at you like you already belong to him. And two, Sey told me that he refused to void the contract when you spoke to him."

"You and my guards are becoming quite familiar it seems."

"Do not be angry with them."

"I am angry with you. How dare you insert yourself into the affairs of my country! There are things here that do not concern you."

"Oh, but they do concern me," he said in a calm tone though hints of his own temper were evident.

"They do not! I do not know what makes you think that the affairs of my country involve you but-"

"I couldn't care less for the affairs of your country!" His voice was full of fury. "You are my concern." He took a deep breath and looked away, visibly uncomfortable with his outburst.

Aela rubbed her temples and took a deep breath. In a softer voice, "I had every intention of discussing this with you."

He stood up and moved to sit in the chair next to hers. His hand covered one of hers in a gesture of comfort. "I'm surprised that the elders did not tell me of the engagement...or of the fever."

She laughed a mirthless laugh. "I'm not surprised that they held their tongues regarding the Phoenix Son; you are a foreigner and not to be trusted with such privileged knowledge. But I am surprised that they did not tell you about the fever. I thought that would have been the first deterrent they tried."

Her body relaxed as his fingers moved in slow circles over her hand. "It does not matter."

"So you said."

They sat in a calm silence, the anger between them melting away.

"Your fiancé was not pleased at being refused."

She gave a short laugh at his smug tone. "No, he was not. I fear that the Immortal will find very little about me that will please him."

"I don't know about that," Tarr squeezed her fingers before releasing her hand. She missed his warmth immediately. "He looked quite pleased by his potential, future wife." Her lack of awareness of her own attractiveness amused him greatly.

"I am going to request that the Immortal Council retract the contract."

He leaned back in the chair, stroking his chin thoughtfully while she continued.

"It was made without my consent. I cannot marry you and him, but I cannot refuse you the terms of the game. He cannot be married to a ruling monarch. When the contract was made, I was intended to be a priestess and Kesh the high king. But it did not turn out as intended."

"The Council may not care about your first concern, but the other two are points they will most definitely have to consider."

She nodded and then said in a quiet voice, "I never wanted to be the high queen. I wasn't properly prepared for it."

He smiled. "You are not as unprepared as you think. You ordered an Immortal to bed, against his wishes."

She returned the smile briefly. He watched as her expression turned thoughtful.

"Why did one of the elders imply that your family has lost the Great Wave's blessing?" The comment had surprised him. He did not understand the beliefs of her country as well as he would like, but he failed to find a reason why the elder thought so.

"My being queen was not meant to be."

"Why is that?"

"Two of my cousins were born around the same time I was. The Head Priestess at the time had divined a prophecy from the Great Wave shortly before our births. The prophecy told that three of great power would be born; one to the season of stormy seas, one to the season of calm seas, and one to the season of changeable seas. Ishea was born to the calm seas, Aine to the changeable seas, and I to the stormy seas.

"It was said that the three of us were born with great power and potential for becoming high priestesses. In Dovkey, there is no greater honor than being chosen as a priestess. So, the three of us were prepared to become priestesses from the moment we could speak. My mother was the Healer Priestess in Shu'esh before becoming a Princess of Dovkey. She instructed us until she became sick. She was greatly respected." Aela's attention wandered as if lost in a thought.

Tarr waited patiently for her focus to return, content to drink in the sight of her.

She shook her head and turned back to him.

"Shortly before the priestess trial-"

"I've heard this term, but I don't understand what it is."

"Not everyone can become a priestess. A young woman must pass a series of tests, each focused on the varying levels of priestesshood. The tests that a girl excels at determine what kind of priestess she will be. However, she must be able to display her connection with water magic." She paused, remembering the story that she had never had to tell before.

"Before the trial in which the three of us were to display our 'great power', another prophecy came from the Great Wave. 'One will fail, one will serve, one will betray.'"

AELA PAUSED AS SHE remembered the past. She had spent many years with her cousins under the instruction of her mother. As children, Aine and Ishea had shared the same beautiful golden hair and delicate features. People knew even at a young age that they would grow into slender women with grace and beauty. However, for all their similarities, the two could not have been more different.

Ishea had been a shining star of sweetness and energy. She brought a smile to everyone's lips, and though she did not always seek attention, she was often the focus of everyone around her.

Aine preferred to stay to herself. She was called shy, though those closest to her knew that it was rather a complete lack of interest in others. She had shown very little interest in the training. She did everything she was told and excelled at every task put before her, but Aela knew that she had no great desire to become a priestess.

Aine had been close to very few people. Most did not even try to get close. She had deep blue eyes that seemed to hold secrets, both wonderful and dark. Such a look in a child was not comforting. Kesh, who knew Aine better than many others, told Aela once that Aine had the great gift of prophecy. She could see the future without practicing the rituals of divination. Images just came to her, whether she wanted them or not. He told her that knowing a person's future was an uncomfortable and disturbing feeling, especially when the future did not hold fortune.

"Who failed, who served, and who betrayed?" Tarr's question drifted into her memories, making her aware of his presence once more.

"Ishea is the one who serves, obviously. She is the Healer Priestess, having taken my mother's place. Aine disappeared the morning of the trials. She never even came to the beach where they were held. Many suspected that she would be the one to betray."

"Why is that?"

Aela looked at her companion and noted the seriousness in his expression. "Aine was quiet and mysterious. She was not close to many, and it was quite clear from the beginning that she did not want to be a priestess,"

Aela's expression became solemn as she thought of her cousin's disappearance. "We never knew that happened to her. Her parents had died when she was very young. My mother unofficially adopted her by the time our training began. We sent people to search all of Dovkey for her, but she was never found. Some of the elders think that she went to Frin'gere or Gildia. She did have a great aunt in Gildia."

Kesh had been so devastated, though he had refused to talk about it.

Tarr stared at her, waiting for her to finish. Never had she said the words out loud to another. The outcome of the priestess trials had spread quickly throughout the country. Her shame had become the shame of her house and the people she was born to serve. No one spoke of it to her.

"I was the one who failed."

"How did you fail?"

Memories that she tried not to relive flooded her head. She stood on the beach watching Ishea complete all the tasks put before her, excelling at each one. Her final test was to prove that she knew the magic of water, to prove that it had connected with her.

The waves beat against her as she waded waist-deep into the ocean. She held a small knife in one hand and used it to inflict a small incision on her wrist. Red droplets dripped from her arm. She dipped the knife into the water, bringing a string of salt-water drops with it. With the knife held over her bleeding wrist, the water fell into the cut.

Ishea chanted softly to herself, and the stream of red stopped. She came back to the shore and revealed that she had used the magic to close her wound. Not even a scar remained. It was immediately decided that she would be a healer priestess. Ishea had smiled and bowed her head in honor; though, Aela remembered the look of disappointment in her eyes. Ishea had always wanted to become the Head Priestess, the one who answered directly to the Great Wave.

"I passed the tasks, but I could not demonstrate an understanding of the magic," she replied, though she could not look at him while she said it.

Yes, she had passed every task just as impressively as Ishea. Having watched her cousin so easily perform the true power of her magic, Aela felt relieved.

"What was your demonstration?"

"I tried to create a dome of water. I went out into the ocean and tried to call the magic to me, but it did not answer.

"The three of us were all meant to be great priestesses, but Aine refused to become one, and I had no connection to the magic," Aela turned to him, forcing a smile on her face.

"We both know that isn't true."

"Visions sent by the Great Wave and the ability to control water magic are not the same thing."

He narrowed his eyes at her, appearing to disagree, but did not say anything.

She continued, "The elders and the priestesses decided that I had lost whatever gifts I was born with after getting the fever. I came so near to death that I must have lost something." Bitterness edged her voice.

"Kesh said that it affected your eyes. I have not noticed any deficits."

"My sight was not affected; my eyes lost their color though," she said simply.

"They lost their color?"

Aela smiled a sad smile, and with a sigh, "I cannot even remember what color they were. It does not matter anymore." He was on the verge of objecting. "I was not meant to lead the people. I am the failed one." She said it without sadness or self-pity, having accepted the truth of it years ago.

Tarr looked at her thoughtfully. "Have you ever considered that this just hasn't finished playing out?"

The question took Aela by surprise. She could understand how it would appear to him that she had given up hope too early, but years of disappointing those around her were compelling enough evidence. She had never felt comfortable with herself until she had settled in Masia. Her life up to that point had been a constant chase of things that she could not catch. She had been like an awkward actor in a drama.

"I spent so many years being trained and groomed to become one thing and then another, but I was never those things. No matter how I studied or prepared, I could not be those things."

She took a deep breath, and in a rare moment of vulnerability, released the strict posture of her spine. Leaning forward, she put her head to the table briefly. A quiet groan escaped her lips. She felt Tarr's warm fingers in her hair. The sensation was new but surprisingly soothing.

She turned her head to look into his dark eyes. "Tarr, I'm in an impossible position. I cannot be promised to two men, but I am. I cannot refuse either without horrendous consequences. I cannot be married to the Phoenix Son and rule Dovkey."

She paused as a sharp emotion shot into her chest. "My line is dead. I am the last of the Gero family, with no hope of producing an heir. Even if I did rule, the monarchy would end with me. The elders would pursue their Reformation agenda in the end no matter what."

His fingers continued playing in her hair, occasionally stroking the surface of her cheek. "Why not rule and let it end after you?"

The question was so gentle. His touch was so comforting that she felt the despair seep from her eyes in the form of tears.

She lifted her head, pulled away from his touch, and wiped the tears from her eyes. "I was sent to Masia after the fever and the trials. At first, I was ashamed and hurt, but I never felt such peace with myself until I settled into life there. Once I accepted that I was the fated failed queen, I was free. And happy."

She turned her watery eyes to him, and he cradled her face in his hands. "There is no cause, no country, no duty that is more important than your happiness."

The statement was said with such honesty that Aela was taken aback and unable to respond.

Tarr pulled away from her and leaned back in his chair folding his fingers in front of him. "Being the selfish man that I am, I wouldn't tolerate anyone interfering with my happiness."

"Are you suggesting that I do the same? Not allow anyone to interfere with my happiness?"

"Yes, that is exactly what I am saying."

"I want to serve my people. I want to watch my country prosper, and I want to welcome the next house that the Great Wave approves. I want..."

"Don't stop now. Get it all out," he said with an encouraging smile.

"I want to end this constant fighting with the elders and the priestesses. I want a Dovkey where anyone can feel the power in the water or hear the voice of the Great Wave in the sea. I want the tangled mess of laws created by the Reformation to go away."

"So many wants for a woman who doesn't think she was meant to be queen."

"The Phoenix Son implied that he would find something to offer you that would make you relinquish your claim."

Tarr's eyes narrowed in amusement. "He can think that if he wants, but nothing would tempt me to relinquish my claim."

Aela was briefly confused. "Nothing? There is nothing that would tempt you?"

He leaned towards her. "I doubt anything would have swayed me before, but having met you, I know with perfect certainty that nothing would sway me." She continued to stare at him.

His amusement deepened, and he laughed at her look of continued confusion. "You have no idea, do you?"

"I'm tired, Tarr. It has been a long day, and tomorrow will be even longer."

Tarr helped her stand, walking behind her as they headed towards the exit. Aela's hand was on the handle when Tarr turned her forcibly around. He looked down at her, his expression intense and his voice low. "There is one more thing that we need to discuss."

Aela stared at him in confusion. "Oh?"

"I have never left a woman unsatisfied, and there is some doubt as to your satisfaction the last time I kissed you." His arm wrapped around her waist, and she felt the insistent tug as he drew her body into his.

"Tarr," she said it as a warning, but he ignored her.

His hand was in her hair, dislodging pins. The tiara tilted on her head as strands fell to her shoulders. She thought for a moment that she should object, push him away. However, she wanted to experience again the softness of his lips.

With each encounter, Tarr broke down more of the wall she had erected between herself and the rest of the world. He knew the hidden passages into her heart, going straight to the only place she allowed herself to be vulnerable. He crept into the most secret of places inside her, not as a marauding warrior, but as a faithful knight. The understanding she found in his eyes warmed her, but the unfamiliarity of it made her feel weak and exposed.

"I don't believe I said one word of complaint," she said breathlessly when he pulled away.

He paused with his face just inches from hers. "You laughed."

She smiled at his almost petulant tone. "Out of bewilderment, out of joy, out of surprise."

"Surprise?" He raised a brow.

"Having never been kissed before, I was surprised at how enjoyable it was. I thought it might be, but I didn't realize how much." She felt slight embarrassment revealing that to him.

Tarr seemed to sense it, for he pulled back to study her. "A beautiful woman should be kissed often and well."

"There are some luxuries a queen does not get to have."

With his lips just above hers, he whispered, "A queen should have all the luxuries. I'll give you any luxury you desire."

She pulled back to look at him and could only guess at the depth of his promise.

"Should I tuck you in, Your Majesty?" He whispered seductively.

Aela smiled. "No...not tonight."

Tarr lifted her hand to his lips, placing a gentle kiss on her skin. "Then, I wish you a pleasant night, my queen. May you have dreams full of all the luxuries." His smile was mischievous as he left the room.

Aela felt his absence, but she refused to contemplate the significance of it.

Mar, Ter, and Anut waited outside the door. Sey would see to it that Tarr was safely ensconced in his room before returning to her. They walked the halls, eerily empty. Aela knew that many discussions were taking place in secret throughout the palace.

Perhaps, the elders had not thought of the possibility that Aela would be forced to forfeit her right to rule, but they were thinking about it now. For good or bad, they would have to seriously reconsider her contract with the Phoenix Son. She hoped that they would side with her desire to nullify it.

Memories of the past were hard to rebury. Telling Tarr about the prophecies and priestess trials dragged the shameful, ugly bits of her past to the surface. Restlessness filled her, and though she knew she needed sleep, she avoided her bed for too many hours.

When she finally settled enough to sleep, she laid her head on the pillow. The ocean breeze blew over her skin, and she prayed to the Great Wave...*I would never have chosen to fail you.*

Chapter 18

The hour was late, and the darkened halls of the palace were empty and silent. The occupants were already asleep, except for two dark figures who met in secret.

The taller of the two leaned casually against the wall as if his presence wasn't the least bit dubious. The cigar between his lips flared red as he inhaled, illuminating the dark goatee. He exhaled a cloud of smoke into the air with the pretense of a man who had no cares in the world, yet the tension of his body was visible.

A figure approached him with caution.

"Why was I not told about the engagement to the Phoenix Son?" His voice was low and cold as he exhaled another cloud of smoke.

The other replied in an even lower voice, "I have no idea."

"Was Kesh aware of it?"

"I don't see how he couldn't have been aware of it, but I see no reason he would have kept it secret from you."

His laugh was harsh. "Kesh was a man of many secrets. I imagine he kept even some from you."

His statement was answered with silence, and again he laughed. "Just as I thought." Amusement was a low rumble in his chest as he drew on the cigar once more.

"He neglected to tell me about the state of the affairs here in the palace."

"He was not here often. It's possible he wasn't aware."

The dark figure flicked the ashes from his cigar and tsked at his companion. "Now, now, we both know that isn't true. He was a schemer, a master manipulator, and did nothing without truly understanding all the possible complications. The Phoenix Son is a complication."

"Yes, he is."

"The queen is a complication as well."

Surprise and anger filled the response, "The queen is the reason you are here!"

"I understand that, but it does not change the fact that she will make things more difficult." There was a tell of irritation to his tone.

"Why, are you starting to like her?" Amusement this time.

A moment of silence passed between them as he exhaled another breath of smoke. "How could I not," he responded quietly. "But he knew that." A sharp laugh. "Of course, he knew how this would play out."

His companion laughed. "Kesh did not know everything."

"Are you sure?"

No answer to his question.

"There is no question that he omitted things," the man stated. "What of her guards?"

"They are of no concern."

A dark brow rose, "Is that so?"

The other figure smiled. "You do not appear to be having any trouble getting close to her."

"You know what I mean," a disgruntled murmur.

"Do not worry. I will see to it that they are not a problem when the time comes."

"Very well." Silence again.

The other hesitated before responding, "Will you try to persuade her to leave? You can be very persuasive when you want to be."

"No, that is not an option. She could never be persuaded to leave, no matter the danger."

"Then you will have to try harder," said the other in a firm tone. "I will not see harm done to her too."

The dark figure laughed, "Even my charm has limitations."

His companion responded with unsuppressed anger. "I did not know that the king's death was part of this."

"That was his doing, not mine." He replied. "I did not suggest Seer's Fortune." A hint of anger filled his voice.

Again, there was silence. "I did not expect our first meeting to be like this."

"Neither did I, but so much of this has not been what I expected." Wary amusement lightened his tone.

"What do we do now?"

"We continue with the plan."

IN A DIFFERENT PART of the palace, another figure also waited in the darkness. The light of a single candle illuminated his face as he spoke to someone unseen.

"I've adhered to the plan thus far, but there is a complication."

"What complication?" A faceless voice inquired.

"Her betrothed. His arrival was not expected, and he has the power and influence to interfere with our plans."

"Then eliminate him."

"We cannot so easily remove such a person."

"Then we enact the next part of the plan."

"Are you sure?"

The voice scuffed. "Of course, I am sure. We have been planning this for years. Waiting so eagerly for this moment. You cannot fail."

"I will see it done." The words were said with deep conviction.

The faceless voice ended the connection with the accomplice. He had been useful in achieving their ultimate goal. Without his personal ambitions to rule Dovkey, they never would have gotten this far. The knowledge he had shared early on was paramount to where they were now.

While their partner thought only of Dovkey, together they would have the world. Years of waiting patiently for the pieces to fall into place had only stoked the fire within. The desire to burn and conquer was so strong now.

It was weeks since the queen's favored city crumbled to ash with a strike of their magic. The scope of devastation was wondrous. Fully being able to test the limits of their power was exhilarating.

And watching the queen's sorrow at the destruction was like tasting a decadent dessert after a rich, indulgent meal.

More pain and suffering would come to the queen of Dovkey before the end. Her advisors did not believe that a powerful evil was in their kingdom. Her struggles to convince them brought a smile to the wrangrent's face. They would savor every moment of it, relish the shock as the truth was revealed.

The queen would watch everything she loved turn to ash before she too was consumed by the wrangrent's fire.

Chapter 19

"Your Highness, I would have a word with you."

Aela paused at the sound of Aluz's voice. Three of her guards surrounded her closely, but she could see the Immortal approaching from down the hall. His face was set with determination. Aela sighed, realizing that he would not be put off today.

She waited while he approached. Despite the upcoming confrontation with her advisors, she felt relaxed and content, something that she had not felt since coming to the palace. Reluctantly, she admitted to herself that much of the peace she felt was due to Tarr. His words had offered her comfort and support.

She had not realized how much she missed having someone to discuss the difficult decisions with. Kesh had once been her confidant, but he had become distracted and absent with his frequent trips to Frin'gere. She often spoke of her thoughts and feelings with Menony, but her closest friend was hesitant to give any opinion regarding matters of the state. However, Tarr had barged into her life, demanding to know every thought and feeling, every memory, every aspect that made her who she was. It was undoubtedly disconcerting, yet she found a person who somehow knew her in a way that no other did.

"Good morning, Lord Phoenix Son," Aela said with a smile as her guards parted before Aluz.

He smiled briefly with a quick bow of his head. "I would talk with you this morning."

She was irked by his insistence but managed a pleasant tone. "So you said."

With a wary look at the massive guards surrounding them, he took her elbow in a firm grip. Though it was not painful, Aela did not appreciate the high-handedness of the gesture.

"I can see that I have arrived at an opportune time. There is great disorder in your life and in the country as it were."

His words and tone were so presumptuous that Aela wondered if it was an acquired attitude of Immortals. She contained her irritation only with effort.

"Much has happened in the last few months; however, some of the concerns that Dovkey faces now have been with us for a long time. The ideals and aspirations of the Reformation have never been far from the minds of the elders."

"I will not let this injustice happen. I swear to you that I shall use my influence as an Immortal to assure that your interests are protected."

The conversation with Tarr last night gave her an unexpected surge of courage. "I'm not sure if you understand what my interests are. I think it would be obvious that voiding the betrothal contract is in the best interests of Dovkey, and in turn, myself." Her voice was low but firm.

Aluz stared at her, surprise evident. "I don't know what you mean."

"If I am required to follow through with the contract, I will have no choice but to abdicate. Otherwise, you and I both are in violation of Immortal Law. Furthermore, the consequences of Seer's Fortune will fall upon me and possibly the people of Dovkey. That is not something that I wish to see happen."

He looked stunned as he stared silently at her. "I understand this is your birthright."

"Yes, it is."

"But your destiny lies beyond just Dovkey."

Oh, how she was tired of hearing of destiny and of making arguments for it. He knew nothing of her destiny.

"How do you know that this is not the reason that you failed the trials? That you did not become a priestess because you were meant to become so much more."

His query rendered her speechless. "I had never considered the outcome in that light before."

He eagerly started to further his argument, but Aela interrupted. "However, that does not change the fact that I do not want this for my life. I do not wish to be an Immortal." She held up a hand to still his protests. "I have lost the last of my family in only a few months."

She sighed, knowing by the look in his eyes that he was sympathetic but not understanding. "I have survived a fever that no one thought I could. I have fulfilled my part of a prophecy made long ago, and I have lost the person closest to me. I seek now only to see my house finish its service to the Great Wave. I would do this to the best of my ability. I have no desire to speak of destiny. This is the fate of Dovkey. I believe with all I am that the Great Wave has made this abundantly clear."

He was still as he considered her with kind eyes. "I have no argument for what you have said. It is evident that you cannot be swayed, though I will admit that I cannot understand how you undervalue yourself."

Aela bristled inside at his words. Reluctantly, she admitted that there might be some truth to them, and that alone allowed her to contain her temper. "Do you still wish for the union between us? It is against the Immortal law."

"I am aware of the Immortal law." He looked away from her briefly. "I have sent word to the Council and am awaiting their instructions. Will you wait for their response before you act on any decision?"

"Of course, I will await their guidance on the matter of our contract. The matter of Lord Tarr and Seer's Fortune still awaits resolution. Honestly, I do not see a union between us coming to pass without horrible consequences for all involved. What is that you want, Lord Phoenix Son?"

He did not answer immediately, his amber eyes narrowed in thought. The warmth of his face vanished and was replaced by fierce determination.

"As of this moment, with the situation as it is, I cannot have what I want...for I wish to be joined with you, yet I do not wish for you to be robbed of what is rightfully yours. The Immortal Council will have to govern the outcome of this situation."

Aela was not pleased by his answer.

The Immortals were revered and sought in times of need, but their purpose was to interfere as little as possible in the fate of mortals. The Phoenix Son suggested that the Immortal Council be given the full responsibility of deciding the fate of her country. She was not in support of the Reformation and the changes its followers wished to enact, but she was even less in favor of outsiders governing the fate of her people. Outsiders who were removed from the everyday lives of her people, of all people. Outsiders who shared the same cold, distant superiority of the Immortal standing before her.

"It is your place to seek guidance from the Council; however, it is not the source that I seek guidance from. Only the will and purpose of the Great Wave affects the outcome for the Dovkeyen people. The only answer I seek from the Council is whether or not our betrothal is null or if they know of another way to satisfy the terms of Seer's Fortune."

"Do you wish to be with the Frin'geren?" he asked softly.

"No," she lied. "I only wish to be of service to my people. I had no desire for a husband, and I have in such a short time acquired two potentials."

He seemed eased by her admission, though not entirely happy with it. She nodded her head in respect and continued down the hall for her confrontation with the elders.

HEAVY TENSION FILLED the room. The priestesses' indignation came off them in waves. The elders opposite them shifted anxiously in their seats with their eyes never focused ahead. Aela sat on the dais watching the scene, amused that she was the one most at ease despite the impact today would have on her future.

"Today, we will discuss the ramifications regarding the betrothal contract with the Phoenix Son. First, however, I want any news from our eastern border. Have there been any reports of ash?" Aela addressed the room.

The room was silent. "There have not been any sightings of ash, Your Majesty," Berto stated.

Aela nodded and turned to the priestesses. "What messages have come from the Great Wave?" Surely, the protector of their nation had guidance for his people.

Bena suddenly looked uncomfortable. "There have been no messages since King Kesh's burial. The waves have been silent."

"What does that mean?" George asked with worry as he leaned forward in his chair. "That cannot bode well."

"It is neither good nor bad. We must simply wait for the Great Wave to bestow wisdom on us,"

It was rare for the waves to be silent. There was always some message of small or great importance that traveled with the waves. Their silence was unsettling. Aela wondered if the Great Wave was still holding a period of silence to honor Kesh's death, and that when the grieving of their deity had passed, the waves would carry messages once again.

"This is more concerning, indeed," George murmured as the elders began whispering amongst themselves.

Elder Malcolm stood, gaining the attention of everyone in the room. "Last night, an alternative was placed before us."

The room waited with bated breath for him to continue. Aela felt a weight in her stomach, certain that she knew where the elder planned to steer the meeting.

"Our queen is promised to an Immortal. It has long been intended that she would join with him, and in doing so, become a member of the Council herself. It has been many generations since Dovkey has had a member on the Council."

"Council members leave behind any familial ties and loyalties to land and country. You know this, Elder. A member of the Council who originates from Dovkey does not provide any particular benefit to our country," Bena stated.

He raised his hands in a placating manner. "Yes, I am aware of that. However, allow me to speak what is on the minds of many of us. It is a great honor to be selected."

He peered earnestly around the room until several of the elders nodded in agreement.

"Our country has long prospered under the rule of the House of Gero. The very house blessed by the Great Wave himself." He paused, and Aela suspected his next words would strike hard.

"We have a queen who does not carry the favor of the Great Wave though."

The priestesses gasped, and Bena spoke with ice in her tone, "And, how do you know this, Elder? Have you consulted the waves?"

"I have not that ability, Priestess."

"No, you do not. So, you cannot know what favor the queen has or does not have."

Malcolm bowed his head, one of the few times he had ever given Aela a true show of respect, before turning back to the room.

"Have there not been signs all along? The fever and infertility, the failed trials...and we cannot ignore the present circumstances. Recent events have given us much concern."

"And let us not forget the prophecy. It was a priestess who foretold of the one who would fail the Great Wave," Elder George added from his seat. The men around him nodded gravely in agreement.

Aela was unsurprised; she knew the elders would use the prophecy against her. However, the priestesses seemed taken aback.

"The prophecy spoke of three. One who would serve, one who would betray, and one..." Bena's gaze briefly shifted to Aela before coming back to the elder, "who would fail."

"And is it not evident who those three became? Ishea serves as the Healing Priestess. Aine abandoned us before ever completing the trials. And our queen failed the trials. Is that not enough of a sign from the Great Wave?"

"We have not received any messages conveying that our god does not approve of the queen." The assertion was firmly stated, yet Aela could hear the wavering conviction in the priestess's voice. She felt the first chills of apprehension.

"What do you conspire to, elders?" Another priestess asked.

Malcolm, the great blustering man that he was, managed to feign innocence. "We conspire to nothing, priestess. We have simply discussed the many concerns that face us now- the losses, the prophecy, the Frin'geren and Seer's Fortune, and the Phoenix Son. There is much to be concerned about. Yet, the waves have told you nothing."

He glanced at Aela, and she knew he was ready to strike the final blow. "Is it not in the best interest of everyone that the queen be relieved of her responsibilities and allowed to seek the honor of becoming an Immortal? Does this not benefit Dovkey to appoint a ruler the Great Wave favors while also allowing the House of Gero to end in dignity?"

Waves of anger and fear crashed inside Aela as she listened to the elder's suggestion. She had never had the favor of the elders, but for them to move against her so fiercely was inconceivable. Unable to recall a time in their history when a monarch was removed, Aela looked anxiously to the priestesses for reassurance.

"It has not been done," Bena said stonily.

"But it is not unlawful," Malcolm responded calmly.

Aela was unaware of what he referenced. She was not a scholar of the law, yet she had never heard of a law that would allow the elders to take the throne from her. In the years since the Reformation, they had worked hard to limit the power of the monarch, but no changes had given them the power to abolish the monarchy, though that had been their goal all along.

Crushing pressure in her chest stole her breath as she realized that her failures could be the end of her house, the monarchy, and many of the traditions of Dovkey. Never had she felt the title of the Failed Queen as powerfully as she did now.

The door to the room opened, and the Phoenix Son entered. He paused before the elders, acknowledging them first and then the priestesses.

"Forgive my interruption, but I felt that I must inform you. I have sought out the guidance of the Immortal Council. My messenger left at dawn. I expect that only a few days will pass before we hear from them."

Though she resented his intrusion, Aela was thankful for his timing at least.

"What counsel have you sought, my Immortal lord?" one of the elders asked.

"I have presented the complications of the betrothal and of the Frin'geren's claim."

"It is not a claim," Aela said impatiently, drawing the attention of the room to her. "Lord Tarr is the rightful winner of a game of Seer's Fortune. All the appropriate proof of that game has been provided. An attempt to discredit that is reckless." She was shocked at how often they conveniently forgot about the consequences of Seer's Fortune.

"Of course," Aluz bowed his head to Aela, his voice soothing and calm. "I did not mean to imply that Lord Tarr was in any way deceiving you."

Aela doubted the sincerity of his words.

"Will the Immortal Council know of a way to circumvent the outcome of the game?" George asked with obvious hope.

"If there is a way, I believe that someone among the Immortals will know it."

Other questions were asked about voiding the contract made by the game of Seer's Fortune. Aela was not surprised that the option of ending her engagement to the Phoneix Son was not brought forth by the elders. However, they had made their agenda clear enough.

"Are there other matters of concern?" Aluz's questions silenced the room. Aela, who had lost track of the questioning, focused on the Immortal. She was on the verge of replying, ready to dismiss his concern, when a priestess answered before her.

"We await the guidance of the Great Wave."

Aluz's gaze sharpened, and his realization of this statement's significance was evident. "Do not the waves speak to you now?"

The silence of the waves was once again discussed to Aela's disapproval. The will of the Great Wave did not concern the Phoenix Son.

However, he argued that as an Immortal, he was learned in many mythologies, and was said by some, to be closer to the divine energies of the world. Immortals were said to be above the failings of man. They had progressed past feelings of greed, selfishness, lust, and hate.

Years of existence and their rebirth by an Immortal force had taught them the uselessness of war and violence, and because of that understanding, they sought to bring peace and understanding into the world. On and on he went.

Aela did not doubt any of the tales regarding the Immortals, but she loathed the thought of an Immortal having any in her country. She disagreed with the elders eagerly telling him of Dovkey's problems.

"I understand why you would be alarmed," he said cautiously, "this is undoubtedly another issue that should be addressed with the Council."

"No," Aela said. "The Immortals have no more control over the Great Wave than we do."

"Yes, of course...but there may be those among the Council who can contact your deity," his pleasantness irritated Aela. The pretense of civility and humbleness in direct opposition to everything she said was insulting.

The room was divided on the Phoenix Son's proposal. The elders were quick to agree to anything the Immortal suggested as if his every word was wisdom. The priestesses, however, were not so content with the proposal. It was long their sacred duty to be the only link between the people and the divine. They studied and trained for years and endured the harsh ritual of the priestess trials to have the honor of communicating with the Great Wave. Aela could see the discomfort in their stances and the distrust in their eyes. She could sympathize completely.

From the moment the Phoenix Son had arrived, he had attempted to take charge of her life and her country. No doubt, he was used to being consulted as an Immortal, but it seemed that he excelled in giving his counsel even when it was not sought.

Furthermore, his insistence that the Immortal Council be notified of the happenings within Dovkey deeply concerned Aela.

Her country had existed in its quiet corner of the world, without the influence of others, and though the internal power shifts that had taken place were upsetting to her, she had no desire for Dovkey to be exposed to the conflicting pressures of the world.

The ongoing debate around her was a reminder of how ineffective the two guiding factions had become. She respected the role that each group played in the governing of Dovkey, but their rigidness was detrimental to her people.

"When will you receive word from the Council?" one of the elders asked.

Aela looked to the Phoenix Son, who seemed pleased by the deference and attention. She wondered briefly what kind of man he was before becoming an Immortal.

"I expect that it will take several days for the Council to confer."

Several days, Aela thought. That seemed like a lifetime; she was loath to have Council's involvement. However, she needed them to approve the voiding of her contract with Aluz.

"Since the Immortal Council's guidance is needed in the resolution of this matter, we will speak no more of it until we have received word from them."

The room hushed. Despite the quiet, Aela knew a storm was brewing. She had feared another ash storm, but now, it was apparent that a political tempest brewed in its place.

Chapter 20

Later that night, Aela stood in the darkened room looking out at the sea. Without the rays of the sun to pass through the waterfall, the dancing rainbows were absent. Tarr found that he missed them. Though she had sought this place for comfort, the magic of the afternoon they had spent here was not present.

She avoided him again today after she met with the elders and priestesses. Even though he was a foreigner, he easily discovered the palace gossip, and it was not good. The elders had seen their opportunity and had struck ruthlessly to further their agenda. Their argument appeared logical on the surface, but the scope of what they proposed was far more devastating than one woman's life. And he didn't believe for one moment that they had considered how their power play affected that one woman.

Convincing her guards to take him to her had been surprisingly easy and concerning. Though neither word nor expression betrayed their concern, he knew that they were worried about her. Thus, the reason he was standing in the doorway of her secret room.

He held a lantern aloft as he entered. The only acknowledgment she made of his presence was to wipe quickly beneath her eyes.

Setting the light on the ledge, he stood silently next to her. Unwanted tears crept rebelliously from her eyes no matter how many times she cleared them from her face.

He knew the elders currently were honoring the Phoenix Son with another feast. Unsurprisingly, they neglected to invite him.

However, he wondered if she too had been overlooked or if she had made some excuse to avoid them.

None of that was the reason for her tears though.

"A beautiful woman standing alone in the dark is a thing of concern."

She closed her eyes at the sound of his voice.

His form blocked most of the light cast by the lantern.

"My lord." Formality provided her some distance, a wall that she could put between them. He imagined the events of the day had left her feeling raw and vulnerable.

"My queen." He stood next to her watching the river fall to the ocean. They stood in silence, and though she tried to hold them back, the tears continued their silent descent.

Instead of drawing attention to them, he opened her palm, his fingers rubbing circles into her skin, before gently dropping a small cloth-covered square into her hand.

She looked at him, but he remained silent. With her free hand, she unwrapped the bundle and revealed a small dark square.

"If you're going to be alone in the dark crying, you should have a little chocolate. It enriches the experience."

She managed a smile. "Thank you." They stood in silence again, her eyes fixed on the delicacy. "This is not Dovkeyen chocolate."

"Of course not," he said with mock outrage. "If you're going to indulge, you need the best. It's from Domea."

"This is illegal."

"I won't tell anyone."

"Perhaps I'll save it for later."

"Afraid not. A beautiful woman crying and eating chocolate should not be left alone."

She gave a weak laugh. "Go ahead. Indulge. Those are tears of bitterness, I think. Take something sweet to balance it."

Her eyes closed as she took a bite, and then moaned at the sheer wonder of it.

"I have not had this in a very long time," she said.

Beside her Tarr gasped. "You mean this is not the first time you've had illegal contraband?"

She smiled at the false astonishment in his voice. "I'm afraid not."

Her smile deepened at his laughter.

"The first time that Kesh came back from Frin'gere, he brought Domean chocolate with him. It's still the most delicious thing I have ever tasted. Thank you." She took another bite and let the delicacy melt in her mouth.

They remained in comfortable silence. Tarr thought of the week of silence they had spent together, and the kiss they had shared in this room. With great effort, he kept his hands to himself. He wanted to envelop her in his arms and kiss her until the tears dried up.

Instead, he asked, "What are you thinking about?"

She hesitated, and he wondered if what she said really was what occupied her thoughts. "I was wondering how you and Kesh met. You should tell me the story."

He raised an eyebrow at her commanding tone. "I would be more than happy to; right after you tell me about how you came to have four very unusual guards."

His gaze held a challenge as he suspected that was a story she would not tell.

"Perhaps another time," she said.

"Yes, another time." He waited for her to relax again. "The elders are conniving, old bastards."

She laughed even as the tears started to fall again. "Yes, they are," she said quietly. "I suppose I should not be surprised. They have been working towards this for a long time."

"Do they have the power to remove you?"

"I didn't think so, but something said between Malcolm and Bena makes me think that there is something the elders know that I don't. I'm going to talk with the priestesses tomorrow."

"How is your fiancé...the other one?"

Aela started laughing, but it uncontrollably turned into crying. "I'm sorry," she said between gasping sobs. "I'm not sure what this is. I'm so sorry."

He put an arm around her shoulders and pulled her into his body. Her head rested on his shoulder. "This is everything. Grief, pain, fear, anger...just everything."

She let him hold her. "I don't want to lose my throne."

The shuddering breaths that followed her statement revealed how cathartic they were for her. He wondered if she had ever said those words out loud if she had ever let herself want something. At that moment, he realized he wanted to give her everything she wanted. He would do what he needed to ensure that.

"Of course you don't, and you won't."

"You don't know that," she whispered.

"Why do you think I'm here?"

"The Phoenix Son has involved the Immortal Council. I knew that I needed them to deal with the contract, but the thought of them coming in and taking over terrifies me."

"That's not what the Council does."

"That's what the Lord Phoenix Son is trying to do," she said bitterly.

"Yes, he does seem quite ambitious for an Immortal. Aren't you glad you won't have to marry him?"

Her face was pressed against his chest, but he felt her lips part in a smile. "That has not been decided yet."

"I will call upon all the avenging power of Seer's Fortune to see that it does not happen," his words were harsher than he intended, but he meant every one of them.

"I'm beginning to understand why Kesh chose Seer's Fortune."

Her brother's decision to play Seer's Fortune almost guaranteed that Tarr could not be parted from Aela. Even against an Immortal contract, it stood unbreakable.

"Why hasn't the wrangrent attacked again?"

"Destroying Masia took a great deal of power. Even a wrangrent would need time to recover and build back up his power."

"I keep waiting for reports that another town has been turned to ash. I fear every day that it will happen, and the elders still refuse to acknowledge the threat. They still think that it was a Frin'geren attack. They have soldiers camped out at the border, but I know somehow the wrangrent won't attack near the border again."

"No, he will not attack at the border. The next attack will hit closer to the palace... closer to you." She nodded as she tilted her head back to look at him.

"I will be by your side." He felt more than his words could convey. He would protect her against all threats. His commitment to stay with her was more than just the promise he had made to Kesh. Yet, the words remained trapped on his tongue.

She started to pull away, and he tightened his hold on her. So many things he should say, and what he said was, "Why don't we find our rest together?"

Her eyes widened momentarily, and he wanted to believe lust was the emotion there. "I do not think that there would be much resting."

He stared down at her, his hands resting on her hips. "No, there wouldn't."

"Your offer is tempting," she whispered to him. "I need rest. I need to stay alert and focused. I wish you good night."

She stepped back and his grip loosened. His need for her was great, but he had to fulfill his own duties above all else. Protecting her was his mission. Wanting her was the complication.

Leaning forward, he gently kissed her forehead. "Then go rest."

She turned to leave, pausing when she stood in the doorway. "Thank you for the chocolate. I think it did balance some of the bitterness."

"Sleep well, my queen."

AELA TOSSED AND TURNED for hours, but sleep eluded her. When daylight filled her room and Menony prepared her clothing for the day, Aela had gotten only three hours of sleep.

She stared at her reflection as her friend pinned her curls up for the day. Dark circles under her eyes betrayed the lack of rest. Her skin was pale and dry, reminding her that she was not taking enough care.

Menony fussed over her but refrained from commenting. She applied extra creams and salves to her face. She changed her original choice of dress as the soft pink washed out her complexion. Instead, Menony dressed her in a deep green dress with long sleeves and a high neck. The extra coverage felt like armor, and Aela was grateful for the feeling.

She left her room, and three of her four guards fell into step beside her.

"You did not sleep," Mar said.

She glared at him for a moment before muttering, "Obviously."

"Dreams?"

"No. Too many thoughts."

"They are moving against you." She knew that he spoke of the elders.

"There is an ancient Dovkeyen law, my queen. The elders met in secret last night. They spoke of this law, which states that the priestesses may contest the reign of a monarch that is out of favor with the Great Wave. The elders are preparing a proposal for the priestesses to review and decide whether that favor has been bestowed on you." He paused, "They summoned the Healer Priestess to weigh in on the issue."

"They called Ishea to the palace?" Aela's voice shook with anger. "I am going to see the priestesses now."

Mar nodded. She did not ask how he knew this. The guards knew all the secret passages that she did, and probably a few more. She assumed Ter was the one who had spied on the elders. He had broken off from the rest of them just before they had reached her room last night.

She found the priestesses gathered in the new temple room. Lingering outside the room, she dreaded facing them.

The temple room predated the Reformation by only a few years. The ancient temple pools had long been deemed inconsequential and forgotten. The new room with its high ceiling and clean white stone was circular. A large open window looked out onto the sea. Though the waves no longer pounded the white cliffs violently, the sea continued to rock the palace, a reminder of the Great Wave's displeasure. The priestesses knelt in a circle discussing some matter amongst themselves.

As Aela slipped into the room, she bowed her head and waited to be addressed. The required conduct among the priestesses was much different when inside a holy place. Outside this room, she was queen. Inside, she was just another citizen. The women in this room were equal to one another, but to all others who entered, they were superior. This was their domain, and she had been taught long ago to respect that.

"Your Majesty, you have entered the temple space. With what matter may we help you?"

They were words of ceremony only. Aela knew that the priestesses tolerated her as the elders did. Though it was not a personal dislike of her that underlay their cool regard, but rather a deep disappointment. She was the first queen of Dovkey to not pass the trials.

"I come to discuss with you many things, Masia most important among them."

Her words were met with heavy silence.

"It was attacked by evil magic. I have no more proof for you than I had for the elders. I can only tell you that I looked upon the city and felt that something beyond just fire had occurred. Something was not right in the way it stood frozen in ash."

"We have heard your claim that a wrangrent is responsible. That is a heavy claim to make."

Aela stepped further into the room, and all eyes turned to her. "Yes, I know, and I would not make it unless I was sure."

"How can you be sure though, Your Majesty?"

"I felt magic during my training. I know what it should feel like, and I know when a great deal of magic has been used in one place. I may not have passed the trials, but I did complete the training. These things are taught to all priestesses are they not?"

"They are."

Aela waited for more but realized that nothing else would be said.

"The other matters?"

She took a deep breath. "I have been informed that the Healer Priestess Ishea has been called to the White Palace to help you determine whether I have been given the divine right to rule."

Bena's brow tensed, but the rest of her face remained calm. The slight expression made Aela wonder if the priestess approved of the elders' plans. The Head Priestess possibly disliked Ishea more than Aela did.

"Is it true that there is an ancient law that says you can denounce the monarch if just reason shows she has not been chosen by the Great Wave?"

Bena looked down for a moment as she released a long exhale. She looked back to Aela. "It is true. And the Healer Priestess is on her way here. We will convene on the topic as soon as she arrives. The elders have put forth a declaration of question regarding your right to rule. We have no choice but to see the inquiry through."

Her words confirmed Aela's fears. "Thank you, Priestess Bena. You have been a great help." She turned to leave when Bena spoke out once more.

"It does not weigh in your favor, Your Majesty. You know this?"

Aela turned and nodded. "Yes, just as you must know that the Great Wave lashes out on our white cliffs not in disapproval of me, but in grief for what has been done to his people. I implore you, priestesses, to listen deeper to what the Great Wave tells us."

With that, she left the room.

Chapter 21

"Is it done?" the faceless voice demanded.

"Yes, it is done, just as you instructed. I was in her room earlier, and she does not suspect."

"Good," the voice purred with satisfaction.

"Will the spell kill her?"

"Slowly, painfully, yes. Oh, come now. You don't really have feelings for her, do you? It was only to be an act, but is it something more now?"

"No, of course not. I just don't see a reason to kill her."

The voice laughed. "Who would take you for such a soft heart! Be careful, my friend. We have a purpose, and it does not involve Aela. So, while you convince her that you truly care, you must not allow yourself to fall for your own lie. I am giving you everything that you ever wanted. Soon, you will be a king. Remember that when you stare into those unnatural gray eyes of hers and feel yourself begin to waver."

"You are right. I will not succumb to the few charms she has."

"Good. I had hoped to catch her in Masia, but our timing was off. Unfortunately, I did not see directly the pain in her eyes when she gazed upon her beloved city turned to ash."

"I believe she was truly broken by it."

"Hmm, perhaps it would be better not to kill her outright. Perhaps, I will draw it out so that I may see her suffer as I destroy her country bit by bit."

"I CANNOT UNDERSTAND why you are still sick, Ony. Your seasickness usually resolves in a day," Aela said as she pulled the pins from her hair.

Her meeting with the priestesses was followed by more meetings with the elders. Neither meeting accomplished anything useful to Aela's thinking. She had told herself that she would sneak away and nap, but the opportunity never came. The Phoenix Son had insisted that she dine alone with him that night. Though spending time with him was not something she enjoyed, it was her duty to entertain the Immortal, especially when he requested her company.

She had not seen Tarr that day and felt a hint of sorrow for his absence. His humor amused her, and his presence comforted her. Thoughts of his offer to stay the night were among the troubles that kept her from sleep. She had not lied when she said she was tempted. Even now, as she undressed for a relaxing bath, her thoughts strayed to him.

"I do not understand either," Menony said as she picked the queen's dress off the floor. She was pale and paused in her movements to clutch a hand to her mouth. Her eyes closed as she breathed through the nausea, and then she continued with her tasks.

"Menony, you need to go to bed," Aela said as she rose from her vanity.

The brunette shook her head with an expression of stubbornness. "No, I'm fine." She turned a stern expression on Aela. "You need to go to bed. Right after this bath. Let it relax your body so that you can just fall into sleep."

Aela smiled sadly. "My body is not the problem."

Menony stopped what she was doing and hugged Aela tightly. "They cannot take what is yours. They cannot prove that the Great Wave does not approve your rule because there is no proof."

"They will use the trials and the prophecy as proof."

Her friend hugged her tighter. "Prophecies and visions are tricky things, Aela. You know that. They are not always clear. Sometimes they are only a warning of what could pass, not what will." She pulled away and smoothed Aela's hair behind her ears in a maternal gesture. Her loving gaze filled Aela with warmth.

"Oh," Menony said as she turned her head away. "It's relentless," she muttered as she again held her hand to her mouth.

Aela steadied her by the shoulders. "You, my friend, need rest to cure whatever this sickness is that has been lingering for weeks now."

"I promise it will abate," she said as she pulled away from Aela.

"Not if you do not take care of yourself."

"I will help you with your bath, and then I will lie down." Aela wanted to argue that she could take her own bath, but Menony's determined expression told her it would be a waste of energy for them both.

"Fine. And, then I will see you to bed."

Menony smiled and went to gather the toweling.

Steam rose from the clear water that filled the tub. Aela reached out to graze her fingers over the surface but stopped abruptly before touching it.

A series of images flashed through her head so quickly she could not be sure what they were. She stared at the water, unsure of why she suddenly felt wary of it. Reaching out again, the same images assaulted her.

Flashes of ice and fire. A small vile of light blue liquid. A fragment of a memory from ten years ago. The sharp cry of an infant.

Her fingers hovered over the water as her heart began to beat heavily in her chest. Something was wrong, but she didn't know what. The water contained a message, but the feeling was different from the other times. Before, she had been drawn to the water. As she now stared at it, her instinct was to pull away.

The message was there though. A warning.

It remained out of reach. Despite her aversion, she decided to submerse herself since that was how the visions usually came.

"Aela, is something wrong?" Menony asked as she reentered the room with a pile of towels.

"No, I'm fine," Aela said with a forced smile.

"The water will cool."

"You're right," Aela said as she dropped her robe and stepped into the tub. The steamy warmth of the bath was exactly what she needed. She closed her eyes and breathed in the comforting fumes.

Sinking deeper into the water as it rocked against her chin, every muscle in her body relaxed. Still, the sense of foreboding would not abate.

The noises in the background faded from Aela's consciousness as the water swayed around her. Entranced by the gentle movement of it, she didn't immediately notice the paralysis of her body.

Her chest touched against the surface of the water as each breath became deeper than the last. Her mind cleared completely for one blissful moment.

An undistinguishable image flashed through her consciousness, there and then gone.

Her chest rose with another deep breath. A sharp pain pierced her sternum and rose up her throat. She opened her mouth, but nothing came out. With another breath, the sensation was gone.

A flow of images flooded her head... the same images as before.

She gasped just before her entire body sank underneath the surface of the water. She tried to resurface, but her body was too heavy to move. Her limbs were unresponsive to her commands. Her chest burned for air.

Blackness surrounded her and consciousness faded.

MENONY TURNED QUICKLY when she heard the water splashing, and Aela's pained cry. She rushed to the side of the tub as she called out for Mar, Ter, and Anut. A sheet of ice covered the water that had been steaming only moments ago, and Aela's image was barely discernible.

"Aela!" she screamed as she started to reach towards the water. Mar pulled her back before she could touch the frozen surface. "Something's wrong, Mar! Something's wrong." She yelled as she fought against him. Panic filled her.

"Something is in the water. Do not touch it," he ordered as he set her on the ground behind him. He swiftly knelt next to the tub and broke the ice. It reformed instantly around his arms. He attempted several times to reach into the water, and each time it formed new ice and kept Aela just out of reach.

Menony cried quietly as she tried to edge forward. Anut was at her side, and gently restrained her. Over and over, Mar drove his hands through the ice as it formed a thicker layer with each break. He pulled his hands and arms out, and Menony could see the skin tinted blue from the iciness of it.

Ter knelt on the other side of the tub. An unspoken conversation took place between them. Mar nodded and prepared once more to reach into the water. He drove his massive fists into the ice several times before there was a break. Ter waited until the break was wide enough for his own arms and reached into the water. Mar continued to break the ever-reforming ice as Ter reached deeper into the tub.

Finally, Aela's head appeared above the surface of the water as Ter lifted her from the tub, gripping her tightly beneath the arms. Mar kept the ice at bay until Aela was pulled completely free of it. Ter collapsed backward with Aela in his arms.

Menony pulled away from Anut and rushed to the queen's side. Aela was gray and breathing slowly and shallowly. Her lips were blue, and ice crystals formed at the tip of her lashes.

"Aela," Menony called out as she hovered near the two. Behind her, Anut laid a hand on her shoulder to remind her it was not safe to go any closer.

"Is she okay? What happened?" She turned to Anut and then to Mar, who still knelt by the tub. His bare skin was a similar shade of gray, but his breaths came in quick gasps.

Having witnessed Aela's previous visions, she knew this was different.

Anut left her to hover at Mar's side.

"I am not affected," came the low reply. Mar looked up to her. "An ice curse in the water," he breathed heavily.

Menony gasped. "No, no, no. Ice magic is twisted magic. That would mean..." She let the statement hang in the air, too fearful that the words spoken aloud would make it a reality.

Mar looked to Ter, who shivered while he held Aela to his body. "She absorbed all of it."

"What does that mean?" Menony asked as she held out toweling to them. Anut would not let her get any closer.

The head guard stood. His arms still held a blue tinge. "The curse is in her now. It cannot be transferred to anyone else."

"Does that mean we can touch her? We can help her? Tell me what we need, Mar. Give me something to do!"

He turned to her. "You are not to touch her."

Menony started to object, but Mar stopped her. "You know why you may not take that risk."

He waited for her to acknowledge his order. "She needs heat. Anything that will provide heat."

Menony nodded and rushed away to call for hot water.

Mar and Anut knelt beside Ter. "I would take her, brother," Anut said softly.

Ter shook his head and held her closer. "No, you must stay clear."

Anut simply nodded.

"I will get water from the Temple Pools. They still contain magic," Anut stood and headed towards the door. "And I will send Sey."

He left the room as Menony rushed back in.

"What does an ice spell do, Mar?" she asked quietly.

"It kills," he replied simply.

Chapter 22

"Surely now, you can see that she was never meant to be queen," one of the elders whispered secretively to the man beside him. They stood together on the outer edge of the crowd gathered outside the queen's chambers.

In a voice just as hushed, Elder Berto replied sagely, "Be careful of the things that you say, Malcolm. We do not know the Great Wave's will."

Berto sighed with a heavy heart as he glanced around at the others, trying to follow the conversation of the priestesses. When the queen had claimed a wrangrent attacked Masia, he agreed with the others that it was just not possible. Wrangents in the past committed atrocious acts of conquest, killing, and destroying all in their paths. Their reigns of tyranny lasted centuries and spanned countries. Dovkey's isolated location, surrounded by ocean and mountains on all sides, had saved the country from the last known wrangrent. However, now, he had doubts, and he wondered if maybe the queen was right to fear.

"Think of the signs: the Exchromy fever, the failed trails, her involvement in this marriage fiasco with the Frin'geren, and now an ice curse! You must agree with me that these are signs and not good ones!" Malcolm persisted.

The ever-calm Berto looked at him with irritation. "The problems of her engagement are in no way her doing. We are more to blame than she is in that matter. We made the Immortal contract, and we let Kesh leave for Frin'gere, allowing for his arrangement with the Frin'geren."

He paused and his expression grew more somber. "The priestesses would know if she was not meant to sit on the throne. They would have seen. It is not our job, my old friend, to watch for signs."

"What if the priestesses are wrong? They were wrong once before." The comment was said so softly, yet Berto felt its impact greatly. He started to refute the accusation but found no words.

"They told us that Queen Aela was meant to be a high priestess, and yet she failed the trials. People see what they want to see, Berto, and no one wants to see her family die out as it has. It has been a good reign, but we cannot blind ourselves to the truth...the house of Gero has perished. There will be no heir from the queen. This is the Great Wave's will." He clenched his fists in front of him.

"Our queen is dying of a curse. This is not the time to speak of such things." Berto turned from Malcolm to listen to the priestesses.

"How do we know that's even true? Her giants haven't let anyone in to see her!" He paused and said more quietly, "The Healer Priestess is on her way. When she arrives, she must be allowed to see the queen!"

Berto turned his attention to the High Priestess, who stood before the unmovable barrier of Mar and Ter. Her statements echoed that of the elders.

"You are not protecting her by keeping out those who would help."

The guards remained unmoved with their gazes fixed on the wall behind her and unresponsive to her demands.

The priestess huffed in frustration and turned her attention to Menony as the woman exited the room. "You must order these...men...to stand down. If the queen is afflicted with a curse, she must be seen to immediately."

"I'm sorry, High Priestess, but I do not command the queen's guards. If they refuse to let anyone in, there is nothing I can do."

The young woman who had loyally served the queen addressed those gathered in the hall. "The queen is unchanged. It does not appear that the ice curse has weakened her any further, though she is still not conscious. When the Healer Priestess arrives, please see that she is brought to the queen immediately. She will be allowed access." Menony looked to Mar for confirmation, and the guard nodded. "Please, there is nothing more that can be done for her at this time."

After a few more moments of grumbling, the elders and priestesses dispersed. As Berto walked away, he noted that Lord Tarr and the Phoenix Son Aluz remained.

TARR STOOD ACROSS THE hall, leaning against the wall with his arms crossed over his chest. Sey had been watching over him when Aela was attacked. Anger filled him, and he wondered irrationally if the situation would be different had all her guards remained with her. He knew it was unlikely.

Aluz strode arrogantly to the door. "You will let me pass."

Tarr snorted in amusement.

The guards held their posts as Menony reentered the room and blocked the Immortal's advance. "I am a member of the Immortal Council, and the queen needs my services."

Still, the guards refused him entry.

"Can you break an ice curse, Immortal lord?" Tarr asked as he watched the scene between Aela's guards and the fuming Aluz.

"Breaking a curse of any kind is a complicated -"

"That is the only service she needs right now." The Frin'geren's dark eyes stared intensely at the Immortal. "Does not a Phoenix Son know a bit of fire magic? That would be of use against an ice curse undoubtedly."

Aluz barely contained his aggravated sneer, but Tarr only smiled at the other man's annoyance. "Not all Immortals practice elemental magic. Some of us have more complicated magical practices."

"Are you referring to the phoenix fire? The one she would enter and emerge as Phoenix Daughter. Is that the 'complicated magical practices?'" He made no effort to keep the contempt from his voice.

"I am surprised that you are familiar with such things. Yes, I could take her into the fire; however, there is a chance that she would not survive it in her weakened state. I feel the risk might be preferable to inevitable death though. It was her destiny all along to join me in the fire."

Tarr smiled, though there was nothing friendly to it. "I think such a risk could wait until the healer has arrived, don't you?"

"I cannot say. Until I have assessed her, I cannot know if the phoenix fire would save her from this curse...or if what ails her is even a curse. The likelihood a curse this powerful was cast in the palace is...it's highly unlikely."

He turned back to the guards. "You must understand why I have to see her."

Still, the guards remained unmoved.

"You are condemning her to death then," Aluz said in rage.

"That seems an overly strong statement...Immortal."

Tarr watched cautiously as Aluz approached him. "They practice fire magic in Frin'gere do they not?"

Again, the Frin'geren smiled. "They practice all magic in Frin'gere; less restrictions there."

Aluz's smile was disdainful, "Yes, very hard to control what is practiced. A wrangrent resulted from that lack of control there once before."

Tarr simply stared at him with his dark eyes. The two glared at each other until Aluz looked away with a huff. Tarr smiled.

Without further objection, Aluz left. Tarr waited until he was far down the hall before approaching the guards. "I have to see her."

No response. The Frin'geren stared with frustration at the guards blocking his path.

The door opened behind them, and Menony peeked her head out. "Are they gone?"

Though the question was not directed at him, Tarr answered. "Yes. The Phoenix Son was not happy about being refused entry."

Menony grimaced. "Well, the queen will not be happy about Ishea at her bedside, so no one gets to be happy."

"Ah, yes, the Healer Priestess. Aela is not fond of her."

"That is an understatement," Menony muttered.

"I never did hear why she dislikes her cousin so," he drawled to Menony. "She is a beautiful, accomplished, and warm woman. Hard to imagine why anyone would not like her."

Menony glared at him, and he fought to keep from smiling. "Do not repeat that opinion of her to the queen. You will quickly lose any favor you hold."

"Jealousy?" He further provoked. "I could see that."

"She is not jealous of Ishea!" Realizing her outburst, she took a calming breath. "Even before the fever and the trials, Aela never liked Ishea. She always felt that there was something...off. Perhaps everything that Ishea has achieved since inspires a bit of jealousy, but the dislike was present from the beginning."

"Aela has good instincts."

"Queen Aela," she corrected. "You are not married yet."

"Soon enough," Tarr teased. However, his jest failed to cheer her. Menony's expression sobered.

"Let us hope that she will have the chance to decide what she wishes to do with you."

"Let me in," Tarr pushed against the guards.

"I can't," she looked up at the guards. "You will have to convince them, Lord Tarr." She returned to the queen's room once more, closing the door softly behind her.

Tarr argued, pleaded, and threatened the guards for over an hour, but to no avail.

Despite his objections, Sey continued to guard him.

"I could be of help. This was why I was sent here."

The guard looked down at him. "You were sent to break an ice curse?" Sey asked with a hint of suspicion.

Tarr groaned. "Yes and no. I could not have known that an ice curse would befall her, but Kesh sent me here to protect her."

"In that, we have all failed," the guard responded solemnly.

Tarr hated that he felt the same.

A heavy hand patted his shoulder. "We will allow the Healer Priestess to try first. If she is unsuccessful in removing the curse, then we will consider other options."

"Do not wait too long," Tarr warned.

"It has been our duty to protect her much longer than it has been yours," the guard warned back.

Despite his frustration with her guards, he respected their loyalty. Furthermore, he trusted them to do everything in their power to protect her. With reluctance, he resolved himself to wait for the Healer Priestess and remain ready to intercede if needed.

THE HEALER PRIESTESS arrived within three days of Aela falling under the ice curse. Only Berto, Bena, and Menony were on the dock to meet Ishea.

As the boat pulled up to the dock, she disembarked even as the crew finished tying up the vessel.

"Has her condition worsened?" Her pale green eyes filled with concern as she looked from the elder to the priestess. She paid no heed to Menony.

"No, she has been stable for the past few days as far as we know. Her guards will not let anyone into the room."

The elder and priestess looked to Menony.

"No, her condition has not worsened," she said as she bowed her head to the Healer Priestess.

Bena stepped forward and took Ishea's hands in her own and gently kissed each. "Thank you for coming, Ishea." She turned to Aela's friend, "Menony is the only one who has been allowed to see the queen. She has reassured us that Queen Aela's guards will allow you entrance though."

Ishea smiled at her and returned the gesture. "It is an honor to be of service to the High Priestesses, the elders," she smiled at Berto, "and of course, the queen. I must see her immediately."

"Of course, Healer Ishea, right this way." Berto stepped to the side, allowing Ishea to follow Bena as she led the way to the queen's quarters.

They walked quickly down the halls. "Surely the elders can do something if the queen's guards insist on barring entrance to those who would help?"

She looked over her shoulder at the elder.

He took a moment to reply. "We could order the palace guard to overtake them, yes. There would be injuries and possibly causalities. We have done our best to avoid such extremes. Menony updates us on her condition and has assured us that she will inform us if there are concerning changes."

Ishea peered over her shoulder. Menony could feel the priestess's vibrant green eyes studying her in a way they never had before. "I see," she said in a soft voice. "The queen is fortunate to have such a loyal servant in you, Menony."

She nodded in response to the priestess's statement, not allowing the irritation to show on her face. Truthfully, she was Aela's servant, but never had the queen or her guards treated her as such. Aela was her friend and family, and she knew the queen viewed her as such too. However, many viewed and treated her like a devoted servant.

When they arrived at Aela's door, they found Tarr and Aluz waiting. Tarr stood off to the side, muttering something to Sey, while Aluz paced directly in front of the door. He looked up at the arrival of the group.

Tarr's sharp gaze was the first to notice them; however, Aluz spoke first. "Ah, Elder Berto, do you have any news to pass on?"

The elder smiled at the Immortal. "The Healer Priestess Ishea has arrived. She has immense experience in dealing with ailments of this nature."

Aluz looked to the priestess and smiled warmly. "I believe that we have met before. Were you in Domea a year ago dealing with the Reginigi Fire?"

"Yes, it is an honor to see you again, my lord. Our country is blessed to have you marrying our queen." Ishea bowed her head.

"I am eager to see her," he said.

She nodded. "As any devoted betrothed would be." Her attention turned to Tarr, and she smiled again. "Lord Tarr, it is a pleasure to see you again, though the circumstances are less than ideal."

She stepped away from the Immortal. "Will you excuse me? I would like to see the queen now."

Ishea stopped before Anut. He did not move. "I must see the queen. I am here to help her," Ishea explained calmly.

Still, Anut did not move. He gave no indication that he was even aware of her presence.

"Does he understand?" She asked with concern as she turned to Berto. "I cannot help her if I cannot see her."

Menony heard Tarr snicker.

Berto nodded as he approached the guard. "Please, you must let us in. She is the Healer Priestess. She could be our only hope of saving the queen. You must let her in."

Anut turned his gaze to Menony. The gazes of everyone else followed. She wondered if Anut had overheard the priestess's words and now sought to establish that Menony was more than a servant. She smiled briefly at the gesture.

"We must let the Healer Priestess in. She is here to help." She looked at Ishea and bowed her head. Then she stepped around the priestess and entered the room. Shortly after, the Healer Priestess was also allowed entry.

A huge fire burned in the brazier and candles filled every available surface. The room was hotter than the hottest summer day, yet Aela's body shivered under layers of heavy wool. Ishea crossed the room and knelt beside the queen. She gently removed the layers of blankets and touched the skin at the base of the queen's neck. Menony knew that Aela's skin was colder than the winter sea.

"It is without a doubt an ice curse. Can you tell me how you think she came under it?"

"She went to take a bath. After only a few minutes in the water, she complained that she was freezing even though the water was still steaming. I helped her to bed and went to fetch her robe. When I returned, she was unconscious. We have not been able to wake her since," Menony explained. She told the story that she and the guards had agreed upon. Revealing that Mar had been unaffected by the curse was not information that he or his brothers wanted to be revealed.

Menony resumed her place on the other side of Aela, applying the hot compresses to her forehead.

"Thank you, Menony, but that will no longer be needed," Ishea said indicating the hot towel. "I am afraid that it does not help her. I fear that it may be causing her to lose more of her own body heat."

"But it has been helping for the past..." Menony allowed her objection to die. Instead, she smiled and rose from the bed.

"I have a small matter to see to. I will leave her in your care." She exchanged an unnoticed look with Mar and Ter, who stood by the door before leaving the room.

Ter followed her. As the door closed behind her, Aluz, Tarr, Berto, and Bena waited for news.

"I am afraid that her condition has not changed since last night. Are you sure there is nothing that you can do to help?" she directed her question to the Phoenix Son.

He shook his head. "I am sorry to say that I know very little of water magic and even less of corrupted water magic. I have tried to contact the Immortal Council, and I am still awaiting a response. As soon as I receive any information, I will put it to the best use."

Menony knew Aela was both eager and fearful of the Council's response. The delay in their reply worried Menony most, especially now that the wrangrent had attacked the queen directly.

"Thank you, my lord," she said with a sad smile.

Behind her the door opened again, and Ishea stepped out. The Phoenix Son stood directly in front of her, blocking Tarr from view.

"It is worse than I suspected, but I do not think that she will die. I am afraid that it will be a long recovery for her. I am sorry that I cannot give you more comforting news."

Aluz nodded and thanked her before returning to his quarters.

Berto also thanked Ishea and invited her to join the elders for dinner.

"Thank you, but I would like to rest before I return to the queen." The group dispersed, and Berto showed the Healer Priestess to her room.

Chapter 23

By morning, the queen's condition was no better than the night before. By the second day, the Healer Priestess announced that the queen was failing. The ice curse was too strong. She promised to do all in her power but was not hopeful of the queen's ultimate outcome.

Menony watched helplessly as her friend slipped closer to death. She agreed with the guards that it was time to try something different.

"We cannot wait any longer. She is getting weaker each day; even Ishea is losing faith that the queen will survive," Menony said quietly to Tarr as they stood cautiously on one of the balconies.

"Ishea spent the entire night with her, did she not? I cannot help her if the Healer Priestess is beside her all night, and it cannot be done during the day. We must do this after midnight," he replied. "The elders will not permit the use of fire magic in the palace even if it is to save the queen."

"She will leave tonight. I will find some way to get her out, but assure me once more that you can do this?" Menony's voice and face expressed the intense worry that filled her.

Tarr put his hands on her shoulders to offer comfort. "I cannot guarantee that it will work. I have not even seen her yet. I base all my assumptions on what you have told me. In the end, it is up to Aela. A great deal of what I will do depends on her own personal strength."

Menony smiled a weak smile. "We have nothing to fear then. She is the strongest person I know. The priestess will be gone by midnight."

"What of the guards?"

"They agree that this must be done. The Healer Priestess was not as effective as we had hoped. You will have no trouble entering the room tonight. They will not leave their posts outside her room but have agreed to leave the room. As you requested, I will not be there either."

"It is for your own safety that I ask this. Do not fear, Menony, I will save your queen... if she lets me," he hugged her tightly.

She pulled away and wiped her eyes before the tears could fall. She allowed him to leave first. After waiting several minutes, she returned to Aela's chambers.

ISHEA SAT WITH AELA all day. She performed every healing and purifying spell that she knew. However, nothing seemed to take effect. Menony stayed with her throughout the hours of daylight and into the night helping in whatever way she could. While the priestess chanted or performed the intricate parts of various spells, Menony tended to the candles. She made sure that none of them went out and replaced those that were spent. The intense heat of the room exhausted her, but she refused to leave Aela.

The heat affected even the guards. They broke their rigid postures and leaned against the walls. She noted that their movements were more sluggish than normal. Menony did not know where they came from, but she was sure that they were not from a climate of extreme heat. To save each other from the uncomfortable warmth of the room, they began rotating watch, disappearing for hours at a time, until finally, they could not even stand to be in the queen's chamber for more than a few minutes.

"Menony, we must take a break from this heat," Ishea finally said. Streams of sweat flowed down the sides of her face, and her white gown was drenched.

"We will make ourselves sick if we stay in here any longer tonight, and she needs us too much to risk that. Come, the candles will last the rest of the night, and her guards are here to maintain the fire." She stood by the side of the bed, her soft face filled with concern. "She has survived so much; I cannot bear the thought that she will not survive this." She leaned over and placed a gentle kiss on the queen's forehead.

"Sleep well," Menony murmured.

Ishea looked up.

"Please, Menony. You too must rest." She crossed to the other side of the bed and lightly put her hands on Menony's shoulders.

"I would stay with her all night if I could, but I am no good to her exhausted. I will rest and then return to her in the morning." Her voice was low and patient. "Come, rest if only for an hour or so, then you may come back. That is an order from the Healer Priestess," Ishea joked lightly as she led Menony out of the room.

Menony allowed the priestess to think that she was reluctantly being led from the room. In truth, she planned to leave anyway. Keeping the heat in the room at such unbearable levels was not safe for her, but she knew that it would wear the priestess down and ensure that she left for the night.

The door shut behind them, leaving the blistering room silent. They passed Mar and Ter standing guard outside the room. Menony prayed silently to the Great Wave that Tarr would succeed, that tomorrow they would all awake to the news that the queen was conscious and well.

TARR CREPT DOWN THE hall towards Aela's room. Thanks to Sey's scouting, the occasional palace guards were easily avoided. He insisted on coming at night to avoid the elders, priestesses, and Phoenix Son who lingered on and off throughout the day. Sey had assured him that very few people came to Aela's room at night.

He approached where Mar, Ter, and Anut guarded the door. Mar's hand fell heavily on his shoulder as he entered the room.

"We give you this opportunity out of desperation. Know that should greater harm befall her you will not live to see the terms of Seer's Fortune fulfilled. We will endure whatever consequences come. This our vow to you."

Tarr nodded in acknowledgment, feeling a shiver of fear. He knew with certainty that his death would come swiftly and painfully if they believed he had harmed their queen.

Mar's hand fell away, and he stepped forward. A thick hand on his chest barred his way. Turning to the other side, he stared into the shadowed face of Anut.

"Know also that there is no place in this world where you will not be found. I can see you, no matter where you flee."

Despite the threat, Tarr smiled as he responded. "I understand."

Anut studied him for another moment before releasing him. Tarr slipped through the door, closing it softly behind him. He scanned the room, eying the many candles that burned and the crystal bowls of water that hung over the bigger flames, giving the room warmth and moisture. The heat was intense, and he removed his leather vest, allowing it to fall to the floor as he approached the bed.

Aela's pale face and blue-tinged lips were the only parts visible. Her form shivered even buried underneath layers of warm wool. Pulling back the layers, he saw a body weakened by the spell and lack of sustenance.

He ran his fingers gently across the cold skin of her forehead. She immediately responded to the warm touch, moving her head as much as she could toward his trailing fingers. He smiled and stroked her forehead again.

"My lovely queen," he whispered, "I warn you that this will not be pleasant."

He stared at her a moment longer. Then, with one hand, he flung all the coverings completely off her body.

Only a thin white garment clothed her. Her limbs shook violently with the wool layers removed. Her jaw chattered and white breath escaped her lips.

He hated seeing her in such pain and discomfort, but it only strengthened his resolve to break the curse inside her. He slipped one arm underneath her shoulders and the other under her knees. With little effort, Tarr lifted her from the bed and pulled her into the warmth of his body. He carried her to the long desk by the blazing fireplace and gently laid her out on the wooden surface.

"Someone filled your body with ice. I will fill it with fire."

He stared at three large candles that burned brightly on the mantle above the fire. Under his concentration, the yellow flames dimmed progressively more and more until extinguished. He closed his eyes and held a tight fist in front of his body. Barely audible words of a foreign tongue fell from his lips as the sensation of magic built in the air around him. The weight of it intensified until the magic siphoned all the heat of the room into his closed fist.

His eyes and fist opened together. Three flames danced on the surface of his palm, joining together into one. He held his hand over Aela's stomach and stared at the deepening blue darkening the edges of her lips.

Tarr pulled his hand away, but the flame continued to float in the air above her. With a single word, the flame responded to his command and spread through the air. A fiery sheet of blazing yellow and orange hovered above Aela. He held his hand above the flames and pushed them down onto her body. The fire burned on the surface for a few minutes before sinking into her skin and disappearing completely.

He waited and watched. Tarr had never attempted to infuse fire into another's body. His own body had trained for years to accept the flames without burning. He had never seen done what he now attempted. However, a healer once told him of a man whose frostbitten limb was saved by infusing the leg with fire magic. In theory, filling Aela's body with fire magic would burn out the curse.

His eyes narrowed in concern as the queen continued to shiver. Suddenly, Aela's skin flushed a bright red, like an intense blush. Her chest rose with a deep breath, so deep that it lifted her ribs from the desk. Her red skin faded to purple, though pools of red remained in splotchy patches on her body. Minutes passed as her skin flushed red and purple several more times.

Though the fire no longer touched him, he felt the magic battle under her skin. He felt the flares of heat and the iciness of the curse as the two waged war. And underneath those dueling forces, he felt something else. Something different from anything he had ever felt before. A force that was fluid and unbreakable at the same time. Its influence was faint at first but grew stronger as the fire burned hotter. He suspected the unknown magic was Aela's. Together, her magic and his overwhelmed the ice.

Finally, the shivering stopped, and her skin glowed as if lit from within. Again, she breathed deeply, and the glow faded, leaving her skin its normal milky shade.

"The ice spell was strong, but you were stronger, my queen," he whispered in her ear. He rested his forehead against her temple. His breaths came quickly as relief filled him.

AELA CONTINUED TO BREATHE deeply, though she did not regain consciousness. Dreams of fire and ice occupied her mind. She had been locked in ice for so long, unable to determine how much time had passed, but then there was fire. It spread throughout her body like a flame on oil. First, a pleasing warmth covered the surface of the ice, and she felt it break through the endless cold. With the surface broken, the fire seeped into her body, threatening the ice and awakening the magic slumbering deep within.

Initially, she had not trusted the fire, but as the icy grip on her magic melted, she realized its intent was to free her. She willed that sense of water she felt to work with the fire until there was not a trace of cold left.

Still in a state of half-consciousness, she rose from the desk and wandered to the door like a sleepwalker. Her eyes remained closed, but images of the future, past, and present flowed through her mind's eye like a lazy river.

The door opened just as she reached it. She felt the presence of Ter and Mar standing outside. She paused in the doorway, then turned to the left and continued down the hall. The two guards followed closely behind.

Aela unknowingly led them down hall after hall. Servants who rose early to prepare for the day, watched in awe as she sleepwalked through the palace. Whispers spread quickly and soon a crowd followed in her wake.

Anut and Sey joined them along the way, and the four guards formed a protective circle around her. Still, she continued to walk in the physical realm while her mind remained ensconced in the realm of visions.

Standing in the ceremonial cave where she had last stood at her brother's funeral, she stopped only when the cool sea breeze hit her warm skin. It filled the entrance of the cave, and the sound of the waves hitting the steps echoed softly. Aela took a deep breath and slowly descended the steps toward the water. Unknown to her, Anut and Sey stood at the edge of the water watching her while Mar and Ter guarded the entrance even as a crowd formed.

Her foot touched a step half-submerged in the water, and she paused. Her grey eyes opened for the first time in days. Before her was the sparkling blue-green sea, swaying gently. A wave hit her shin, and the water seemed to wrap around her.

She took another step. Thunder unexpectedly filled the air, shaking the palace awake.

Aela looked down at the few steps that remained visible under the water's surface. Her eyes widened as she watched the water separate, revealing more carved white steps. The sea continued to pull back, forming walls of water on either side of the stairs, until far below a sandy white path was revealed. Aela took each step slowly as she descended lower and farther into the sea than any other ruler before her.

She came to the last step but did not hesitate to put her feet on the damp white sand. Thirty feet of water loomed above her, but she was not deterred. Though she was conscious, she felt as if her mind lingered between this world and the other.

Her body was weak from the days of inactivity and sore from the descent down the white steps. Drawn by an unseen force to follow the uncovered path beneath the walls of water, she continued forward. Thunder continued to shake the sky and flashes of lightning lit the indigo clouds.

IN THE CAVE ABOVE HER, many gathered. The elders, many still clothed in their nightshirts, stared in disbelief at the phenomenon happening before them.

"What is this?" One of them grumbled as his eyes remained locked on the sea ahead of them. Aela was now forty feet down and almost fifty feet away.

Bena and the other priestesses knelt on the steps just above the water level. The High Priestess responded with a tone of awe, "The Great Wave has revealed the path to the White Beach."

"Is she dead then?" Malcolm asked bluntly.

"No, she is not dead," the Phoenix Son said as he stepped lower. He stood only a few steps above the priestesses with his gaze as focused and intense as theirs.

"Has your god ever given the path to a living being before?"

"No, not in our entire history has this happened," Elder Sam answered.

"So, is she healed?" Another elder asked as the Healer Priestess pushed to the front of the crowd.

"You told us that there was no change in her condition," Malcolm turned on the priestess.

"There was none when I left her. Menony and I were reluctant to leave her because there was no change," she searched for Menony to verify her claim.

"It is true. I did not want to leave because I feared that she was even worse than before," Menony answered. She stood next to Mar.

A brilliant strike of lightning captured their attention and silenced the onlookers. The water ceased parting, and Aela stood before a wall of ocean.

SHE WAS NOT AWARE OF the thunder or the crowd as she stared into the simmering sea and saw a sight that no other living person had ever seen before. The White Beach.

Sands shimmering like thousands of diamonds spread in all directions, and beautifully polished pillars of coral lined the white

THE FAILED QUEEN

path that led further into the ocean. Floating lights gathered near the edge of the water. She stood motionless as a hand extended from one of the glowing figures.

The figure laid its palm on the surface of the water. "You are so strong, my dear sister. More powerful than you could ever know."

Her consciousness returned fully, and tears filled Aela's eyes as she listened to her brother's voice.

"Kesh?" There was no answer, but she did not need one. She put her palm against his, though she felt only water.

"Promise that you will not let the House of Gero die. Do not let our family perish," his voice pleaded.

"I don't understand, Kesh," Aela objected.

"You will. Now claim this blessing from the Great Wave and confirm for all the House of Gero's right and duty to rule. Accept the crown of Dovkey."

His hand pulled away, and the glowing figures drifted farther from her. She watched as everything faded. Even her view of the White Beach faded, and all she could see was water.

A flash of lightning and a boom of thunder drew her attention to the sky. Three walls of water loomed over her.

With tears still rolling down her cheeks, she proclaimed in a voice loud enough to carry to the people in the cave, "Great Wave, protector of Dovkey, ruler of the White Beach, give me your blessing to rule the people of Dovkey. For three hundred years the House of Gero has protected your people and made the land you guard peaceful and prosperous."

The sky boomed and water shook all around Aela. "I, Queen Aela Vantia Gero, daughter to King Ingrand and sister to King Kesh claim with the blessing of the Great Wave the crown of Dovkey."

Lightning hit the water, sending great waves in every direction. The flash was so bright that the crowd in the cave was forced to look away. Only a few looked back in time to witness the walls of water collapse onto Aela.

"OH, GREAT WAVE, NO," Menony whispered as she watched in horror. Water flooded into the cave, wetting even those who stood on the higher steps.

"What happened?" Malcolm asked as he opened his eyes. However, he did not need the answer as he looked out over the still sea.

"She went all the way out there to die?" Aluz asked with disbelief. He waded into the water to search for a body. "It does not make sense," he said to himself. "There can be no reason why your god would allow her to claim the throne and then..." he could not finish the sentence.

"He gave her just enough strength to let her and her house die in glory," Ishea said, though none seemed to be listening to her.

"Look," Menony yelled as Aela's body surfaced. Before the elders could reach her, Mar had already waded fully into the water and guided her to the stairs. Sey stood far down on the steps as the water reached his waist. He lifted her body from the sea.

Before anyone could ask the dreaded question, Berto, who stood nearest to them, exclaimed, "She's breathing. Thank the Great Wave, she's breathing!"

A chorus of relief filled the cave as Sey climbed the steps out of the water. He held Aela's dripping form close to him. The remaining members of the queen's guard closed in around Sey, Aela, and Menony. Together, they left the cave, leaving a group of stunned and relieved onlookers.

Berto turned to the man beside him and said in a voice that only the two of them could hear, "You wanted signs; I believe that was a sign from the Great Wave himself that we have the right queen."

Chapter 24

Aela opened her eyes to the beautiful glow of the indigo sky. A sea breeze blew through the open windows, welcoming her back to good health. She closed her eyes again and breathed in the salty air. A soft shuffling sound from somewhere in the room revealed the presence of another. "Menony?" she called softly.

Her friend sniffled as she started to close the window nearest to Aela.

"No, leave it open. This room is so hot," her voice was soft as she smiled at Menony. Tears gathered in her friend's eyes.

"We were terrified, Aela. I feared that..." She attempted to smile, "but we are just relieved now that you are better." She sat on the bed beside Aela and kissed her friend's hand.

Aela gathered Menony in her arms and held her as sobs wrecked Menony's body. Her hands gripped Aela almost painfully. Minutes passed before she was done.

Pulling away, Menony wiped under her eyes.

"How long have I been out?" Aela asked with concern. "It must be early afternoon."

"It is. You've been asleep for about six hours." She bent down to help Aela stand. However, Aela's expression turned blank as she paused.

"I went to the White Beach last night," she whispered. "I saw Kesh."

"You did?" Menony suddenly grew very pale and knelt before her. Aela reached out to steady her.

"Are you alright?" She asked.

Menony nodded and asked in a whisper, "What did he say to you?"

"He told me to claim the throne... and he told me not to let our family die." She looked at Menony and saw tears streaming down her cheeks. She turned to her friend and held Menony's face in her hands. "What is it?"

"I'm so happy that you were able to see him. After everything that you have been through, it was a great kindness you deserved. I'm truly happy it happened." She wiped the tears from her face and managed to smile.

"Oh, Ony, what would I do without you?" She stared tenderly at her friend before pulling her into another hug.

Menony brushed away the tears. "Let's get you dressed and call for some food." They steadied each other as they stood and walked towards the vanity.

"What was it?" Aela asked hesitantly as they moved past the tub. "What happened in the water?"

Menony eyed her with curiosity. "You don't know?"

Aela shook her head.

"An ice spell was in the bath water. Your body couldn't keep any heat. The spell prevented you from warming up even though we had a huge fire and candles all throughout the room. Eventually, you would have frozen to death."

"Ice, yes, I remember that now," Aela said to herself.

"Well, Ishea arrived. She was on her way here already, and she tended to you." Menony paused to watch the queen's reaction.

"Why?" Aela's expression darkened.

"Because she is the Healer Priestess, and they said she had experience dealing with something similar."

"Something similar to an ice curse?"

Menony shrugged at her irritated question. "She stayed with you the night before and almost all yesterday. Late last night, she and I left to get some rest, and the next thing we knew you were walking the path to the White Beach."

"That's good," Aela said to herself. "Let everyone believe that it was Ishea who cured me. There'll be fewer questions that way," she commented thoughtfully.

"Wasn't it Ishea who saved you?" Menony asked slowly.

"It's hazy. I can only remember flashes of images. But then fire broke through the ice." She turned to Menony and said firmly, "It was not Ishea who removed the spell."

"Who was it?" Menony leaned forward.

"It must have happened sometime after you left. Someone came into the room. He came to me, and I cannot remember what he said, but I know that his voice was the first I had heard in a long time. I was carried from my bed, and there was fire all over me."

"All over you?" Menony asked with alarm.

"I cannot remember everything. All I have are the bits and pieces, like the remnants of a dream." She paused, collecting as many details as she could. "He spread a blanket of fire over me and it burned on my skin, but it did not burn me." She had a far-off look in her eyes as she relived the night's events. "My body absorbed the fire, and the fire must have broken the ice spell.

"He whispered something in my ear, and then I was standing in the water on the steps. It parted for me, and I saw the entire stairway to the White Path. I didn't think. I just walked and walked until there was a wall of water in front of me. I saw the White Beach and the souls of those who have gone. That's when I saw Kesh. The rest is a blur."

"I know the rest. You claimed your right to rule, lightning struck the sea, and the water fell all around you. Mar retrieved your body from the sea, and to the surprise of all of us, you were alive. We brought you back, and you slept the rest of the morning."

"I am the rightful ruler of Dovkey," Aela whispered the words.

"You were always the rightful ruler."

"Yes, but now no one can challenge it. Not now that the Great Wave has sanctioned it."

"All thanks to a mysterious man," Menony added. She watched Aela's face wrinkle with thought. "Who was he?"

"I don't know. I did not see his face, but his voice... it lingers on the edge of consciousness. I cannot retrieve it, but it is there. I have a feeling of who it might be."

SEVERAL HOURS LATER, Aela emerged from her chamber to find all four of her guards waiting. Mar stepped forward; his arm crossed over his chest as he bowed deeply to her.

"You were worried, weren't you?" Aela asked softly. Though no response answered, she knew it to be true. She touched his shoulder.

"We failed you," came a deep reply.

"Of course, you didn't. There was nothing that you could have done to prevent it. None of us guessed that the wrangrent was already so close. You kept me safe while I was ill though."

"It was not the Healer Priestess that healed you."

Aela's face tightened as it always did when she thought of Ishea. "No, it was not."

Mar stood before her, but it was Sey who spoke. "To the Frin'geren's room?"

Aela smiled. "Yes, that's exactly where I want to go."

ELDER BERTO INTERCEPTED her on the way to Tarr's room. The elder wore a smile of genuine relief as she approached him. "I cannot tell you the relief I feel now that you have recovered, my queen."

Aela smiled in return. "Thank you, Elder Berto. I too am relieved."

"Many are curious about your recovery and your trip to the White Beach."

"I am told that Ishea saw to my care while I was under the influence of the spell. I can only assume that it was her talent for healing that saved me. I do not remember much, but I can tell you that I do remember the deathly cold.

"Then, without reason, my body began to warm. It must have been Ishea's counterspell taking effect. I awoke with only the thought of getting to the stairs. When I got there, the water began to part, and I was overtaken by the presence of the Great Wave. I know that it was He who led my feet. The rest you saw for yourselves."

"Did you see the White Beach?" Berto asked quietly, still in awe of what had happened.

"No, I saw only water."

His expression briefly showed a hint of disappointment. "Nonetheless, we have much to be thankful for, especially Ishea's timely arrival."

"Yes, I am most grateful." The words did not come easily for Aela, but she managed to make them convincing.

The elder's smile faded. "I do not wish to burden you with such things when are you still recovering, Your Majesty..."

"Please, I wish to know what concerns you, Elder."

He hesitated. "Despite our best efforts, word of Masia's destruction and your illness has spread throughout the country. A civilian army has started to gather, my queen."

"Truly?"

"Yes. Many of them have already arrived at the palace. The elders have met only once with a man named Tevor, who has been appointed as their leader."

"I know Captain Tevor. He sailed with me to Masia. What happened at this meeting?"

Berto cleared his throat. "There was much debate on the issue; however, it was decided that an army is not needed at this time."

"Oh?" She was careful to keep the anger out of her voice.

"I do not agree with the decision, Your Majesty, but I'm afraid that I and those who agree with me were outvoted. Most of the elders do not feel that there is sufficient enough threat to warrant the creation of an army."

"What about Masia? What about the ice curse? Surely, they see now that there is a wrangrent in Dovkey."

"I'm afraid, my queen, that the Phoenix Son has convinced many of the elders that these two things might not be connected and that the events of late do not necessarily indicate the presence of a wrangrent."

Heat crept into her cheeks. With a deep breath, she contained her temper. "They are fools, Berto, to ignore this danger."

She knew what she asked for next was a risk. "Elder Berto, I need you to do something for me."

"Of course, my queen."

"I want to meet with the army and Captain Tevor. Can you see to it that they are not dismissed until I have an opportunity to talk with him?"

"The elders have already dismissed them, but they will not leave until they have talked with you. They are loyal to the queen only. But, a word of warning, my queen, it is against the law for you to command an army without the inclusion of the elders. Do not give them a reason to try you. With the happenings of this morning, the elders cannot move against you without cause."

Aela watched Berto carefully. She saw only loyalty in his eyes. "Thank you. Tell no one of this conversation."

He nodded and assured her that he would arrange a meeting with Tevor. He wished her a good night before leaving.

"They will persecute you to the fullest," Mar said behind her as if he knew that she was presently contemplating how to best use this civilian army for Dovkey.

"I will have to be very careful."

The grunt of approval from her guards as they continued to Tarr's room made her smile.

HE OPENED THE DOOR at the first knock. "I thought our time together was done," he said with a smile.

Sey stared down at him and responded with what might have been a laugh. "The queen would see you."

"Would she? Well, I am always available for the queen," sarcasm laced his tone.

Sey stepped aside. Aela stood with the other three guards surrounding her. She stared at him as if years had passed since their last encounter. Quietly, she asked, "May I come in?"

His eyes took in the sight of her like she was a lush oasis in the middle of the desert. She felt the heat of his gaze like the fire that had broken the ice spell, consuming and ardent.

"You look well." The roughened edge of his voice was like an accelerant, and she felt her body warm even more.

"I am well...thank you, Tarr."

He revealed nothing, merely stepped inside and gestured for her to enter. The guards waited outside.

Tarr's room was larger than the first one she had visited. The great windows across from her were open and looked out on the river. A cluster of candles illuminated the sitting area with two sofas and a glass table. To the left, she could see into the bedroom where the lanterns she had seen last time burned with a soft glow.

Aela turned back to Tarr. He studied her with his unreadable eyes. She felt exposed and wished desperately that his face would betray some emotion, any emotion. Unable to hold his impenetrable stare, her eyes wandered down his body. The loose white shirt he wore opened at the neck, revealing the upper half of his chest. Tight black pants clothed his legs, and his feet were bare. His state of undress stirred unfamiliar feelings of longing.

"Is this an official visit, my queen?" he asked, drawing her attention back to his dark eyes.

"It's not meant to be," she said simply, neither her voice nor her expression revealing her thoughts or emotions. She watched the corner of his mouth twitch in irritation at her vague answer.

"Well, let's have a drink then."

He sauntered into the other room. Aela could hear him rustling in his chest for something. After a few minutes, he returned, carrying a cloth-wrapped bundle. Gently, Tarr slide the cloth down to reveal a bottle of light brown liquid.

"What is that?" she asked as she sat on one of the sofas.

Tarr smiled. "This is Domean olive water. There is no drink out there stronger than this or so I've heard," he added with an expression of mock innocence.

"Are we playing a game, Tarr?" The question was harsher than she intended. His mood was mercurial, reminding her that he was a man of many secrets and hidden motivations.

His smile faded. "You have questions. I have questions. Let's share the bottle while we take turns asking our questions."

"Do you agree that there are no terms on what questions can and cannot be asked?"

He nodded.

THE FAILED QUEEN

She watched as he poured two glasses of olive water. The clear, brown liquid carried a briny smell. He set one of the glasses in front of her and took the seat opposite her.

Raising his glass, "To your health... my queen." He appeared relaxed, but his eyes focused intently on her, and his smile was shallow.

Aela raised her glass to him and took a drink. It tasted as horrible as she had heard it described, and it reminded her of seawater. She set the glass down and found Tarr staring at her over the rim of his glass.

"It gets better the more you have," he laughed at her sour expression. "I will let you ask the first question." He stared at her in silence before lowering his drink. "Have you ever been drunk before?"

Aela could not keep from laughing. "Yes, I have. Why? Were you hoping to get me drunk?"

He had a sudden look of disappointment that caused another eruption of laughter from Aela.

"Yes, I was." He seemed surprised by his answer as if that was not what he had intended to say. "Have you played cards, gambled, and whored the night away too?"

Aela smiled as she took another drink. "Cards yes, gambling yes... 'whored the night away,' most definitely not." He seemed pleased by her mirth.

"I am surprised," Tarr said as he finished his glass and poured them both another drink.

Aela stared intently at his glass and then at her own.

"I promise I poured equal amounts into each," Tarr teased.

Aela looked at him thoughtfully. "Did you break the ice spell, Tarr?"

He took a drink, but his eyes never left hers. "Would it matter if I did?"

"You cannot answer with a question."

"I would be admitting to breaking the law."

Aela grunted and looked down at the liquor in her hand, "That has never concerned you before." Only two fingers in, and she could feel the tingling effects of the Domean olive water.

Tarr peered into his drink as if the answer lay at the bottom of his cup. With a heavy sigh, he put the glass down, "I find that I cannot lie...yes, I broke the ice spell."

"How did-"

"Oh, no," he said with a smile as he leaned forward, "it's not your turn anymore." He ran his finger slowly over the rim of his cup. "Where are your guards from?"

Aela blinked in surprise at the question and started to say something but found the words would not come out. Many times, she had answered this question with a carefully crafted lie, but her tongue refused to voice the falsehood. She took a drink and tried again. Still, she couldn't find her voice. She relented and told him the barest form of the truth. "They came from the sea."

Tarr raised an eyebrow at the brevity of her answer.

"How did you break the ice spell?" she pushed on before he could ask another question.

"With fire magic. How did they come to be your guards?"

Now, they were playing a game. "I agreed to watch over them, and they chose to serve as my guards in exchange."

"Aela," Tarr said in an annoyed voice.

"What did you wager in Seer's Fortune?" She leaned into the space between them.

Tarr stared intensely at her before sitting back. "Ask a different question. Seeing as I cannot lie, and I refuse to tell you what it was, I simply won't answer the question."

"Why won't you answer it?"

"Because I swore to Kesh that I would never tell you. Why is it that I can't lie, Aela?"

"I would assume it is for the same reason that I can't." They stared at each other.

"Where's yours?"

Aela hesitated, "There's a truth spell in your Domean water."

"I didn't realize you were capable of that," he sounded surprised and impressed.

Aela scoffed but did not look offended. "I did complete the priestess training. Priestesses served as judges once upon a time in Dovkey; the truth spell is still taught though we no longer assist in trials. Where is yours?"

"The candles," he said with a look down. "Aren't we a trusting pair?"

Aela held her cup in both hands looking at what remained of her drink. She looked up again and sought his eyes. "Can I trust you, Tarr?" She had not meant to pour all the vulnerability she felt into the question, but it had seeped out, nonetheless.

"Yes," he said without pause. "Do you?"

"Yes," she responded just as quickly.

"You're in danger, Aela. That was not an insignificant spell. A great deal of power was put behind it and a great deal of malevolence too. The wrangrent is determined to harm you. I don't think that it is any coincidence that Masia was attacked."

"Yes, I know. I cannot figure out if it was destroyed to hurt me, or if I was supposed to be there when the city was destroyed."

"I would venture to say that it was intended for you to die in Masia, and when you didn't, the curse was employed." Aela nodded. "Surely, you suspect by now that the wrangrent is here in the palace."

"Or has an accomplice in the palace." She covered her face with her hands and let out a frustrated groan. "I don't know how to uncover this threat though. Mar and the others are more determined than ever to never let me out of their sight. Sey refuses to leave me. I don't like that you have no one with you."

Tarr laughed. "I can take care of myself. Don't worry about me. Frankly, I'm relieved that they will all be watching out for you. Be careful of any water you encounter. Don't accept drinks from anyone." Aela raised a brow as she stared pointedly at him.

He smiled and winked in response. "Unless they're from me."

Aela's faint smile faded. "I don't know what to do, Tarr. I had hoped that the Phoenix Son would contact the Immortal Council, but I have not heard any news. I don't even know if he did. But why wouldn't he? It must be apparent now."

"I don't trust Aluz."

"Why?"

"Gut feeling. Something about him has never felt right. There are other ways to contact the Council. I know someone who could get a message to them."

"Do it. They are needed here; we cannot take on a wrangrent alone."

Tarr nodded. "I'll have to leave the palace for a few days."

"I'll convince Sey to go with you."

"No, all your guards need to stay with you. Besides, I can move faster and attract less notice if I go alone." He stood. "I'll leave tonight. I might be able to return by midday the day after tomorrow."

Aela stood also and took steps towards him, her balance slightly off. His hands on her arms steadied her. "Be safe...and return quickly."

He smiled before pulling her against him. His lips were on hers, kissing her with such passion she felt her body melt from it. Even as her balance wavered, his strong arms held her tight. Need flared to life, and she allowed herself to feel it as she pushed all the fears away.

Years of indoctrination had made her cold and closed off, subjecting her to loneliness of the deepest kind. In Tarr's arms with his lips on hers, she wanted to experience the intimacy of surrendering to another. She longed to be only a woman with wants and needs. As he deepened the kiss and his hands began roaming over the curves of her body, she let go of all thought and just experienced the ecstasy of his touch.

FROM THE FIRST MOMENT, he had wanted her. She was a promise made to his closest friend, a task that needed to be accomplished. However, she had become an answer to a prayer he had not known he had made. She was the fulfillment of a dream that he locked away years ago. The desire for her had only deepened. It burned hotter within him with every moment he spent with her. Need took on new meaning with this woman.

Seeing her frozen and dying had broken something inside him. He felt fear, unlike anything he had ever experienced. Unable to watch her slowly succumb to death, he used his fire magic. Unsure if it would work, he had desperately filled her body with flame and heat, praying to any god that would listen for success. When the glow of health had returned to her skin he had taken his first breath of relief.

The wager in Seer's Fortune was meant to ensure that he could stay close to her for as long as needed. Tarr had always intended to release her from it when the threat Kesh had foreseen resolved. Now, he knew he could no more step away from this woman than he could stop breathing. That realization terrified him.

He broke the kiss and pressed his forehead against hers. "You almost died," he whispered the words.

"I did," she breathed into the space between them. "But you wouldn't let me."

"Never."

He closed his eyes and absorbed the smell of her, the warmth of her skin, the faint buzz of magic that now radiated from her body.

He would happily stand there forever feeling her healthy and safe in his arms.

She pulled away, and he opened his eyes to look down into her gray eyes. Her hands cradled his face as she slowly brought her lips to his. He allowed her to control the kiss, though he felt the desperate desire to consume her in every way.

Aela's hands moved from his face down to his shoulders, and her arms wrapped around his neck as she pulled her body tighter to his. His hands gripped her hips. They ached to explore every inch of her, but he kept them still, not wanting to push her.

She whispered, "I want you. I want to feel your touch everywhere. I want..." She smiled. "I'm not even sure what all I want."

He smiled, perfectly ready to give her what she knew she wanted and all the things she did not know yet to want.

"Then I'll just have to give you everything, my queen."

His lips gently kissed her temple before trailing down her cheek to her jaw. Her eyes closed with a sigh, and her head tilted to the side, giving him access to the graceful column of her neck. He continued placing soft kisses on her porcelain skin as he traveled down her neck to her collarbones. His lips brushed against the strap of her dress.

He wanted her skin bare, wanted it against his bare skin. He took a step back and smiled when her eyes stared at him with confusion. Reaching behind him, he grabbed the linen shirt and pulled it over his head, exposing his chest to her. Her confusion turned to appreciation as her eyes surveyed his exposed body.

With tentative hands she reached for him, shying away just before making contact. He felt a slight tremor in her hands as he grasped them and placed them on his body. Slowly, her fingers skimmed the planes of his chest, tangling briefly in the patches of dark hair. Her touch was tantalizing and teasing in its gentleness. As her fingers coasted over his nipples and then his abdomen to where a trail of hair led under his pants, he stepped closer, stilling her exploration.

His fingers traced smooth lines up her arms to the straps of her dress. He paused to look at her. Seeing only need and eagerness, he carefully pushed the dress off both shoulders. The weight of the garment pulled it down her body to pool on the floor. She loosened the tie on the short drawers and pushed them to the floor to join her dress.

His eyes feasted hungrily on the sight of her naked body. Her breasts were small and tipped with pink nipples. The elegant lines of her torso curved in at the waist and flared at the hips before tapering to long, beautiful legs.

Tarr wrapped his arms around her as he kissed her roughly. She responded with a need equal to his as she circled her arms around his neck. His hands glided down her back until he clasped both buttocks in his hands. He lifted her then, and without instruction, she wrapped her legs around his hips.

He carried her into the other room and laid her out on the bed. Staring down at her uncovered body, he breathed one word, "Beautiful."

The smile she gave in return was breathtaking.

He leaned over the bed with a dark smile on his face. "I'm going to worship every part of your body." And then, he proceeded to do just that.

With lips, tongue, and teeth, he lavished attention on every inch of her starting at her mouth and down to her feet. She made soft sounds of pleasure as he loved her breasts, and Tarr smiled at the thought of making her lose her restraint. He imagined with excitement the sounds she would make when she finally let go completely.

When his lips settled between her legs, her body tightened.

He stroked the inside of her thighs, "Trust me?"

"Yes," she sighed.

With a smile, he proceeded to bring her to climax with his tongue and fingers. She arched her long body and moaned softly as pleasure overwhelmed her.

He stood above the bed, taking in her relaxed state, and realized that he was never going to let her go. She was his.

THE WAVES OF PLEASURE faded slowly, and Aela realized the heat of Tarr's body was missing. She opened her heavy eyelids and found him standing next to the bed. She expected to see lust and hunger, but instead, she saw resolve and something deeper than just affection.

His gaze met hers, and she lost her breath at the look of possession in his eyes.

"Tarr," she breathed.

He smiled. "Yes, love."

His hands pushed the black pants down his body, and she watched with bated breath as his powerful body was exposed to her. She had seen a man's naked form before, but nothing could compare to the strength and pure male beauty of his body.

Tarr's knee pushed into the bed and then he was over her body crawling higher onto the bed. "I haven't finished giving you everything."

Sparks of anxiety and anticipation filled her as his lips found hers. She waited for the pain that she knew came with a woman's first time. Yet, his attentive hands and lips again explored her body with distracting enthusiasm. When he finally pushed slowly and patiently into her, she was so aroused she barely felt the pain.

And when he pushed deeper, she gasped from the intimacy of having his body within her own. Giving her time to adjust to his penetration, she found that despite the discomfort she wanted more.

She wanted all of him. The realization was quickly forgotten as he moved in and out. The tension of another orgasm built, and she finally understood how two people could forget where one began and the other ended.

IN THE AFTERGLOW OF their lovemaking, she lay with her ear pressed against his chest, listening as his heart rate slowed. His fingers never stopped moving as if the feel of her fed an insatiable hunger. He held one of her hands in his against his abdomen. She closed her eyes and simply enjoyed the feeling of being with him.

His fingers on her face and the deepness of his laugh brought her back to consciousness. "I would stay here with you in this bed forever, but I need to leave soon if I'm going to use the cover of night to my advantage."

She groaned, and he laughed again. "I'm going to take that as a testament to my skills."

"I don't think that you were ever in doubt of your skills," Aela said as she sat up and looked down at him.

He pulled her back down and rolled on top of her. "My skills are of no importance if you, my love, were not pleased beyond measure."

She smiled. "I was…pleased beyond all imagining."

He smiled as he leaned forward to kiss her. "You do know how to stroke a man's ego."

Aela sighed and moaned softly as he kissed her passionately.

"I could devour you," he said huskily against her lips.

"I think you already did."

"Again and again." He pulled back and looked at her. "Getting out of this bed may be the hardest thing I have ever done."

She laughed as he grudgingly stood, helping her up in the process. His playful demeanor grew more serious as he helped her dress. As he pushed the final strap of her dress into place, he placed a soft kiss on her shoulder before stepping away to put his pants on.

His fingers interlaced with hers as he led her to the door. She turned to tell him something, but the words were lost as he pulled her into his body and kissed her deeply once more.

He finished the kiss, leaving her breathless, and rested his forehead against hers. "I never expected this."

Neither did she, but before she could respond he took her face in his hands and tilted her face up to his. His voice was serious and commanding.

"Be alert. Your enemy could be anywhere." She nodded.

He kissed her before pulling away with obvious difficulty.

"I'll leave you to get ready," she walked to the door, his hand resting protectively at the base of her spine. She turned to him before opening the door. "You stay safe, I stay safe. Agreed?" she demanded.

"Agreed." He opened the door. Her guards waited outside.

Tarr turned to Mar. "Let no harm come to her." His expression was severe, and his voice unyielding.

Mar and the other three crossed their arms over their chests giving Tarr their vow. Aela wondered if he knew the significance of the gesture. No one other than herself had ever been given such a thing.

He acknowledged it with a nod and watched as Aela and her guards disappeared around the corner. Walking away from him might have been the hardest thing she had ever done.

Chapter 25

Aela ignored Tarr's absence and skillfully changed the subject when he was mentioned. The events at the White Beach and Masia caused a great deal of excitement and fear throughout Dovkey. Aela spent most of the following two days with the elders and priestesses addressing the public outcry. She balanced her thoughts of Dovkey with her thoughts of Tarr.

He returned two days after they had made love. His return to the palace the same way he had left it seemed to go unnoticed. However, unbeknownst to Aela, an ambush of palace guards in his room awaited him. Under orders from the elders, Tarr was detained. The elders held him under suspicion for the destruction of Masia and the attempted assassination of the queen.

No amount of arguing or pleading could change the elders' decision to imprison Tarr. Aela explained repeatedly that he could not have been responsible for the destruction of Masia as he had spent almost every moment with her on the journey there. She argued that she would have known if he was casting a spell of such magnitude. They dismissed this by pointing out that she was not capable of magic, and thus, not capable of detecting another's use of it.

She argued that he had no reason to want her dead, that it benefited him in no way. Again, the elders were ready with a rebuttal. If he was the wrangrent, he wouldn't be concerned about the trivialness of Seer's Fortune, something that had not seemed trivial only weeks before.

Aela even went so far as to testify that it was Tarr who broke the ice spell. This was met with angry objections over Aela's lack of gratitude to the Healer Priestess. They adamantly proclaimed that it was Ishea who had saved her. When they asked how she could be sure it was Tarr, she explained that he had told her himself.

The information was ultimately used against Tarr with the elders citing that his knowledge of fire magic was an admittance of guilt. Suddenly, the elders saw so clearly that Tarr had turned Masia to ash with his magic. They argued that Aela was too trusting to see it.

The Phoenix Son poured fuel on the fires this his own conjectures. The Immortal expressed his concern that the Frin'geren had deceived their vulnerable and grieving queen. That she could not see what was so plain to everyone else, that the Frin'geren had caused the death of their king, and he was now bent on the destruction of Dovkey. He argued that all the evidence pointed to Tarr, that he was the wrangrent, and the elders were now willing to acknowledge that one even existed. They hung on the Immortal's every word and expressed their gratitude repeatedly for his valued insight.

The priestesses, to her great relief, reserved judgment. They refused to accept that the Frin'geren was guilty of the crimes for which he was accused. At their insistence, a trial was arranged to try the foreign lord.

Aela stormed down the hall, having just left another meeting with the elders in which they refused to hear her defense of Tarr. Her guards trailed behind her as she rounded a corner and almost plowed into the Phoenix Son. Uncaring if he heard, she groaned with annoyance at seeing him.

He blocked her path. "Excuse me, my lord." She tried to go around him, but he succeeded in blocking her path again.

"Aela, I must speak with you." She hated his patronizing voice and the familiarity with which he said her name.

"I have things to see to." Still, he refused to move.

"It concerns the Frin'geren," his voice more forceful than before. She was angered that Tarr was referred to as 'the Frin'geren', always with a hint of disdain. Every time she heard him to referred as such, she fought to keep her temper in check. He was a lord in his own right and a person who deserved the same rights and courtesy as anyone else.

"What regarding Lord Tarr?" Her guard began to close in around her, but she stayed them with a gesture. She was curious to know what the Immortal would say.

"I can understand how confusing and frightening this must be for you, but you must come to terms with the truth. The Frin'geren is not who you think he is. He took advantage of you when you were helpless and alone. He gained your trust only to get close to you, while all along he planned destruction and death." His voice was condescendingly calm again.

"Is that what happened?" Aela asked darkly. "I'm such a weak and feeble-minded creature that he seduced me so easily?"

"You have endured many... disappointments," the word dripped with pity, "in your life. It left you susceptible."

She bristled in response to his words. "Where is the Immortal Council? Why have they not come if they're aware of the happenings here?"

Aluz's eyes narrowed just slightly, though he managed a tight smile when he spoke.

"Of course they are aware, but I have assured them that everything is in hand. We have the wrangrent in custody, and when the trial is held in three weeks' time, there will be other members of the Council here to see to his conviction."

"Why three weeks?"

"It is customary to give the accused time to prepare a defense."

"Ha, and how is a man to prepare such a defense from the confines of a cell?"

"We cannot release him, Aela. It is too dangerous. You have seen for yourself the things he is capable of." He must think her foolish indeed to believe a wrangrent could be contained by iron bars.

"And the betrothal contract? What has the Council decided regarding that? I received the blessing of the Great Wave, and I will rule as He intends."

Aluz sighed, taking the expression one does with a petulant child. "There are greater concerns right now. The contract will be addressed when other matters are resolved."

She took a step closer to him. Her eyes bore into him with all the dislike she felt, though her voice remained calm.

"You are an Immortal lord, and you may still be my betrothed, but you have no say in how my country is ruled. You have no authority to instruct me in how I will or will not conduct myself."

"I believe those very things give me the power to do just that," he said with menacing calm.

She realized that she could talk herself breathless before he would change his views. Though her temper burned with his assumptions, she knew it was best to walk away.

"Are we done?" Aela felt the thin control she had over her temper slipping.

His nostrils flared with an angry breath, but she did not wait for him to respond. As she moved around him, she felt his harsh grip on her upper arm. Her guards moved to restrain him, but she again stopped them with a gesture. The tension in their bodies conveyed their displeasure, but she would not have them detained as well for assaulting an Immortal. Aluz was not above doing such a thing. She met his gaze as he stared down at her with fire in his eyes.

"Perhaps I should instruct the elders to arrange for our wedding ceremony...in two weeks' time."

"Absolutely not," Aela said in a frosty voice.

"Would you break the contract, Aela?"

"Would you risk the wrath of Seer's Fortune?" she countered. "By Immortal Law, you cannot be bound to a ruling monarch."

His grip on her arm tightened painfully, but she refused to show any signs of discomfort. The usual warmth of his expression was gone. His eyes were like ice, clearly conveying his displeasure with her.

"There is only one thing other than a winner's refusal that nulls the terms of Seer's Fortune, and that is a conviction of an unpardonable crime. Crimes such as a wrangrent's practice of unnatural magic."

"Oh, Great Wave," Aela whispered to herself. "So, it's not just a neat way of sweeping a messy problem under the rug, but also a way to ensure that you get exactly what you want."

"I am concerned with what is best for Dovkey, and you, of course, before all other things." His voice lacked sincerity.

"Your hands are quite cold, my lord."

They both looked down to where he gripped her arm. Her skin paled under his fingers. He lifted them away, and the tint of blue in her skin faded quickly.

"Careful how you tread, Your Majesty. The elders would love nothing more than to dethrone and discard you. I am the only ally you have. It would be advisable not to offend me." His voice was as icy as his touch.

Aela stared into his fiery eyes. "I'll remember that, Phoenix Son." Without another word, she strode away from him, allowing her guards to close in on all sides. The cold lingered in her skin where he had touched. It was a familiar cold. She had felt it only days ago coursing through her entire body.

The Phoenix Son was right; she did need to tread carefully.

THE TERRIFYING AND exhausting dream left Aela breathless upon waking. The heavy pounding of her heart and the shallow, suffocating breaths held her pinned to her bed. After a few minutes of initial panic, she focused on deep breathing. Her heart rate slowed, and the movement of her chest evened until both were steady. However, her body continued to shake.

The first light of day was still hours away, but she could not return to sleep.

The moon projected eerie shapes on the walls, but the remnants of her dreams continued to haunt her. Even shutting her eyes for a moment brought an abrupt flash of images. She threw the covers off. The thin fabric of her white nightgown clung to her skin as she struggled to sit up. After pacing the room several times and failing to calm her restless thoughts, she wandered towards the room connected to hers.

Menony slept peacefully. Aela watched her chest rise and fall slowly and smiled as she gazed at her friend's tranquil face. The sight of Menony's peaceful sleep brought relief.

However, she would not find such restful sleep tonight. She feared closing her eyes again.

Menony shifted and released a soft moan. Aela hoped that her dreams were pleasant. Without making a noise, she returned to her room. Looking around the dark space, she decided she wanted to be somewhere else, anywhere else. Opening the door, she found Mar and Anut staring down at her, their concern visible in the tension of their broad shoulders.

"You are not well?" Mar asked softly.

Aela felt like a small child as she shook her head and answered, "I had unpleasant dreams."

Anut shifted his weight and straightened uncomfortably. "What is it?" she asked with alarm.

"Visions like this have come before," he said softly.

Aela looked away from both guards and stared down the dark hall before responding. "I know..."

"And unpleasant events followed," Mar quickly interjected.

Silence filled the space between them as Aela continued to stare down the hall. Few rooms existed in this part of the palace where only the royal family slept. To the right and several feet down was Kesh's room. The door had remained shut since his departure for Frin'gere.

When the nightmares so common to childhood had awoken her as a little girl, she had raced to her brother's room. She had not wanted her parents to know she was afraid; so, she would stay the night with Kesh, who always kept her secrets.

The painful ache of sorrow filled her chest as she briefly thought of running towards the closed door. *Kesh will not be there*, a cold voice inside her head said. She blinked the tears out of her eyes and looked back to the concerned guards.

"We are here to listen," Anut said.

"Or would you wait until the daylight?" the other asked.

"The light of day will not make the images less terrifying." Aela considered telling them. "Thank you, but I want to calm my nerves before I relive the dreams."

She held out her shaking hands. Anut nodded, and Mar unexpectedly encased her hands in his massive ones.

"The kitchen will hold something calming." It was dark, and though she could not see his face, Aela could sense the guard's reassuring smile.

"Sweet cream is best," Anut said from beside her. Aela smiled despite her distress.

Anut jerked his head to the left and held out his elbow. Aela slipped her arm through his and allowed him to lead her in the direction of the kitchens.

He stopped outside the darkened room and stood guard, though Aela doubted anyone would disturb her this early in the morning. The walk with Anut had calmed her considerably. They said very little to each other, but the mere presence of the calm, giant guard helped to put the terror of the dreams far from her mind. She entered the kitchen more at ease and ready to analyze her dreams for meaning.

However, she noticed a small light at the far end of the room. The dying embers of the hearth fire glowed, and the candlelight moved towards her.

"Aela?" a soft voice asked.

"Why are you here, Ishea?" Aela asked as if exhausted by the question.

Ishea appeared not to notice her tone as her smiling face became visible. "I would assume for the same reason as you. I cannot sleep."

She waited for Aela to respond but continued when it became clear that the queen had no intention of responding. "I have not seen you since you were sick. I hope that you are doing well?" She stared at Aela with concern.

Realizing that she could not escape the conversation with the priestess, Aela carefully considered her reply. "I am fine... all due to your healing." The tone of her voice did not match the pleasantness of the comment.

The priestess's expression darkened as she finally took note of the queen's coldness. "I am very relieved to hear that, though, I must admit that I was surprised by your sudden recovery. I have dealt with similar spells, and sadly, it often takes weeks for the person to recover."

And so, it begins, Aela thought.

The Healer Priestess was only a few months older than the queen; however, that had never prevented Ishea from treating Aela like a child. Many people had told Aela that the priestess was overly concerned with everyone's wellbeing. She was known to act like a worried mother caring for a sick child. Aela's father often said that Ishea's intense questioning was simply her way of showing concern. Aela had never felt comforted by the explanation.

"The Great Wave must have wished for a swift recovery and given us strength beyond our normal bounds. Who are we to question the workings of the Great Wave?" She tried to relax, but again her body was tense.

Ishea smiled radiantly, another attribute that greatly irritated Aela. The priestess was a stunning beauty with her smooth tan skin, straight hair, and soothing eyes.

"You are right. The Great Wave does do amazing things, and I am honored to be the vessel through which He wields His power. But you are also a vessel... Your Majesty."

Her musical voice was filled with sweetness. "Especially now that you are the Blessed Queen. The palace priestesses explained to me that you are the only living person to see the White Beach," she whispered the name with awe.

"I'm afraid that's not entirely true." Upon seeing Ishea's confusion, Aela explained, "I did not see the White Beach. I saw only the wall of water in front of me."

"Ah," Ishea's expression became thoughtful. "What led you to the sea? When I left your room, you were completely unresponsive. How did you feel upon awakening?" Her intense stare was almost too much for Aela.

"I'm sorry, Ishea, but may we continue this conversation at another time? I was hoping to find something that would help me return to sleep. I trust that you of all people understand how important sleep is to my full recovery."

"Yes, it is exceedingly important. I have many sleeping drafts with me. Would you like me to retrieve one for you?" Ishea offered eagerly.

"No... thank you." Aela wanted nothing from her cousin. "I think that a glass of milk will be sufficient." Her response was far too quick, so she tried to amend it with, "Thank you, Ishea, but please do not let me keep you from sleep any longer."

"I will retire only if you promise to find time tomorrow for a quick assessment. I want to ensure that there are no lingering effects of the spell."

"Of course," Aela almost breathed a sigh of relief as she managed a regal smile.

Ishea's smile faded, and her expression became very serious. "Aela," she began tenderly as she placed her hands on Aela's shoulders, "I am only trying to help you. I know that you have often felt threatened by me, but I only do what I do out of service to my country and my queen." She smiled dimly. "Good night, my queen." With a bow, she left the kitchen.

The confrontation with Ishea left Aela feeling more unnerved, and she realized that there was only one person she wanted to talk to.

TARR'S CELL WAS HEAVILY fortified, and his anxious guards explained that visitors were forbidden. Aela reminded them with unquestioning authority that she was the Queen of Dovkey. If she wished to see the prisoner, she would see the prisoner. Between her threatening tone and the towering figures who accompanied her, the guards allowed her to enter the dungeon cells.

He was in the second cell on the right. Light from a blazing torch hung on the opposite wall and moonlight spilled through the bars. As Aela approached, she felt the wards cast by the priestesses. The familiar feeling of water in the magic. She stepped through them and encountered another ward; this one was burning cold, so much like Aluz's touch during their encounter the day before. She knew immediately he had cast the second ward. As she stepped through it, she felt the chills up and down her spine, far too similar to the ice spell.

First, she saw his fingers reach out and wrap around the bars and then his face, which looked ghostly in the moonlight.

"I was told there would be no visitors," Tarr said as he smiled at her.

His eyes drank in the sight of her beautiful face. He had not seen it for days, and he realized he was starved for contact with her. However, as he looked closer, he saw the signs of missed sleep and rising stress. He angered knowing that what she faced outside these bars was equally as unpleasant as his experiences behind them.

"I'm the queen," she said with authority. His smile deepened at the confidence with which she spoke the words.

"Damn right, you are."

Her smile was radiant.

"I brought you something."

"A key? A way to disengage the wards?"

"If you were truly the wrangrent, those wards would not be able to keep you in," she said with disdain.

"You walked through them without difficulty."

"They are not set against me." Sadness filled her response.

"Why are you here, Aela?" his voice was low and soft.

She approached the bars. Her eyes darkened with sorrow as she looked around the cell.

"I can't get you out of here. I have argued with the elders but nothing-" she stopped at the sound of his mirthless laugh.

"No, I wouldn't expect you to be able to. They've decided that I am a danger...and a convenient scapegoat."

"I should have seen this coming."

Tarr reached out to run his finger across her cheek. Her skin was cold, chilled by the heatless dungeon.

"You couldn't have stopped it."

Aela stepped closer to him, seeking comfort in his touch. Their bodies pressed against either side of the bars. Her eyes closed for a moment as he stroked the side of her face.

"I had a dream tonight. It was like the vision of Masia." The words were a whisper.

His hands moved down to her arms, and he continued to stroke lightly. Her body relaxed at his touch.

"There was fire and destruction, people crying out in pain. I felt like I was surrounded by a cloud of smoke so thick that I couldn't get through it even if I had been able to move."

"You couldn't move?"

"No. I could just hear people dying and then, in some moments the smoke would clear, and I could see the terror around me."

Her eyes popped open, and he saw the terror. She looked away as the images resurfaced in her head.

"How were the people dying?" Aela barely noticed his hand cupping her face. He gently pulled her gaze back to his.

"Some of them were choking on the smoke, I think. Others were burned by the fire. They tried to put out those who were on fire, but the flames wouldn't go out no matter how much water they threw onto them." Her voice and expression were distant. "Those poor people, fighting the fire and the smoke and the men dressed in black and orange."

"There were men dressed in black and orange?" The eagerness of Tarr's question caught Aela's attention.

"Yes, does that mean something to you?"

"Many parts of Frin'gere carry banners of orange and black. What else?"

"There were two children. Those two children," she whispered to herself.

His body immediately went rigid. "What about the children? Were they hurt?" His intense curiosity unsettled her.

"I don't know. I woke up before I saw what happened to them."

"What did you see of them? Was someone after them?" Unconsciously, his grip on her tightened. When she winced, he forced himself to relax.

"I don't know," she said with more frustration than expected. "I just got images of them, two little boys staring at me, with a fountain behind them."

She paused. "The fountain," she whispered to herself.

"What about the fountain?" He asked as her gaze became unfocused.

"I'd forgotten that. It's important...somehow."

Aela stared into Tarr's eyes. Her stare was focused and wary. "What is so important about those children?" She used a stern voice, one that exuded her authority as queen.

He met her stare as his hand continued to caress her cheek.

"Don't lie to me, Tarr." He hated that her trust in him was threatened for even a second.

"I'm not sure I understand what your dream means."

Her eyes narrowed. "The wrangrent is going to attack a city... if he hasn't already."

"Yes, I understand that part," he said with a weak smile. "I don't understand the children."

"I think they are important, but I don't know why."

He hesitated. The secret was not his to tell, but with her newest vision, it was paramount that she knew. "You need to tell Menony of this."

"Why?" She looked at him in confusion as she realized he knew something she did not.

"I know of one child, but not the other. Menony will know what the second one means."

She pulled back from him. Her expression was full of pain, and he wished desperately that he could have spared her. She swallowed once and then twice. He watched as she struggled to respond.

"Aela," Tarr began softly as he cradled her face in both his hands, "Kesh was married to Menony, and together, they had a child. That child is in Shuesh right now."

"No, no," Aela shook her head in denial even as she tried to pull away from him. "Why would they keep such a secret? Why would they not tell me?"

He hated the look of betrayal in her eyes. "I was sworn to secrecy. Believe me, I did not want to keep this or any other secret from you."

She continued to pull away. "How could I not know?"

Tears slipped down her face.

"They didn't want anyone to know. Kesh said it was safer for Menony and the baby," Tarr tried to comfort.

"How do you know?"

Every word he said was a stab to her heart, but he refused to keep anything more from her. "My brother was a witness at their wedding. I met Kesh through him. Years ago, Kesh brought a Dovkeyen woman to my brother's home. He told Jathe, my brother, that she was Kesh's cousin and needed a safe place to hide. He did not mention at the time that she was also my brother's future wife...but Jathe figured that out soon enough," Tarr smiled at the memory.

"Aine?"

He nodded. "Yes."

"All this time, she's been in Frin'gere, married to your brother?"

Again, he nodded. "I have three nieces."

Her head dipped as she tried to contain the sobs.

"She and Kesh saw something of the future all those years ago, and they knew that she would not be safe in Dovkey. I don't know what they saw. Neither would ever say."

Aela sobbed harder, her body leaning heavily on the bars. Tarr's arms came around her, keeping her on her feet.

"So many secrets! So many." She sobbed until her breaths turned to gasps. He held her as best he could while offering comfort through his touch.

"The child, oh Great Wave, the child!" She cried as she pulled away from Tarr. She ripped herself from his arms.

"The child is in Shuesh, and that is where the wrangrent means to attack next. My nephew! I must stop him. I have to protect the child!"

"Aela, wait!" Tarr called as she pulled away, but with the bars between them, he could not keep ahold of her. "Those men that you saw, the ones in orange and black…Aela, please come back!" He called as she rushed back down the hall. His words were lost. She was too far to hear. With frustration, he slammed his hand against the bars.

Chapter 26

The secret felt like a betrayal even as she wanted to deny it. However, Aela knew in her heart that it was true. The older of the boys she had seen in her vision was around four years old. She remembered four years ago, Menony had gone to Shuesh to take care of her ailing mother. Six months she had been gone. Enough time to finish a hidden pregnancy and give birth.

Other incidences came to mind. The looks that had often passed between Kesh and Menony. Aela had always thought them to be looks of concern regarding her, but now she cursed her foolishness. She remembered the grief and pain in Menony's face when Kesh had returned on the black ship.

Mar and Anut remained silent as she returned to her room. She wondered if they had suspected when she had not.

Menony stood in the center of the room, one of the queen's robes draped over her arm. She looked up when Aela entered and smiled at the queen.

"I couldn't sleep so I thought that I would check on you, but you were up before I was. The guards were gone with you, so I assumed all was well. I haven't been able to sleep well lately. I'm sure whatever it is will pass soon though."

She talked as she continued to arrange the disorder of Aela's room. Aela wondered how she had never noticed before the maternal softness of Menony's voice. Her friend had always been attentive and supportive, but in the last few years, her demeanor had turned more nurturing.

Aela stood with her back to the door studying this woman who had been her closest friend for so many years.

Menony looked at her with concern. "Are you okay?"

Whatever she saw, alarmed her. She dropped the garments in her hands onto a nearby chair and approached the queen.

"What's wrong? Is it the ice spell? Are you feeling its effects again?" Her hands hovered over Aela, wanting to give comfort but wary.

"I had another vision. This time of Shuesh. The wrangrent will attack there next." Aela watched as the color drained from Menony's face.

"There were two children in my dream. Two little boys. Tarr said that he knew one of them."

Menony's eyes teared, and her shaking hands went to her belly. Aela's eyes followed their movement.

"You won't feel better for another few months, will you, Ony?" Tears formed in Aela's eyes.

"I'm sorry I couldn't tell you. I wanted to, but Kesh said it wasn't safe. I'm so sorry, Aela."

They stared at each other in silence for several long moments. Aela closed the distance between them. She gently laid her hands on Menony's abdomen, and she felt the small swell. She placed one on each side and gently rubbed her hands around.

A brief flash of a soft pink background filled her head as she closed her eyes and the gentle thudding of a small heartbeat against her hands. She opened her eyes as she looked at Menony.

"Do you remember when I told you about one of my first visions? A baby was crying, your baby... Kesh's baby," Aela said softly.

She knelt before Menony and rested her ear on her pregnant belly. She listened to the soft thudding as grief consumed her. All the pain, all the fear, and all the sorrow poured out of her as Menony gently cradled Aela's head against her body.

AELA WANTED TO SPEND hours with Menony hearing stories of her and Kesh, of her nephew. However, her vision failed to give any clue as to when the attack on Shuesh would happen. She knew she had to act quickly if she was going to protect the city and her last remaining family.

Convinced they had the wrangrent imprisoned already, the elders would be of no aid to her. She knew the risk she took by not involving them, but she would not allow for their incompetence to delay action. Their continued reliance on the Phoenix Son concerned her.

She did not trust him.

Her steps were silent as she hurried down the hall, but Anut had no trouble keeping up with her. They walked in silence.

The image of the fountain repeatedly flashed in her head until she was sure that it was the same one she had seen when she was eleven. It stood in front of the healing temple, a place of learning for young priestesses. Her mother took Aela there before contracting the fever. It was one of the last memories she had of her before the illness.

Aela could see her mother so clearly still; a tall, beautiful woman with cascading hair of gold and honey. Her soft brown eyes and warm smile instilled a comfort in everyone she met. A kind woman who never forgot that kindness sometimes had the greatest healing power, Princess Vantia had been a goddess in her daughter's eyes. On that visit to the temple, an eleven-year-old Aela wanted nothing more than to become one of the priestesses just as her mother had once been.

The fountain was ancient and built before the White Palace. Shuesh was the site where the Great Wave first appeared to the people of Dovkey even before they had reached the sea. It was built over the spring of water, said to be sent by the god. However, water had long ceased to flow from the stone. The circular foundation was cracked, and the entire structure was stained a pale gray by time. Nevertheless, the fountain was revered, and the young priestesses of the temple dutifully tended to it.

It was the pride of Shuesh, just as pearls had been the pride of Masia. Shuesh represented Dovkey's longstanding relationship with the Great Wave and the power he gave to his chosen followers. That pride and significance made Shuesh a prime target for the wrangrent.

"Shuesh is a place of great spirit," Anut said as if he could read her thoughts.

"Yes, I'm sure that is one of the reasons that the wrangrent plans to attack it. There are many young priestesses in training there as well."

She refused to voice the other reason she feared Shuesh was targeted. She would not say out loud that she feared the wrangrant also knew of the Dovkeyen heir that secretly lived in the oasis city.

After leaving Menony in the early morning hours, she told her guards of her dreams and the two children she saw. It had not been a surprise to them that Menony was with child; however, none of them seemed to have known that Kesh was the father.

Menony had agreed to seek out Elder Berto, her movement around the palace being less conspicuous than that of Aela's guards. By noon, Menony returned with a message that conveyed that Captain Tevor would meet with Aela at dusk. She arranged for one of her guards to meet him outside the palace and ensure his coming and going went unseen.

Along with arranging the meeting with the civilian captain, Berto had sent a message of warning and informed Aela that the elders were being pushed by Aluz to try Tarr within the week.

Berto was not hopeful as to the Frin'geren's fate. The Phoenix Son planned to aggressively prosecute Tarr regardless of his innocence, but Aela knew that she would not allow them to try Tarr. The elders followed the Immortal in blind faith. They desperately clung to the hope that convicting Tarr would make the horrible threat of a wrangrent go away. Even now, she had Sey secretly watching Tarr. The guard was prepared to implement her escape plan for Tarr if the elders moved too soon.

She split her guards despite their refusals. Sey was assigned to Tarr, Ter to Menony and Anut with her. Mar had been sent on a special mission. After which, he would escort the captain to their meeting.

So many plans to organize and execute, Aela thought as she headed towards the assigned meeting place. She had chosen the temple pools. It felt like the only safe place in the palace, the only place uncorrupted by the elders and the Phoenix Son. It was also the only place that guaranteed complete secrecy. She trusted Anut to ensure that they were not followed as she took the familiar path to the ancient room.

Mar and the captain awaited her as she entered. Anut stood guard outside while Mar stayed inside.

The captain ran a hand through his dark brown hair as he stared at the room in wonder. Aela studied him silently. The faint lines around his eyes told that he was not as young as he appeared from a distance; however, he could not be more than forty years old.

"You are now captain of a civilian army?" she asked as she approached. His gaze shifted swiftly to her, and she was satisfied to see the intelligence in his blue eyes.

He bowed deeply. "Yes, Your Majesty. I speak for the men gathered in your service."

"Why have you gathered outside the White Palace?"

A flash of confusion showed before he answered. "I witnessed for myself what happened at Masia. I stood through the storm that proceeded our arrival."

She knew from the darkening of his expression and the sudden grief in his eyes that he was remembering the ash city. "I have seen things that I never thought possible," he said softly.

"The things that happened in Masia should never be," she said gravely.

"Many are dead, many more are gone without a trace of their bodies. It was nothing but ashes, everywhere."

He stared at the waters of the temple pools. "Something very evil attacked there. I don't think that it will stop at Masia."

"No, it won't. The destruction at Masia is the work of a wrangrent."

"Many share this fear, Your Majesty. And when word spread of the curse that befell you, even more, questioned what was happening in Dovkey." He bowed his head. "Thanks be to the Great Wave for your recovery."

She smiled and gestured for him to continue.

He hesitated briefly. "We have requested a meeting with the elders, to hear what is being done, but our requests have been refused. Is it not their place to answer to us, the people of Dovkey?"

Aela's smile was without mirth. "It is indeed their duty. I fear they have forgotten that. Currently, they hold Lord Tarr in a cell, awaiting trial for the destruction of Masia."

"Lord Tarr? He sailed with you to Masia. He stood through the same unnatural storm I did." She nodded. "They think they hold the wrangrent in a cell?" Disbelief and censure filled his voice.

Aela smiled again. "Yes, they think that they can hold a wrangrent in a cell with a few water wards."

"You do not believe that he is the wrangrent?" The captain asked carefully.

"No, I do not. Tarr was the one to break the curse afflicting me so recently. He came to Dovkey with the sole purpose of protecting me, sent by my brother. I have no questions as to his loyalty...or his character.

"I'm afraid he's an easy scapegoat. The elders don't want to deal with the real threat to Dovkey. They want to hastily wash their hands of it and move forward as if it never happened."

She saw anger in his face now. "What I say next, Your Majesty, is dangerous... but the elders have long led Dovkey astray. They seek out personal agendas and not the welfare of the people. I was trained as a soldier, but the elders dismissed the soldiers in a time of obvious need. Negotiations and contracts cannot protect against a wrangrent. He sighed. "I do not seek war, but there are times when war comes regardless, and we must fight. The elders leave us weak."

"War is coming. The wrangrent is not sitting in a cell, and he is not done with Dovkey. You think your words are dangerous, but the words I am about to say are treason." She waited for his reaction. He stood attentively, the resolve clear in his alert eyes.

"My allegiance lies with the Queen of Dovkey; not the elders."

"Before you swear any allegiance, I must know something. The wrangrent will strike again and soon. I know where because I have seen it in a vision. Do you trust this? Will the men you represent trust this?"

The man before her did not waver. His grave eyes remained fixed on her. "I was with you when you had visions of Masia. I know that you see the truth. You have been to the White Beach, my queen. We have all heard this and know that you are the one blessed by the Great Wave. I trust your direction without question. You command it, and we will see it done."

Aela felt the tightness in her chest loosen at the captain's words. She did not doubt that he would follow her commands, and she trusted his words that the army would also follow her lead.

"The wrangrent will attack Shuesh next. I do not know when, but time cannot be wasted. I have seen an army attacking the city and turning it to ash. The people must be warned and protected. I believe the wrangrent has chosen this place because of the fountain-"

"The first touch of the Wave, that is what we call the fountain," he said softly. "I am from Shuesh. That fountain represents the birth of Dovkey as a nation. It was when our wandering ancestors came together as one people." His voice was filled with emotion.

"Yes, and it represents our connection to the Great Wave. Aside from the White Palace, Shuesh's fountain and temple are the most sacred emblems of Dovkey's prosperity and history."

"Masia was easily accessible, but Shuesh is not on the rivers. It would not be hard to move an army into Masia without detection. If a ship captain understands the waters he sails, he could come down the rivers quickly enough to catch a city off guard. But not in Shuesh. An army would have to leave the water and march on foot a very long distance. They would be spotted in time to give warning." He looked back to Aela. "Do you think that is why Masia was hit first?"

"There are many reasons why Masia was hit first. It is close enough to the border that some would easily assume that Frin'gere is the attacker. Masia," she paused as the pain entered her voice, "was very dear to me. It was my home for many years."

She motioned Mar forward. The guard unrolled a weathered map of Dovkey and held it open between her and the captain.

Tevor nodded, "Shuesh would know of an army's approach before it would be in range to attack."

"That would be true if we were dealing with a normal army. The wrangrent will cloak any forces he sends to Shuesh. We have seen his power. I do not know; however, what forces work with the wrangrent. Whatever they are, they move slowly; otherwise, there would have already been an attack...or he is rebuilding his strength for the destruction he plans to unleash on Shuesh."

"You wish to send men to protect the city?" Tevor asked.

"Yes, however, no one is to know that you are going. The people of Shuesh are not to know that you are there. You will watch the city from a distance and prepare to counter any offense. If the wrangrent gets wind of your presence, he may choose a different target. We cannot afford to lose this advantage of knowing where he will strike.

"In sending the army to Shuesh without the elders' counsel, I am moving directly against them. Should this action be discovered, they will have reason to move against me. I wish that what I ask of you was not an act of treason, but the elders are blinded. They will not sanction this act. You have seen with your own eyes the destruction. You know what is at stake. I must ask this."

Tevor's gaze was unwavering. "We were trained to defend our country in times of need. Dovkey is in need. The elders are ineffectual; it is not to them that I give my loyalty. I follow the Blessed Queen and so do the people." He crossed his right arm over his chest, a closed fist thumping against his shoulder. "We will need to leave immediately for Shuesh."

"Yes. I advise that you leave at nightfall. Send a message to the elders that you are disbanding per their orders."

"I would leave a small contingency of men with you, my queen."

Aela smiled at the statement. "I have my personal guard; I will be well protected. The people of Shuesh will need all your men." She paused and said almost to herself, "I would go to them if I could, but I cannot rouse the elders' suspicions."

"The men will understand, Your Majesty. Many preparations must be made."

"Yes," Aela sighed with relief. She looked at Mar and nodded.

He rolled up the map and went to the door. Anut entered the room. "I am sending my guard, Anut, with you."

Both Anut and Captain Tevor inhaled sharply.

Before her guard could object, she turned to him and said quietly, "I need you there. You can communicate with me as the others cannot. Men cannot be trusted with messages."

Tevor studied the guard but said nothing.

Aela expected an argument, but Anut simply bowed his head.

As she stepped closer to him, he bent down even further so that she could speak only to him. "You know who is there, and you must protect him. Find him and keep him safe. You will aide Captain Tevor and keep him in contact with me, but most importantly, protect the child."

Anut nodded again and then bowed deeply before her. He turned and went to stand next to Mar. They communicated quietly.

She turned back to Tevor. "He will convene with the others in my guard and join you before you depart. Anut can contact me at almost any time so do not hesitate to call on me if needed. May the Great Wave bless you."

He bowed deeply before leaving. "And you, my queen."

Chapter 27

If the elders noted the civilian army's departure, Aela did not know. She had made what arrangements she could for Captain Tevor and his men, though it did not seem like enough. He and the army departed in the night, confident and committed to their mission.

Anut voiced no objections to going for which she was thankful. Aela watched with tenderness as her guards gathered on the dock, expressing in their silent way their farewells. It had been many years since they had been separated, and though she did not like to be the reason for their separation, she had no choice. She needed Anut in Shuesh.

The soldiers had departed several hours ago, and the palace slept peacefully unaware of the events set into motion. Aela led what was left of her entourage into the old parts of the palace.

Sey, Ter, and Mar walked behind her, moving silently despite their size. Menony held a bag slung across her shoulders, walking between Aela and the guards. Her head hung as she cried quietly.

Aela spared her a quick glance and noted the silent tears sliding down her friend's cheeks. She slowed enough so that they walked side by side. She took Menony's hand and gave it a reassuring squeeze.

I will not let anything happen to him," Aela said softly.

Menony answered with a smile. "I know that you will do everything that you can."

They walked in silence.

"What's his name?" Aela asked.

She realized that though she had seen the child, he was still not real to her. She knew who he was, yet his existence still seemed to be a wishful dream.

Her friend smiled. "Nico."

After my grandfather, Aela thought.

"Who...where does he stay? Does he know?"

"He's only four, but he knows that I am his mother and that Kesh is, was, his father. He lives with my sister. She does not know the reasons for the secrecy, but she understands that there is a need. I have visited him as often as I could without drawing too much attention. Kesh did the same. It was more difficult for him. Though. Both to get away and to keep the distance. We did it at his insistence, but I think he knew his time was limited."

Aela thought back to their time in Masia. Menony left every few weeks for a visit to her sister and mother. At the time, Aela had thought nothing of it, having been under the impression that Menony's mother was ill with limited time left. Now, she realized the true reason for the visits.

"Did Kesh know of this one?" Aela asked with a look at Menony's belly.

The other woman smiled a smile of deep tenderness, one that only a woman feeling the growth of a fragile life inside her could.

"I didn't tell him, but he knew."

"How do you know?"

"Kesh saw so many things. I know that he saw this," she paused, her smile turning sad. "And still, he did what he knew he had to do."

They walked through the waterfall room. No rainbows danced on the walls here at night, but Aela could hear the vague voices of the river. She felt torn about listening deeper to them. Undoubtedly echoes of pain and suffering cried out from the water, and those she didn't want to hear. But there were other voices too. New voices from all the people who lived by the rivers. People she had never met, but people whom she was ultimately responsible for.

"Why did he have to play Seer's Fortune?" Aela heard herself asking.

"He was afraid that when you finally asked me that question you wouldn't be able to understand the answer. He wanted you to understand, Aela." Menony took a breath as they paused in the waterfall room. "Kesh was a seer. He saw things even from a young age. I can't imagine being that young and seeing the things that he saw. Aine was a seer too. I don't know the things that she saw, but something made her want to run away, and Kesh helped her. He took her to Frin'gere, helped to get her settled there.

"Yes, I heard," Aela said with a small smile. "Tarr told me he has three nieces."

Menony smiled. "She knew that she would love and marry Jathe. She told Kesh to take her there. He was hesitant at first, but she assured him that she would find only happiness. And she did. She has been very happy."

Aela rarely thought of her quiet cousin, who she knew so little of, but knowing that she was happy filled her with relief.

"Kesh said he always knew that you were meant to rule Dovkey, and he was meant to provide the heirs that would continue his family line. I was in love with Kesh for years," a sweet expression lit her face as she thought of it.

"When I realized that he felt the same, it was every dream come true, but it was years before Kesh felt we could be together. Nico came soon after we were secretly married. By that time, Kesh had told me some of the things that he saw. His visions of the future became less clear in the last few years. He had a vision years before, when he first helped Aine leave Dovkey, that the house of Gero would die out, and that something evil would attack Dovkey."

She hesitated. "He saw his death and your death. For years, he tried to discover the meaning. He sought out seers in Frin'gere, but he could never make sense of it. Finally, he met one who put him in a deep trance that lasted for days, and Kesh found the meaning he had searched so long for. 'A sacrifice of the house of Gero will be made for the blessed queen to rule, and in her reign, the people of the wave will prosper for centuries. Should the seer fail the queen, evil will blacken the wave and spread through the waters to poison all.'"

Aela watched Menony tense as she repeated the prophecy. She felt chills skitter down her own back.

"Kesh was the seer sacrifice. I argued with him for months that he couldn't sacrifice himself. That he must have misinterpreted the message. I'm ashamed to admit that I suggested Aine be the seer sacrifice. But she is not of the House of Gero. I even raged against the Great Wave for requiring such a thing. But Seer's Fortune had the power that no one could refute. It would ensure that Kesh's man was near you no matter what. If he could not be there to help you, he was going to make sure that someone he trusted was."

"Tarr," Aela breathed.

"Yes, Tarr."

"Did you know Tarr before this?"

"I had heard of him, but no, I did not know him until that day that you met him." She smiled. "He was not what I expected."

Menony's sad eyes connected with Aela's. "I hope that you can understand this. Kesh believed that you were the only one who could protect Dovkey and his family. He felt that his part in this was so small compared to what you would need to do. I hope, Aela, that you know this was done out of the greatest of love."

Aela felt the familiar aching in her chest, mingled with a sense of dread that she would fail her brother, and his sacrifice would be for nothing.

"I do understand." She cleared the sorrow from her throat as she grabbed Menony's hand. "I will protect his family...my family. Come, we must go."

***

THEY STOOD ON THE PLATFORM from which Aela had first seen the black current. The water was no longer black, but it was not calm. The waves had ceased their violent assault on the White Palace, but their displeasure was still strong. The choppy waters splashed up on the stone as Aela and Menony stood with the wind blowing past them.

Mar and Ter had dived into the water a quarter of an hour ago, but the two women waited patiently, their hands clasped together. Aela worried as she stood with her friend that this would be the last time they would see each other.

Menony's words had brought her a bit of peace, but they had also made it painfully clear how much the fate of everything she loved depended on her. For so many years, she had lived with the notion that she was the weak one, the failed one. However, Aela could no longer believe that that was her destiny. The trip to the white beach had proved it to herself and everyone else.

The knowledge did not bring her much comfort. There were still trials ahead. Battles to be fought. Sacrifices to make. She could fail as she once had. In that moment of the trial when it mattered most, she had failed.

No, Aela refused to believe that she would fail this time.

She saw Mar first as the two guards lifted their heads out of the water. Even in the moonlight, she could see the gray skin of his face with its delicate scale pattern. The features were completely those of a man and traits passed on from his mother. The eyes were a startling melding of both lineages; perfectly ordinary in shape and size but otherworldly in the iridescent blue-green shade. Where a man would have ears, Mar and Ter had small, ruffled fins. Just below their jawlines, she could see the semi-functional gills closing against the air. Despite scaly grayish skin and massive size, they resembled men in all other ways.

She remembered when she had first seen them. They had just reached their maturity, but even in the stoic silence, Aela could sense their pain and awkwardness. She knew intimately their unspoken feelings of rejection and loss. She was as alone and unwanted as they were. Together they formed a refuge from the harsh reality of having nowhere to belong.

Aela had been in Masia for only two years when the Sea King himself, ruler of the Mer-people, had come to her seeking a place of safety for his half-mer children. She learned later that coming to her in his changed form had cost the king greatly.

The Mer king told her the story without shame or anger and related the events of their lives as if discussing the weather. As had happened many times before, he had become enamored with a mortal woman. And as he had before, he wooed her, thinking nothing more of her after their short affair.

Unlike before though, she became pregnant. This had never happened with the king's other mortal lovers. The son born was half merman and half man. Excited by this child who could live on land and under the sea, the king again joined with the woman. Again, she gave birth to a son. She gave him two more sons before dying in childbirth with the last.

However, his half-children were regarded with distrust at first. The king urged his court to watch the growth of these special children. Soon, the distrust turned to envy, and envy turned to hate. The court was full of the king's other children, and they would not tolerate the half-breed sons. The king realized that his half-Mer sons would not be safe when they reached maturity. At such a time, he would not be able to protect them.

They would have to make their way in the world of their mother. It was not a world that they knew, and the king could provide little in the way of instruction. Remembering the alliances he had once had with the Dovkeyen kings of old, he decided that the House of Gero would aid him.

Selecting Aela had been easy. She was removed from the center of Dovkeyen politics, and she was far from the king's ocean realm. He had no doubts that she would do this favor for him.

He was right not to doubt. When the Sea King had come to her, Aela had been awed. The Mer were a myth to her people. Centuries had passed since the two were allies, and mortals had forgotten the truth. She asked the king what she should do with his sons; he said give them a purpose.

They had decided on their own purpose, taking it upon themselves to be her personal guard. She had done all in her power to teach them the ways of their mother's people. Together in Masia, they had healed and faced or repressed whatever demons had haunted them.

Mar placed his hands on the stone ledge and hefted his massive body out of the water. Ter did the same.

Aela looked expectantly at Mar. "Well?"

Mar needed a few moments to acclimate to breathing air. "He is coming."

No sooner had the words left his mouth when the waters began to churn in small glowing whirlpools. Aela placed a protective hand in front of Menony, gently pushing her away from the edge. She may have done a great favor for the Sea King, but it was always best to be wary of the mer-people.

The whirlpools grew, combining into bigger ones until there was only one. The wind blew in symphony with the turbulent waters. Aela pushed away the strands of hair that whipped at her face. The light under the water grew brighter as it neared the surface.

THE FAILED QUEEN

Aela saw the white coral spirals of the king's crown before she saw him. The water parted for him as he emerged. He was larger than mortal men, more massive than even her guards. Shimmery blue-gray and green scales covered his face and torso. Stiff fins fanned away from his face, and the crown of uneven coral spires rose above them. Larger fins protruded out of his shoulder blades and rose to the height of his face before curving down to his chest. Fins collared his thick neck. Gills on either side of his neck gasped hungrily for air and the narrow slits of his flat nose flared. He stared at her with his large iridescent, humanlike eyes. His overall shape was that of a man, but there was no doubt that the creature before them was otherworldly, powerful, and dangerous.

Aela stepped forward and bowed deeply. She straightened and looked directly into the eyes of the Sea King. She shouted to be heard over the noise of the whirlpools.

"Great king, I am honored by your presence. Peace and prosperity to your kingdom of beauty and splendor." She had learned from her guards the importance of looking directly at the king and complimenting his domain.

The Sea King smiled; his blue lips were those of a man, but his jagged teeth were those of a shark.

"Such pretty words I love to hear." His laugh was like distant thunder. "Fair was once your kingdom, but ugly in despair it is now."

"Yes, my people have suffered a great loss recently."

"Loss is not all. Evil ash poured down from your palace. Evil ash polluted my waters." The water grew more violent with his anger.

"I am sorry that you and yours were touched by that."

"We are all touched by evil so great. Like a tempest it rages; life it takes. It comes for you, Blessed Queen."

"Yes, I know, and that is why I called you here. Once, you asked me to protect those dear to you. Now, I ask that you return the favor."

She reached out for Menony, firmly grasping her hand. "She carries a future king of Dovkey."

The Sea King's eyes glowed with amusement. "To me, you trust the heir to the White Palace?"

"Yes," Aela said without hesitation. She knew that she could not show any weakness to the king.

His eyes darkened now. "For how long will I keep your treasures? Indefinitely?"

"I ask that you only harbor them until the wrangrent is no longer a threat."

Dangerous amusement filled the king's voice. "Like fire, this evil burns; where will you stand Queen of Dovkey?"

"In the fire."

His eyes glowed like embers of a cool green fire. "You will burn."

She knew he was challenging and testing her. "I am the Blessed Queen of Dovkey. Nothing shall burn me."

Luminous green eyes bore into her with approval. "You have been to the White Beach, even the sea knows of this. Those of the sea have not seen what you have. The Great Wave has wisdom beyond all; you will serve him well, mortal queen."

His webbed hand reached into the water and emerged with a small vessel made of rough coral, spires growing in all directions.

"An island only the Mer know of; there your princess and unborn king shall wait. Unknown, unseen, and untouched."

"Ter will go with Menony," Aela said as the vessel floated towards them.

"The Mer do not love this son of mine."

"Like all your sons, Ter is a warrior...on land and in water. Be proud of these children, Sea King. They have served me well."

She turned to Ter and said more quietly, "I need you to ensure that nothing happens to her. She is my hope."

Ter nodded and bowed. She had not expected an argument from him. He and the others knew that she had too many people to protect. To save the men and women of her country, she would have to turn her focus away from those she loved. Doing so put them at great risk. For her alone, her guards would do this.

The vessel rocked against the stone platform, and Ter reached out to steady it.

Menony turned to her with tears in her eyes. "I'm afraid. Not for me or him," she said with a quick glance at her belly, "but for you. The wrangrent is powerful."

"I have been given this fight. Kesh saw it; all those who saw the waters of the sea part saw it. I cannot deny what I must do."

"I know." Menony cleared the tears from her eyes. "You must defeat this evil."

"And I will."

Aela was pulled into a tight hug. "I do not know how you will do this, but I know you will."

"I love you, my dear friend. I will see to the other and send him when it is safe." She pulled away. "Go now."

Ter helped Menony into the coral boat. She stood on the platform long after the Sea King had said his farewell and the boat bearing her friend disappeared into the night. She stared out at the ocean even as the wind battered her. She prayed that she had the strength to see this through.

Aela prayed that the Great Wave had not been mistaken.

Chapter 28

Shuesh was unlike any other city in Dovkey. It was a pearl among the vast fields of dark green and deep purple. The white stone of the city's circular outer wall had been cut from the sea cliffs and hauled across the country.

Two towers, one facing west and the other facing south, rose above the twenty-foot wall of white. Nestled against the two semi-circle inner walls on the north and south of the city were the vendors and artisans from every walk of life.

Shuesh's marketplace circled the healing temple. The tranquil round building, made of the smoothest bleached stone, opened to the east and west, allowing the morning and evening sunlight to illuminate the sacred fountain within the city center.

The people of Shuesh had resided together peacefully for hundreds of years. No walls marked the divide of the estates, and the livestock of one of the southern estates often roamed onto their neighbor's land. The northern end of the city had been given to the growing of flowers and herbs from which oils were made.

The estates to the east grew the city's grain, vegetables, and fruit. Because of its remote and disconnected location, Shuesh established long ago the means to be self-sufficient. Once a month, a caravan carried trade-able goods to the river where they were sold and shipped to other areas of the country. Among the most successful of Shuesh's products were its finely woven cloths and its rare oils.

None of these fine wares left the city on this day. Both city gates closed, and soldiers replaced residents on the edge of the city wall. The battle that Aela had dreamt of loomed on the horizon.

Tevor's men had made good time, arriving at the outskirts of Shuesh before any signs of trouble. They camped outside the city in a nearby forest waiting patiently to act. However, when a great cloud of smoke approached from the west, they abandoned camp. Slowly but steadily, the cloud drew closer to the city.

Having grown up in Shuesh, Captain Tevor was familiar with the leaders and was easily received. With their understanding and approval, he moved his men into place.

With the soldiers' aid, the city's leaders quickly organized and evacuated the outer edge of Shuesh. Containing the panic was by far the hardest task. With news of Masia still fresh in the minds of many, the fear of succumbing to a similar fate spread rapidly.

Every soldier entered his career knowing that war was a possibility. However, Dovkey had been at peace with its neighbors for so long that the possibility seemed remote. Tevor wondered how many Dovkeyen soldiers before him had lived their entire lives without seeing true battle. That he and his comrades should see it was a sobering thought. Unlike his father before him, his sword would sing and carry the stain of lives taken.

Such thoughts did nothing to weaken his resolve. He believed in his country and his god, trusted that he served the Blessed Queen, and remained fully committed to giving his life to protect those things. Fear battled inside him to overcome his devotion, but he pushed it aside as he prepared to face the approaching evil.

After setting the city to action, he found the queen's guard, Anut. The solemn behemoth of a man had traveled with them in silence. His presence unnerved many of the men though Trevor's assurances that the queen unwaveringly trusted Anut diminished some of the trepidation.

Now, the guard stood over a large glass bowl of water. The surface turned opaque before revealing the queen's worried visage.

AELA HAD WAITED ALL day at the temple pools for word from Anut. She leaned over the central pool as the water stirred restlessly. Swirls of misty color clouded the surface before condensing into the image of Anut and Captain Tevor. The city behind them was blurred, but she knew they were in Shuesh.

"What is happening?" she asked without greetings.

"The wrangrent is almost upon us," Anut's voice called from the water.

"Clouds of smoke approach from the west. We made our presence known shortly after realizing that they were not storm clouds. The outer edge of the city has been cleared. The people are gathered in the market area and around the temple," Tevor informed the queen.

"No," Aela said quickly. "Do not gather them in the center. That is where the fighting will occur. They will be safer tucked away in their houses."

Tevor's confused face was visible in the pool of water. "Will the wrangrent not attack the homes as he enters the city?"

"He might pause to attack those closest to the gate, but his purpose is the temple. He will destroy that first and work out from the center," Aela responded.

"How do you know this, my queen?" Tevor asked.

"I have seen it. The fighting will center around the temple. You must move the people back to the outer wall."

Tevor nodded and relayed an order to a nearby soldier.

"We have little time," Anut said. He had moved out of view.

The sound of thunder followed before Aela could voice her question. The images in the water wobbled.

"The city walls shake with great force, and clouds of smoke glow red like fire," Aunt told her.

Aela put her hand to the surface of the water, and she could feel the force of vibration. "What's happening?" she demanded.

"He is here," Anut replied.

"Has the attack started?"

Before Aela's questions could be answered another wave of sound hit the city so hard that the bowl of water between which both parties communicated, wobbled on the small table and shattered upon hitting the ground.

Aela stared at the smooth dark surface of the water. "No!" she cried as she touched the surface of the water again. "I need to see. I need to know what is happening."

She submerged her hand completely and gasped at the power she encountered. The water magic filled her fingers, crawling up her arm, and spreading across her body. It filled her with the gentle and violent energies of the sea.

All her life encounters with water magic were fleeting and weak. The visions of late had grown in strength, being the most direct experience she had with the magic. Her eyes closed as she focused on the power of the water. It was the steady, swift current of the river, the soothing sway of calm seas, and the destructive thrash of tempestuous waves. The magic was neither good nor evil. It was neutral, existing in both extremes of creation and chaos. Its existence was free of intent, but malleable and ready to match the motivations of one who could wield it.

Her eyes shot open, and she stared in wonder at the water beneath her hand. The image of Shuesh's outer wall appeared. Cautiously, she removed her hand, fearful that the image would vanish.

However, the image only grew clearer, and Aela leaned forward to study the pool.

Wipsy black and gray clouds hovered near the city. With each thunderous boom, they flashed red and orange. The strength of the thunder shook the city walls. Stone dust floated in the air, but the walls stood steadfast, constructed of thick slabs.

She could hear in the distance the frantic cries of people. Soldiers yelled instructions as the image shifted, and she saw people rushing to leave the center of the city. Terror filled their faces as they clung to each other in desperation.

Her view of the city blurred, and then she was looking at the outer wall. A line of flame circled the perimeter, and men dressed in black and orange emerged from the fire. A small army gathered outside Shuesh, and the flames from which they emerged died as quickly as they had appeared.

These were the men from her dream. Just as it had been in her vision, it was unclear if they were friend or foe.

She willed the water to show her more of them. Her sight focused on one man in particular. He was tall and heavily built. A long black beard obscured part of his face, but Aela recognized his features. He looked like Tarr, possessing the same black hair and darker skin.

She thought immediately of Tarr's brother Jathe. The man who had married her cousin and stood as witness to her brother's marriage. Disbelief was her first reaction.

The man in her vision walked amongst the others with an air of authority, giving orders as the men around him hurried to fulfill them.

They carried blue glass bottles full of liquid. She watched with confusion as they set them several feet from the wall. For the span of a moment, she feared what was contained in those bottles. Tevor and his men were not prepared to fight both the wrangrent's magic and that of the Frin'gerens.

The city continued to shake with the wrangrent's fury as the Frin'geren soldiers completed setting the circle of bottles around the perimeter. As one man set down the last of the bottles, a bolt of lightning erupted from the cloud of smoke and seared a path toward him. The bottle nearest to him burst, and the fiery bolt disintegrated.

Fellow soldiers in black and orange gathered around the man and guided him towards the South gate where a large Frin'geren force waited inside the circle of bottles.

Again, the wrangrent shot a bolt of fire towards the Frin'gerens, and again a bottle burst nearby. Strong thunder shook the ground, followed by several bolts of fire. The sky lit with lightning.

Each strike raced toward the city with violent intent. However, none of the strikes found their target. Before contacting the wall, multiple bottles burst, and the bolts sizzled in midair without causing harm.

Mar edged closer to the pool and stood opposite Aela. She looked up at him. "They put wards around the city. Why would they do that?"

Initially, he gave no response. He stared back at the pool as more wards burst with the continued assaults. "Are these men with Tarr?" Mar finally asked.

Aela watched as bolt after bolt of lightning rained down on the city. Each one evaporated before hitting, and another blue bottle ruptured. She wondered at the wards but smiled as she remembered that Jathe was married to her cousin. Aine knew water magic, and Aela was certain that she was the creator of the wards.

The attack continued for over half an hour, but the time between strikes lengthened. Finally, the last bottle burst, and the clouds glowed a deep red. Thunder rumbled incessantly as if the sky itself growled with displeasure, but nothing shot out at the city below. The wards had weakened the wrangrent, but Aela knew the battle was not over. She had seen ash. It was yet to come. This was only the calm before the storm. The wrangent was regrouping and rebuilding his strength.

The grinding of stone against stone drew her attention to the door.

Mar had left the room, and now he reentered. "The elders are looking for you. They have heard word of an army marching across Dovkey, and they are not happy."

"They will have to wait. Do not let them find me," she ordered.

"You will have to face them soon," Mar said as he knelt beside the pool.

She stared at him in silence, before drawing a deep breath.

"I've acted without their approval. They will seize this opportunity to remove me from power, blessed by the Great Wave or not. I knew this." She paused. "I know I have to face them, but they will have to wait until I am ready," Aela said calmly before returning her attention to the pool.

"Sey awaits orders."

She knew what Mar was asking. Unsurprised and unconcerned that the elders knew of her actions, she had prepared for this inevitability. Once she was stripped of her crown, Tarr would not be safe. She did not trust the elders or the Phoenix Son to deal with him fairly.

Reaching into the water, she disturbed the image momentarily. Her cupped hand reemerged with a sphere of water. With intense focus, she infused her will into the water. Though she had never used the water magic in such a way, she allowed her instincts to guide her. The surface hardened like glass, and the interior briefly glowed a bright white. Satisfied that it would do what she intended, she handed the sphere to Mar.

"Give this to Sey. It should help with the wards placed on Tarr's cell. Sey is to get him out no matter what."

"The Frin'geren will object."

Aela nodded. Tarr would undoubtedly object to leaving her alone to face the displeasure of the elders. She did not care. Those she loved would remain safe. She would ensure it with her very last breath.

"Whatever he must do, he is to get Tarr out of the palace."

With a nod, Mar left the room.

Aela sat next to the temple pool. She felt powerless despite the well of power in front of her. Her army was hundreds of miles away fighting an evil far greater than anything her generation had ever seen. She was separated from her loved ones and could only pray that they remained safe. Even her guards who had been a constant for many years were gone. She was very alone as she pulled her knees to her chest and waited for the wrangrent's next assault.

Chapter 29

"No," Tarr's voice shook with anger. "I am not leaving her."

"My orders are to get you out by any means needed." Amusement filled the guard's voice, "I will knock you unconscious and carry you out if needed. Willing or not, you are leaving, and my queen's orders will be fulfilled."

"It is not safe!" Tarr exclaimed. He neglected to lower his voice, though he doubted it mattered. Sey's presence alone indicated that the guards were incapacitated.

He'd been curious when he heard a scuffle outside the dungeon door and then shocked when he watched the guard approach. Sey held a faintly glowing sphere in his hands. It flashed and then evaporated as the guard passed through the wards. Instantly, Tarr felt them drop away.

"It is not safe. Not for you, not for her, not for anyone." Tarr heard the anger in Sey's voice. "She has been burdened with this undertaking, and you would add to the weight with your stubbornness? She does this not just for you but for herself."

Guilt filled him. Tarr wanted only to protect her, but he understood Sey's meaning. The guard wrenched open the door to his cell without the key. The hinges strained under the force of his pull and surrendered with a creak as they fell to the ground with a clank.

"I cannot abandon her," Tarr said earnestly as he stepped out of the cell.

Sey snorted and stepped back. "Foolish Frin'geren. We do not abandon our queen."

Staring at the guard with confusion, "You said we are leaving? That you are taking me out of here?"

"I am taking you out of your cell, yes. We are leaving the dungeon, yes, but we are not leaving the queen. We will stay unseen in the palace."

"We are going to hide somewhere in the palace? For how long? Why even hide?" He spewed the questions rapidly in his frustration.

Sey invaded his space, towering over him, but Tarr did not back away. He stared into the shadowed face.

"If the Phoenix Son finds you, he will use you against her. So, he will not find you."

Sey turned and started towards the door. Tarr watched him walk away, immobile with anger.

The guard paused and said over his shoulder, "One way or another, Frin'geren. It matters not to me how we do this."

He considered for a moment his chances of overpowering Aela's guard. They were not in his favor. Besides, he realized the wisdom in Sey's reasoning. He could be used against Aela. The better option, the more strategic option, was to wait for the opportune time to strike. Though it went against his need to go to her and stand by her, he followed Sey as they slipped out of the dungeon. Three palace guards lay unconscious on the ground, and he stepped over them.

They turned down one hall and then another entering parts of the palace that he had not seen before. With so many forgotten passages throughout the White Palace, it was no surprise that the wrangrent had been able to enter undetected.

"Has the wrangrent struck yet?" He asked quietly.

"Yes. A group of men in orange and black warded the city against the first attack."

Tarr's gaze jerked towards the guard. "That's Jathe. My brother. Those are his men. She needs to know that they are allies."

Sey chuckled. "She suspects so already."

THE CITY CONTINUED to shake from the thunderous clouds above, but no further attacks came. It was only a matter of time before the next onslaught.

Captain Tevor had watched with trepidation as the men in orange and black appeared and surrounded the city. Now, he suspected that they were allies. It was clear the blue bottles blocked the wrangrent's strikes.

He was not sure where the men had come from, but he was not about to turn away any help.

"Open the south gate," he called to the men stationed on top of the wall.

A soldier looked warily at the new arrivals and back to Tevor before relaying the message to the next post. Not waiting for the order to reach the gate, Tevor descended the wall as the city took another beating of thunder. He raced to the south gate and arrived as the unexpected allies moved into the city.

A man of dark brown skin rode in front. His black hair was pulled into a tight knot behind his head, and his icy blue eyes surveyed the Dovkeyen soldiers. His formidable size and fierce countenance made him an intimidating presence.

"I am Jathe, Lord of Avengere. I have brought my forces from across Frin'gere to aid the Queen of Dovkey."

He bowed his head, the men behind him following suit, and waited to be addressed.

Tevor stepped forward. "I am Captain Tevor, leader of the Queen's forces here at Shuesh."

He studied the man in front of him.

"I was unaware the Queen had allies in Frin'gere."

The Frin'geren lord scrutinized Tevor before he burst into laughter. "She's engaged to my brother. That makes us in-laws if not allies."

His deep laughter died away, and his face turned fierce once more.

"Though I did not come at the queen's personal request, I am here to serve her." His white teeth contrasted greatly with his skin. His smile was no less intense than his eyes.

"If you did not come at the queen's request, then at whose request did you come?" Tevor asked cautiously.

"I swore to King Kesh before his death that I would come to the aid of Dovkey should the need arise."

Tevor immediately wondered how Jathe knew Dovkey was in need. However, the Frin'geren answered before the question was asked.

"My brother, Lord Tarr, sent word that the queen needed assistance, that there was a wrangrent rising to power. I came not only to fulfill a vow but also to protect my own interests. A wrangrent is a danger to all."

Tevor nodded his head. "You warded our outer walls, and for that I thank you. However, if you prove to be a threat after we have defeated our common enemy, I will deal with you then. Until that time," he held his arm to Jathe.

The Frin'geren eyed it with seriousness, then laughed and locked wrists with the other man. "Smart man. Never trust a Frin'geren completely."

He released the captain's hand, and his smile faded. "The wards are spent. Only a temporary defense really," he looked up to the sky, "though they may have worked to spend some of the wrangrent's magic."

He pursed his lips. "Or maybe just succeeded in angering him." He turned to Tevor. "Could be both. There's a fight still to come."

Tevor nodded. "We move to the center of the city."

Jathe's brow perked in confusion. "The center?"

"The queen foresaw the battle taking place at the temple, which is in the center of the city."

The other man nodded. "Lead on."

⁂

AELA WATCHED SILENTLY, unaware of the exchange taking place between the two men.

Mar had returned and stood over her watching the pool too.

Her mind wandered, and her attention on the pool slipped. She fought the rush of images. Scenes of Masia and her visions bombarded her. She closed her eyes and pushed her palms against her temples. She fought to clear her head, but in the barrage of images, the fountain emerged again and again.

"My queen," Mar's gravelly voice drew her attention.

The room was silent. The thunder had stopped.

In the pool, she watched as ash began to fall like snow from the smokey clouds. The sight of it was deceivingly peaceful.

She gasped as she realized that the wrangrent's true assault was just beginning.

⁂

ANUT LOOKED UP TOWARDS the silent sky. Ash floated delicately on the slight breeze. Even before it touched his skin, he felt the evil.

Upon seeing the falling ash, Tevor and Jathe urged their forces forward.

"We must hasten if we are to make it to the city center," Tevor shouted to the men, his pace quickening as he spoke.

"It is just as the queen predicted," Anut said as he ran beside the captain.

"Let us pray that the city officials were able to return the people to their homes," Tevor said as he drew his sword.

A few feet away Jathe also drew his sword. His men moved stealthily behind him as they navigated the alleys between buildings.

The ash continued to fall, gathering in piles on the streets. Fire on the rooftops above drew the soldiers' attention. They watched in horror as it spread rapidly across the city's buildings.

Distracted by the flames above, they did not notice the forms rising from the piles of ash.

A tortured scream filled the air. An unnatural creature rose from the ash and reached for the nearest soldier. The sound of sizzling flesh filled the air as it touched a soldier's arm.

He dropped his sword, grasping the blackened flesh of his arm. His eyes filled with terror as he tried to retreat, but the creature reached out again and grabbed the soldier's face. It held on until the man in its grasp turned to ash.

Anut and the others watched in frozen horror until more emerging ash creatures spurred the soldiers into action. They plunged their swords into the ashy beings, but their swords proved useless.

Tevor and Jathe's men fought with everything they had, but the creatures kept coming.

One came for Anut. He sidestepped it, driving its head into the nearby wall. The contact burned through his gloves and reddened the top layer of his scaly skin.

"They are guarding your temple," Anut said to Tevor as the captain dodged an attack.

"Yes, but how do we get past them without turning to ash ourselves?" Tevor paused as another of his men turned to ash beside him.

He turned quickly, but not quick enough. The fingers of one of the ash men scraped along his spine. He cried out at the burning pain that spread across his back.

Anut quickly pulled him behind the column of a building. He propped Tevor against the column and examined his back. Jathe joined them.

"I have never seen anything like this, and I have seen a lot of magic in my life. This is beyond fire magic."

The skin on Tevor's back was not red and tender as a normal burn should look. Instead, it was black and crisp like the burnt edges of paper.

Jathe pulled a small bag from his sword belt and poured a fine white powder into one hand. Then, he rubbed it onto the burned skin.

"I do not know what good this will do."

A man's scream alerted them to the prevailing horror rendered by the ash men.

"We must find a way around them and get to the wrangrent. If we kill the wrangrent, we kill them." Tevor pushed himself away from the column and pulled a dagger from his belt.

"Not so easy a task," Jathe muttered as he followed closely behind Tevor and Anut. They crept from behind the column, unaware of the creature that stalked them.

"Behind you, captain," a soldier yelled before falling to another ash man.

Tevor turned quick enough to push Jathe out of the way as the creature that stalked them lunged forward.

The ashy hand reached for Tevor's heart but closed over a vile of water hidden under the captain's shirt. The vile burst against Tevor's chest, and the creature screamed in pain as the water dissolved its hand.

Tevor watched in awe. "Can it be that easy?" he said to Anut.

Jathe was close enough to hear.

"There is only one way to know."

He raced for a clay urn that stood nearly as high as he did and pushed it over. Water poured onto the ground, running in streams towards the ash men and soldiers who continued to fight. The feet of the ash men dissolved underneath them, forcing them farther into the water until nothing remained.

"Find whatever water you can," Tevor ordered.

They pushed over urns of water, until a barrier formed between them and the ashy creatures. Through a stroke of luck, the soldiers of Dovkey and Frin'gere ended up on the right side of the barrier. They were free to continue towards the temple.

As they made their way closer, the soldiers threw water behind them, in front of them, and at whatever creature came close enough. When they finally made it to the temple, they found it empty.

The smoke above them rumbled and ash once again fell over the city. It gathered in the puddles of water, clumping together, and moving. To the soldiers' horror creatures again rose from the ash. However, these ash creatures were no longer vulnerable to water.

"What do we do?" one of the Frin'gerens shouted at Jathe as ash men forced them to retreat into the temple.

"The water doesn't work anymore," another soldier shouted. The watery ash men moved slower than their previous counterparts but were seemingly indestructible.

"What do we do?" the question rose from the group as they put their backs together while drawing closer to the fountain.

THE CITY WAS ON FIRE. Flames engulfed the rooftops of shops and houses surrounding the temple. The thatched circular roof of the temple was also ablaze, and the ash men from her dreams sprang to life from piles of falling ash. Aela watched in horror as her nightmare became reality, and the screams of Shuesh filled the room.

She watched as the men retreated further into the temple, pursued by the wrangrent's creations. They met in the center, dead-ending at the sacred fountain.

"The fountain!" Aela shouted, suddenly realizing its significance.

"My queen," Mar's voice stirred her attention away from the scene unfolding before her. "They are searching the entire palace for you. They have begun searching for Menony as well."

"They can wait," Aela said as she turned back to the pool.

"They will not wait. They mean to imprison you. When they come, I will bar the door, but for how long?" Mar asked.

Aela looked away from the pool. Her thoughts were a blur. She needed to focus on Shuesh, but clearly, the elders were closing in.

"They have the palace guard with them," Mar said.

Mar was skilled, but he could not fight the entire palace guard. Even if his odds were better, she would not risk him in a skirmish with the elders' men.

"Block the door for as long as you can. If it appears that they are close to breaking through, you escape down the stairs to the ocean. Do not let them imprison you."

She stared at Mar for a long, tense moment before he nodded and took a position against the door.

Thankful that he had not argued, Aela turned her attention back to Shuesh.

"The fountain," she shouted. "Strike the fountain."

She strained to feel the magic in the pool and the water that surrounded her men. All water was connected. Reaching into the power of the Temple Pool, she pushed through it to connect to the water in Shuesh. She commanded the soldiers repeatedly to strike the fountain.

"DO YOU KNOW ANY MAGIC that will harm them?" Tevor asked though he already knew the answer.

"If I did, I would have employed it long before now," Jathe responded as he watched the creatures shuffle towards them.

"What about the wards that you brought? They held off the wrangrent's attack. Can you not recreate something similar?"

Tevor knew that they were the people's only hope. Once the wrangrent was done with them, the ash creatures would spread throughout the city and destroy all those in Shuesh.

"I did not create the wards, and the person who did is not here" Jathe's face was strained as he watched the enemy edge closer.

The water on the ground trembled though there was no thunder.

"*Strike the fountain.*"

The voice was barely audible, and Tevor was unsure if he had truly heard it.

Again the water shook, but more forcefully this time.

"*Strike the fountain*"

Certain of what he had heard this time, he looked around and saw all gazes turned towards the fountain.

"Do you hear that?" another soldier asked.

"*Strike the fountain.*"

"There it is again," said a Frin'geren.

"Our queen commands," Anut said as he approached the fountain. He beat his massive fist against the stone.

Tevor and Jathe turned to the fountain behind them.

"Nothing has flowed from this fountain in over a century," Tevor said.

"Perhaps, it is time that something did," Jathe responded.

He raised his sword over his head and looked to Tevor.

"YES!" AELA EXCLAIMED. She heard the sound of stone being struck though it was not from Shuesh. The palace guards were demanding entry into the room. They banged the stone door again.

"We know that she is in there," it was the voice of one of the elders. "She must face us and explain her actions!"

"If you do not allow us to enter," the voice of another elder ordered, "then the palace guard will have no choice but to move past by any means necessary. Do you understand?"

Mar stood with his shoulder braced against the door. She called his name quietly. His head shook from side to side.

"We did not want to resort to this, but there is no other choice," the elder said. "Move into the chamber."

"It's time, Mar. Go now." He hesitated. "Go now," she repeated softly.

He stepped away from the door as the guards on the other side grunted with effort. Her friend and guard bowed before her and then moved quickly down the stairs and out of the room.

Aela turned back to the pool but waited for the sound of stone on stone.

She heard steel on stone.

JATHE AND TEVOR STRUCK the fountain together with their swords. Nothing happened, yet the unseen voice urged them to continue. Other soldiers and Frin'gerens joined them. Their swords sparked as they hit the stone. Still, nothing happened, but the men continued to strike even as some of their comrades fell behind them.

STONE AGAINST STONE, sword against stone. Aela could hardly tell the difference anymore as the two sounds pounded her ears one after the other. The magic gathered in her hand and spread throughout her body. She had never felt such a thing before.

She held her hands in front of her, unsure of what to do with the swelling power.

They needed water magic in Shuesh, but without blessed water, there would be no victory. Swords continued to beat against stone and stone ground against more stone as she realized what she must do.

She held her hands over the water, now shaking from all the power, and plunged them deep below the surface calling out, "May blessed water once again flow from the fountain of healing."

As the last word left her lips, so did the magic leave her body. Its release was stronger than she had expected, and though the stone chamber around her cracked and the stone door crumbled to rumble, she remained kneeling beside the pool.

WATER SHOT FROM THE fountain with such force that it threw the men around it backward and blew through the flames of the burning temple roof. The swell of water fell back toward the ground, raining down with fury on the ash creatures. It hit the ground collecting in force to flow through the city like waves. It was destructive, destroying everything of ash and fire, and carrying with it the remains of all that the wrangrent had unleashed.

Chapter 30

The soaked defenders of Shuesh watched as the water rose throughout the city. The fountain continued to flow until the ash was purged, and the city cleansed.

"Where did the water come from?" Jathe asked as he cleared the spray from his face.

The wave had stilled, and now the soldiers waded through the knee-deep flood, shouting victory.

The Frin'geren sank down on the fountain's edge next to Tevor. Anut stood over them.

"It was the queen's voice we heard, wasn't it?" He directed the question to Anut.

The guard nodded.

"She urged us to strike the fountain," Tevor explained through heavy breaths.

"It was your queen who did this?" Jathe asked with astonishment as he looked around at the city. "It takes a great deal of power to do this."

"She is the Blessed Queen," Tevor responded.

"It would appear so," Jathe said absentmindedly as he nodded. His expression hardened as his gaze fell on the burned body of a fallen Frin'geren. "The wrangrent was not defeated, you know this?"

"I know," Tevor replied with equal gravity. He rose and held his hand out to Jathe. "Your aid is greatly appreciated, Lord Jathe. We would have suffered greatly at the beginning without your wards.

THE FAILED QUEEN

Your men fought bravely against the wrangent's creatures. I will see to it that the queen knows of the service you did our country."

Jathe laughed heartily as he shook the captain's hand. "I always enjoy a good fight. My wife keeps me penned up. It's been far too long."

Tevor shook his head. "Again, you have my thanks. I'm going to see to my men. Many are undoubtedly injured," his expression saddened. "Some will be unaccounted for. I would like to make sure they are honored for their sacrifice."

Jathe wished him well and watched as the captain walked away to join a group of his men. Without looking up, he said quietly, "You are one of the queen's guards, are you not?"

Anut's head turned in his direction and nodded.

Jathe's smile was fierce. "Saving this city was not my primary reason for coming to Dovkey."

"You owed Kesh this service."

The Frin'gern laughed. "I owed Kesh more than I could ever repay in a lifetime. Bastard made sure I did." His expression softened as he remembered all the things that Kesh had done for him. Among them was bringing Aine, his beloved wife, to Frin'gere.

"Fighting these creatures of ash was not my task."

"You know what is in this city, do you not?"

It was a tense moment before Anut responded. "I do."

Jathe just smiled. "I have to leave Shuesh now, before the wrangrent recovers from his loss. If he knows that I am heading to the palace, he will try to stop me by any means possible. I must get there quickly and without being seen," he said in a hushed voice.

"By river or land?"

He considered it before responding. "The river is faster, is it not?"

"I will ensure that it is," Anut responded gravely.

Jathe nodded. "Very good. We must collect our precious cargo and sneak out of the city."

"Do you know where to find him?"

Jathe slapped Anut's arm even though the queen's guard towered over him. He pondered it was a strange sensation to be around a man larger than himself. Usually, he was the giant in the room.

"Of course, I do. I've been to dinner three or four times." Jathe laughed and led the way. He whispered orders to his men as he passed, and they stealthily retreated from the joyous Dovkenen soldiers. Then, he navigated the streets of Shuesh with ease, proving that he had indeed been there before.

THE WRANGRENT'S HANDS burned with black flames. Ash swirled in the air as they wrung their hands in frustration. Shuesh was meant to be another silent attack. One that would be discovered long after they had retrieved what they needed from the city. The people of Dovkey would whisper about it as they did Masia. In fear and awe.

Stolen! Ruined!

People would talk about victory...the queen's victory. Sing her praises far and wide.

No one would talk about their perfect creations of ash and destruction. No one would remember and tremble at the clouds of smoke that shook the walls of Shuesh.

Somehow, she had known. The Blessed Queen of Dovkey had been a step ahead. The thought of it was intolerable.

Aela was intolerable.

She had stolen the wrangrent's victory, and if she was not already in possession of what the wrangrent sought, she soon would be.

This queen was meddlesome. Interfering with their great plans.

But no more.

The game was over.

Now, she would feel it at the heart of what she loved.

She would be stripped of her power, left defenseless and alone. They would make sure of it. They would take away her loved ones. Kill her defenders. Reveal her for the falsehood that she was.

A smile curved the wrangrent's lips. Yes, the time had come.

With a tilt of their head, they studied the ash swirling in front of them. The game was not over. It was merely changing.

They laughed with manic glee. The next battle would not be as dramatic as the one at Shuesh. Though they loved to display their power, for this next confrontation they would be a threat unseen. Manipulating the people around her just as they manipulated the magic running through their veins.

Aela would not survive their next encounter.

Chapter 31

The door to her cell opened, and Aela jumped at the abruptness. An elder stood in the doorway, flanked by nervous guards.

"Your Majesty, if you would follow me." He stepped aside with a slight bow.

Aela strode to the door and stared down at the man. He failed to meet her stare. She walked past him and allowed the guards to lead her from the dungeon.

The Reformationists had waited decades to strip the monarchy of its power. Now, the last monarch of House Gero was on trial. The elder behind her did not seem to relish the moment as much as she expected.

Nevertheless, she stood by her decisions. With her chin held high and the posture befitting her status, she entered the throne room.

She knew the charge. A law created during the Reformation stated that the king or queen could not order military action without the support of the elders. She knew the consequences of her actions. Even though the elders' foolishness had driven her to such measures, she would face the charges and stand trial. Perhaps then, they could focus their time and attention on the real threat.

The reception was not as cold as she expected. The elders stood to the right with hands clasped behind their backs. Malcolm and Hans met her stare with a satisfied smile, but the others' eyes shied away when she looked at them. Clearly, not all of them agreed with the proceedings.

Berto looked at her with understanding. She gave him a small smile of encouragement, for it looked like he needed it more than she did. Looking away from the kind elder, Aela continued past them with her head high.

The priestesses stood veiled on the left. She could not see their faces, but their stiff postures conveyed discontent. She wondered briefly if they disapproved of the trial or of her actions.

Aela realized that this was the second trial of her life. She had so greatly feared failing the first. Though she was certain of this trial's outcome, she was not afraid.

By law, she was guilty of treason. She acknowledged that laws kept chaos at bay. Order allowed peace to flourish. She had violated those tenants.

At one time in her life, her belief in the law had been as black and white as the ink and paper on which they were written. She felt no moral constraints in following them to the letter. Now, she saw the grays of the world.

On her throne, the Phoenix Son sat. She did not doubt that in the ten years since the signing of their betrothal, he had longed for his chance to take that place. Their betrothal was never about her despite his attempts to make her believe otherwise. She felt her skin redden with rage as she thought of his manipulative abuse of power.

If he noted her anger, he made no indication of it. He stared down at her with stoned-faced superiority. With a regal gaze, he nodded at the guards standing on either side of her. They lead her with shaky hands to stand before him.

She met his gaze and in a cold voice greeted him, "My lord."

Aluz seemed pleased by her use of the honorific.

She had never seen a criminal trial, but the ancient traditions of her forefathers guaranteed that it would be lengthy and riddled with pompous ceremony. She had questions that needed answers, questions that could not wait until the trial was over.

"What news is there from Shuesh?" she asked the room.

A hushed silence was the immediate answer.

She could feel the warring emotions of those gathered behind her. Sadness, shock, disapproval, fear. They all swirled in the air.

"Queen Aela," one of the elders began, his voice shaking with an emotion she could not distinguish, "you do realize that you are on trial for treason? That your first thoughts should be of your own fate?"

She took a calming breath to steady her voice and asked calmly, "What news has come from Shuesh?"

"Shuesh is not of concern to you at the moment." Elder Malcolm stepped in front of her. His condescending eyes bore into her, but Aela would not be intimidated.

"Considering that my actions regarding Shuesh have led to this trial, it is my concern. Someone will tell me the outcome of Shuesh." The calm was gone. Now, she demanded.

He breathed deeply, color rising in his bloated face. "Do you confess to the traitorous acts you have committed?"

Oh, no, Aela thought. *That was too easy.*

"That has yet to be proven, and until that time, I am still the reigning monarch." She addressed the room. "I will ask one more time. What news have you received from Shuesh? How many perished in the fight? What is the state of the city? Has any relief been sent?"

Malcolm's face tightened in anger as he prepared his retort; however, another answered from behind them.

"We have heard no news of Shuesh. The messengers sent out two days ago have not yet returned."

Aela turned to find that it was Berto who answered. The look of hopelessness in his eyes penetrated deeper than the rage, and she tried to give him a small smile of encouragement. "Thank you, Elder Berto."

She returned her attention to Malcolm. "You may proceed with the trial now."

They did not need her permission and would continue without it, yet she enjoyed the satisfaction of issuing the order.

Aluz chose that moment to step forward, likely realizing the impending explosion of Malcolm's temper. With silent acknowledgment to the Immortal, the elder returned to his seat.

As Aluz approached Aela, he spoke to the room. "I have been asked by the elders to stand as a judge in this trial. I am not entirely familiar with the legal customs of your people, but they have agreed to steer me in the right direction should I wander."

He had not mentioned the priestesses who still stood rigidly united against him.

"It is not the place of an Immortal to judge a queen of Dovkey. Only the Great Wave may judge her," Bena's stern voice rang out. The priestesses beside her murmured their approval.

Aluz held up his hand to silence their opposition. "You, the spiritual advisors of Dovkey, and the elders who protect the power of law and order are divided. I am more a mediator than a judge truthfully."

She watched with surprise as the priestesses heatedly objected to his words. The more vocal elders, such as Hans and Malcolm, had their own arguments in favor of the of Phoenix Son's involvement.

He leaned close to her ear, saying softly, "It saddens me to be in this position, Aela."

She glared at his false concern.

Still, his voice projected remorse and concern, "I hope that we can prove you innocent of the charge."

Aela barely refrained from rolling her eyes but could no longer endure his stare without her own temper exploding.

The trial was a waste of time, especially with a battle-torn city awaiting aid and many other vulnerable cities left unprepared for attack.

She stepped away from Aluz and addressed the room.

"There is no need for this trial." Her words silenced both groups. "I freely admit that I am guilty."

The room erupted with objections, gasps, and curses. Yet, Aela continued in a raised voice that overcame the noise, "I sent a group of soldiers to Shuesh without consulting the elders. I did send them with the intent of engaging the wrangrent. My intuition proved correct as the wrangrent did attack the city shortly thereafter."

Malcolm, unable to control himself, stepped forward so that they nearly stood nose to nose. "And how did you come by this knowledge? Why did you not share it with the elders?" His shouts managed to quiet the room.

"Did you act under guidance from the Great Wave, my queen?" Bena called as she too stepped forward.

They waited in tense silence for Aela to answer.

"The Great Wave showed me that Shuesh was in danger. As his favored queen, I was obligated to act. I believed the elders incapable of realizing the threat, and acted with haste, in the best interest of the Shuesh."

The elders roared in protest.

"How did you receive this knowledge from the Great Wave?"

"We can hardly acknowledge a threat when we are unaware of it!"

"You make us ineffectual by withholding information!"

Aluz struggled to quiet the angry men.

"Quiet. Be at peace, elders. We must proceed calmly and detached of personal insult if we are to discover the truth."

No outbursts followed his words.

Aela took advantage of the silence. "If this trial is merely to prove that I violated the law by sending soldiers to Shuesh, then we need not proceed. I confess to my guilt, and we may move to the punishment. No more time should be wasted on this when we still have heard no news from a city that has just survived a skirmish with the enemy.

"However, if this is a trial to determine whether or not my actions were validated by the circumstances and outcome, then let us proceed. I stand firmly behind my decisions."

She heard whispers among some of the elders and priestesses, and it gave her hope.

"No," Aluz said firmly. All attention shifted to him. "This is a trial to determine if the law was broken."

"I have already admitted that it was," Aela retorted.

"The trial shall proceed," he turned from her. "One elder and one priestess have been assigned to advise you in representing yourself."

With a flourish of satisfaction, Aluz resumed his seat above her. She watched in disgust as his hands subtly caressed the throne.

"You will not take my confession?" She cried out angrily.

"No. I do not believe that you are allowed to testify until after the opening ceremony and the presentation of the crime is made. I have been given a great responsibility and intend to see that no more laws are violated."

He looked away from her to those behind her. "We will start with the opening presentation."

Aela stared at him in silent shock. He was drawing this out, stalling for some reason she could not understand, and that scared her. She knew in her gut that something even worse than this trial motivated his actions.

As the opening arguments proceeded, a startling thought occurred to her. The trial was a diversion, allowing the wrangrent to regroup and coordinate his next attack position unnoticed.

The question of the Phoenix Son's involvement could no longer be denied.

Until this moment, she was unconvinced that he could be involved with the wrangrent. He was an Immortal lord. It was his duty to protect the world from twisted magic.

However, she had repeatedly seen evidence of his worldly desires and the strength of his contempt for being an Immortal. Yet, she had not believed that he coveted such things so much that he would betray even the Immortal oaths.

The rest of the day proceeded in a blur. The pomp and ceremony were honored just as Aluz had decreed.

As she was not allowed to speak again until her defense came, in another two or three days, she paid little attention to what was said. It was of little consequence to her. Lost in her thoughts, she became a prisoner in her mind as the hours passed.

One word though, three simple syllables, drew her back to the present. "Menony..." It echoed through her head.

"Menony, the queen's personal maid, will testify two days from now," Aluz confirmed. "She will be the first of the witnesses called against the queen, is that correct?"

He looked to the elders for confirmation.

Aela turned in response to their silence. They looked amongst themselves. Their discomfort was obvious.

Finally, Malcolm spoke. "The queen's maid has not been seen for over a week. She cannot be found in the palace, my lord."

Annoyance flared in Aluz's eyes and betrayed the calmness with which he spoke. "And a thorough search has been conducted?"

"Yes, my Immortal Lord," Malcolm responded with a bowed head.

Aela watched the smooth face of the Immortal tighten in displeasure. The intensity of his reaction and his strong desire to know Menony's whereabouts alarmed her.

"I am aware that there are many secret places to hide in a palace this old." He smiled at Aela. "I was told that the temple pool where the queen watched the Shuesh scene was also a long-kept secret, known by only a few of you."

He returned his attention to the elders. "It is possible that there are other such places where she may have secluded herself. She is an extremely loyal servant," the last word said with an almost undetectable touch of disgust. "I trust that she would not leave her mistress, though she is no doubt scared. We must find her and ensure that every measure to ascertain the queen's innocence is taken. She must be found as she is one of the few people to know what happened in the hours leading up to the offense in question."

His voice, which had been the perfect tone of benevolence, turned cold and stern. "We agree that she must be found, do we not, elders? And that another search of the palace will begin again tonight?"

The elders murmured their agreements.

"You are exceedingly wise and fair, my Immortal Lord. Menony will be found. I promise to have every corner, every alcove, every inch of the palace searched until she is," Malcolm assured.

"The truth must be known," Aluz stated grandly. "The opening ceremony will resume tomorrow. Your Majesty, I must now ask that you be escorted back to your cell."

Guards appeared on either side of Aela. She continued to stare at Aluz. He bowed his head in a gesture of respect, but she could see the smugness in his smile. It was not wise to fight this battle. There would be others. She suppressed her temper and bowed her head to the Immortal before she was escorted out.

As she reached the doorway, Bena announced loudly, "We will endure this farce only until the Great Wave has spoken." Her veil was pulled back, and Aela saw the anger in her eyes. She directed her words at the Phoenix Son.

Turning to Aela, her expression softened. "We will pray all night to the Great Wave, my queen. Until he answers."

Aela smiled and nodded in gratitude. As she returned to her cell, she marveled at the acceptance and support she had finally earned from the priestesses.

Chapter 32

The next day preceeded much the same as the first. Aela retreated to the inner realm of her thoughts. She had often thought the elders a silly group of privileged, old men, but never would she have thought them so weak-minded to have fallen in with the Phoenix Son's autocratic takeover.

Admittedly, he was an Immortal, a position that demanded respect and was defined by leadership. Yet, she remained baffled as to how they could not see his power lust, a trait that was condemned by the Immortal Laws. It was against the Immortal code for any Immortal to hold any political position in a territory of mortals.

The priestesses sat in heavy silence through the proceedings. The Great Wave had not spoken. They waited for a sign, for reason to stop the trial, but it did not come. Fear and worry deepened the severity of their expressions with the lengthening time of silence. Aluz asked every day if they had guidance from the Great Wave. They were forced to report that they did not.

Days passed and still no news of Shuesh. No messengers to confirm that the city still stood. No witnesses to support Aela's actions. She expected by the fourth day that Captain Tevor would appear. She was disappointed.

Aela worried about the Great Wave's silence and the fate of Shuesh. She also wondered about Tarr and her guards. She had seen Mar escape the Temple pool room. She had not received confirmation that Sey had succeeded at escaping with Tarr. Out of fear, she did not mention either. She would not draw attention to them.

She listened with half an ear when Aluz concluded the opening presentations by the elders. Tomorrow, they would present the case against. He outlined, with great accuracy, how the rest of the trial would proceed. Aela smiled despite herself as she wondered if he had been coached by one of the elders or if he had indeed diligently studied Dovkeyen law as he had once told her.

She forced herself to sleep that night despite the nightmares that frequently woke her. Images of Masia on fire, of people calling out in pain, and ash falling from the sky like snow flashed through her dreams with increasing intensity. She woke frequently with screams echoing in her head.

Grief washed over and consumed her in the dark hours of the night. Alone for the first time in years, she opened herself to the deep pools of emotion she locked away.

Snatches of her life in exile, surrounded by the warm welcoming people of Masia. She remembered the peace that came with being so removed from the palace that she did not have to care about its politics. She remembered wading in the shallow waters of the Greater River as a lost and confused girl and feeling again a renewed awareness of the water. In the currents of the river, she experienced her first visions and reconnected with the Great Wave.

On the docks of Masia, she stood with her guards, teaching them her language while learning their own. Walking through the lazy streets, they learned to be men, and she learned to be a woman, growing together so that they became inseparable in spirit. The tears washed over her like a cleansing rain, and Aela let the pain of the loss flow away. Between the nightmares and tears, she managed little sleep.

BERTO AND BENA REPRESENTED her. Their loyalty warmed her heart. Unsurprisingly, Malcolm argued against her.

He presented his case with such ferocity and efficiency that Aela was quickly reminded of the elder's tenacity and intellect. He merely needed a pursuit that suited his passion. Apparently, persecuting Aela was among his passions.

She forced herself to focus on his speech.

"Not only did the queen violate the balance of power when she sent soldiers to Shuesh, but it was witnessed by the elders that she illegally practiced magic." Malcolm measured his pace perfectly as he stopped in front of the elders and turned back to pin Aela with a scathing stare.

"Illegally?" Aluz interrupted, clearly confused by the charge. "How was it illegal?"

Aela turned to him and smiled. Obviously, his knowledge of Dovkeyen law was not as vast as he boasted.

"It is illegal for anyone other than the priestesses to perform magic of any kind in Dovkey, and they may only practice water magic," Aela answered for Aluz. "It is common knowledge."

His confusion was replaced with a look of irritation. However, before he could respond, Malcolm seized upon the opportunity.

"You see, she is a persistent breaker of the law despite her in-depth understanding of it. Your Majesty, I would remind you at this time that you are not allowed to speak until you have been asked to voice your defense, and we have not yet called for that."

Aela kept her gaze on Aluz as she took a calming breath. "You do understand the conditions of this trial, Queen Aela?" Aluz asked haughtily. "You are not to speak."

Aela raised a brow as he stared at her. The room quieted.

Finally, with a huff of annoyance, Aluz said, "You may answer the question. Permission is given for you to speak."

A small smile pulled at Aela's lips. "Yes, my Lord, I understand."

They stared at each other in silent challenge. Aluz looked away first. "Very well. You may continue, Elder."

Malcolm smiled. "Thank you, my Immortal Lord. As I was saying, the queen must be tried for not just the act of treason, which is a grievous crime indeed, but for the use of magic.

"It is known by all here that the queen undertook the priestess trial at the age of thirteen and failed. We believed her to be at the time unable to do magic. A great disappointment to all, but not a misdeed. Yet, we were deceived. Queen Aela purposefully failed the trial and hid her abilities from us."

"We do not know that she intentionally failed the trial."

Malcolm turned to find Berto as his opposer. The older man had stood and glared at the younger. "Many priestesses come into their abilities at an older age."

The priestess sitting next to Berto nodded in agreement. "Elder Malcolm, I am afraid that you are painting an inaccurate picture of the young woman on trial."

Several of the elders murmured in agreement. They were clearly divided. Tension hung in the space.

Malcolm recovered quickly. "It is rare for a young woman to acquire abilities after the age of thirteen, which is why the trials are conducted at that age. However, had the queen come into her powers later as you propose, Elder Berto, it was her duty in to inform the Head Priestess, which she did not do." He turned to Bena for confirmation.

The priestess grudgingly agreed.

"We need not wonder though. All we must do is ask the queen herself." He looked to Aluz to ask the question; the Immortal could compel her to speak truthfully.

"Your Highness, did you acquire your magic after the priestess trial?" Aluz's question held the room in suspense.

He had not used the Immortal power to compel her, for which she felt a small gratitude.

Aela could have lied, and Aluz could have forced her to answer truthfully, further tainting her character. She sighed before answering truthfully, "No."

The response of hushed murmurs was immediate, yet Malcolm's voice carried over all of them. "So, you admit that you possessed the ability to use water magic at the time of the trial and purposefully failed?" His question struck like a wounded viper.

"Yes, I could perform the magic during my training but could not do so during the trials," Aela answered.

Berto spoke out, "That has nothing to do with this trial."

"Of course it does!" Malcolm countered as he stood in front of the elders. "It is about establishing a tendency towards disrespectful violation of our laws!"

"You are trying to slander the queen's character," Berto retorted hotly.

"I am merely presenting the facts. Her character speaks for itself." Malcolm walked away from the elders smugly.

Aela turned back to watch the reaction of the elders; however, her attention shifted instead to the figure in the corner. Familiar green eyes watched the interplay of the elders with a perceptive intensity that was unnerving.

Aela had always been disturbed by the way her cousin seemed to absorb every detail of a situation. Behind the beautiful face was a mind that sorted, assembled, and analyzed, yet few but Aela thought of Ishea that way. She was the benevolent Healer Priestess, the one to save the children of Dovkey.

Aela continued to watch her cousin while wondering at Ishea's observations.

Aluz's gaze also drifted to Ishea. He called out her name in surprise, and as attention shifted to her, the deep concentration was replaced by a look of sorrow. So quickly the transformation happened, Aela knew she was the only one to witness it.

One of the elders rushed to greet her, fawning over her outstretched hand. She smiled warmly at him. "We are honored by your presence."

"As always, I am touched by the warmth of your welcome, Elder Fred." Her hand remained in Fred's grasp as she turned to Aluz. "Forgive me for interrupting. I know not what matter of state you are conducting, but I have brought urgent news from Shuesh."

Aela rose from her seated position.

Hans spoke before she could question her cousin. "We are involved in a matter most disturbing. The queen is being tried for treason."

Ishea looked with shock and deep concern toward Aela. She pulled her hand from Fred and rushed to Aela's side. Grabbing her cousin's hand, she addressed the room in earnest.

"That cannot be. My Immortal Lord, elders, revered priestesses, I know my cousin is not capable of such an offense. She is a true servant to her country. For as long as I have known her, she has been an ideal of virtue. Forgive me for speaking out of turn, but I must stand as witness to my cousin's character." She squeezed Aela's hand and gave her an encouraging smile.

"Healer Priestess, your testimony is highly valued though entirely out of turn. We have not reached the defense part of the trial yet. However, I will suspend the hearing so that we may know what news you bring from Shuesh. The lack of news has been very distressing to us all." Aluz gestured for her to continue.

Despite the warmness of Ishea's demeanor, Aela felt cold. A chill reminiscent of the ice curse crept over her skin. It disappeared quickly.

Ishea's expression turned grim. "I wish that I brought with me more hopeful news; however, it is only the truth that I can share with you. Shuesh has been destroyed."

"No," Aela shuddered and withdrew from Ishea. "That is not possible!"

"I am so sorry, my queen, that the news was not more heartening." The priestess turned her saddened eyes to the elders. "The city lies in ash, just as Masia."

The elders gasped as they accepted the priestess's account.

Aela listened as Ishea described how the wrangrent had left Shuesh a mess of crumbled stone and ash. According to the great Healer Priestess, no survivors could be found among the wreckage. The wrangrent's attack had been swift and lethal. Even the great fountain had been destroyed.

"The symbol of our deity lies in pieces because of the wrangrent's fury. He means to attack the heart of our people by destroying our center of healing," Ishea continued to explain.

"The fountain wasn't destroyed by the wrangrent," Aela said.

Ishea turned towards her with narrowed eyes.

"I assure you; it has been destroyed, my queen. I have seen it myself," Ishea said slowly.

Aela looked at her with sudden conviction. "Yes, it was destroyed but not by the wrangrent. The Great Wave destroyed it when he washed the city clean after the battle. First, our men struck it, and then blessed water flowed out and cleansed the city of ash."

She turned to the others. "Why has no other news come from the city? There were survivors." Looking back to Ishea, "How is that only you have come with news?"

Ishea's eyes dilated, but her surprise was quickly disguised.

"It is as I said. There were no survivors to bring the news. I was in the port of Nysea when I and my fellow priestesses noticed the unnatural clouds that moved east in the direction of Shuesh. We rode out immediately. However, it is a two-day ride to the city, and when we arrived there was nothing left to aid."

She stared at Aela before carefully asking, "Why is it that you think such things happened at Shuesh? You seem quite sure."

"I saw it," Aela admitted reluctantly.

"You saw it? How?"

"I viewed the battle using one of the ancient temple pools. Through it, I saw everything, from the arrival of the unnatural clouds and the Frin'gerens to the wrangrent's army of ash men, the flooding of the fountain, and our victory."

"The queen illegally used magic to watch the events at Shuesh," Malcolm explained as he approached the two women.

"It was actually the matter we were discussing before your arrival," Aluz added.

"I see," Ishea said softly.

She looked away from the Immortal Lord and studied Aela intensely. "But I did not think that you possessed the gift of water magic, cousin." There was a sharp edge to her voice, barely detectable, and it made Aela's gut churn in warning. "You have kept a great secret from us."

Ishea continued to study her, talking slowly as her mind put the pieces together. Aela watched suspiciously, wondering at her cousin's calculations. The unease in her stomach grew until Ishea turned to the Immortal with a look of concern.

"What magic was performed at the pool?" Ishea asked Aluz.

The Immortal responded quietly, "I am unable to say as I did not witness the event, nor am I learned on the subject of water magic."

"Who did witness, any with training?" Ishea asked.

Several of the elders explained what they had seen, but Ishea did not appear satisfied. "Were none of the priestesses present?"

"I believe Feone was there," one of the elders called out. All attention shifted to the priestess who stood bowed in the corner.

"Feone," Ishea began softly, "you will tell me exactly what you witnessed."

The priestess looked to Aela and spoke only after the queen gave her a nod of encouragement. "The queen stood next to one of the ancient temple pools."

"What are the pools used for?" Ishea asked.

"They are said to have been a concentrated source of water magic. Pure power that could be used to perform any ritual, but they were lost after the Reformation."

"Go on," Aluz encouraged gently when she paused. "What did you see?"

"The queen stood next to the pool and an image of Shuesh reflected in the water."

"How did you know it was Shuesh?" Ishea continued to soothingly interrogate.

"I saw the fountain. During my training, I was required to spend time at the Temple of Healing, so I know what the city and the fountain look like. Her Majesty stood there with her eyes closed and hands held out to the water, in deep concentration."

"Then what?"

Feone narrowed her eyes suspiciously at the other priestess. "The fountain burst."

"You mean the image was gone?"

"No," Feone straightened her shoulders and took a deep breath. "Water erupted from the fountain in the image and from the temple pool."

A series of gasps followed the admission.

"Feone, have you ever...performed magic like what you witnessed the queen doing?" Ishea asked with a concerned expression.

"No, it takes a great deal of power to communicate any bit of magic over even a small distance. I know of very few priestesses who can do it." She turned to the queen. "I'm so sorry, Your Majesty."

Aela gave her a weak smile. "It's the truth, Feone. Do not be sorry for that."

"It appears that the queen not only deceived us about being able to practice magic but is more powerful than could be expected," an elder stated venomously.

"The queen was blessed by the Great Wave and through her, he wielded his power," Bena defended.

The gasp beside her drew Aela's attention.

She watched as Ishea tried to conceal the small smile on her face while infusing her voice with confusion and worry. "How can it be though? The prophecy would have to be wrong. The Great Wave would be wrong. No, it cannot be." She said firmly as she stared at Aela.

"One to save the children of Dovkey, one to fail..." she drew the words out slowly as if realization had just hit her. "And one to betray."

She whispered the last words, yet Aela knew that not a single person in the hushed room missed their implication.

There it was...the final crime brought against her. So softly, so subtly that she had not foreseen her actions reflecting in such a horrific way.

"No," she whispered softly to the accusation. "No, no, no," she continued to object in disbelief. "I am not the wrangrent."

Ishea took a step back, her eyes watering with tears. "I would never have thought you capable of such things."

She turned pleadingly to Aluz. The Immortal stood with genuine shock reading as clearly on his face as Aela's.

"I...I do not know what to say," he stuttered as he looked from Ishea to Aela. "I do not..." He looked remorsefully at Aela.

The elders and priestesses stood in shocked silence, hatred, and anger in their eyes. Ishea alone looked expressionless and betrayed nothing as she stared intently at Aela.

"My Immortal Lord, I would like to petition that the trial be adjourned today considering what has been revealed. The Immortal Council will have to be alerted immediately."

"But we have a trial to conduct," Malcolm objected.

Ishea silenced him with a gesture of her hand. He looked like a reprimanded child as he held his words. "The Council will try her for crimes much greater than this trial." She paused. "And punishment fitting those crimes will be greater than any we could enforce."

"I am not the wrangrent!" Aela grabbed her cousin's wrist.

Both women visibly shuddered at the contact. Aela felt ice twist up her arm like a creeping vine, and a chill seeped into her muscles. She broke away quickly and stared back at Ishea in stunned disbelief.

Ishea was visibly shaken, and Aela was sure that it was not entirely an act. Looking down at her arm in disbelief, Ishea withdrew and turned her wide eyes to Aluz.

"My lord, I believe it would be safest for everyone if you bound the queen so that she cannot perform magic against us."

Aluz stared at her for several moments before nodding. "Yes," he agreed as he moved toward Aela.

She continued to stare at her cousin even as he stood next to her. He said her name several times before she complied with his wishes and thrust her wrists towards him. She let him bind her without another objection. It was useless to resist now. The evidence had been greatly turned against her. Even those on her side would find it hard to trust her innocence.

Two anxious guards stood on either side of her, afraid to guide her to the prison cell. However, Aela did not need their guidance as she turned from the horrified faces and headed towards the door.

The fools, Aela thought as she was followed from the room. They thought they had finally revealed the wrangrent, and they had. However, it was not the woman bound and on her way to a prison cell.

Chapter 33

She stood in the doorway and took great delight in seeing her foe detained in the archaic prison. The tower room had been unused for centuries, reflecting a time when her ancestors embraced barbarism with relish. She had often sought out this place to feel the dark nature she secreted away reflected in its torturous purpose.

Metal rings with broken chains lined the wall opposite Aela's cell. A rotting square table in the middle of the room held spikes and hammers of various sizes, shackles, prongs, and jagged blades. A cold hearth stood in the corner of the room, ash and broken bone in the grate. Time had ground scent and stain into the stone so thoroughly that only hints of odors and hues remained.

"You know, they weren't even aware of this room." Aela's bowed head popped up, and her gaze locked with Ishea's.

As she sauntered to the middle of the room, Ishea savored the sight of Aela behind bars. Her pristine white robes dragged on the ground. She cared little of the hems soiled by the gathering grime.

Smiling cunningly at Aela, she continued, "I'm not surprised though. A bunch of Reformationists, all of them. So ready to forget the times before the Reformation, so eager to look away from the ugliness of the past... as if it has nothing to offer us." Ishea picked up one of the spikes and examined it. Fantasies of using the barbaric instruments filled her with excitement.

"There is a lot to be found in the ugliness though." She looked to Aela. "Don't you think?" She gave the spike one last look before carefully replacing it. Perhaps she would use it on her cousin later.

Aela started at her in stony silence.

"I found this room when I was just a child visiting your mother."

She circled around the table towards the blackened hearth and held out her hands in front of it as if warming them. Ash and bone swirled slowly, gradually gaining speed. The ashes sparked and gathered to form small, black flames that converged hungrily on the bits of bone.

Aela gasped.

"I was always fascinated by ashes, you know." Ishea smiled as she watched the pain flash across Aela's face.

"These bones and ash taught me so many things. I wouldn't be who I am today without that knowledge."

She remembered exploring this room, fascinated by the chains, hammers, and other implements of torture. Her lessons with the priestesses bored her. In this forgotten room though, her imagination gorged on the possibilities.

She had sifted the ashes through her fingers so many times, marveling at how substance could be turned into something so delicate and fleeting. And then, she felt it. The crackling magic contained in the broken bones and ash. It sizzled along her nerves faintly that first time. Every time after, the sensation intensified until she felt the electrical current buzzing on her fingertips. Years would pass before she could do more than just experience the crackling energy.

She turned back to Aela, and the two women studied each other. The hatred and distrust in Aela's eyes excited her.

"I assume," Ishea looked away first with a gleeful little smile, "that you learned your magic in much the same way. Not from ash of course, but what was it? The ocean waves?"

She slowly approached Aela, dragging her fingers across the rusting prison bars as she went. "No, it couldn't be. You were sent away after the trials...to Masia." She stopped to study Aela's reaction and was pleased by it.

Raw pain and anger flashed across the queen's face before she could contain it. Ishea laughed.

"Ah, Masia. We both have happy memories of that place. It was your sanctuary, your place of refuge and healing after the failure and the plague. It was the first demonstration of my power to the world, and it was quite the show, wasn't it?"

Aela threw herself against the bars as she reached with murderous hands. Ishea's laugh only further enraged her.

"It was the rivers, wasn't it? The currents taught you to use water magic. There you were growing up on the outpost of the kingdom, out of sight and out of mind, and becoming everything that they thought you incapable of."

Ishea bowed her head. "What a great deception! Mine was nowhere near as good as yours. You were the rare survivor of a plague that killed hundreds. The great Healer Priestess, your very own mother, died nursing you back to health. Sacrificed herself for you. But then the trials came, and you failed. You always did struggle during the lessons, didn't you? Did just enough to pass. Was it really any wonder that you failed?" she emphasized the last word. "You were the failed queen, teaching yourself magic from the river currents," she laughed to herself. "They all knew I had great power; just unwisely chose to believe I would use it in their favor."

AELA FELT THE RAGE growing inside her as Ishea pushed harder and harder to elicit a response. She didn't understand what her cousin hoped to accomplish or if she simply enjoyed the pain that she caused Aela. It was easy to believe that Ishea simply enjoyed the infliction of pain.

Yet, despite the storm of hatred growing in her heart, she felt restrained. As if her magic had a consciousness of its own. It contained her, kept her still and quiet. She did not understand it, but the ancient magic of her people was beyond her understanding. Within it was the wisdom of the Great Wave. Aela trusted in that.

Ishea noted Aela's restraint, and it only fueled her efforts to inflict a deeper wound.

"It was beautiful that morning." Her voice was soft, but her eyes were hard as she watched for the injury. "The clouds had parted, and the sunlight hit the pearly stone of the city. It danced on the water. I watched it from across the bank. They were preparing for a festival, celebrating your visit. The banners were rainbows strewn throughout the city. Such a lazy city, everyone walking around like there was no reason in the world to hurry through life.

"It was mid-morning, and the divers were preparing for their treasure hunt. There was one in particular that must have started early because as the others plunged into the waters, he emerged.

"A child, female, with soft golden curls, sat on the pier, her chubby toes teasing the current. She giggled when the diver swam to her, her father no doubt. He held up a rough pearl of pink and lavender. Her eyes enlarged, and she reached tentatively towards it, smiling when her father placed the pearl in her tiny hand. 'That pearl is for the queen,' he said. 'The first from Masia. Our queen will wear it in her crown.'"

The tears poured down Aela's cheeks, and still, she felt the invisible magic wrap tightly around her, containing her pain and anger. She desperately wanted to lash out and strike Ishea. She imagined using the magic like a blade, one that could end her cousin's existence. Yet, with each vengeful thought, the magic wrapped her tighter until emotion rolled inward, unable to escape.

"I think her dress was yellow. A bright yellow. Like daffodils in the spring. I remember a scrap of it swirling in the wind after the ash had settled...no more bones to burn."

Her body was frozen and bound, but her lips parted, and the pain was allowed release. She screamed in agony as the painful images flooded her head. For so long, Aela had been nothing but numb, and now, she wanted only anger. Her existence was pain, her own, and the pain she shared with her people.

Ishea smiled in triumph. She turned away, satisfied with the misery she elicited. She sat on the table facing Aela.

Aela's body had bent from the pain, and she knelt on the floor of her cell as tears silently fell from her eyes.

"I wasn't the only the only little girl that went exploring though, was I? You found the temple pools. I never thought they existed. Otherwise, I might have sought them out. There was a great deal of power in them."

Aela looked up Ishea's last statement. "Was?"

Ishea raised a brow. "You didn't know? Of course not, they've had you imprisoned since that night. Whatever power they once held, you gathered it and unleashed it in Shuesh. I wondered where all that magic had come from. I knew that it couldn't have been all you." She tilted her head to the side with a thoughtful expression. "Though none of us are sure of your potential now."

The pleasantness left her voice. "I checked them after the elders told me what you had done. There's nothing but residuals. Whatever was there, was ancient and potent." Anger darkened Ishea's eyes and her nostrils flared with a few deep breaths.

"Did you feel it, Ishea?" Aela provoked. "When it washed over your army and defeated you, did you feel how ancient and...pure it was?"

"Aine was a curious little girl too."

Aela started at the abrupt change in topic.

"You found the temple pools, I found this room, and Aine found me. She was everywhere, wasn't she?" Disgust laced her voice. "Every time I turned around, there she was just silently watching me. She was so quiet, never betraying a thing."

Ishea's gaze became unfocused, and Aela watched as her cousin seemed to go to another place, lost in memory.

"Nothing, I never saw anything in those big dark eyes that seemed to see everything. I was afraid that she would tell someone. She didn't though, so I let her watch. Who cared, really? That little mute wasn't going to do anything. But one day, those eyes of hers weren't so blank. I'd been twirling ash in a ball just above my hand. She's seen it before, but she saw something else that day."

Ishea looked at Aela, and she saw the insanity that Ishea always hid so well.

"I remember looking over my shoulder, thinking- there she is again, watching. But her eyes widened, and they were black and empty. When they cleared, it was the first time ever I saw something in Aine's eyes. Fear. She'd seen so much; I couldn't figure out why she was suddenly afraid. It was days before I realized that she had seen something beyond me in that chamber. She had seen the future. I wanted to know so badly what she'd seen, but she was never alone.

"And then she was gone. The trial came, and she ran. Later, when I realized what I was destined to become, I knew what it was she had seen." She laughed and for once it was not musical or soothing. It was deranged. "For so long, I thought that Aine was the savior of Dovkey. I knew who I was in the prophecy. Aine had seen me becoming a wrangrent, and I believed that she was the only one who could defeat me.

"I waited many years, trapped in the priestess training, unable to stretch my magical abilities. But when my missions began, I searched the entire county for her, but there was no trace of where she had gone."

Ishea tilted her head at the same odd way as a bird, but her face began to smooth, looking less demented. "It took me a long time to tie the two of them together, Aine and Kesh. He helped her run away to Frin'gere, you know. He set her up with a family, attended her wedding, and the birth of her first child."

Ishea's fingers curled in anger. "I can thank her for those water wards the Frin'gerens placed around Shuesh. Even after all these years, they felt like her. I imagine she enjoyed making them. Probably even saw how well they'd work against me," Ishea muttered to herself as her hands clenched and unclenched.

She turned back to Aela, her gaze sharp.

"I think he had sight similar to hers, maybe not as powerful." Ishea began to examine objects of torture once more though her thoughts were obviously elsewhere.

"You think Kesh knew about you?"

"She must have told him there would be a wrangrent, but she never told him who, I'm sure of that. Though I don't think he was always comfortable around me. But we will never know the truth, will we? The king of nobility went and sacrificed himself, but for what?"

"So, it started with those ashes. You didn't learn everything from them though." Aela attracted Ishea's attention once more.

The priestess smiled and leaned back against the table. "Aren't you clever? You keep reminding me of how foolish I was to overlook you."

Displeasure darkened her expression at the reminder of her mistake. "I guess it doesn't matter though, does it? I have you where I need you, and even though you cost me a defeat at Shuesh, I will be merciful."

She regained her wicked smile. "I think that I shall let Aluz convince the elders tomorrow that you must be punished as soon as possible. You are too much of a threat for us to wait for the Immortal Council."

Ishea pushed away from the table and grabbed the bars on either side of Aela's face. In a conspirator's tone, "The Council is not coming, you know. Aluz never called them."

"I suspected as much," Aela replied. "When did the two of you come together? I assume that he was the one to teach you the basics of fire magic that you then merged with the ash magic."

Ishea smiled as if she had been waiting for the question to be asked. "I met him the same time that you did, just shortly after your mother died. He had just been betrothed to you. I found him in one of the gardens, obviously considering the ramifications of the engagement, and distracted him with question after question on fire magic. We did not see each other again for many years." She paused to consider. "Yes, it was after I became a priestess and was on my mission of healing. I sought him out. By then, I knew so much more, and Aluz's frustration with his chosen future had grown greatly. It took little persuasion to bring him into the web of my plans." She tapped the rusty bars with her nail.

"Aluz wanted so much to be king," Ishea snickered. "He's an Immortal, and all he wants is to rule a bit of land. I had only to promise him Dovkey. Marrying you did not seem to upset him either."

Aela felt the bile rise in her throat again as she thought of the Immortal's betrayal and his control over the elders. According to Ishea, she might very well be executed tomorrow. She would not think about that now. She pushed down the fear, knowing it was useless to her.

Ishea reached through the bars and ran that same slender finger down Aela's forehead to the tip of her nose. "What thoughts are gathering in that head of yours? Were you thinking about how silly you were to trust that pretty Immortal? Are you upset that once again you will not be allowed to be queen? It's just one thing after another for you, isn't it, cousin?"

She waited for a response and received only cold silence. Aela refused to be baited.

"You know if you had not proved to be so troublesome, I would have let Aluz marry you and keep you as his little pet. He is a little fond of you."

Unable to get a rise out of Aela, Ishea's smile faded as she gripped the bars with white hands. Her eyes darkened, and the madness showed once more.

"Where is your maid, Aela?" she demanded in a hard voice.

Aela's brows rose slightly in response. "I have no idea."

Ishea slammed her hand against the bars. "You are lying! I want to know where she is."

"Why?" Aela leaned forward, meeting her cousin's anger head-on.

They glared at each other for several tense minutes. When Ishea spoke again, her voice was calmer.

"Because she is carrying the heir of Dovkey, and Kesh's child would be invaluable to me. Not surprised? So, you do know. I'd wondered if they had let you in on that little secret. It took me quite a while to figure it out. Of course, when Aluz told me she was pregnant, my long-held belief that they were lovers was confirmed."

"How did Aluz know?"

Ishea smiled again. "Immortals, it seems, can discern the presence of a person's soul. Some are more gifted than others, but all are taught to read auras for clues to the soul. A woman with child carries a separate aura, that of her unborn baby. Aluz can see the auras; unfortunately, he is not very good at reading them. If so, he might have seen something important in yours."

She turned away, her causal demeanor failing to mask the intensity and desperation. "Once more, where is your servant?"

"What do you want with her child?" Aela asked in a hard voice.

Ishea sighed as she leaned against the table. "Kesh was a very powerful seer; I am sure of it. His child could be as great if not more so. I need a seer." She paused, considering whether to share the next bit of information. "The more power you attain, the greater your chances of losing it. You're more vulnerable to attack, yet the harder it becomes to see all the directions you can be attacked from. With a seer of my own, raised to love only me, I would always be able to see the next attack and prevent it. I would never have to lose anything."

"Your tower will eventually fall, no matter what measures you take," Aela warned.

Picking up one of the spikes, Ishea twirled it in her hand. "I can torture it out of you, Aela."

Aela approached the bars, grasping them with both hands. "You can try."

⁂

ISHEA'S EYES NARROWED. Aela's will was strong. She would be hard to break. Though the process was likely to be enjoyable, she felt the familiar irritation she had with her cousin. So poised, so determined...so pure. The queen of Dovkey disgusted her.

Ishea wrapped her hands around Aela's as she crushed them against the bars. Her whisper dripped with hatred. "You are all alone. Kesh is dead, your servant girl missing, your loyal guards gone, and even that Frin'geren dog has abandoned you."

Aela smiled.

Ishea growled. "You knew that too, did you? Is he with Menony? When I find them, will I get the pleasure of murdering him in front of you? Aluz said that you were in love with the Frin'geren. I won't make it quick, Aela. I'll drag out his pain for days."

"You would have to find them first." She smiled. "I am never alone, and no matter what you try to do to me, I will not give you anything you want. Ever."

Ishea took a deep breath. "I think I'll kill you myself, Aela. I'll turn you to ash just as I turned your beloved city to ash. In front of all Dovkey, I'll show what I am, and I will show that their Blessed Queen is still nothing but a failure.

"Tomorrow morning, Aela, I'll have the elders march you out to the stone steps where the waves can wash away your remains."

She leaned closer to whisper in Aela's ear. "Know this though, I will find Menony. I will have Kesh's child. I'll track down that Frin'geren and every one of your guards, and I'll let the wind scatter their ashes all over the land." She pulled back, looking into Aela's eyes once more. "I will win, Aela."

Chapter 34

The long narrow slits that let light and air into the room had gone dark long ago. Aela sat in the darkness contemplating what would happen next for her. The knowledge that Tarr and her guards had escaped filled her with relief. She had worried that they would not obey her request. More importantly, Menony and her unborn child were safe. The only other thing that Aela could hope for was the safety of her people.

She did not doubt her cousin's threat. Aela was certain that tomorrow Ishea would unleash the full extent of her power with the intent to eliminate Aela once and for all.

"Things could have ended differently, Aela."

His voice came from the doorway. Though Aela could not see him, she recognized the Phoenix Son's voice.

"Yes, they could have," she responded to the darkness.

A glowing ball of flame appeared. She shielded her unaccustomed eyes as it floated toward her. As her eyes adjusted, she saw the man behind the fire.

Aluz looked disheveled. His hair hung loosely and unkempt at his shoulders. His tunic hung open to reveal the skin of his chest. His feet were bare. He looked lost, and the arrogant superiority was replaced by confusion and sadness.

"I did not want it to be like this," he said as he stood in front of the bars, looking down to where Aela sat on the floor.

"What exactly was it that you didn't want, Aluz?" She stood to face him. "The death of hundreds of people, the destruction of an entire city, the reign of terror that Ishea plans to unleash?" Her voice grew louder with anger.

"Sometimes change brings with it a degree of loss."

Aela's laugh was without mirth. "What a heartless description of what happened in Masia," she said softly.

"It is not Ishea's intention to rule with terror."

Aela grabbed the bars between them. "Can you honestly be so foolish? Do you not think the people of Masia and Shuesh felt terror when she attacked?" He gave no answer. "My execution tomorrow will be terrifying no doubt."

Aluz looked at her then. His fiery eyes burned with despair. "That is why I have come. I have observed your compassion and your dedication to your people. I believe that Dovkey would be enriched by the influence of such a queen."

Aela stared at him in confusion.

He stepped forward and grasped her hands. "I want you to be my queen still. When I rule Dovkey-"

"Over my dead body!" Aela tried to pull away, but his grip was too strong.

Aluz's temper flared. "That is exactly what will happen, Aela, if you continue to be stubborn!"

She stared at him as he regained his composure with a few deep breaths. "If you tell me where your maid is, Ishea has agreed to release you...into my custodianship."

Aela laughed. "Oh, what a bargain. Life bound to you as what, some sort of slave?"

Fire erupted all over the Phoenix Son's body and flames danced in his eyes. Aela managed to pull free her hands and stepped away in alarm. A murderous gleam lit his eyes.

The room glowed from the fire that burned around the Phoenix Son. He closed his eyes, obviously trying to calm himself. The flames grew.

"I could take you into the phoenix fire right now, Aela. You would be untouchable and immortal."

"And still bound to you," Aela said as she looked around for anything that might save her from the growing flames.

"Yes, bound to me in the most intimate of ways. Did you know," he said as the bars began to melt beneath his hands, "that a fledgling phoenix is completely dependent on her creator? She is loyal and obedient."

Aela's eyes filled with fear as the fire flared shades of blue and red, spreading into her cell, and the bars collapsed in front of the Phoenix Son.

She looked around for an escape but saw only more bars. Looking back at Aluz, she questioned if the threat was real. She feared that his threat was honest and that the fire circling around them was in fact the phoenix fire.

"It won't hurt, Aela. When it is over, I will care for you."

Aela tried to retreat to the back of the cell, but the fire closed the circle around them. The room glowed with the blaze, and Aela looked around one more time for any chance of escaping Aluz. She found no way out, and the fire continued to creep towards her.

TARR STALKED INTO THE room, a lit torch in one hand and a sword in the other. First, he and the guards had searched the dungeon for her. Not finding her filled him with fear. As he crept through the palace, he overheard snippets of conversation and was reassured that she was alive. However, finding her proved difficult.

When the unkempt Phoenix Son wandered past his hiding place, his instincts told him to follow. He was led to an unfamiliar part of the palace. Following carefully at a distance, he silently climbed the stairs unseen behind the Immortal.

He unsheathed his sword and used his magic to light the torch while Aluz threatened her.

When he finally entered the room and saw her surrounded by the Phoenix's Son's flame, he unleashed the power of his own fire. The torch fell from his hand and landed on the floor where flames crawled along the ground and slithered up his body.

Aluz turned to him. "I suspected that you knew fire magic. Far better at it than I had anticipated." His face and voice hardened. "Why did you return, Frin'geren? You were given a reprieve; it was foolish to come back."

"I couldn't leave without my fiancée, could I?" He smiled at the Immortal though the threat was clear enough.

"She was never yours."

"Not according to a little game of Seer's Fortune."

Aluz laughed as he turned from Aela and faced Tarr. His smile was demented. "You put far too much faith in a game."

Tarr's smile was viscous. "Are you denying me my winnings, Aluz?"

"Aela will not be yours," Aluz said with equal viciousness.

"Even without Seer's Fortune, I would strike you down." He raised his sword and charged toward the Immortal.

Aluz laughed and met his assault with a bolt of fire.

Tarr dodged and swung his sword in a wide arch catching Aluz in the arm. The Immortal stumbled backward, momentarily stunned by the blow. Tarr took the advantage and landed a kick solidly in the other man's chest. Aluz fell to the ground. His fall created an opening in the circle of flame, and Tarr gestured for Aela to exit the cell.

She rushed forward only to be pulled back by a flame wrapped around her ankle. She cried out in pain as the burn shot up her leg.

Tarr rushed into the cell, flames dancing all over his body. She pulled away from him instinctively, but he wrapped an arm around her waist anyway. He urged his flames to warm her, and he trusted that his magic would not burn her.

Fire moved down his other arm and covered the blade of his sword. He swung it at the flame gripping her ankle. It severed the flame with one swing.

Aela pulled free from the surrounding fire that crackled with hues of blue now. She limped with every step, but Tarr supported her as they headed toward the opening once more.

The Phoenix Son rose in an explosion of flame. He burned blue, and the outlines of his body blurred in the flames. Murderous rage filled his eyes.

Tarr pushed Aela behind him. Raising his sword in defense, he stood ready for the assault. "You cannot win this, Aluz."

Evil laughter erupted from the burning form. "I am an Immortal. You cannot defeat me."

Another fiery bolt shot towards Tarr. He met it with his fire magic. The two flames crashed in the space between, filling the air with crackling and popping. They swirled around each other, trying to consume the other. Finally, they shattered and fell to the ground like glowing embers.

A single sliver of flame soared through the air again and caught Tarr in the shoulder before he could counter. He groaned as his body took the blow, and he urged his fire to converge on the wound.

Aela attempted to assess the wound, but he firmly pushed her behind him again. A volley of fiery bolts shot through the air towards them. Tarr blocked each one with his sword, sending flames in all directions.

Freeing his right hand from the sword, he shot another bolt at the Phoenix Son. It broke into smaller bolts just before hitting the Immortal.

Aluz managed to block a few, but the majority slammed into his chest. He staggered backward.

Tarr pulled Aela with him as he used his foot to sweep away the blue flames in front of another set of bars. He moved them without inflicting damage on himself. Red and orange fire moved down his free arm and wrapped around the bars as he reached out for them.

Turning to Aela, he said, "When they burn through the bars, I want to you get out through the other cell. Your guards are waiting for you; they'll get you to safety."

"No! You are coming with us, Tarr," she pleaded.

"This was my whole purpose for coming here," his hand cradled her face. "To keep you safe."

"You have to come with me to fulfill that promise. You can't die here."

He smiled with amusement. "Who said anything about dying here?"

"Tarr!"

"Go," he pushed her through the melted bars and into the other cell.

AELA TURNED JUST IN time to see Aluz's burning fist swing towards Tarr. She called out, but it was too late. The blow landed on Tarr's right temple, and he went down, disappearing beneath the flames.

Aluz stood over him, a bolt of fire in his hand.

Aela looked around for water but found none. Eyeing the torture implements on the table, she rushed out of the cell toward them. Blue fire licked at her as she skirted past it.

Her movements distracted the Phoenix Son. He eyed the spike in her hand as she held it in front of her threateningly. Turning fully towards her, he left his back open to attack.

Tarr rolled away, kicking his legs out toward Aluz's knees. The impact bent the Immortal over, and Tarr struggled to his feet. He brought his fist down on Aluz's upturned face, driving the Immortal to his knees. Tarr's foot connected with the other man's abdomen and then his ribs.

He swayed on his feet but managed to stay upright as Aluz collapsed onto the ground in front of him. Side-stepping the body, Tarr staggered out of the cell towards the table where Aela stood with a deadly spike in her hand.

"I love how well you listen," he remarked as he took the spike from her. "Let's go."

She nodded and started towards the door.

Blue fire flashed up in front of her, and she heard Tarr groan behind her. The Phoenix Son's fire engulfed him, extinguishing the red and orange fire magic.

The same flames rose up to wrap around Aela. They contained her, unlike the fire that burned Tarr. She called out to him as she struggled to go to him, but the bands burned with her attempts to break free.

She watched in horror as the spikes on the table rose up into the air. They hovered and then turned. With astonishing speed, they flew through the air toward Tarr. Her scream was deafening as she watched helplessly. The spikes spread out just before hitting their target, penetrating the fire that burned all around Tarr.

A great cry of pain filled the air.

The blue flame retreated from her body and gathered into a shape that stood behind Tarr. The flames converged, and Aluz became visible as the fire absorbed into his body. The ancient spikes that had once been used for torture protruded from Aluz's shoulders, chest, leg, and the center of his forehead. His eyes glazed over, and his body slumped to the ground.

Tarr limped forward as Aluz collapsed behind him. Only Tarr's red and orange fire burned in the room. He called it back into his body, leaving the space around them cold and dark.

Aela tentatively stepped closer to the fallen Immortal. The color leached from his skin as pools of blood formed under his body and spread slowly across the floor.

Aela gagged at the sight, and Tarr pulled her head to his chest, blocking her view of the dead body. He shushed her, his hand running soothingly up and down her hair.

"We must leave quickly. That will not have escaped everyone's notice."

Together, they limped from the room. Outside, Sey and Mar waited. The cloth that usually covered their heads was gone. Mar stood on her side, offering aid while Sey did the same to Tarr.

"It will be harder to get out now. I had not intended to get into a firefight with the Immortal," Tarr groaned as they rushed down the hall.

"You defeated an Immortal," Sey said with a smile.

Tarr looked up at him, taking the hand offered. "Just one of my many feats you could say."

The guard laughed and thumped his big hand on Tarr's back eliciting another pained groan.

"The temple pools," Aela said. "We can escape the palace from there."

"The temple pools?" Tarr asked incredulously.

"Yes, there's a passage that leads to the ocean. You can swim, I hope."

Tarr nodded. "I can swim, but not well," He sighed.

"We will get you both through," Mar said. "Now, we must go quickly."

Chapter 35

With Mar and Sey's help, Tarr and Aela moved undetected through the palace. A black wound wrapped around Aela's ankle, shooting burning pain up her leg. She limped, but otherwise, was unharmed.

Tarr's wounds were more extensive. His shredded clothes hung loosely off his bowed frame. Beneath the burnt edges, his exposed skin was blackened. Blood trickled from his arm and his leg, and a raised bruise formed at his temple. He struggled to keep his eyes open, and Sey supported most of his weight. Aela frequently cast worried glances at him as they raced towards the pools. She would not lose him.

The rainbow chamber was dark and cold, and for the first time in a long time, Aela did not hear the voices of her people in the waterfall. The silence felt ominous.

The broken stone door partially blocked the entrance to the temple pools. She supported Tarr while Sey helped Mar to remove the rumble. When an opening formed, they climbed through. Against Tarr's wishes, Sey lifted him from the ground and handed him through the opening to Mar.

Aela guided them through the room, but when she reached the stairs that led to the ocean, she found the passage completely blocked.

"What happened?" She turned to Mar.

"I left through this passage," he said simply.

The passage was thoroughly blocked. Even with Mar and Sey's strength they would not be able to get out.

"Is there no way out?" Tarr called from the top of the steps.

Aela and Mar turned from the blocked passage and rejoined Sey and Tarr in the temple pool room.

Tarr leaned heavily against the wall, his breaths labored. "Where to now?" He panted.

Aela's eyes scanned the room. Scorch marks marred the stone. She placed her hand against the nearest one and felt the chill of her cousin's magic. Ishea had mentioned coming to see the pools. The walls and passage bore proof of the effects of her displeasure.

As she continued to look around the room, she realized that Ishea expected her to come here. That was why she had destroyed the passage. Overhead, they could hear the faint sound of raised voices. Aela knew the palace was awake and looking for her, which meant Ishea knew of her escape.

"The pools go to the ocean, do they not?" She turned to Mar.

His iridescent eyes met hers. Without the head wrap, she saw his face tighten with concern.

"They do, but the pools are deep, and the passages are long." His gaze shifted to Tarr. "He will struggle."

"Can you get him out?" she asked.

"I will get him through," Sey said as he joined the conversation.

"Ishea knew we would come here. We cannot go back the way we came, and we are quickly running out of time."

Aela knelt beside the main pool, the one that had given her the first vision of the wrangrent. She trusted the pool would lead them out, but she worried about Tarr's state. He slumped against the wall, his face tight with pain.

Gesturing for Mar and Sey to join her, they assisted him to the pool. He collapsed to his knees staring disconcertedly at the water.

"How deep?"

"Deep," was all she said. He turned to her, and she saw a flash of despair. He did not believe he could do it. The pain of his injuries showed in his face, and his shallow breathing came faster with every minute.

"What if this is the wrong one?" he asked.

"We get lost in the pools," Aela responded as she assessed him.

He managed a smile despite the pain. "I guess it's a good thing I have absolute faith in you then."

She cupped his face briefly. He closed his eyes and leaned into her touch.

"Sey will swim behind you. Get out through the tunnel as quickly as you can. Once you are in the ocean water, he can help you, but you have to get yourself there first."

He turned his face into her palm and kissed it gently. "I will. I will get through the tunnel." He assured. With a stronger voice, he commanded, "You do the same."

"I'll see you down there." She turned to Mar who knelt beside her. "Shall we?" He nodded.

Aela plunged headfirst into the water, feeling it rush up against her. A weak current pushed her back toward the surface. With all her strength, she swam against the current. The light above faded, and the tunnel darkened until visibility was lost. She knew that once she reached the ocean she would know; the undertow would sweep her out not up.

Lost in the darkness of the water was a surreal feeling. Fear clawed at her mind, demanding that she breathe. Her chest tightened with the need for air. Her arms weakened with each stroke, and she felt her body floating back up.

Mar would be behind her, but the tunnel was small enough to limit his movement. He would not be able to swim to his full ability until they were out. She only had to make it there, and then she could trust her friend to get her to land. With renewed determination, she pushed her body to keep swimming.

The pressure built. Her lungs ached, and she felt lightheaded. She was out of air.

Keep swimming, she told herself. Just as she thought that she would lose consciousness and be swept back up the tunnel, her body was whisked sideways. The undertow carried her deeper into the sea.

She was free of the tunnel. Her thoughts blurred, and she forgot everything but the feeling of weightlessness that surrounded her.

A hand gripped her waist, and with a great surge of movement, she was propelled upward. Her head burst through the surface of the water. Cool air hit her face and signaled her lungs to draw deeply. Waves lapped against her, and she coughed as a spray of water hit her in the face. Mar held her higher above the surface, allowing her to take greedy gulps of air.

"Where..." she attempted to ask as Mar effortlessly towed her through the waves. "Where are we going?"

"There is a hidden grotto that the Mer people use. It is for our use now per the Sea King."

She relaxed in his hold as they drifted below the white cliffs. Trusting him completely, she closed her eyes and let her body relax. She was unsure of how far they had gone when he warned her that they would have to dive deep to get to the grotto. She followed his instruction to take a deep breath before he dove down.

One arm held her tightly against his body while the other guided them down with side strokes. Each powerful kick of his legs propelled them deeper.

Mar swam many feet down before the opening became visible. With the grace of a fish, he swam through and up a short tunnel. They emerged in a clear pool that glowed with pale teal light.

The stone was white, and the chamber was warm. Mar helped Aela to dry land, leaning her against the wall. His somber eyes watched her until she assured him that she was well. He left her to dig in a small chest that sat off to the side. Returning with a blanket, he wrapped it around her shoulders.

"You had this well planned," she remarked. He smiled slightly.

She reached out for his hand pulling herself to her feet. "Thank you, Mar. For everything, for always being there."

A few silent tears ran down her cheeks as he enfolded her in his massive arms. He spoke no words, but she felt the love through his touch.

He pulled away as he adjusted the blanket. "You will need to be strong for tomorrow. Rest now. I will find Sey and the Frin'geren."

She nodded and brushed away the tears.

He dove back into the water, and Aela waited for her loved ones to return to her. It seemed that hours passed before Mar and Sey emerged with Tarr between them. They carried him out of the pool and laid him next to her.

He coughed heavily as they stepped away. Aela rushed to him. He rolled onto his side as he expelled more water from his lungs. He looked up at her and sighed in relief.

"I almost didn't make it."

"Me either," she said as she pushed the wet hair from his face.

His hand came up to cradle her cheek, a small smile playing on his lips. "You are a fine sight to see after an exhausting day."

She laughed and let Sey carry him further from the water.

Aela stripped Tarr of his shirt, which earned her a lecherous comment or two. She fussed over him, critically examining each wound. None were life-threatening.

"Aela, I need to hold you," he said weakly. His eyes refused to stay open.

Carefully, she sat between his legs and leaned against his chest. "Does this hurt?"

He snorted. "Everything hurts, love." She started to shift position, but his arms wrapped around her. "You are perfect, just stay right here... in my arms."

Eventually, she allowed her eyes to close and her body to relax against his. Mar wrapped another blanket around them.

She smiled and whispered her thanks as he walked away. Behind her, Tarr's breaths evened and deepened with sleep. Slowly, his heat returned and soaked into her.

Unexpectedly, he kissed her temple. "I love you, Aela." He whispered the words in her ear as his eyes closed again, and his body relaxed.

She rested her head on his shoulder. "I love you." His arms tightened around her, and she smiled at his acknowledgment of her words.

Exhaustion prevailed, and she fell asleep in his arms, knowing that for this night at least, she and those she loved were safe.

***

AELA AWOKE IN TARR'S arms, comforted by the warmth and strength of his body. His breathing was slow and deep, the sound of it a soothing song to her ears. She remained still, hesitant to wake him, but the incessant pain compelled her to move.

Gently lifting his arm, she maneuvered out of his hold and gently rested his arm against his chest. She smiled at the peacefulness of his face in sleep.

With a slight limp, she made her way to the clear pool of pale teal water. Sitting at the edge, she dropped her feet into the pool. The water was cool and soothed the pain slightly, and Aela was grateful even for the tiniest relief.

A movement off to the side caught her attention. Sey stirred from his position in the dark corner of the grotto. He moved gracefully and soundlessly towards her, sitting at the edge next to her.

"Mar?" she asked, looking around and not finding him.
"He is scouting. We will have to leave today."
Aela nodded. They could not stay in the hidden pool for much longer. Even beyond the most basic needs of food and water, they could not stay. Ishea's anger over their escape and the death of the Phoenix Son would be felt by the people. Dovkey would feel her wrath.

"I don't know where we will go, but we will have to get word to the Immortal Council. We must report Ishea and inform them of Aluz's death." A tiny shiver of fear ran down her spine. Punishment and revenge were unlikely, yet the Council would not be pleased.

She sighed, "It will not be a pleasant encounter, I fear."

Sey placed his hand atop hers where it rested on the ground. She turned to him.

"Thank you, Sey. For watching over him," she said with a look back at Tarr. "And me."

"He is amusing," the deep voice rumbled. Sey smiled as he shrugged.

Aela laughed softly. "That he is."

"He is wounded badly. I almost did not get him out of the temple pool." She believed that. "He was determined to make it to you though."

She looked at Tarr again. Burns from his fight with the Phoenix Son covered his torso. "I did not think a fire caster could be burned."

"Different types of fire magic," Sey responded.

She studied the burn that wrapped around her ankle. It was not a normal burn. Pain continued to shoot up her leg. She wondered if this, like her eyes, would be another mark of the things that she had survived.

She swirled her foot in the water, the movement of it against her skin soothing. Almost hypnotized by the rippling, Aela let herself relax. Though she tried to think of the journey ahead, she found that thoughts escaped her. All thoughts expect one.

Suddenly more alert, she reached into the water.

"Take your feet out for a moment, Sey."

He obeyed the command without question or comment.

The water around her fingers warmed as she moved them in small circles. Energy built with each circle she completed. Slowly, she pulled her hand from the water and watched in awe as it followed. The water formed a ball in her palm as she rotated her hand. It continued to swirl inside the ball, and Aela watched the glow in the center pulse outward.

Taking her ankle from the water, she turned her back to Sey and rested her foot on the white stone. She pushed the ball into the burn that ringed her lower leg. It pulsed and swirled around her ankle.

The pain intensified, pulsing in time with the glow of the water. The pain and the glow faded together as her water magic healed the damage done. When the burn faded from her skin, the water evaporated into the air. Aela smiled over her shoulder at Sey.

"That is new," he said simply, though she saw the awe in his eyes. "I did not know that you could do that."

"Neither did I."

A shadow in the water moved closer. Sey and Aela shifted away from the pool as Mar's head broke the surface. He pulled himself out just as Aela heard Tarr awaken with a start behind her. She went to calm him; he seemed momentarily confused by his surroundings.

"The waves are restless," Mar said as he cleared the water from his face. "And the rivers carry death."

"Ishea unleashed her anger last night," Aela said as she helped Tarr to stand. He groaned and swayed as he came to his feet.

"We have to leave," he said.

"We will and soon. First, though, I'm going to heal these wounds."

"Yeah?" He questioned with a raised brow.

She guided him to the edge of the pool, performing the same water magic she had done to her ankle. His injuries were more extensive, and the healing more painful. She did not pause despite the muffled groans of pain he made.

"I cannot heal all of it. The Phoenix Son's magic was strong, but I think that they will heal with time. Do you feel better?" she asked as the last of the magic swirled and glowed around his chest.

He nodded and stretched. "Even if I didn't, we would have no choice but to leave quickly. My brother is on his way here with Kesh's son."

"What?" Aela drew back in horror.

Tarr pushed into a sitting position with the magic's healing completed.

"I sent word to Jathe to bring the child here, where he could be under our protection. I had no way of knowing that the wrangrent was already here."

"He was at Shuesh? It was his men in the Frin'gern uniforms?"

"Yes. He arrived in time for the fighting. Not the timing he was hoping for, I'm sure," he said with a smile as his joints popped from the stretching.

"I do feel better," he said with a slight smile and a quick kiss on her lips.

"We have to go now and intercept them," Aela said. She looked at the pool and then at Tarr. "Your brother...will he take Nico to Frin'gere and guard him until Ishea is dealt with?"

Tarr's expression was severe. "Yes, he will."

He hesitated only a moment before adding, "We will all go to Frin'gere." He continued even as Aela shook her head. "It will not be safe here for any of us. Until the Council can contain the wrangrent, you cannot stay here, Aela."

"I am not leaving my people."

"She will destroy your people to get to you. You will not be safe here."

"I am not leaving." When he would have objected, she added quickly, "First, we ensure that Nico is safe. That is our only concern at the moment. And to do that, we have to get to the surface and find them. How were they coming?"

"By river," Tarr said. He disapproved of her choice, but he suspended the argument for the time being.

Chapter 36

Aela and Tarr made it out of the grotto with assistance from Mar and Sey. As the four of them swam along the cliffs, Aela felt the restlessness that Mar had reported. Voices echoed in the water, like the ones she often heard in the river. They were more distant and harder to distinguish. Straining to hear more, she felt as if she knew the voices.

They found the steep path that led up the cliffs. Unlike the swim, they all struggled. She and Tarr with the steepness, and Mar and Sey with the narrowness of the passage. They made slow progress up the cliff and needed to stop occasionally for Tarr.

Deepening dread filled Aela as she continued to ascend the path. She feared that Jathe and her nephew were nearing the palace, bringing within her grasp the one thing that Ishea wanted most.

She felt darkness and death the higher they climbed. The stirring of the waves below warned of the same violent sorrow that had pounded the cliffs after the destruction of Masia.

Mar reached the top of the cliffs ahead of her. He helped her over the last ledge, pulling her body level with his. As he leaned down to do the same with Tarr, Aela looked towards the White Palace. Grimy, gray streams flowed over the stone near the water's edge and ash fell from the windows like snow blowing off a mountaintop. The scene was eerie and silent.

"Oh, Great Wave," the prayer left her lips on a gasp.

"What has she done?" Tarr's shock matched her own.

"Someone suffered because of our escape last night. Some defenseless soul paid the price of her wrath." The guilt made it hard to breathe.

"Whatever she has done, it is not your fault." Tarr gently cupped her cheek.

Though she nodded, Aela did not feel absolved of the guilt.

"Let's get to the river." She swallowed the pain. "There is nothing else we can do here. We must intercept your brother and make sure Nico gets to safety."

She turned away from him and began walking over the dark green hills towards the river. Mar immediately followed. Sey wordlessly laid a hand on Tarr's shoulder, expressing their shared frustration that their queen suffered. Tarr acknowledged the gesture with a nod. Together, they too followed.

The ash continued to fall around them gathering on the ground in small piles. Aela tried not to think of it even as delicate gray flakes stuck to her hair. She refused to cry.

The restlessness of the river called to her as they approached. Ash floated on the dark surface, dancing to the erratic current underneath.

"There is a lot of ash," Tarr said as he stared out at the river and the White Palace.

She heard the faint echoes again like the ones of Masia. Without consciously choosing to, Aela stepped into the river.

───※───

TARR MADE TO STOP HER, but Sey stayed him with a heavy hand on his shoulder. "It calls to her, and she must answer."

He nodded, viscerally uncomfortable with her among the ashes. In his time with Aela, he had learned that there were times he could not intervene no matter how much he wanted to.

"What happened here, Aela?" he asked instead.

She stood near the bank with the water swaying around her knees. Her hands shook as they reached toward the ash. Screams of pain, pleas for mercy, prayers whispered in fear, and hopelessness filled her head as her fingers touched the ash. She wanted to pull away immediately but recognized the voices that had once belonged to people who were nothing but ash.

Berto.

Malcolm.

George.

Feone.

Bena.

The elders and the priestesses.

There were others; palace guards, maids, cooks, and docksmen. All of them now trapped in the ash of death.

The anger burned what tears she had, and in a gesture of rage, she scooped up the ash and flung it toward the palace. A cry of pain and sorrow, of despair and retribution filled the air. She did not know how she could ever make her cousin pay for this atrocity, but she vowed that she would find justice for all the souls that had perished in the blaze of that evil magic.

She relaxed her fisted hands, and her fingers grazed the surface of the water. Her anger was so great she almost missed the message the current carried.

A ship approached. It passed the juncture of the two rivers and now sailed with great haste down the Joining River.

Her nephew was within Ishea's reach.

Aela turned to the shore where the others waited.

"Jathe's ship is close. Mar, Sey, swim out to the ship and turn it back to the Lesser River. Tarr and I will travel on land and meet you upriver."

They hesitated. "Go now! You will swim faster without us."

They waded into the water and dove beneath the surface and out of sight.

"Will they make it in time?"

"Yes, they will have no problem swimming against the current."

Aela pushed through the water as she made her way to the shore where Tarr waited with an outstretched hand. The air around them shook with soundless thunder. Aela's balance faltered as did Tarr's. They fell away from each other, Tarr to the ground and Aela into the river.

She was lost under the water and caught by the current. It carried her toward the palace. Pushing to the surface, she took a quick breath before being submerged once more. She struggled to the surface, able to keep herself above this time. Aela fought to swim against the current as it carried her to the palace docks.

Ishea stood in pristine white robes.

"I must stop underestimating you, Aela. Just when I think you'll die quietly, you remerge more troublesome."

The falling ash began to swirl with agitation around Ishea. The air shook again, and a fierce wind blew towards the palace. Gray clouds formed in the sky, and Aela thought of the storm that had preceded her arrival in Masia.

Aela looked back down the river and realized the wind pushed Jathe's ship ever closer to the palace.

Unwilling to fathom the possibility of the ship getting within Ishea's grasp, Aela stood in the water. She pushed her feet into the warm mud and called upon the magic to support her feet even as the water pushed against her chest.

With every ounce of magic she had, she drove her hands into the river and urged the current to stop. She felt the tremendous strength of the river as her body shook with the effort to stop it.

She too felt its willingness to obey. Slowly, the current stopped, and the waters of the river became still.

THE FAILED QUEEN

The menacing laugh beside her threatened her concentration for only a moment.

"Impressive for one who failed her trials. Though you are not the only one who knows water magic, or did you forget all those years we trained together, cousin?"

Ishea also stood chest-deep in the water several feet away from Aela. Her hands clawed at the surface, and the current reluctantly responded to her pulls.

Aela felt the movement against her hands. She felt the unwilling current being helplessly pulled by the strength of Ishea's magic. Aela pushed against it, again calling on all the magic within her and around her. The current slowed to her push and quickened to Ishea's pulls.

"You're not strong enough, Aela."

Aela followed her gaze as the ship came into view. Ishea smiled and continued to drag the current closer with her hands.

She used all her power, and still, Aela was not strong enough. Her body was inching closer to the palace as the water pushed against her.

She needed more strength, more magic. The river was not enough to overpower Ishea. Keeping one hand pressed against the current, Aela reached the other towards the palace...towards the ocean.

Unsure of when she had become so attuned to the magic that had evaded her years ago, Aela closed her outstretched hand and felt the small backward surge of water. She tightened her grip on the current and felt another surge, stronger this time.

Ishea felt it too as the water began to pull in the opposite direction. One current pushed against Aela while the other obeyed her pulls.

"Oh, clever, cousin," Ishea said as she pushed against the backward-flowing current Aela had started.

They stood facing each other, pushing and pulling in opposite directions. The strain showed on both their faces, yet Ishea smiled.

"What are you going to do, Aela? Pull back the river? Call up the ocean? Even if you could do it, you'd destroy the White Palace in the process. Is that what you want? Think of all the lives you'll take."

"Are there any lives left?" Aela grunted, struggling to maintain the push and pull.

Again, the evil laughter jarred her concentration. "You killed Aluz. I was fond of him, and he had his uses. After discovering his body, I couldn't help but vent a little frustration."

"Your frustration was worth all the lives you took?"

"These lives," she looked to the groupings of ashes, "were worth nothing," she spat but the smile reappeared.

"I thought you would be happy, Aela. I got rid of those condescending old fools and the meddlesome priestesses for you. If only you could have heard their cries and screams...but you can, can't you? You always heard voices in the river."

The ash floating around her reverberated loudly with the voices of Ishea's victims. Aela fought to keep her focus even against the deafening cries.

It slipped, and she felt the current hit her as Ishea took advantage.

She regained her position and again, she stood facing her cousin as they both fought the pull of the other. Aela realized that she could not continue to do both. She would have to decide to either hold against Ishea or pull on the full power of the ocean.

"You won't just destroy the palace. You'll destroy yourself. You can't pull the river back, and you're not strong enough to call up the ocean, Aela. Give in," Ishea taunted.

Aela knew there was a grain of truth to what her cousin said. As she glanced at the White Palace, she knew that she would destroy it.

Though it had never been a home, she knew the loss of it would be saddening.

She also knew that she might not survive the expenditure of magic it would take to accomplish this. There was no other way to stop Ishea from getting to the ship though. Once her cousin's grip on the current was broken, Mar and Sey could swim the ship far enough upriver to be safe from Ishea. Her nephew would be safe; Tarr would make sure of it in her absence.

Aela studied the palace once more; it would fall on them as it crumbled into the river.

So be it, she thought with steely determination. Closing her eyes, she gave herself over to the magic in the water and sent one last prayer to the Great Wave.

I am your vessel. Let the power of your domain flow through me and in this last act, I will not fail.

At peace with her decision, she opened her eyes to stare into her cousin's. A look of understanding followed by angry disbelief passed over Ishea's face. Moving quickly, Aela turned her body to the palace, arms stretched out, palms up and open. She called back the river and commanded the ocean up.

"No!" Ishea's scream seemed distant.

The current against Aela's back almost submerged her, but she fought to stay upright. With a great rumbling, the river rushed back through the passages under the palace. The sound of stone breaking under the force of the rapids thundered in the air.

A sound, hushed at first, grew and a great wave, greater than any Aela had ever seen, rose over the cliffs. The water glittered blue and green as the wave hung suspended over the palace.

In perfect sync, the wave crashed down, exploding out the windows of the palace and the rapids flooded backward, pulling both Aela and Ishea under while white stone crumbled under the onslaught of ocean and river.

Aela lost consciousness for a moment as the rush of water violently tossed her body. A sweet unfamiliar voice, the voice of the river itself, urged her awake. She fought against the pull of stones sinking to the bottom and swam upward towards the light. Her head broke through the surface, and her body gasped for breath immediately.

The thunderous sound of the river and the wave left her hearing muffled, making her more disoriented as she bobbed in the water. The splashes of falling stones alerted her to the danger of staying where she was. She searched for the riverbank.

Swimming with the little strength she had left, she drew closer to the bank, careful to avoid the debris. She pulled herself onto the shore and rolled onto her back. Her breaths came desperate and deep as she closed her eyes and willed her body to calm. She lost sense of time as she lay there, focused solely on breathing.

Burning pinpricks all along her skin forced her eyes open. Ash fell from the sky, and she felt it burn as it touched her skin. She brushed away the flakes, but they continued to fall.

"Do you see how great my power is, Aela?" She turned towards the voice. An ash figure slowly condensed into the image of her cousin. It hobbled down the bank towards her.

Aela rolled onto her side and tried to stand, but the figure was already on her. She was pinned on her back, and a hand glowing like embers wrapped around her neck. She fought to pull the hand away, but her fingers burned from the contact.

The hand tightened, and she struggled to breathe.

"Even as my body lay broken at the bottom of the river, I live on in the ash I have created." Ishea tightened her grip, her expression crazed. "You cannot defeat me."

Aela struggled harder but was unable to remove the strangling hand. "You don't get to win, Aela."

THE FAILED QUEEN

She gasped as her vision started to blur, and her head felt light. Her chest burned from lack of air. She could not overpower Ishea.

Realizing what she must do, Aela used the last of her strength to dip her hand in the river. She focused intently on the water.

Praying that she was right, she flung a handful of it at Ishea, slapping her wet hand against the chest of the ash body.

Ishea laughed, "A little bit of water won't hurt me." Her smile faltered as the ash dissolved beneath Aela's hand.

Ishea pulled back to stare down at her chest. "What is this?" Her attention returned to Aela. Her hand stayed tightly clutched around Aela's throat, making Aela's words barely audible.

"What did you say?"

Aela struggled to remain conscious as she once more tried to voice the words.

Ishea's grip loosened only slightly, enough that Aela could take a breath. "Blessed water," she managed to gasp.

The features of the ash face tightened. "Blessed water," she said slowly. "You used up all the blessed water in Shuesh."

The hand tightened again. Aela fought with everything she had until Ishea's grip loosened once more.

"Blessed...queen..." She gasped a word with each breath.

Ishea smiled. "Oh, yes, you're the blessed queen. With the power to bless water, is that right?"

Aela felt both of Ishea's hands close around her neck. The water she had flung at Ishea had done damage, but it was not enough. She would need more water to destroy the ash body her cousin possessed.

The river was close. She would have to submerge Ishea. Grabbing both of her cousin's arms, she pulled the ash body on top of her own though the contact burned. She rolled both of them into the river, the current pulling them to the center.

Ishea lost her grip as they sank under the water.

The water eased the burning in Aela's chest, and her head cleared. Her eyes opened, and she watched Ishea's disintegrating body struggle to surface.

Her body was stronger in the water than Ishea's. She gripped her cousin's ankle and pulled the ash body deeper. They were face to face, and for a moment, Aela saw Ishea's face as it had once been.

She thought of blessed water and knew that there was no water more sacred to her than that of the river. She was the Blessed Queen, and she alone could bless the water.

Ishea struggled, the last of her air bubbling past her lips as she soundlessly screamed. The water around them glowed, and Ishea's ash body broke apart. The clumps of ash glowed briefly before disappearing completely.

Aela swam to the surface. The ash that had floated in the river disappeared all around her as the water glowed.

Dovkey was free of the wrangrent once and for all.

Chapter 37

Tarr waited for Aela at the shore. He looked tired and stunned. As she swam toward him, she wondered if the fall had knocked him unconscious.

"Is she dead?" he asked as he helped her from the water.

"She is," she responded with grave certainty.

Aela did not savor the killing of her cousin. However, the immense relief she felt almost brought tears to her eyes. She did not understand where the strength and power had come from to defeat Ishea.

"You sure?"

She nodded as she stretched out on the bank. He lay next to her.

"What makes you so sure?"

"Nothing impure could survive in that river and never will. I blessed it."

Tarr smiled. "Didn't know you could do that kind of magic."

Her eyes closed, but she smiled. "I'm the Blessed Queen."

"Look at us- the Immortal killer and the wrangrent slayer," he jested.

Aela smiled faintly. "I'm still not sure how I did it, Tarr," she said softly.

Strands of wet hair were plastered to her face, and he gently pushed them away.

"You were always destined to this, Aela."

Her eyes opened. "Without the blessing at the White Beach, I would not have defeated her. It's the might of the Great Wave that overpowered her."

He smiled with amusement. "You stopped the river's current, pulled it back over a cliff, and rose a great wave from the sea. Give yourself some credit, love. That was all your strength." His gaze turned serious. "Everything you had to endure to come to this moment, that took strength too, Aela. A different kind of strength."

He turned his attention to the crumbling palace. "Kesh said things would have to unfold a certain way for his children to survive and his country to prosper. I guess they did."

He turned back to her. "He was willing to do anything to make sure that you arrived at this point. He had no doubts that you would defeat the evil he foresaw."

After pausing a moment, his dark eyes met hers, and he said in a soft voice, "Do you want to know what I wagered in Seer's Fortune?" His voice was barely a whisper.

She sat up, taking his hand in hers. "You said that you swore not to tell."

"Now that it is done, I think Kesh would approve. He was unsure if he could cheat the game. Seer's Fortune is a mystery that few understand. He counted on losing, to ensure that I would stay by your side through all of it, but just in case...".

His fingers intertwined with hers as he struggled to say the next words. "If he won, I owed him a boon of his choosing. Anything...he could ask anything of me, and I would be bound by the game to complete his request. I already knew that he wanted me to come to Dovkey to watch over you. It wasn't until after we played that the bastard told me what he really intended. If Kesh had won, he would have commanded me to kill him."

Aela gasped, her hand closing tightly around Tarr's. "What?"

"He believed so strongly in the prophecy and the need for a seer sacrifice." He smiled sadly. "He must have known that I would never be able to do so without being magically compelled. I felt great sadness and relief when he lost."

"And Kesh swore you to secrecy because I needed to trust you in all of this?"

"Yes."

She turned away from him with her gaze not focused on anything in particular. Tears gathered in her eyes. The love she felt for her brother had never been greater.

"Ishea told me that Aine saw something when they were younger. I wonder what she saw when she looked at Ishea."

"Aine will never tell you. Kesh asked, my brother has asked many times, and she refuses to say. We'll never know."

"But she knew who she was in the prophecy the whole time."

"Maybe, maybe not. Perhaps Aine saw what Ishea would become and had the opportunity to prevent it. Instead of fighting that battle, she fled. Perhaps, that is how she failed."

Aela nodded.

"I do know this, Aela. You had to fail the trials. Had Ishea seen you as a threat, she would have eliminated you long ago."

Aela fully believed the truth of that statement.

"You had to doubt yourself so everyone else would too. The Great Wave's blessing signaled that the time had come to put away that doubt."

Reviewing the events of her life, she understood why Kesh had insisted that it play out as it did.

Had she never gone to Masia, would she have met her guards? Would Menony have been able to sneak away so easily to birth her and Kesh's child in secret?

Had a Frin'geren not been bound to her, would she have survived the ice curse? Would she have made a fateful trip to the White Beach?

"Your promise to Kesh has been fulfilled. I am safe, and the wrangrent is dead. You are not obligated to marry me anymore."

He eyed her as if she were a puzzle he couldn't figure out.

"Tell me what you want, Aela. You're not obligated anymore either."

She looked out on the land again. The evidence of the wrangrent's defeat was everywhere. Broken slabs of white stone littered the river. It glowed faintly with her blessing as it continued to flow around the rubble. She wondered if it would always retain that glow.

The land to either side of the river was dark green, and Aela knew that further east, the farmers of Dovkey enjoyed a good season. They would have a profitable harvest.

Shuesh was no doubt repairing the damage done by the fight with Ishea's ash army. Its people lived and would continue to have the opportunity to prosper. Life would return to normal once again.

A wave of sorrow washed over her as she thought of Masia. She wondered if people would people return and rebuild. If there would be divers once more to collect the freshwater pearls that could only be found in that spot of the river. She wanted to believe that a little girl in a yellow dress could walk out on the dock to wait for her father to surface.

Aela desperately wanted a future where Masia was real again, and she had the power to make it happen.

Finally, she turned to the remains of the White Palace. The towers had crumbled and little of the palace that had been built above the river remained. The great dock was buried in rock, and the water found new paths to the sea. White foaming rapids brushed against the stone. Some of the old palace possibly still existed; the rooms carved into the cliffs and the spaces beneath the river. The waterfall room would have survived, and that thought brought a smile to her face.

The White Palace was not the only thing that had been destroyed. The elders and the palace priestesses were gone. So much history, knowledge, and culture was lost in the cruel tantrum of her cousin. These things too would have to be rebuilt, but like the White Palace, she would not rebuild them in the exact image of what they had been. Instead, she would create a system that represented who the people of Dovkey really were. The Great Wave had given her the power to destroy and create, and she would build something better. This was the destiny she was meant to have, and she was ready to embrace it as she had never been before.

"We won't have a palace," she said as she looked at Tarr. He turned to her slowly, amusement lurking in his eyes.

"Not right away. I have plans though." He lay next to her, also braced on his elbows, looking out at the land.

"The palace isn't the only thing that will need rebuilding."

He nodded. "I was thinking about a summer home near Masia, something by the river."

Aela smiled and looked back at the glowing water.

"The elders will have to be replaced." She noted his raised eyebrow from the corner of her eye. "With limited powers, of course. They'll be advisors and representatives of the people as they were meant to be."

"And the priestesses?"

"I'll search all of Dovkey to find those who hear the river and waves as I do; young or old, it won't matter."

"What about the priestess trials? Are you going to do away with them?" Amusement filled his voice.

Aela thought on the question. "Yes, I think that I am."

He laughed, "You are the queen. The Blessed Queen. Does this make me the blessed king…or rather prince? I have to say I'm not happy about this prince title."

She laughed, but her eyes were somber.

"The trials, like the elders, were ineffectual. How could we find the women most connected to the magic of the Great Wave when we forbid the practice of it? And not every girl comes into her magic at the same age. There must be better ways to determine who will be a priestess and who won't. I'll find the ways and start by getting rid of that stupid law about who gets to practice magic."

"What will they say about this radical queen? Next thing you'll do is declare drinking and gambling legal."

Aela laughed. "I find I enjoy the drinking. I'm strongly considering the drinking. The gambling…eh," she turned to him. "I'm sure they'll say that I've been corrupted. They'll say that the queen is too heavily influenced by her Frin'geren prince. That is if you want the position."

"Change it to king, and we have a deal."

She was warmed by the laughter that bubbled up in her chest, the laughter that he could always bring her.

"That is not changing. Prince…take it or leave it."

He looked mildly annoyed. "I'll be a prince to an infant king." Aela nodded, and Tarr sighed, "So be it."

Turning serious once more, "We won't have children, Tarr. Are you okay with that?"

"You're the Blessed Queen; anything is possible." He took her hand and laid a kiss on the back of it. "You know what I want."

She shook her head.

"I want you. The palace, the title, a child…it's all appreciated but unneeded. When I made that promise to Kesh, I never doubted that I would fulfill it, but I also never thought I wouldn't want to be anywhere but here. I renounce my claim from the game of Seer's

Fortune." He gave her that devilish smile. "Aela, my love, will you marry me?"

"I never thought I would say this, but yes, I will marry you, Tarr."

He pulled her into a passionate kiss. "It's a pity you destroyed the palace. We'll have to seal this deal out in the open now."

She laughed as he kissed her again. When she pulled away, she was breathless.

"First, I have to call Mar and Sey back. And retrieve Menony from the Sea King. I trust him to keep her safe, but I'd rather not leave her with him any longer than necessary."

Tarr helped her to stand. "If you insist. Business now, pleasure later." He grunted. "You know, you are going to make my brother ridiculously happy."

Aela took his hand and began to walk upriver. "Oh, why is that?"

"He can say he's related to royalty."

"Even if it's only a prince."

Tarr frowned. "This matter is not settled. After you've spent a night in my bed, I'll ask you again...and I expect a different answer."

Aela laughed, filled with hope and love, as they walked to find his brother, her guards, and her nephew, the future king of Dovkey.